Diamond Head

A Novel by Peter Gilman

DIAMOND HEAD

Coward McCann, Inc.  New York

Library of Congress Catalog
Card Number 60-9500
Fifth Impression

MANUFACTURED IN THE UNITED STATES OF AMERICA

This book is dedicated to
Nina Shipman and Dave Smith.
And to the memory of Sarah Park.

"Come tread with me a little space of paradise. Sweet land of palms and peace, love and song . . . and yet, those who knew her in days gone by would walk sadly now in well remembered haunts. Old faces are missing, and faces resembling them are few. The Hawaii of yesterday passes, and it makes even the stranger pensive to see the changing. To one who views her from the height of the heart, a bright commercial future is cold compensation for the irreplaceable loss of Old Hawaii."

—Charmian London

Prologue

MAUNA LOA is a sun volcano; a proud, hoary throat-of-thunder rising nearly three miles above the Hawaiian sea. It is a dark mountain, the color of pocked buffalo hide, its flanks scarred with the black ribbons of lava flows. It is a mountain more massive than a legion of men, more graceful than any maiden—less predictable than either. Hills fit into hills like lovers and robes of cloud bed them quietly for their moment, then drift away, leaving them sharp and naked brown against the washed blue sky.

There is sugar cane to 1,500 feet, then dense fern jungles of wild, incredible greens. Farther up there are rain forests of sandalwood and lehua and the sudden flash of wild rose. The air is sweet with burning cane.

Past Red Hill cabin to the summit at Mokuaweoweo, the winds send music lapping through your brain and the pili grass crackles under your feet like restless bugs. The slopes are corroded with ash and cinder, the sad detritus of time; further still, with winter's snow.

From the summit, Mauna Loa is a strange, hauntingly silent bowl of fire and coiling gas and the hot dark miracle of creation. It is like being present at the beginning of time.

There is a moment, at the summit, when you can witness the Specter of Brocken—a phenomenon that occurs when the sun is low and you stand between the sun and the clouds and you see your shadow upon the clouds encircled by a rainbow; something like the halo of Jesus. If the specter appears, then according to native legend you will be blessed with the glories of earth: love and the end of loneliness. If it does not, you will be left to the eternal fate of man.

Part One

Chapter One

AARON HOWLAND felt the tremor of the volcano as he pressed flat against the rim of the summit. It was the second tremor he had felt that day and the fear grew sick inside him. He shuddered a moment, feeling the cold shock of the snow against his stomach and hips. Then he worked his way carefully up the slope until his head and shoulders were beyond the lip of the crater and he could, if he wanted to, look down into the fire pit. But not yet, he warned himself. Don't look down yet.

He sucked in his breath and waited for another sign: a stronger quake, an earth tilt, a rift opening up along the wall of the crater. But Mauna Loa remained silent. The only noise Aaron Howland could hear was the sad dull echo of the wind and the muffled drums in his heart.

I wish I weren't this scared, he thought. I shouldn't be this scared. A man considering suicide, a man testing himself with the idea of suicide, should be beyond fear.

But he knew he was not beyond it. Quite to the contrary, all his senses were suddenly alive to fear, quivering with the conscious realization of his own mortality. It was this realization that had brought him—driven him, really—alone to the rim of the volcano.

If you are afraid to die, if you are afraid to face death, then you do not deserve to live, he thought; considering, a moment afterwards, that if you are afraid to live, afraid to face life, then perhaps you do not deserve to die. Earlier that day, he had been afraid to face death. Earlier that day, he knew he had proven himself a coward.

He had started out from the Howland Ranch four days before, he and the big Hawaiian, Dean Kahana, moving the horses easily through the coastal grazelands and down across the brutal sprawl of the Kau Desert toward the volcano slopes. They had each gotten a wild goat, Aaron with the high-powered Winchester rifle and Dean Kahana with bow and arrow, and shortly before sundown yesterday they had reached Kulani at the five-thousand-foot level and Aaron had gotten the first wild boar.

The boar had broken from thicket at their approach; black, big-headed and muscularly lean beneath the coarse, matted fur. He trotted uphill several yards, rooting his way through scrubs of panini cactus; then he turned and headed for open country with an amazing burst of speed, until Aaron's first shot crushed his shoulder, somersaulting him down the slope. When they rode up to him he charged wild-faced, running awkwardly with the pain, running on rage more than on muscle, his tusks catching the sun like polished scimitars, Aaron's second shot splintering one of the tusks, the final shot ripping through the chest to the heart.

They camped up above Kulani that night, waiting out the soft evening rain that drifted through the forest. After the rain there was an hour of darkness, then a young moon rode up into the sky from behind the dome of Mauna Loa.

"I've often wondered what it's like up there," Aaron said.

"At the summit?"

"Right up at the crater. At the top of the world."

"It don't look like no top of the world," Dean Kahana said. His voice was deep and slow in the night. "Looks more like some kind of hell. You get up there and you're all alone and you look into that fire pit, and it gives you a bad feelin'. Makes you feel hopeless; like it was laughin' at you, tellin' you how you ain't gonna live forevah and even though you'd like to do something good while you are alive, it don't really mattah too much. It just ain't no good up there." He shook his head. "It's like death."

"In a weird way," Aaron said, "it must be beautiful."

"Maybe."

"Even death has beauty."

"Not for me."

"That's because you're afraid of dying."

"Yessuh."

"I'm not," Aaron said. "In a way, it would be a kind of relief."

"Haw, that ain't no way to talk," Dean Kahana said. "Lemme tell you: once, when I was a kid, I got lost up there at the summit. You remember—your dad had to come get me. Him and some of the ranch hands. The lava lake was eruptin' and fire fountains was leapin' a thousand feet into the sky. Auwe, I was scared! It was like bein' all alone at the end of the world."

Aaron had an uncomfortable memory of the incident. It had taken place just before the great eruption of 1935. He had been with his father in the searching party, but he had quit long before they reached the summit. Quit because he had been afraid.

The fine boar ribs had been wrapped in koa leaves and roasted in a bed of hot stones lined with koa branches. They were grainy but had a full flavor. The two men ate in silence. Aaron wondered moodily why he felt a compulsion to finish a pint of bourbon with his dinner. Feeling the liquor, he said:

"It's curious how a man, if he stops to think about it, realizes that somehow he's missed out on life. Most men do. A man reaches the halfway point, like me, and he starts needing to try all the things that, for some reason, he's never tried before. Like now I want to go up to the fire pit. I was born and raised on this island, yet I've always been afraid to go up to the summit; to see the fire fountains that built my own island. Now I want to. I feel as if I have to."

"If you really want to that bad, we can go up tomorrow."

Aaron turned sharply. "You think I'm still afraid?"

The Hawaiian's grave eyes studied Aaron. "No, Mistah Aaron. I didn't say that. I'm just suggestin'—"

"I don't want to go up tomorrow," Aaron said, angry at the sudden chill in his voice. "But someday I'd like to go up alone."

An hour after sunrise they were up in the scarred, desolate reaches of the mountainside, leading the two pack horses carefully across cinder and swirls of pahoehoe lava crust, when the first tremor hit them.

"Holy God, watch out!" Aaron cried out.

"The horses—"

But Dean called too late. Aaron's mare shied, lost her footing and spilled down the slope. The crack of her foreleg could be heard above the deep subterranean roar that accompanied the quake as it ground its way through the mountain. A whole section of cinder cones, built up like a shallow mesa, was shaken loose and poured down at them. Spatter ridges were rocked apart, and huge chunks of lava rumbled down the slope, kicking up a pall of thick gray dust.

"Pehea oe?" Kahana called out. "Are you all right?"

Aaron got up slowly and shook himself. There was a dark bruise swelling above his right temple. "Yes," he said, a little uncertain. "I think so."

Kahana fought to control his horses. He tightened his grip on the halter rope, pulling the pack horses close and steadying them.

"Are you suah you're all right?" he said, riding toward Aaron. "That was a bad fall."

"I'm okay," Aaron said sullenly. "It'll take more than a lousy fall from a horse to keep me down." But he was trembling. His face was white and bloodless and he was fighting an urge to run. He wanted to run very bad and he wanted a drink very bad.

"Let's get the hell out of here," he said, suddenly aware that the earthquake was over. The dust was settling and far to the north he saw the lava flow that he knew was the killer flow of 1859 glistening in the early sunlight like a silver river winding its way to the sea near Kawaihae. "We'd better hurry," he said.

"No point in hurryin'." Kahana grinned. "Ain't no place to go."

"Away from here," Aaron snapped. "We're probably on a central rift with the whole goddamn volcano set to blow. We're in a hell of a spot if there's any big activity going on up there." He nodded toward the volcano.

Dean Kahana gazed up at the dome of Mauna Loa. He had noticed, all day yesterday and during the morning, that the heat of the vapor columns seeping up through cracks in the mountainside had become more intense as they had ridden to higher altitudes. The lava streams that made up the inner mass of the mountain must be hotter than usual, he thought. And there had been minor quake reports all week. If an eruption was starting in the summit crater, a lateral pressure on those inner lava streams would force them out at a weak point in the mountain, cracking and rending the whole flank from the summit to the place of ejection. But it was improbable that lava would eject at this low a level. Even though that quake seemed strong enough. And awful close.

"We're pretty safe here," he said easily. "Ain't no point in worryin'. We'll luck out."

"I never depend on luck."

"Sometimes you gotta. Byanby, everyone needs a little bit of luck," Kahana said.

He was a tall, big-shouldered man not yet twenty-five, with long powerful arms and hands like slabs of granite. His skin was the warm rust color of the Polynesian, his hair a sward of heavy black grass falling across his forehead. His eyes were dark and curiously sensitive, like the eyes of a child. His face wore an expression of watchful innocence, and it had in it all the heavily carved features of his people: a low forehead with a ridge of bone protruding at the brow; a thick, prominent nose, hooked slightly like the nose of an American Indian; wide, full lips framing an easy smile.

He dismounted and crouched over the injured horse, testing the leg.

"Broken?" Aaron asked.

Kahana nodded. "We'd more bettah take care of her," he said quietly.

Aaron took the rifle from the saddleboot, waited until the mare's painful curiosity ebbed and she lay still; then he fired.

When the echo of the rifle shot died away, the volcano seemed suspiciously still. Too damned still, too damned silent, Aaron thought. He realized with distaste that he had broken into a cold sweat. He could feel it spring damply in the palms of his hands and his plaid cotton shirt was sticking to his back. He felt through the saddlebag and took out the flask of bourbon, cursing his need for it, cursing the way the silence scoured his nerves.

The eerie, warning silence, he thought. Like the silence of ghosts on God's sea. Or that bitter, heartbreaking silence so many years ago, the silence that came before the great Tsunami wave that killed little Aaron Howland Junior.

He took two big swallows of bourbon, then offered the flask to Kahana.

"Kamau." Kahana grinned, his broad white teeth gleaming against his dark face. He drank sparingly, wiped the lip of the flask with the tail of his shirt, and returned it to Aaron.

The sun had heaved up higher into the yellow June sky, sending long shafts spilling over Mauna Loa and out across the ocean. A lone Hawaiian hawk was flying so high that it caught the sun on its breast and shone like a spark.

"I don't know how you feel about it," Aaron said, after he had switched the saddle to the lead pack horse, a scrawny, sure-footed blue roan. "But I've had it. I'm for heading back to Manoalani, as fast as we can. That damned earthquake—" He shook his head.

"No sweat, Mistah Aaron." Kahana laughed good-naturedly. "I don't think Pele will cause any more trouble."

Aaron remembered the old Hawaiian legend of Pele, goddess of the volcanoes. At the beginning of time she visited each of the Hawaiian Islands in turn, starting at the northwestern end of the chain, and her eruptions built up the land mass above the sea. Strangely enough, modern scientists agree with the geophysical facts of the legend: that the great underwater volcanoes erupted in the depths of the Pacific millions of years ago, pushing the summits above the surface and thus forming the entire archipelago, from the northwest to the southeast, and that this was the order in which the peaks appeared above the sea. At present, all the volcanoes are dormant except Mauna Loa and Kilauea on the Island of Hawaii, largest and youngest of the chain, and the only above-water island that is still growing, due to continued eruptions. Pele's home is in the fire pits of these volcanoes, and when she is angry, she causes an eruption.

"For my dough Pele's a manic-depressive," Aaron said. "And I don't trust her moods."

"She'll be quiet now," Kahana said. "But if you say so, we'll go back."

"I say so."

They rode single file down the mountain. Aaron dropped behind, brooding, feeling somehow guilty, feeling that in some less than obscure way he had shamed himself, and that Dean Kahana, whom he knew had never been overly fond of him anyway, now thought him a coward. He kicked his horse into a trot and pulled up alongside the Hawaiian. "You can make it back across the desert by yourself, can't you?"

Kahana looked curiously at him. "Where are you goin'?"

"Up to the summit," Aaron said flatly.

"By yourself?"

"Yes."

"That can be verra rough, all alone. Be more bettah I go with you."

"Goddamn it, I want to go alone! Can you make it back okay?"

Dean Kahana thought of the long trek across the scoriae and old lava flows that marked the Kau Desert. There would be no trick to getting across. It would take all day and it would be lonely, but there would be no trouble. Unless there really was some action going on up in the fire pits—either in Mauna Loa or Kilauea. Then there would be trouble. Then he would have to make a run for it. And it might prove to be one hell of a run.

He studied Aaron, puzzled by the confusion and intensity in the haole's eyes. But after a moment he grinned and said, "*No pilikia*. No trouble, Mistah Aaron."

So Aaron turned and started up along the volcano trail by himself, passing scorched koa trees and shrubs of wild akala raspberries, and farther on the trail steepened so he had to dismount and guide the roan across the cinder so her hoofs would not sink through the crust. The air became so thin that he could hardly breathe. By midmorning his desperate flush of courage deserted him and he started working on the bourbon again, telling himself that if he made the summit, his feeling of cowardice and sour shame would wash away.

He passed glacial scratches along the trail, and a pile of chipped rock and primitive tools in the mouth of an old lava cave where centuries ago Hawaiian warriors chiseled their battle adzes and spear points from the hard, cokelike lava called clinkstone. He remembered reading that during a major eruption, Mauna Loa had hurled eight-ton chunks of clinkstone more than a half mile from its pit.

Early in the afternoon he crossed beds of green basaltic limu and the fine, grasslike filaments of lava called Pele's Hair, and he knew that he had, at last, reached the vast mottled plain that was the summit; a cold, barren land that looked like God had abandoned it. Several times, he thought the crater was just ahead. But the undulations of the plain fooled him, one desolate, corroded hill after another, until, hours later, he finally saw the telltale cloud of steam hovering silently over Mokuaweoweo. The lava beds became too jagged for the roan, so he tied her to a cluster of clinkstone and went the rest of the way on foot, scrambling up across pahoehoe blisters and then at last the ice ridge, and just before he reached the crater the second tremor threw him down hard against the talus slope and he waited there for another sign, his heart pounding thick and cold in his throat. Then he crawled on his belly to the rim of the crater, his lips twisting with some inarticulate prayer for the volcano to be still.

Don't panic, he warned himself. Just take it easy, boy.

But he was not a boy. He was thirty-five years old, and he was beginning to curse time. He was a broad trunk of a man, ruggedly built, but he had grown suety through years of easy living. The muscle ridges through his back and shoulders were slabbed with fat. His barrel chest curved down to rest on low hips and thick, gorilla-muscled legs. His hands were hard and capable, and his forearms swelled beneath the gabardine parka. His shoulders narrowed into a bunch with his thick neck.

Strangely, no emotion showed in his face. It was a flat mask, fleshy and softened by sun and whisky. His hair was like thin damp strands of straw. His nose was long and twisted slightly where a tiny white scar seared the bridge. His wide mouth was thinly carved, the lips curled tight with inarticulate resent. His eyes were small and stale gray, the color of donkey's hide, distant, vacant and dull. Lately, there was always a troubled pulse of liquor behind those eyes.

He was still a strong man. All the drive was still there, the hint of harshness. But the direction of his drive had been changed: the purposeful, careful road he had followed all his life had suddenly looped into one of those superhighway cloverleaves, with each loop beginning and ending with himself. And he had known, for some time now, that any road he selected would lead into a head-on crash.

He twisted and leaned up on his elbow, letting the rifle cradle against his hip, and reached into the shell pocket of his hunting parka for the flask of bourbon. His hands were clumsy from the cold, but he finally got the delicate silver lid unscrewed and tipped the flask to his lips, drinking deeply and welcoming the rich burn of the liquor as it flowed through his body.

From the summit, the vast shaggy sward that was the Island of Hawaii spread out before him, its crude prairie of cane and coffee and cattlelands dipping and pitching endlessly toward the Pacific. A bank of moveless cloud slept in the east, covering Hilo and the thunder cone of Kilauea. But the saddleback was clear, and far to the northwest he could see the great sweep of the Howland Ranch, his father's home, his own birthplace, way out past the brilliant green waves of cane; and beyond, he could see the smooth bend of Kailua Bay and the Kona Coast, with the sea moving slowly in against the coast with a curl of blue that could break his heart.

He wiped the lenses of the rifle sight with a handkerchief and screwed the eyepiece around until the ranchland showed clearly and he saw the familiar rise of the mansion, Manoalani, looming in the distance. He set the safety on the rifle and took aim.

Now, he thought, if we were only closer, and Laura was to walk out on the lanai . . . He pressed the trigger.

Then he set the rifle down in disgust. The idea was contemptible, he thought. Like teasing yourself with that petulant notion of suicide a little while ago. A man who talks about committing suicide seldom does. It was a grandstand play. Trying to make other people suffer for your own disillusionments.

He checked his watch. Five-thirty. Right now at Manoalani, Senator Howland was probably out pacing the lanai, brandy in hand, the old fabled rage working up through him as he waited for the Governor's call. Proud, ambitious old fool. Aaron grinned, thinking of his father and all his dreams of leading Hawaii to statehood. Since Delegate Stinson's death in Washington earlier that week, the old man had been seething with anticipation. He had even worked over an acceptance speech, just in case. Well, if the power boys of the Big Five and the Republican Party brass around Iolani Palace had decided to give old Willard Howland the nod for the delegacy, he would have heard by now. At any rate, it would keep the old man too preoccupied to pay any attention to Laura.

Dear sweet lovely Laura, the most charming wife a man could have, Aaron thought bitterly. Except that the marriage had no voltage. During the last few years, something had gone out of the marriage. He was not an adolescent fool who expected the magic to last forever. But he expected a little more than what was left. Where there had once been magic, there was now little more than stylized responses. Where there had once been a tumbling middle-of-the-afternoon spontaneity, there was now a staleness; a habit of ultimate but savorless intimacy. Once upon a time there had been a lovely, zesty girl in gay chiffon, dancing close to him, her eyes filled with expectancy and urge. Now there was, in her place, a nervous, resentful woman, sixteen years older and twenty pounds heavier, who had uncomfortably replaced the gay chiffon gowns for drab, somber-colored things. The glow had given way to a withering of flesh about her face; the coronet braids had given way to the short, currently stylish Italian bob, and her hair had lost its gloss. The exuberant girl had given way to the discontented American housewife, and until recently, the only stumbling block on the way to the divorce court had been her pride.

He had used her pride, he had used his knowledge of her reluctance, to convince her to take a week's vacation at Manoalani. Time to think things over. And then, if she really believes that divorce is the only solution—then the hell with it. God knows, she has reason enough.

He took another slug of bourbon, feeling dizzy from the combination of alcohol and altitude. With some contempt, he studied the ornate inscription on the flask:

To Aaron
on his 35th birthday.
With love, Laura

It had all started so casually that night. So damned easy.

The party was at their home in the swank Kahala district of Honolulu. Laura had invited the crowd from the Oahu Country Club and some friends from Castle & Cooke to help him celebrate. He had been against the idea. He wanted to forget his thirty-fifth birthday. There was something ominous about it; something that brought with it the sense of soon being forty years old.

He had never had that feeling of age before. He had taken the years in stride, letting his thirtieth birthday pass by with little notice. He was still a partner in youth. He swam at Waikiki almost every day in the year. He played a steady game of golf with the younger crowd at Waialae. His singles game at the Pacific Club courts was adequate enough, although he was cutting down in preference to doubles. He found he could play four hard sets of doubles and not be as pooped as from one set of singles.

He had let the years pass by with nothing more than a vague feeling of discontent that he believed to be universal with all men as they moved through their thirties, and it was not until the night of his thirty-fifth birthday that he felt a rather sharp resentment against age. All along, he had believed that man conquered Time. That night, he became curiously overwhelmed with the possibility—perhaps the strong probability—that Time conquered man; and that in the final reckoning, Time would conquer Aaron Howland.

And that night she came to his party. He saw her and all his sour spirits vanished. Looking at her, he realized that the feeling had been building within him for years. The aimless, hungry restlessness. The sharp, anticipatory shiver in his guts when he had watched the young gold-skinned girls with their supple bodies switching mysteriously in their cotton dresses as they strolled along Bishop Street in the late summer afternoons. Before he danced with her, before he even spoke to her, he decided that with her he could conquer Time.

Her name was Lei Villanueva. She was a cosmopolite—part Hawaiian, part Chinese, part Filipina, part Portuguese. She had warm, coppery skin. Her slanted, brandy-colored eyes seemed oddly mocking. Her wide, full mouth gave a suggestion of savagery to her sullen, vital face. Her hair was the color of midnight, long, the way he liked it, falling in glossy ropes of ebony to her bare shoulders. Her ripe body seemed so incredibly curved in a light silk dress that it looked as though she could burst it with one indolent stretch. She moved with a sinuous grace, full of rich, slow promises. She hit him hard where all his curious, restless hunger lived.

She danced a hula for them early during the party, and about midnight, when the liquor had done its job on most of them, she let loose with a torrid Tahitian number, Aaron staring at her all the while with the slightly apologetic air of a hungry dog. She felt his eyes and, turning, stared frankly at him across the living room and smiled in a way that suggested they were both alone among all these people and both very much aware. Later, they danced together.

"That was quite a sensational number you did for us. As host, I'd like to thank you."

"I hope it didn't shock you." Her voice was pleasantly low. It had a smoky quality he liked.

"Not at all. Maybe it shocked some of my stuffy guests, but they need to be shocked. I was crazy about it."

"Good. It's a Tahitian love dance, and it's supposed to make a man a little crazy."

She was lithe in his arms. As she moved he could feel the smooth warm muscles slide beneath the velvet skin of her back. They danced in an easy rhythm. He was not holding her close, yet her body moving next to his seemed frankly erotic. He felt there would be no pretense about her.

"Should I take the bold chance and tell you how much I'd like to see you dance again?" he tried. "Or should I discard that idea?"

"Discard it."

His grin was a bit shamefaced. "I hope I didn't offend you."

"No."

"Then what?"

"I'm a little disappointed."

"I'm sorry. I only meant that it was a beautiful dance and I think you are a beautiful woman . . ."

"And you'd like to see me again."

"Yes."

"How quaint."

Her slow bold stare of appraisal made him feel peculiar. "Why does that disappoint you?"

"Because it's so trite," she said. "It's automatic. A tired old gambit. You're saying things you think you're supposed to say. You've been following me around all night, your eyes glued to me with a kind of forlorn but greedy glitter as if I were a rare food and while your hunger is all there, you're not too sure your digestive tract could handle it. Say something that sounds as if you haven't babbled it a million times before."

Aaron felt defeated. He had the uncomfortable knowledge that she could see through him as he stood there, pleading dumbly for adventure.

"You've stumped me," he said weakly. "What can I say?"

"That's for you to decide." There was a trace of a smile on her wide, savage mouth. "It's your birthday, Mister Howland. Take a chance."

"With you?"

"Sure." Her grin was almost childlike. "I've been watching you. You look all twisted up inside. Desperate. Ready to explode."

"I am ready to explode."

"What about?"

"You."

When the dance was over he fixed bourbon and sodas for the two of them. He felt pleased with himself at the ease with which he maneuvered her outside. The breeze, sweet with the scent of ginger, was cool on their cheeks. They strolled quietly to a corner of the garden where a little Yeddo-type Japanese bridge arched across a fishpond to a miniature pagoda. A giant banyan sheltered the corner in darkness. The only sound was the murmuring of the warm, moonless night on the waters of the pond.

She was leaning against the banyan, facing him boldly in the dark, her arms folded beneath her breasts. She was putting any approach squarely up to him, yet he did not know just how to go about it.

"Do you believe in predestination?" he said, trying to make his tone sound casual. When he saw her face pucker up he realized how paltry he sounded.

"You mean like you and I were scheduled to meet tonight for some particular purpose and as soon as the setting is right you're going to show me that purpose?"

"Well," he stammered, "that's not exactly . . ."

"No, not exactly, but close enough," she said. "I don't go for it anyway. It's just another tired, worn-out gambit."

"Everything's a gambit to you. You're impossible."

"No, quite the opposite," she said, her voice amused. "Ask anyone."

"You're playing a game."

"Play with me."

He saw in her eyes a strange mixture of tenderness and deep rich laughter. His heart was pounding. If he missed this chance, she would have contempt for him. He would never make up the lost ground. He grabbed her wrists and pulled her body tightly into his and kissed her. But somehow, the kiss didn't come off.

"No. No games," he said. "I've wanted to kiss you from the moment you walked into my house."

"Yes, I know."

"You know exactly what I want."

"Yes." She looked at him with that curiousness in her eyes. "Do you always get what you want?"

"I always try."

She laughed. "That's the second time you've been honest."

"I'm honest about wanting you."

She became quite solemn, almost passive. She sipped her drink, her eyes inspecting him over the rim of her glass. "Want me as what?" she said, in a different voice. "Want me as excitement? Want me as a plaything? As a brand-new toy on your birthday?"

"You know it's more than that."

"Do I?"

"Oh hell, Lei, I want you as a woman." He pulled her close again. "I need you that way. I've got to have you that way." And he realized how much he meant it. The temerity, the shame of the beggar that had been inside him vanished now with a swelling of blood and need, and he knew he would run the risk of rocking his entire structure for her. "I swear I need you so bad—"

She moved into him then. And he felt the full impact of her body: a body that made him think, crazily, of a rumpled bed; of hot dark meadows where love lay waiting; a body that could be tender and pliable with him one moment, and burn the mattress the next. She wore a heavy perfume with the scent of musk, and when she moved into his arms he felt weak, almost sick, with desire.

When he kissed her again he could feel her respond with a wild and muscular abandon. There was a hard glitter of excitement in her eyes.

"Come on," he said, in a thick, dry voice. "I'll take you home."

"No, not home. I know a place."

And that night, with Lei Villanueva, he started having his Great Adventure. He started conquering Time.

A crazy thing to do, but not a pointless thing; not a totally regrettable thing. There were moments with her that he would not trade for the world.

But he should have had more sense than to risk everything. He had known from the start that she represented trouble and the risk of ruin. He had heard of men ruined by similar infatuations that were, at their base, nothing more than tremblings in the groin; weak, fleshy incantations to the shadowy depravities of lust. He did not believe it could happen to him: a respected, successful man with a lovely wife, a fine ocean-view home in Kahala, a twenty-five-thousand-dollar-a-year vice-presidency with Castle & Cooke, close and important friends throughout the Territory; the scion of one of the oldest and most prominent Island families. But it was happening. The entire structure of his life was tottering, ready to collapse. And with it, his self-respect. A man's ruin, he thought, is a staggering monument to his self-indulgence.

Having money in the bank had made it so damnably easy. A nice apartment facing the ocean off Kalakaua Avenue, just far enough up from Waikiki to be fashionable and near enough to his Kahala home so he could open the throttle on the ice-blue Jaguar and race down there in five minutes. Clothes and a television set, a hi-fi, some coldly modern furnishings, a king-sized bed with a black silk spread and a colorful fleet of pillows at the head. It was the first time he had ever kept a mistress.

There had been moments of doubt, moments of self-derision when he riled himself for being a playboy panting in the scent of girl flesh. There were moments of guilt, when he thought of Laura, but he chased these moments away. He would grow restless in the late afternoons, and in the soft tropical blue dusk he would feel that familiar reluctance to drive home to Laura and the passionless routine. Instead, he would speed past the Royal Hawaiian and the Waikiki strip, past the dull green sward of Kapiolani Park, to the place where love lay waiting for him. He had been calling it love for some time.

Laura would never find out because he would be careful. Laura would never find out because he would quit it soon. Just a temporary fling. He would quit it as soon as he had had his fill. Maybe next week. Next month.

But there was that magic to her that was unlike anything he had ever dreamed. She was charged with some sort of pagan voltage that brought him to sensual delights he never believed possible. And he never did get his fill. Not even after Laura found out. Not even months after Laura battled him about it. And the night Laura finally told him she wanted a divorce, Lei Villanueva told him she was pregnant.

The Great Adventure, he thought sourly, crouched at the volcano. Name and self-respect and wife and marriage. All over now and there's nothing left but parts of people waiting to be put together whole again.

He shut his jaw so tight his teeth ached. Don't think that way, he told himself. Don't gloom it up all out of proportion. The answer to everything is patience. Let time take care of it. Laura seems to have simmered down. The thing to do is patch up with Laura and convince Lei that an abortion is the best way out. Then pick up the pieces with Laura and start all over again.

He had been so tense that the knuckles of his clenched fists gleamed white like the joints of quartered beef. Relax, he warned himself. Just ease out of it all.

It had grown intensely cold. Far to the west, the soft gold shawl of the sun burned out beyond Keahole Point. He watched it for a moment and remembered the legend of the Specter of Brocken. Maybe Dean Kahana was right, he thought. I need a little luck. A little pat on the back by fate.

He stood up and turned his back to the sun, his eyes searching the eastern sky where a warm purple light poured over the Island like wine and a prairie of cloud rolled in against the summit on the sundown winds. But the clouds were dark, carrying rain, and he could not see his shadow upon them.

A sudden twilight moved into the sky's arena. Far below, a scar of a moon tracked silently across the ocean. He shuddered a moment as he heard, from far away, the lonely caw of a falcon cut through the silence like a ragged sword. He crouched at the rim of the crater and stared into the fire pit. It was much larger than he had imagined; almost three miles long, almond-shaped, a mile and a half across at its widest point. It reminded him of a painting he had once seen of Dante's Inferno. The sheer walls dropped more than six hundred feet, and there were narrow veins of ice in the far wall. Cracks in the overlapping layers of lava were smoldering, the sulphur banks smoking. Three cinder cones, the largest of which was more than two hundred feet high, rose from the floor at the eastern end of the caldera, hot blasts of steam and sulphur gases coiling about them. Fiery waves of lava splashed up against the inner walls. It made him think of some project that God had been mistaken about and was still experimenting with, as He might be with the soul of man.

He felt the flesh on the back of his neck prickle and bunch with fear. But he could not look away from the caldera. His eyes burned with a stunned idiocy as though hypnotized; his senses were so drugged by the scene that they were unaware of the third, final tremor grinding its way through the volcano.

The rumblings grew louder in the hot black throat. A tremendous blister swelled up from the liquid lake until the gas pressure within burst the skin, sending cascades of molten lava down along the buttress walls. There was a second upsurge of lava. The fumes leaping out from vents in the crater became thin and blue with the increase of heat pressure deep in the pit. The boiling lava lake, a perfect blood-red now, churned up through the throat of the volcano, seething with impatience. Caldrons formed, collapsed into the red pool, then formed again. The roar of fire geysers sounded like the smashing of heavy seas against the rocks. The spouting columns of white-hot lava shot to heights of four hundred feet, almost to the rim. They turned scarlet as they cooled, then fell back as charred boulders and enormous chunks of congealed cinder. There was a sharp tilt to the earth, accompanied by a fresh blast of gas. The lava lake contracted. It dropped as one great caldron deep into the bowels of the pit. Then, as Aaron watched, his face sagged in mute horror, the caldron burst. The earth's hot blood spiraled up from the throat of the volcano, the raging fountain of flame bursting beyond the summit, three hundred feet into the sky above him.

He did not know when he started running. He did not know that he was screaming. The thunder of the eruption muffled his screams. A taste like old brass churned up from his stomach and made him vomit. His lungs ached, ready to burst. His legs felt like cotton. But he continued running, stumbling, staggering to his feet to run again. The first ropy gush of lava had spilled over the summit.

Chapter Two

SENATOR WILLARD HOWLAND twisted impatiently at the lens regulator of the Zeiss binoculars he held to his eyes. He fingered the disc a moment more, until the summit of Mauna Loa showed clearly above its bed of cloud. Slowly, he moved the binoculars, tracing a line from the summit down to the general vicinity where the radio announcer had reported the lava outpourings.

"I can't see a damned thing."

"Try farther east," Dean Kahana said. "Farther to your right."

"The clouds are beginning to roll in all over now."

"Is the summit clear?"

"It won't be for long."

"Do you want me to take a look?"

"If there was something to see, I could see it," old Howland said. "I wish we'd got out here earlier. Before the clouds moved in."

"I'm sorry."

"It's not your fault. My own damned fault."

"Should I try the radio again?"

"See if you can get the latest report."

Dean juggled the dial of the small transistor radio he held in his hand. "I wouldn't worry too much about Mistah Aaron," he said.

"I agree with you. He's not worth worrying about."

"What I meant was that I don't think he'll be in any danger."

"Damn fool thing to do," the old man muttered. "What did he think he'd find up at the summit? What was he trying to prove?"

"I'm not suah."

"Damn fool kid stunt," Senator Howland said irritably. There's been a queerness in Aaron lately, he thought. A hint of breakdown.

"Does he know we all have to fly to Honolulu tomorrow for Delegate Stinson's funeral?"

"Yessuh, Senator. He's plannin' on it."

"What in hell could have happened to him?"

"Probably nothin'. He probably stayed at the observatory for the night. Must of seen a great show from there."

"Unless he was part of it."

Dean tuned the radio until the static cleared and an announcer's voice cut through the still morning air with a staccato insistency:

"We repeat the latest bulletin from the Hawaii National Park Observatory: there is no immediate danger resulting from last night's shocks along the eastern rift of Mauna Loa. Three tremors were recorded at the observatory yesterday. Volcanologist Norton Jaeger said the seismograph in the cellar of Mokuaweoweo registered a southeasterly tilt at six A.M. *yesterday, again at five-ten* P.M.*, and a major quake accompanied by caldera activity at six-forty-seven last night. A two-mile concentric rift opened up along the volcano's southeast wall at approximately six-fifty-five last night, causing lava outpourings along its length. Dr. Jaeger said that the main seismograph at the observatory early this morning recorded a definite reduction of gas pressure in the source tunnel. He added that the underground lava flow had changed direction, starting to*

move along with the gas columns in a westerly course sometime about three A.M. *today. The liquid lava lake in the crater overflowed last night but is now reported to be at the seven-hundred-foot level without fluctuations. The geophysical laboratory chief said there was no danger that the Hilo, Puna or Pahala areas would be under threat of flow. Dr. Jaeger added, however, that additional minor disturbances could be expected today and throughout the week, and that there is a strong possibility of a major westerly eruption sometime in midwinter. This is the eight o'clock news from station KHIL in Hilo . . ."*

Dean clicked off the radio. "A westerly eruption?" he mused. "That don't sound right."

"It's ridiculous," Howland muttered. "Damned announcer doesn't know east from west. No active rift zone on our side of the mountain."

"It's possible, though."

"Damned unlikely. That's about all Manoalani would need."

"The grazeland couldn't take it."

"Neither could I. I'd give the whole damn ranch back to Bishop Bank." He made a last sweep of the volcano with his field glasses. A rack of cloud blanketed the summit. "Well, we won't see anything now," he grumbled, slipping the binoculars into the leather case that hung from a strap about his shoulder.

"I'm sorry I couldn't get to you earliah," Dean said. "Me and Aaron split up about six yesterday mornin'. Right after the first quake. I was goin' to come back through the desert but I cut down to the Parker Ranch instead. Left the horses with Tavares at the west pasture and took his jeep in as fast as I could."

"No, it's my own fault. I should have listened to the news reports last night. I've been so damned busy with—with Joe Stinson's death; with the funeral tomorrow. Waiting for the Governor's call."

"I was goin' to ask you about that," Dean said, studying the old man. "Have you heard anything yet?"

"No," Senator Howland said.

"The Governor hasn't gotten in touch with you?"

"No."

Howland bowed his head, relaxing the muscles in his skinny, corded neck. He balled his hands into thin brown lumps of fists and knuckled the strain from his eyes. Lately, it seemed that everything placed a strain on him. He could scan down a mental list of all the unfinished projects—the new airport terminal at Kona, tourist development at Kailua, the new breakwater at Hilo Bay, funds for dredging the deepwater harbor at Kawaihae, the Governor's failure to open additional homestead lands, cattle troubles, coffee troubles, the water shortage, the one thousand and one problems of the rich sugar lands along the Hamakua Coast, plantation problems at Honokaa, Hakalau, Honomu and Peepeekeo: there had been days when he was certain that the only thing that kept him going in his office was the trinitro toluene. Last winter, when he had led the Hawaii Statehood Commission's debate in Washington, the angina got so bad that he didn't think even the TNT tablets would do it. He had mixed them with straight nitroglycerin tablets, the tablets Dr. Judd warned him to go easy on, and he had taken enough to—well, he wasn't quite sure: to last long enough to see the statehood bill passed in Congress, he told himself. Now, Joe Stinson's death capped the strain; gave it something to chafe against. Delegate Stinson was a casualty in the long, heartbreaking struggle for Hawaiian statehood. And Stinson had come very close to winning the struggle. With the delegacy suddenly vacant, Willard Howland felt the old furious urgency well up in him again. Maybe now he could win the final battle.

He turned to the Hawaiian. "We might as well start back."

They picked their way through sun-bleached kiawe scrubs to a shadowed crevice where they had tethered the horses.

"Come along, Baron, Miss Brett," the Senator said softly to the collies that had risen and started circling at his approach. He swung up into the saddle with an old weary grace and the big, bluff-chested white started down the trail, the collies loping easily alongside.

Dean mounted and followed them, studying the proud, almost insolent figure of Willard Howland, erect and moody in the saddle, cantering slowly ahead, the ancient stallion moving with a marvelous grace beneath the canopy of poincianas and shower trees that lined the sea road leading toward Manoalani.

The sea was drawn calm and glittered in the early morning sun like a slick jewel. They rode out into a square of sunlight and Dean could make out more clearly now the singular figure of Senator Howland, already a legend in his land; dressed as always in a tailed white linen coat that flapped like a sheet about his shrunken frame, his coattails spreading behind the cantle, the white linen trousers, cuffing worn, wrinkled boots, the bowstring tie rippling like a slender black flag past his shoulder, the brim of his woven Manahiki hat swept down to shield his fierce but weary old face—a lean face with famished hollows beneath the high cheekbones, and a sharp nose jutting out like a spear above the white-gold mustaches that flared downward at the corners of his mouth; a face of flint, deeply lined yet curiously warmed now with the sunlight touching and mellowing it with a dignity—a magnificence, really—as if it had been selected by the gods for a statue in some later age and consequently had to endure beyond time.

Somewhere in that burred face, Dean thought, was the seed of the untamed giants who came here and carved from these islands their empires of pineapple and coffee, and sugar cane weaving as far into the sunset as eye can see, and cattle sprinkled like grains of cinnamon across a thousand hills. And Willard Howland, the last of that breed, riding across those hills, his dark gold eyes sweeping his empire like some rude, tattered king, turning finally from the sea road onto the macadam that curved slowly beneath a guard of royal palms to Manoalani: the Senator straight in the saddle, riding in his old proud way, the big white lathered by bursts of his fading, arrogant prance, the pelts of the collies dark with sweat, the dust of time beaten into every part of them.

Like its owner, Manoalani itself seemed worn but indomitable; hewn from some stronger, more vital age and destined to endure. It stood a quarter mile in from Kailua Bay, on a gentle rise of land among silk oak and plumeria, the sun-shot leaves hanging motionless against the massive white-colonnaded veranda. Its lawns were green shimmering washes of velvet, studded with coconut palms, mynas chattering ceaselessly in the highest fronds. Pikaki mounting one end of the veranda had bloomed and fallen, and the drift of its petals lay heavily about the scarred, peeling colonnades. The house itself was solemn, as if its weathered grandeur were reluctantly accepted along with the knowledge that the passions of three generations of Howlands had spent it and now all that was left was to await the desertion of old Willard.

Senator Howland reined his horse and turned from the macadam to a shell path that wound beyond the house through a jungle of fern and Calliandra to a row of stables that were in such utter disrepair they appeared gutted.

"Join me for coffee?" the Senator said, dismounting.

"No thank you." Dean hesitated. "But there is—something I'd like to talk to you about. If you got the time."

"Go ahead."

"I was wonderin' about your plans for tomorrow."

"Tomorrow? The funeral is tomorrow. I'm to give the eulogy."

"Sloan and Paul come in on the *Lurline* tomorrow."

The Senator turned so that Dean could not see the dull anger flush in his cheeks. "Is it so soon?" he said quietly. "I'd forgotten. Seems like they've just left."

"Yessuh. Graduation was Sunday and they boarded that afternoon. They dock at eight."

"Umm . . . Paul had quite a career for himself at Stanford. He should have made All-American. You should be mighty proud of your kid brother."

"Yessuh, we are, Senator."

"Eight tomorrow morning?"

"I was wonderin' if you planned to meet them."

"I won't be able to."

"Then Mother and I will."

Old Howland's tough gold eyes softened for a second as he looked up at Dean. "How is your mother?"

"Good, suh. She sends you her best aloha."

"How does she like living in Honolulu?"

"Pretty good. She's got that little house out in Nanakuli."

"Yes, I know. Tell her we all miss her very much out here."

Dean dismounted and leaned against the railing, scuffing a vague design in the stable earth with the toe of his boot. "We were wonderin' if you'd heard from Sloan. About her and Paul?"

Howland nodded. "Yes, I've heard all right. I know all about their little plans." He made a mental image of Sloan's letter, which was upstairs on his desk, still unanswered. He had tried several times to reply to her letter but could never get started. How can you answer a letter like that, he thought, remembering his daughter's nervous, sprawling handwriting:

Please try to understand, Daddy, and don't let our plans shock you or disturb you. There's nothing shocking about it and it shouldn't even be a surprise. After all, Paul and I have been in love with each other for a long time, and there's no true reason why we shouldn't get married. Nothing will stop us, Daddy, and I know you won't try.

No, there was "nothing shocking" about it, he thought wryly, except that the whole idea of her marrying Paul Kahana was preposterous. And he must not try to stop her, she had suggested; don't stop stubborn, headstrong Sloan Howland. Just sit by idly and watch her smash her life to pieces.

"We were curious how you felt about it," he heard Dean say.

"You know goddamn well how I feel about it," the old man muttered. "And I'm sure your mother does, too. It just can't happen." He turned and scowled through the haze at the distant plateaus of Hualalai. "If Mrs. Howland were alive, God rest her soul, the situation would never have developed." He wondered while he spoke how he had let it develop. Had he been blind to it all along?

"Those kinds of—of situations are developin' more and more these days," Dean said tentatively. "Those kinds of things are—"

"What do you mean, 'things'?" Howland snapped at him.

"Marriages," Dean said. His manner was courteous, but old Howland noted in his voice a faintly challenging ring, a mild defiance. "Those kinds of—mixed marriages are gettin' more common."

"It's common all right! That's the word for it! And it's not going to happen to Sloan, goddamn it!"

"I was just tryin' to point out—"

"Now you listen to me, boy." Howland swung around and glared at him, his lusty old face written with pride and an almost dissolute fury. "I'll be frank with you. I'll give you my honest opinion instead of one that would be pretty to hear. I know just what you were trying to point out. But it doesn't mean a damned thing to me. If these—these mixed marriages are becoming more accepted nowadays, it doesn't make them more correct. It's just a sign of our decaying standards and ideals. A lessening of human dignity for both races involved. And don't let any pelican-chested social moralizer tell you different. It wouldn't be good for Paul, and it certainly won't do for Sloan. And by God I won't let it happen! Not while I've got blood in my veins!" He stopped himself, feeling obscurely guilty. Somewhere along the line, he must have failed with Sloan. But he could not take that failure out now on Dean Kahana. He could not dwell upon the obviousness of race or color or heritage.

"These kids are too young," he continued, switching to another line of attack. "They know the first thing about marriage, but that's all they know. They refuse to believe that living with the person you love is hard and demanding; that a good marriage is one of the most difficult tricks in the world. Especially with kids these days. They're soft and they quit too easily. They want the rewards of a good marriage, they want the rewards of a good life, but they want them the easy way, without bothering to work for them. It's a modern, peculiarly American shortcoming.

"No, I don't think these kids are ready for anything as serious as marriage. Sloan says they plan to get married this October, during Aloha Week. Aloha Week," he repeated contemptuously, "as if the whole marriage would be one big party. I'm a hundred per cent against it." He shook his head. "How else can I feel about it?" He brooded a moment, realizing how Grace Howland would feel about it if she were alive. It would break her heart, he knew. Somehow, he would have to find a way to stop it. "I don't know, Dean," he shrugged with weariness, "I just don't know. Young kids these days . . ."

He let the sentence trail off, thinking perhaps that was the best way to end the discussion. Shrug your shoulders and call them kids and say they don't know what they're doing. Wasn't that the standard line of evasion for today's parental generation? Shake your head and shrug. But how else was he to discuss the situation with a young man like Dean Kahana? As fine a young man as one could ever hope to meet, and a sensitive young man who, Willard realized with a feeling of shame, had been offended by the conversation. The entire Kahana family were among the finest people he had ever known, white-skinned or dark. Doc Kahana, who had managed Manoalani's herds until his death three years ago, had been a hard worker and a dear friend. And Kapiolani, the boys' mother, helped raise all the Howland children. Kapiolani nursed Sloan to her breast after Grace Howland had died bearing Sloan. And Paul?—cocky and a little on the wild side, probably the thing that won Sloan—but a hell of a fine boy. But not for Sloan Howland. Not for the princess.

He studied Dean for a moment, then asked quietly, "How does your mother feel about it?"

"She seemed a little surprised. Knowin' how much she loves both Sloan and Paul, I'm suah she feels awful strong about it, one way or the other. But she didn't volunteer her real feelin's. She kept them to herself. And I didn't ask her."

"And you?" Howland said quite solemnly. "How do you feel about it?"

Dean gazed beyond the stables to where the hot June morning quivered in the garden and soft pieces of the sun moved through the leaves and poured across the mossy lawn. He remembered those days of soft Arcadian peace when he and Paul and the Howland children—not Aaron, he was too grown-up—but Garth and Steven and Sloan, and yes, even Ward Akana (I wonder if the Senator ever sees Ward any more? I wonder what the old man could say to Ward Akana?) used to race through the garden with the rich vague glee of childhood games. A long time ago the garden had been the place of boyhood dreams and secrets and young heroism and first love, and, Dean guessed, a time that would never come again; a time mostly of Sloan Howland running wild on those skinny brown legs, her happy, sudden girl's laughter rippling through the garden:

"Hurry, Dean! Boost me up into the tree!"

"You're too big to hide in the tree. Paul will find you there."

"No no no he won't!"

"You always hide there."

"I like it here. Hurry, we'll climb all the way to the top."

"I'm not goin' to hide up there with you. You don't hide good. You always giggle."

"I won't giggle this time. Promise promise. If you don't hide with me I won't love you any more."

"You don't love me, Sloan. You said you loved Paul."

"I hate Paul! He pushed me this morning and held my head under water until almost I drowned. Please hide up here with me. I'll love you all day long and even after supper."

"No giggling?"

"I promise. We can go all the way to the top and no one will ever find us there."

The sound of her laughter faded away. Dean waited intently,

hoping it would start again, but all he could hear was the lump and feathery scramble of a myna against the leaves.

"Dean?" old Howland repeated.

Dean turned away gravely. "I guess I don't feel anything." He looked at the old man with a faintly sad grin, then gathered the reins and led the horses away. Howland watched him disappear behind the stalls, then turned and started toward the house, the collies trailing behind him as he tramped moodily, with long hungry strides, his six-foot frame bent forward, his hat in his hand, his thick, shaggy white-gold hair falling across his forehead and curling raggedly at his neck, his head low, his shoulders stooped as if he were walking into a strong wind. He mumbled something to the collies and the older one, Baron, stopped and looked up at him gravely and expectantly, awaiting the scratch behind the ear that was given so seldom these days; but after a moment Baron and the younger dog walked away to the cool shadow of the stairs, circled, and found their place.

Howland stood for a while before his house, gazing out toward the slick of Kailua Bay and the open sea, thinking, as he had so many times before, that it was, perhaps, this Kona sea, drawn immense and eternal before him—a restless sea; brilliant, brooding, sometimes tender, sometimes wild, but always curiously sensitive to him, to all of them—that tempered the Howlands and made them what they were: a vibrant, moody clan, equally vulnerable to the most spiraling flights of romance as they were to the shadows which trailed these flights with warm but broken wings.

He mounted the stairs to the shadowy veranda and crossed it and entered the hall. The great house was richly desolate of motion or sound. He stopped in the middle of the hall.

"Coyama!"

The hall was paneled in darkly varnished pine, its deep-bitten grain showing through. The stairway mounted beneath its red carpet in a tall slender curve to the upstairs gloom. A chandelier of crystal prisms hung from the center of the ceiling. The sockets had originally been fitted for candles but long ago had been wired for electricity. To the left of the stairwell was a forty-foot living room, also paneled in pine, with foot-square beams braced across its width. The far wall was built completely of lava rock, with a fireplace big enough for a man to walk into without stooping. The furniture was covered, and it loomed shapelessly in its somber shrouds. A Steinway grand at the corner of the room alone was uncovered. A single bar of sunlight filtered into the room from the division in the heavy dun curtains. The light was filled with dust particles and rested flatly and without warmth on a sheet of opened concerto music on the piano.

To the right of the stairwell was a study, locked now and no longer in use, but which at one time served as a writing room for Mark Twain. This was in the days before the storyteller found fame and he was traveling through the Islands writing stories for the old Sacramento Union. John Howland, Willard's father, was still building Manoalani then and he befriended the writer and brought him to the still-unfinished house to live. The two of them combined several bottles of clipper brandy and their carpenter's talents to carve the koa-wood bathtub in which Willard himself had been bathed as a child. That bathtub too had been since relegated to the locked study primarily because Willard's mother had objected to the gargoylelike Menehunes with which it had been embossed, at Twain's insistence.

"Coyama!" old Howland bellowed again. As he started upstairs, the ancient Japanese cook padded out from the kitchen, his steel-rimmed spectacles perched halfway down his nose.

"Terefono, terefono!" Coyama shouted, shaking a creamed ladling spoon at the Senator and catching the drippings with his apron. "Goldam—two tiam it ring, two tiam! From Honoruru!"

"Was it the Governor?"

"I duhno, I duhno. From Honoruru."

"Did you get a number?"

"Nooo, no numbah. Why for? Him caw back."

Upstairs he tramped heavy-booted along the hallway, on one side of which were narrow windows set with leaded panes of colored glass which made the light passing through them seem richly solemn. Four bedrooms were in the east wing, including the one in which Grace Howland had died twenty-one years before and which now was permanently sealed. He went to the end of the hallway, entering his own bedroom and crashing the door behind him, tramped on through his bedroom to the office adjoining it. He went straight to his desk and, with sudden decision, pushed aside a clutter of old newspapers, government bulletins, Territorial correspondence and a maze of similar documents, and found the telephone.

"This is Senator Howland. I want to speak person-to-person with Governor Balter at Iolani Palace in Honolulu."

As he waited for the connection his eyes fell upon an addressed envelope on his desk:

Mr. Garth Howland
c/o General Post Office Delivery
Papeete, Tahiti
French Oceana

He had written the letter three nights before, but postponed mailing it with the hope that he would know definitely about the delegacy. But delegacy or not, it was high time for Garth to return home. Four years now, old Willard thought, Garth has been drifting aimlessly about the South Seas in that godforsaken damned ketch. *The Seven Little Sisters*—forty feet of rotted hull and a floursack sail. Did Garth plan to spend his entire life aboard that damned boat?

The letter, written in the Senator's recognizable fury of swirls and angry crossing of Ts, was an exhaustive account of the political possibilities resulting from Delegate Stinson's death, plus the usual, time-worn, emphatic request for Garth to return home and manage the ranch.

No doubt this constant, aimless drifting strikes you as a poetical way to dissipate yourself, but it is a bitter thorn in my side, knowing you refuse to return home when you are sorely needed here. I can find no one to manage the ranch. The only person excepting yourself whom I would even consider is Dean Kahana, but he has definitely decided upon a doctor's career and is busy with his premedical studies. There is no one but you, Garth, and I trust I do not have to explain how important the management of Manoalani is to me, to Aaron and Sloan, and to yourself. If I am to become Republican nominee for the delegacy, then I must conduct my campaign with my mind free from any ranch worries. The only way I can be assured of this is to have a Howland managing the ranch.

He had found it difficult to bring the letter to a close. Garth was and always had been his favorite son. Garth the wastrel, the wanderer, the stray; cursed with the search for an unlikely Lorelei.

After several scratched-out sentences, the letter finally concluded:

You are thirty years old now, Son, and if you have not yet found whatever it is you've been searching for, the chances are that it does not exist.

He would mail the letter that afternoon, and hope it would reach Garth, wherever he was.

The office was cluttered with indiscriminate furniture and crammed filing cabinets fathomable only to old Willard. Coyama resolutely refused to enter into the room's mysteries, with the consequence that over the years the dust and debris had never been cleared away but simply changed locations. Behind Willard at his ancient roll-top desk, French windows opened upon a quiet garden shaded by jacaranda and russet Java plum trees, their bloom drifting up from the garden in sweet, nostalgic gusts.

One wall of the office consisted of a recessed bookcase. The law volumes were mildewed and a complete set of Shakespeare had become riddled with termites. Alongside these were volumes of Calderon, Donne and Byron; histories by Gibbons and Toynbee; the works of Plato, a well-read copy of the *Rubáiyát,* several Bibles, volumes of George Bernard Shaw, Proust, Goethe, Henry James, Joyce and Robinson Jeffers that Garth would pore over endlessly but which the Senator had never read; epics by Tolstoy and Dostoievsky that the Senator had tried to read but lost patience with; a complete set of the works of his father's friend, Mark Twain, bound in calfskin, and the South Seas stories of Stevenson, Melville and Maugham, and his old friend, James Hall. In a special dust-covered glass case were the works of his childhood friend, Jack London, with the first edition of *The Cruise of the Snark* personally inscribed.

On the wall alongside his desk there hung an aging brown photograph of Willard with Jack and Charmian London, taken aboard the *Snark* sometime during the summer of 1915, the grin on the novelist's ruggedly handsome face still showing clearly, indicatively. The photograph was signed in ink, *With warmest aloha,* KEAKA LAKANA. Next to it was another large photograph, signed simply FRANKLIN D. ROOSEVELT, showing the former President with Willard and Joe Stinson at the volcano. There were photographs of Aaron's wedding; and the twins, Garth and Steven, taken a short time before Steven was killed at Pearl Harbor. There was a formal photograph of the Kahana family, Doc and Kapiolani and

Dean and Paul, posed in utter discomfort; and a picture of Sloan taken when she was twelve, riding her pony, smiling shyly and gravely into the camera lens. A large oil painting of Grace Howland hung in a chipped gold-leaf frame in the center of the wall. It was a very poor work, done in the fashion of its time with a lush melodramatic background which detracted from the portrait. All the coloring and attitude was wrong, the artist missing the entire concept somehow, everywhere except about the eyes, where he had luckily captured the sad tranquillity that was, in essence, Willard Howland's wife and the mother of his children.

The interisland operator finally got through to the palace, but there was another delay as Howland declined to talk first with Casey Matsuka, the Governor's press secretary, then to Mrs. Isabel Wong, the Governor's personal secretary. Finally, he heard the thick, guttural "Hello, Will!" that he knew to be Governor Mike Balter's greeting.

"Were you trying to reach me, Mike?"

"All morning long. How are you? How's everything on the Big Island?"

"Everything's fine. I've been waiting—"

"Was the eruption last night anything serious?"

"No. I don't know. Look, Mike, I hoped you'd have some news by now—"

"I'm sorry it took me so long to get back to you, but we've been working like the devil over here."

"I understand that, Mike. Have you got any news?"

"These things aren't decided overnight, Will. If it was up to me alone, it would have been a simple matter. Willard Howland is the man for me. But I had to do a lot of checking, get a lot of opinions. From the Statehood Commission, from members of the Oahu Republican Central Committee, from brass around the palace, from Outer Island party chiefs . . . I don't have to explain all that to you."

"Of course, Mike." The color rose in old Willard's face, making his skin, scored by a thousand bisecting wrinkles, look like baked clay.

"But you know me, Will. I wouldn't call you with bad news. . . ."

Howland waited.

"I imagine that you're all set to deliver the eulogy tomorrow.

The plane gets in at Hickam at eight. Services are at Punchbowl at nine. It will be a good opportunity for you. Are you flying in tonight or tomorrow?"

"The first plane in the morning."

"Fine," the Governor said. "All of us here at the palace are stunned. Words can't do justice to a great statesman like Joe Stinson."

"Of course."

"Will," the Governor began, his voice arched in what Howland knew to be the tip-off to a long, overbearing monologue, "Joe died a patriot's death, in the service of his people. And he had nearly won his great crusade. There is a moment, Will, when destiny reaches out and taps each man on the shoulder. There is only one man I know who can fill Joe Stinson's boots in the struggle for Hawaiian statehood. That's what I've been telling the boys these past few days. I think this is your moment, Will."

Howland waited. "Thank you—"

"I've been telling them that we've got a great leader on the Big Island," the Governor drawled on. "A man who has been Territorial Senator from the Island of Hawaii for the past twenty-seven years; a man who during each moment of those years has dreamed of leading his people and his islands to statehood; a man who has dreamed of the justice of sitting in the United States Senate with the power to vote; a man whose dedication and integrity—Will, do you know what I told them?"

"What, Governor?"

"I told them that if Joe Stinson could choose his successor, he'd choose you."

Howland waited impatiently through the Governor's dramatic pause. Then he said, "Thank you, Mike. I mean that sincerely. I appreciate all the work you've done for me. But we can talk about destiny some other time. Get to the point, Mike. What was the verdict?"

After a long pause, the Governor said, "I'm getting to the point, Willard. But it's a little difficult."

"What is it?"

"These are important times, Willard, both for Hawaii and the Republican Party. It's not only a matter of dedication to statehood. There are many internal problems . . ."

"Go ahead."

"Many of our leading industrialists, high-ranking party members, Central Committeemen, myself included, are worried about growing Union difficulties. Not worried, really; perhaps . . . concerned. Contracts for plantation and waterfront workers have been reopened for renegotiation, and it appears they won't be able to settle. It appears, even, that Ward Akana might call a general strike—"

"What's that got to do with the delegacy?"

"Just this: a general strike at this time will look bad in Washington and the Mainland. The big boys don't want it. And before they give you a one hundred per cent nod for the nomination, they want to know if you can control the Union."

"Goddamn it, Mike, no one can control the Union! You know better than that!"

"Yes—I know. But here's what I told them, Willard. I told them that of all the men we could choose from, you had the best chances of—well, let's say, influencing Union leaders."

The Senator bowed his head, his hair spilling like a ragged white mane across his high skull. "Talk plainer, Mike," he said, and his voice was thick and slow. "Talk as plain as possible."

He looked at the receiver for a long time, wondering if there had been a disconnection. Then the Governor's words throbbed inside him, as harsh and as raw as doom:

"Can you control Ward Akana?"

So it had come to that, old Willard thought bitterly, sensing within himself a surge of drab fury against the Governor, against the situation, against himself really, and all the irrevocable accidents of life that never should have been allowed; the wounds that won't heal, the loss of innocence that leaves no peace. By the time we understand the accidents, by the time we understand the pattern of life they have placed us in, the definition we are making of ourselves, it is too late to break out of the mold.

. . . the seed of our destruction will blossom in the desert, the alexin of our cure grows by a mountain rock, and our lives are haunted by a Georgia slattern because a London cutpurse went unhung . . .

"It's—it's not the main issue," the Governor continued, "but it's—well, you know what I mean, Will. If you could control Ward Akana, if you could persuade him, you know; it would put a clincher to everything."

Willard's eyes turned dark and inward, as if they were exchanging with his soul some endless and secret gaze of grief. When he spoke, there was a strange quality to his voice, a tenderness shot through and veined with regret.

"I think I can—reach an understanding with Ward," he said.

Much later he tramped downstairs to lunch: into a high cool room, darkened by shutters but with checkered sunlight filtering through against the far end of the table. The table was heavy mahogany, polished and very large. In the center, a curved silver bowl held a bird-of-paradise spray and a profusion of vanda orchids. A white linen tablecloth covered one end of the table, at which Laura Howland sat awaiting him.

"Is there any news of Aaron yet?" He took his place at the head of the table.

"No, nothing at all." She twisted her lip and looked into the hallway as if she was expecting Aaron to enter. "I suppose he's quite all right. Taking his own sweet time about it all. But I wish he'd get here. Or at least phone."

"No doubt he'll get here for cocktail time. Probably hasn't stopped to consider that we might be worried. He's an expert at not thinking of others."

The guava juice was cold without being iced. The mango and papaya salad succulent. Coyama padded in from the kitchen with a platter of mahimahi steaks.

"Terefono, you getcha?" he asked, hovering over old Willard and placing one of the steaks on his plate.

"Yes, thank you."

"Wuz Guvnah, eh? Wuz numbah one Guvnah?"

Laura looked up at him with interest. "You've finally heard from Mr. Balter?"

Willard nodded. "There are a few things left to be straightened out, but it looks like I'll be nominated for the delegacy."

"Aa-haa, numbah one!" The old Japanese grinned his gums, shuffling back to the kitchen.

"Oh Willard, I'm so happy for you." Laura reached over and gave his hand a squeeze. "We'll be so proud of you."

"It's anything but certain yet," Willard said, easing his hand from hers. He resisted open affection or warmth, no matter how slight. "Then too, there's always the elections."

"You'll win. I'm sure you'll win." She noticed the folded newspaper he had brought to the table. "Is that this evening's paper already? What are those headlines?"

The Senator looked down, surprised that he had taken the paper along. It was the old edition of the Honolulu *Star-Bulletin* he had been reading just before lunch. The banner headline proclaimed in three-inch red type:

DELEGATE STINSON DIES!

Four days before, he had stared at the headline with stunned disbelief. Now, as his eyes glanced down again at the wire story from Washington that told how the Territorial Delegate to the United States Congress, his dear, lifelong friend, Joe Stinson, collapsed in his Capitol office and died of a heart attack in an ambulance en route to Bethesda Naval Hospital, he knew he had channeled his thoughts to accept the fact not only with a sense of personal loss, but also with a cold political practicality of the possibilities that Joe Stinson's death opened up. The second page of the newspaper was devoted entirely to pictures illustrating Stinson's career. One of the photographs was a duplicate of the one mounted in Willard's office. Taken in 1934, it showed Stinson, a portly, balding man who was then Senator of Oahu, and Howland at the volcano observatory in Hawaii National Park. Standing between them, grinning his famous grin, was the first President of the United States to visit the Territory, Franklin Roosevelt. The President had been comparatively strong in those days, and the picture showed neither crutches nor cane, just that confident smile, the optimistic tilt of the cigarette holder, the brim of his fedora curled back from his face.

"I give you gentlemen my solemn promise," the President had said that day, "that these islands of yours will become a member state of the Union. Perhaps this will not occur during my term of office, but sooner than you think, my friends, these islands and their peoples will be granted the full status they so richly deserve."

Well, Willard thought, pushing the paper away, statehood had been promised many times before. And by every President and Congress since. And we're no closer to it today than we were when Roosevelt was alive; than we were, really, when King Kamehameha first petitioned Congress for statehood back in 1854. And all we've ever gotten since are promises. Broken promises which have resulted in an ethical wrong; one hundred years of a moral injustice that has rendered these islands and their peoples into a form of second-class citizenry, the stepchildren of a nation. If he became delegate, Willard thought, it would be a well-gutted battlefield he'd be charging into: a hundred-year battlefield scarred with lies and deceit, political footballing, dalliance and disappointment. Disappointment gives rise to doubt, and doubt to denial. Will the Islands be denied? Will the great nation which boasts to the world of its fair play, its moral justice, its equality of men, continue to deny her own peoples?

He shook his head sourly. "Sometimes I question my own patriotism," he muttered.

Laura looked at him quizzically, but before she could think of some words to soothe him, she noticed that he had become absorbed again in his dreams and his ill-humored picking at his food.

She was an intense brunette with a pleasant wit, and her speech was like the rapid chatter of birds. Although not a pretty woman, she was nice-looking, with a quality of lively, unpretentious charm. Her short-cropped hair was crisp, her pale blue eyes quick and sensitive.

Her father had been a wealthy Maui sugar planter who had packed her off to Punahou and then to Mills College where she had majored in music. She had always wanted to create something of beauty—a tone poem, a light musical score, even an acceptable song, and for a while she worked hard at it. But none of it was any good and she realized without desperation that it never would be. When she married Aaron Howland, in one of the most lavish weddings in Maui's social history, she was satisfied with her conclusion that their love, and the children resulting from it, were to be the beauty and creativity of her life. But at thirty-three she was childless. And after her one pregnancy and its brutal delivery, they had had to tie her tubes for good—so that part of the creativity was out. Several years ago the marriage started going downhill and she knew now that it would never be the thing of beauty she had hoped for. She was left dimly tormented, an uncomfortable woman. She had slid into a black depression upon learning of Aaron's mistress—not even a white woman, but a hapa-haole; maybe not even that, maybe all gook. . . . But at the suggestion of spending a week together at Manoalani, her spirits vaulted to the mountaintops. Then that miserable hunting trip. And all the plans she had for their moments together churned like ashes now in the pit of her stomach. She was flooded with the nervous energies of anxiety. The mental picture of Aaron and his mistress sickened and angered her.

She wondered if she and Aaron could build their marriage into something worth while again, or if it would end in divorce. Divorce takes so much brazen guts. In the tight, critical society of the Islands it took an extraordinary amount of gall. Especially for people like herself. A public admission of failure, after twelve years. And then what? She caught a glimpse of herself in the polished silver bowl. There were those little telltale lines about her throat. They were the first to come, she had heard.

Maybe if she had been stronger they could have tried again. And maybe they would have had another son.

Men like sons, she thought, fighting the memory, as she had so often, of the utter calm of Hilo Bay that first morning of April, 1946: the tide slipping mysteriously out beyond the breakwater, leaving the bay a quiet dune of sand and coral reef, with rays and moray eels and comical pink balloon fish flapping helplessly on the sand, and more than a hundred children, little Aaron Junior among them, racing gleefully and unsuspectingly out across the floor of the vanished bay, collecting fish and shells and coral trees, while the tide kept retreating silently beyond the reef, being sucked into the tidal wave that roared in three minutes later. They were told afterwards that the Tsunami originated with volcanic activity up along the great Aleutian trough near Unimak Island (a place she never would have heard of in a million years) and raced across the intervening 2,300 miles of Pacific at a speed greater than four hundred and ninety miles an hour, until its forty-foot crests crashed into Hilo, killing little Aaron along with a hundred and fifty others. . . .

She bit her lip, trying to snap the train of thought. Her hand raced nervously for a cigarette. Don't think about any of it, she warned herself, lighting the cigarette and inhaling deeply. Think about something else. Talk.

"Incidentally," she caught Howland's attention, "I saw you and Dean Kahana by the stables. I waved to you but you were both so deep in conversation that you didn't notice. Were you settling the problems of the world, or politics, or what?"

"Sloan," he answered her.

"What's new with Sloan?"

"Sloan is adding her own peculiar bullheadedness to the Howland family saga."

"She's due in Honolulu tomorrow, isn't she?"

Howland nodded. "Maybe we can kick it out of her tomorrow night."

"Kick what out of her? What has she done now?"

Willard finished his iced coffee and rang for Coyama to clear the table. "She thinks she wants to marry Paul Kahana," he muttered.

Laura leaned forward. "She *what?*"

"You heard me correctly," Willard said shortly, not wanting to get involved in a long discussion.

Laura was genuinely shocked. "Good Lord! Why that's—that's impossible! You surely don't intend to—"

"I don't intend to do or not do anything about it right now. If you'll forgive me, I don't even intend to discuss it right now."

"This is really incredible!" Laura exclaimed. "Good Lord, I thought Sloan had more sense. What's she been doing all this time up in California? Running around with this—this—" She caught herself as she was about to say "gook," a term she knew Willard Howland would not tolerate, especially as applied to any member of the Kahana family. "Now I've heard everything. What in the world could have gotten into that girl? It can't be true!"

But it is getting to be the rage these days— She caught herself thinking, bitterly, about Aaron. I wonder how Aaron would like it if I started making up to one of them. To Dean Kahana, for instance. Bring Aaron to his senses.

"No, it can't be true, but it seems to be," Willard said, getting up from the table. A siesta would do him good right now. He would be able to work late into the night with a brief nap after lunch. "Maybe if you and Aaron sit down and talk to her tomorrow, you can drive some sense into her."

Laura sat back stiffly. "My God, I'd be afraid to breathe a word of it to Aaron! You can just imagine how he'd act at the thought of his sister marrying—marrying one of them. God, he'd fly into a rage. He'd—he'd kill Paul Kahana!"

Chapter Three

PAUL KAHANA glanced down at her breasts, full and tight against the low-cut formal, and his fingers toyed with the tiny gold football that hung from a chain about her throat.

"Are you happy, Sloan?"

"Crazy with happiness."

"Are you scared?"

"No."

"You're not scared of anything that might happen?"

"Like what?"

"Like old flint-face waging war against us and stopping the marriage?"

"Don't call Daddy that, not even in fun."

"Okay, I'm sorry. I was only kidding."

"Were you kidding when you said he might try to stop us?"
"No. I was serious about that."
"Well," Sloan Howland said, "let's not think about it now. Tonight I don't want to worry about anything. And I'm not scared of anything. I'm too happy to be scared."
They were leaning against the railing of the ship. A warm wind moved down the deserted deck. Tired party streamers and orchids fallen from leis stirred in its wake. A million low stars flooded the sky. The moon was a curl of silver on the shoulder of the sea.
"Do you know what I was dreaming about, a moment ago?"
"Something good?"
"Something wonderful," she said. "I was making believe I was very old, more than fifty, with gray hair and all, and one of my grandchildren—our grandchildren—came to me and asked me what was the happiest moment in my life."
"And what did you say?"
"I said, 'A long long time ago, somewhere out on the Pacific, and I was with Paul Kahana. He was young then, and very handsome. And we were very much in love.' "
His body was strong against hers. When he kissed her she could feel her own body opening, moistening, wanting to be with him again. Her fingers dug tight into the hard muscle of his arm. She moved her hips hard against him, into a high pleasure that was beyond both of them, a mixture of all things.
"You're doing things to me," he said.
"I like to. I'm doing things to me too."
"You little minx! It's only been since—"
"Since hours ago," Sloan said. "Too long. I want you too much to go hours without you." She pouted a little. "We should have gotten a stateroom to ourselves instead of this sharing boy with boy, girl with girl stuff. The ship is the whole world, and everyone in it is asleep except you and me. In the whole world, we've got no place to sleep together. And I don't ever want to sleep any other way but with you. Curled against each other like spoons. Maybe," she grinned at him, "this is what we get for living in sin."
"Do you like livin' in sin?"
"Yes, I love it with you." She rubbed her nose against his throat. "This is the most wonderful honeymoon a girl could ever

have. I think everyone should go on their honeymoon before they get married."

"It might save a lot of trouble," he laughed. "I still think we oughta try your cabin."

"We can't. Ramsey would hear us."

"Ramsey's so drunk from the captain's party that nothin' could wake her."

"We'd wake her. You know the noises we make."

"Good noises. Happy noises."

"Let's jump into one of the deck lounges and start making those noises now. Rock the ship off its course." She looked at him with sudden surprise. "God, I've never talked this way before! I'm talking just like a—like a regular little nymph."

"You're my little nymph."

"No, it's just that I've got so much love to give you. Drown you with it. Am I too much for you?" she teased. "It's all so new to me. I've got so much stored up."

"I'm glad. I'll want all of it."

"I don't know why I ever kept it under lock and key. It's much more fun to use it. I think I'll write a poem about my late and unlamented virginity. I'm so happy I finally lost that silly thing. To you," she added, looking up at him with a face of stars. "I've got to stop talking like this. Just think," she said, "four days ago I was a virgin."

An impatient virgin, she grinned secretly, like all virgins are.

She was a tall and strikingly attractive girl, with a golden beauty that served as a showcase for the vibrant good nature within. Her hair was utterly smooth—the color of wheat, with a faintly glistening creaminess—falling thick and sleek to her shoulders and stirring gently now in the wind. Her brows were darker than her hair and her face was a smooth oval, the gray eyes flecked with gold and spaced gravely, looking curiously and intelligently out at the world from beneath lazy lids and a thicket of dark lashes. Her wide, full lips seemed eager for amusement, and her cheeks were delicately and interestingly hollow. Her throat and shoulders were tanned and firmly smooth above the strapless tube of black silk. The upper slopes of her breasts swelled gently against each other at the bodice of her dress, which was beautifully fitted about the narrow waist, the clean flow of her hips, and the long, wonderfully curved young legs. There was about her a fresh warm glow of fulfillment, as if she had just deserted the unbalanced charm of a girl's world for the more purposeful, and to her, more satisfying world of young womanhood. What surprised her was not the fact that at last she had gone to bed and made love with a man, but rather than she had held off and fought it for so long. She now viewed that past time with a sense of regret, as a waste.

The waste had been their fault, she thought, not hers. For she had met them all, ever since she was fifteen years old and blooming with a high eagerness and the boys first started fighting over her in the locker rooms at Punahou. She had ridden proudly and untouched through all of them: the fumbling crushes of high school classmates, the wise beachboys with their free and easy morals, the collegiate tourist playboys hinting of their future alcoholic dissipation, the carefree big-shouldered athletes, the intense intellectuals who were going to change the world but could not even change her and consequently attacked her rebuffs with pallid innuendos of frigidity. Each time she had gone out with a new boy it was with the hope for the idealized male; the innately good, brave, strong, honest, gentle and true. To all of the young girls of the world, she thought, these idealized white knights came riding out from fairy-tale castles to make the dream come true. It was something she believed in and hoped for and had to have so badly that her disillusion deepened each time as her knights faded into eager-handed but awkward boys pawing furtively for quick pleasure; or else, she thought, they were hopelessly and spiritlessly in love, emotional illiterates grateful for any favor she might grant. They made her feel that sex, which she had always considered as one of the most important and perilous concerns of her life, was merely a bargaining point. She had known several girls who treated it as such. She never had, and she never would. She believed in love and she would give herself in love, lustily and with high pleasure. But the daisy-chain affairs, this living with a swinging gate at your heart, was not for her.

Someone had once tried to condemn her attitude as old-fashioned and prudish, but she knew this to be incorrect. She adhered to no moral code but her own, one in which black or white was rare, but most everything had shadings. Free love was not evil—a man and woman went to bed together if they wanted to, observed a few precautions and decencies, and that was that. But promiscuity was simply not for her. She would wait for love, for her shining white knight. It was not until recently that she admitted to herself that for her, love came as a dark knight.

The plain fact was that she could not fall in love with any of the others because all along she had been in love with Paul Kahana. He had given her an emotional measuring rod against which they all failed. Over the years, it had always been Paul. And she had hidden from it, run away from it, because she knew it would mean trouble. Their close childhood friendship was accepted by everybody. Closeness between the races was healthy and good. It added to the harmony that made the Islands a near racial paradise. But love—especially marriage—was something quite different. She had a feeling that an illicit affair would be less condemned by Island society than such a marriage, which, she knew, would be totally ostracized. Well, she had decided that if her love for Paul Kahana caused trouble, she would face up to it and brave it out. That kind of trouble stemmed from bigotry and fear and false values. She and Paul would conquer it.

Her attitude concerning the matter came only partly from reason, more from an instinctive reaction, like the humping-up of a cat at a dog, and she knew she would not surrender it. Paul was worth it. Their love was something of value. She felt a stubborn pride in barging headlong against society—particularly against the social snobbery that kept alive from age to age the stale and outdated moral code of past generations. Parents, when they are all through with sexual pleasures, tell their children that sex is evil; abstain. It seemed to her that moral standards were not honest representations of present generations' mores, but rather dishonest boasts of morality by past generations.

There is, she thought, a moment in life which is decisive; a moment in which we float upon a current of fate and it swings with us or against us, moving us from happiness or pain to a fuller happiness or more thorough pain. The moment makes a completely different person of us, and there is no going back:

The moving finger writes; and having writ,
Moves on: nor all your piety nor wit
Shall lure it back to cancel half a line,
Nor all your tears wash out a word of it.

The moment may be solely that—a brittle piece of time speared from eternity; or it may be an afternoon, a season, or a year. For Sloan Howland, the moment came when she and Paul Kahana boarded the *Lurline*.

They had shared the fun of the parties of the Phi Delt house at Stanford, the football season heroics, the Big Game weekends, the skiing at Squaw Valley, the wild jazzy nights in San Francisco bistros, the soft splendor of Easter Week at Carmel. But it had all remained on one level of pleasure and no more. It was not until she was curled in his arms as the ship pulled out from beneath the Golden Gate that she understood fully that that level was to be altered, that it would be the beginning of something completely different; that at last the yearning girlhood innocence would give way to the satisfaction of an adult love. And with her curious wisdom, she knew it would be perfectly right.

That first night aboard ship had been a sunburst of love and glory. It was a record shipload, with more than six hundred passengers. Most of them were young people, tourists and college students bound for a summer session at the University of Hawaii. There were parties on all decks, in almost every stateroom. The feeling of carnival reached its zenith at the captain's dinner dance in the main ballroom where, while the sleek bow cut through the waters toward Hawaii, the band struck up "Song of the Islands" and a riot of confetti and brightly colored balloons and streamers cascaded down from the ceiling as hundreds of dancers, the women beautiful in stunning new gowns, the men handsome in white dinner jackets, watched for the first time the rise of the hula moon.

Paul's dark good looks and Sloan's vivacious golden beauty made them the most striking couple aboard, and consequently one of the most popular. The orchestra leader coaxed Paul to the bandstand. Like all Hawaiians, Paul had a deep love of music, and like many of his people, he had a rich, natural voice—a baritone. The crowd became sentimental as he sang "The King's Serenade" while Sloan danced the hula to the ballad, telling the story with the motions of her hands.

Later they were in each other's arms, dancing to a Cole Porter medley.

"I feel as if we're in a goldfish bowl with everyone staring at us," she said. "Does our love show that much?"

"I hope so. Why? Would it embarrass you?"

"No. I'm glad and I'm proud. When I'm in your arms like this, it feels like there's no dance floor beneath me. Let everyone know we're in love." She grinned, looking up at his sleek-skinned, handsome brown face; a hard face of straight lines and flat planes, carved with the same heavy features as his brother Dean's, but leaner, lighter-skinned, his black hair cut close to his head.

She wondered how many girls he had had. Girls had a hard time keeping away from him, she knew. Sure of himself, poised, devil-may-care, he had a cocky charm and a look of appealing, complete and arrogant maleness. Girls looked at him the same way fellows looked at girls, she thought. Girls would look at him and see the lean muscled body. They would look at his heavy, sensual mouth, with its mixture of cruelty and humor, and at his hard hands and guess at how he'd make love. And especially, they'd look into his eyes. You could look into one man's eyes and know that there was no excitement in him. Another man, showing nothing except what was in his eyes, and any girl could sense the male power. The best were the eyes that were power and heat and laughter too. Paul had eyes like that: burning charcoal, bright with power and laughter.

They danced to a corner of the ballroom. She pressed her mouth softly against his throat, feeling a pleasant and shocking freedom that tingled in her remotest nerves.

"Do you love me?"

"Very much. You know that."

"Yes I know, but I like to hear it. Will you always?"

"Yes, and you know that too, you little minx."

"Just with you I'm a minx. Oh Paul, I feel so wanton with you because I'm so much in love with you. I'm giddy with it, I guess. Our love can't be wrong, no matter what anyone will try to say or do. Hold me closer, darling. Hold me like I'm made of meat and bone and flesh and made for you."

He kissed her lightly. Her arm went around his neck and pulled him close again and this time the kiss was moist and hard, bringing on their need for each other, bringing on the spinning craziness.

"Let's get out of here." His voice was thick. "Let's go where we can be by ourselves."

They ducked out of the ballroom and hurried down the gangway to the stateroom she shared with another girl. The blue mists of the moon filtered through the cabin. He locked the door behind them.

"Paul—"

"What?"

"Leave the lights off."

"Sure," he said softly. "Come over to me, Sloan."

She felt suddenly remote, detached from everything, from Paul especially, and from the idea of making love. She had a queer desire to run out of the cabin; to tell him she had changed her mind about the whole thing. A thousand last-minute thoughts—excuses, really—raced through her mind. But she fought against them, knowing that she could not use any of them. They made her feel like some damn fool kid, in over her head. Her sudden fright at the physical shock of love-making unnerved her. All her desire for it fled out of a ragged hole in her heart. She reasoned that everyone was scared the first time. She wished she had had more to drink. Maybe then she would not be so sensitively aware of everything. She was suddenly convulsed with shyness, wanting, at one and the same time, to run desperately out of the cabin, and to plunge into the love-making and get it over with as soon as possible. Should she undress herself? She shuddered with an inexplicable revulsion of being seen naked. Should she wait for him to undress her? Should she—Oh, God, why was she such a damn fool to have gotten into this? What would he think of her afterwards? What would she think of herself afterwards?

"Sloan, come here, darling." She wondered if his voice was really as flat and demanding as it sounded. "Come sit by me, Sloan."

"I'm—I'm scared, Paul."

"I know."

"Suddenly awfully awfully scared."

"I know. And it makes everything all the more important."

"I just don't know what's come over me. I just—I don't know. I love you, Paul."

"Come sit close to me. Don't think about anything. We won't do anything."

She sat on the edge of the bed, across from him, the silk of her dress fanned out above her knees, her long brown legs curled under her, her fingernails nervously stabbing into the muscle ridges on the back of her thigh. He had stripped off his clothes. As he moved toward her through the blue light of the cabin, she could see the outline of the body that she thought she knew so well, and which, she realized now, she did not really know at all. His wide, sloping shoulders were enormously thewed, tapering into a narrow, muscular waist. His chest was deep, his legs were thick bands with the slant of power. Everything about him suggested tremendous, demanding power; every movement hinted of the slow, sure animal grace of the panther. That very strength of him which she had craved so much now frightened her.

"Why am I so scared, Paul? I don't want to be. I want to be good. I want to be expert. I want to be the best. Hold me tight."

He raised her to her feet and kissed her silently until the trembling flowed out of her body.

"I'm embarrassed, I'm such a goof—"

"No no no. Relax. We'll just lie down for a while."

"But I don't want to just lie down for a while. I want to make love. And I don't know how to make love. Please teach me."

His hands moved into the thick creaminess of her hair. He held her face tight and kissed her. Her mouth became eager with his demand. Her fingers clenched into the hard ropy muscles of his arms. She felt her knees begin to give from under her.

She broke from his kiss and pressed her wild hot face against his chest. "Unzip me, Paul," she whispered. "Now, now!" The silk rustled to the floor.

He carried her naked to the bed. His hands covered her body, caressing the vital swelling of her thighs. The skin of their bodies burned against each other. His lips were hungry against her throat, then moved demandingly across her breasts, her belly. He began kissing the soft quivering flesh of her inner thighs, his hands curled over her breasts. She began twisting against him.

She had stiffened with panic at the first thrust of his body next to hers. Then it was a matter of humiliation, of hateful uncoverings, of shocking violation. She lay rigidly resentful beneath the deep astonishment of invasion. With a sense of relief, she felt at last the convulsed thunder of his conclusion. And it was over. A door had closed behind her for all time. And it had not been worth opening. It was absolutely no good; monstrously overrated. It had been awkward and stickily strange with a feeling close to pain—

but nothing else. If this was the fiasco that made the world go round, then millions of people had been monstrously duped for millions of years. Nothing but a vaguely shocking, sweaty, muscular contortion wrapped in labored breathing. Those interminable hours she had spent dwelling upon the act now seemed a ridiculous waste of time and imagination. If there was more gentleness to it, maybe it would become bearable; something you could learn to live with if you didn't think too much about it. If you could do it with a passive acceptance and weren't forced to fake anything. But men resent a mildly passive woman. They brood about it if you don't act as if it was God bursting into you. God—what a fraud!

"Sloan—?" His voice sounded strangely tender.

"Umm?"

"I love you very much. With everything in me that can love. Don't worry about that—"

"Don't worry about what?" She knew she sounded defensive.

"About what happened. What didn't happen. It's my fault. I was too eager."

"Do we have to yak about it? I think we'd better go. Ramsey might come back and—"

"No. Please, Sloan, don't get like that." He leaned up on his elbow and ran his fingers through her hair. He kissed the bridge of her nose with such gentleness that she turned from him and muffled a soft, raw sob into the pillow.

Later, he said candidly, "The only thing that went wrong was that I didn't give you enough time. I was too hungry for you. The first time is usually not so good. We don't know each other's wants or needs or tempo. It takes a little adjustin' and understandin'." He looked down at the clear, delicate articulation of her face. "You'll see," he said, kissing her.

They lay side by side, her head tucked against his shoulder. Through the porthole they could see the moon swing high over the Pacific. Curls of spray shone like lamb's wool beneath the moon. She felt surprisingly comfortable now, lying naked with him on the bed. A cozy, warm feeling. She looked gravely into his eyes. "I—I guess I was awfully afraid at first. Afraid of even letting you see me like this."

"I like to see you like this. I love you, dressed just the way you are."

"Now I do too. It's getting—easier, somehow. I love to have you look at my body. I love to have your hands over my body—Yes, I love to have you do that; it feels so good—" She stopped and held his hands, suddenly remembering. "Paul," she said shyly, "you don't think—well, you don't think any the less of me, do you? I mean, for letting you do it? You don't think I'm—"

He kissed her, silencing her. "Of course not."

"A lot of men do. Or so I heard."

"Naw, you heard wrong. Only boys do."

"It would kill me if—"

"Hush, silly. I love you all the more for it. How do you feel now?"

"I don't know how I feel, I'm so much in love."

"So am I. It's like I waited a hundred years for you, and every second of those years was worth it."

"I'm sorry I made you wait. I'm sorry I made me wait. Ooh, that feels . . . Paul, I'm not scared any more. I'm not scared at all. Please, Paul, don't wait any longer . . ."

They embraced again, with an incredible loveliness, with a kind of singing. She murmured deep in her throat, and the magic started about her. Magic that took his breath. Magic that started with her first taut response; with her fingers digging tight behind his head, pulling his face to her breasts, swelled rich and heated. Her hips churned into a massive warmth against his, her long thighs locking him, frantic with invitation and need. And, as she had sensed it coursing through her nerves, there came upon her a bursting, a shuddering torrent of fulfillment as wave upon wave of sweetness flooded her, moving from sensitive tenderness to tumbling violence, a sweet yet savage orgy that carried her with thundering breath past pain to the high point of pleasure; and while it was happening, while the hot rockets exploded inside her, passing all experience, she understood with sudden wisdom that all her life she had been moving inevitably toward this act with this man and that it was good and true and totally pure.

That had been her moment of decision, Sloan thought, leaning back against Paul now, watching the sea. The dust of the moonlight made the sea look like dark glass. It had been a moment of moving from nothingness to glory, and it seemed almost unbelievable that such a thing could happen again and again. She flushed, looking up at Paul and remembering the crazy pleasure, the litany of love that they had learned during the voyage.

"What are you so deep in thought about?" she asked.

He grinned at her. "Just dreamin'."

"You look a little sad."

"Maybe a little."

"Why?"

"I don't know exactly."

"Because the trip is over? Because we dock tomorrow?"

"Today," he reminded her.

"What time is it?"

"Almost five."

"We've got an hour until dawn. Three hours before Honolulu. Don't feel sad."

"Okay." He grinned and put his arm around her and kissed her and forgot all about what trouble might be coming their way and who might be bringing it.

"We love each other and that's the only important thing," Sloan said. "There's nothing sad about that."

"It's the most beautiful thing I've ever seen," Ramsey James said, gazing through the early-morning haze toward the Island of Oahu. "It just rises out of the ocean with a beauty full of sweet promises; full of love."

"We've changed the old saying, 'See Naples and die' to 'See Hawaii and live,' " Sloan told her. "Look over there." She pointed. "That's Diamond Head, the beginning of home." Diamond Head and home and all that it means, she thought, a flush of sentiment coursing through her with the wonderful warmth of a child's hug. She brushed away a tear.

"Now who's sad?" Paul teased her.

"I'm not sad. I'm just so happy I can't help it. I'm so happy I can't understand why I ever left. It's too lovely a place to leave."

The ship purled familiarly through the deep blue waters of the Oahu Coast. Paul and Sloan had changed clothes and returned to the top deck at dawn to watch the landfall. Ramsey James, Sloan's cabinmate, a college friend who was to spend the summer with her, had joined them. She was a short, strong-legged brunette with a gamin air about her; quite pretty, with pointy little breasts jutting out against the emerald-green sundress that matched the color of her eyes. Sloan was wearing a gold brocade pake-type sundress, and both girls wore a collar of flower leis that came clear up to their chins: orchid leis at the bottom, then a thick carnation lei, a plumeria lei, a white pikaki ginger lei, and on top, a lei of maile and pure white gardenias that Paul had given them. They had passed Makapuu Point with its lighthouse like a white torch against the sky, then the smooth conical dome of Koko Head, and finally Hanauma Bay where the swells piled in like whipcream against the tidal boulders. Now, as the ship rounded Blackpoint and the tawny bluff of Diamond Head, the entire city of Honolulu spread out before them, glowing in the pale early sunlight like a soft pearl.

"What does the name 'Hawaii' mean?" Ramsey asked.

" 'Homeland,' " Paul told her. "It comes from Havaiki, the name of the traditional Polynesian homeland that's somewhere in the Society Islands, near Tahiti. 'Oahu' means 'The Gatherin' Place.' It got its name from its position in the chain—right about the middle. 'Honolulu' has been translated as 'Fair Haven.' "

"It looks like all the homes are built upon the hillsides," Ramsey said. "All of them looking out across the sea."

"That's true," Sloan explained. "Those hills are all old volcano ridges. The valleys are built up with homes too. The main part of the city is straight ahead of you, right behind Aloha Tower. Out there," she pointed, "is Pearl Harbor."

"And there's Waikiki," Paul said, a note of derision in his voice. He picked out the landmark hotels: the chalk-white gleam of the Moana and SurfRider, the Princess Kaiulani behind them, then up the strip to the familiar coral-pink buttress of the Royal Hawaiian. There were several new hotels he could not identify. It seemed that every time he left the islands, new hotels would rise at Waikiki, staggering the skyline. He hoped it would not become a cheap Coney Island type resort as many of his friends were predicting.

"That's where I'll be workin' all summer," he said to Ramsey, indicating a low, green building in the heart of the strip. "The Outrigger Canoe Club. Milk the malihinis."

"What's a malihini?"

"You're a malihini," he laughed. "A newcomer. A tourist."

"What do you call people like you and Sloan, who were born here?"

"Kamaainas—child of the soil; one who belongs."

"Will I ever become a kamaaina?"

"It's kind of hard to say," Paul explained. "Being a kamaaina is a mattah of the heart. A man can live in Hawaii fifty years without becomin' a kamaaina, because somehow he's remained alien; no heart, no warmth, no understandin'. The love of the Islands, like the love of a woman, just seems to happen. You can't plan in advance to love a particular woman; and you can't determine in advance to love the Islands. You see, feel, and understand; and you either love or you don't love. It seems that love of Hawaii is always love at first sight. Those who were made for the Islands, and those for whom the Islands were made, are kind of swept off their feet at the first meeting. They love and are loved back. Hawaii calls its own."

Colors spilled across the island like paint on an artist's palette: the incredible blues of the water, the creamy gold fringe of beaches, the pastel hues of the hotels, the vivid emerald of the hills rolling into the darker forest-green backdrop of the Koolau Mountain range where cotton-colored clouds rolled in against the cliffs on the northeast trade that Jack London called a "very wine of a wind."

It was, Sloan thought, as if the island itself seemed happy and glad, as if just being out there in the middle of the sea was the nicest piece of luck in the world.

There was a time, she knew, that these islands did not exist. When only the great swells of the Pacific rolled through here.

Relatively speaking, the age of the Islands is young, in geological terms. Geologists estimate that the first island appeared above the sea millions of years ago, and the entire chain was well formed by the end of the Tertiary period of time, before the ice age.

The Hawaiian Islands are the summits of a great range of volcanic mountains that stretch nearly two thousand miles down a straight line across the floor of the Pacific. Although this mountain range is lofty, only the highest peaks are visible—the peaks which form the Hawaiian Archipelago: eight main islands and more than fifty islets, reefs and shoals, strung out from northwest to southeast across sixteen hundred miles of sea. The eight large islands are located at the southwestern tip of this range. They are, from northwest to southeast, Niihau, Kauai, Oahu, Molokai,

Lanai, Maui, Kahoolawe (the only uninhabited major island) and Hawaii. They are far removed from other land, truly a "Crossroads of the Pacific"; 2,400 miles southwest of their nearest neighbor, California, and a longer distance south of Alaska's Aleutian Islands and southeast of Japan. Although they do not look very large on a map, their total land area is about 6,442 square miles, larger than Rhode Island, Delaware and Connecticut, and about equal in size to New Jersey and Massachusetts.

The story of the birth of these islands had always fascinated Sloan. . . .

Consider, first, the dark floor of the ocean. Much of it is volcanic. There is a 2,000-mile crack in the bottom of the Pacific, thought to be the juncture between two great blocks which make up the surface of the globe. Starting in prehistoric times, a series of undersea earthquakes poured flow upon flow of volcanic materials along this crack, slowly forming the underwater range of mountains. This process of eruptions continued until, after a thousand centuries of building toward the surface, a volcano head of one of the tallest peaks erupted, sending streams of lava shooting through the ocean surface and up into space. As the lava fell back into the sea, it boiled the ocean water and great clouds of steam blanketed the area. When the steam drifted away, the mountain peak was above water—a newborn island.

For the island that is not washed away, there begins a period of constructional growth. Lava outpourings continue to build the land mass. Wind, rain and tide work over the island, forming valleys, carving caves along the shore, then harbors. The barren rock is ground into sand. The original craters collapse and form plateaus. Marine life appears about the island, and its skeletons form the coral reef that soon builds up to encircle the land. On Mt. Kaala, now 4,025 feet high in the Waianae Range of Oahu, there are bits of coral and weird shells stranded there from the age when Oahu was deeply submerged.

Hawaii, youngest of the Islands, is the only one still undergoing this structural growth, since it is the only island whose volcanoes are still active. Geologists have worked out an average of one eruption for Mauna Loa every three and a half years since 1832. Lava cascades down its slopes. Each new flow lies upon the surface of a much older one. There may be an interval of a few years or perhaps centuries between one flow and the next to cover it. In this manner the Island attained its present land mass of 4,030 square miles, and Mauna Loa has soared up from sea level to its present height of 13,680 feet. Soundings off its coast have reached as far as four miles deep, making Mauna Loa, from its base at the ocean floor to its summit at Mokuaweoweo, the largest mountain mass in the world.

Once the islands had established themselves above the ocean, they underwent a complex cycle of submergences and emergences. These were brought about by an upward and downward movement of the island masses themselves, caused by great pressures on the floor of the ocean—tremendous earth shifts.

They were caused also by the glacial age, which had a great effect upon the islands. During this ice age, the sea level subsided as the ocean waters were frozen into vast peninsulas of ice which piled up on the continents. During that period, Molokai, Lanai and Maui appeared as one island. Oahu, however, appeared as two separate islands. Mauna Kea, the dormant volcano on Hawaii, was covered by a glacier 250 feet thick. Evidence of this frigid period can be found in the moraines and glaciated areas of Mauna Kea above 10,500 feet. The glacier also left its scars in Lake Waiau, highest lake in the Pacific, 13,007 feet up into the reaches of Mauna Kea. At the end of the ice age, as the glaciers melted, the sea level rose as much at 2,500 feet above the islands' peaks. The torrents crashed up against the lowlands, then covered the high plateaus, and finally the mountaintops, and for thousands of years, the islands again waited below the surface of the sea. Ocean currents carved strange shapes from the lava rock. Harbors were broken down, the contour of the island changed, once rugged mountains became softly rolling hills. Then, at last, the Islands emerged complete as we know them: for a moment in our time, the Islands were born. Their soil, crushed by wind, rain and sea, became fertile. Seeds carried by the trades found root and blossomed. Birds came, then man. . . .

And now, Sloan thought, I am returning home. To the only land on earth that offers a physical, spiritual and emotional excuse for returning. I never realized until now how much I missed it; like a long absence from a dear, kind, loving friend. I hope I never have to leave it again.

Three catamarans which had sailed out from Ala Wai Yacht Harbor skimmed gracefully about the *Lurline,* their decks crowded with bronzed, sleek-limbed youths waving greetings to the passengers leaning over the ship's rail. Several sport fishing boats purled lazily in the steamship's wake.

"Look!" Ramsey cried.

Out from Waikiki came a fleet of slender outrigger canoes—each forty feet long, dubbed out of koa logs, the hulls dark, the trims gaily painted, the crafts themselves elegant with their old savage warlikeness, knifing through the swells toward the ship; the Hawaiian beachboys who manned them seemed to be the very embodiment of the royal barbaric sea spirit of their ancestors. A helicopter swooped low across the length of the liner, releasing ten thousand orchids which floated down in a violet haze across the decks. The decks themselves were bright and restless. Strolling musicians and hula girls entertained. Finally the engines were cut, and the big liner which had sailed so proudly across open sea was shoved humiliatingly around by the squat tugs into its pier, like an old fat woman, while the strains of the Royal Hawaiian Band's "Aloha Oe" filled the air.

"Hea—there's Blue Makua," Paul said, pointing down to where the beachboys from the outriggers were diving for coins tossed by the passengers. "There's Blackout and Turkey and Steamboat!" He waved to them.

Sloan tossed a half-dollar into the center of a group of beachboys treading water. "Watch them fight for it," she told Ramsey.

At the splash of the coin, they surface-dove, swimming down through the clear water after the glittering silver. A moment later, a dark giant of a beachboy swam up from the depths, waved the coin, slipped it inside his cheek, and looked about for more of the coins that were sprinkling into the water.

"I'll be damned, Pete Noa got it!" Paul exclaimed, looking down at the beachboy, who was now perched on the ama of a canoe. "*Hea,* Pete!" he yelled. "*Pahea ke piko?*"

The boy looked up and waved at him.

Paul crowded Ramsey James close to him at the railing. "That's Pete Noa," he told her. "You know—the guy I fixed you up with. Numbah one guy!"

Ramsey focused her eyes down the side of the ship until she saw the boy Paul indicated. Even from the height of the promenade deck, she could see that he was a giant. A dark giant, she thought, a little uncomfortably.

"Here." Paul handed her a coin. "Throw it down to him."

Ramsey leaned across the railing and tossed the coin. She watched as Peter Noa dove powerfully into the depths and surfaced, a moment later, waving the coin in his hand.

"*Hea,* Pete!" Paul yelled, pointing to Ramsey. "This is the wahine I was tellin' you about! Fix you up good, huh? Numbah one!"

Peter Noa grinned and blew a kiss to Ramsey. With his fingers, he waved a V-for-victory sign. Ramsey frowned, watching Peter disappear for another coin. He was, after all, much darker than she had anticipated. She had heard all the stories about the beachboys and the young girl "malihinis." A regular Sodom out at Waikiki. She wondered restlessly just what kind of victory Peter Noa had in mind.

As the liner edged into its slip, confetti spiraled through the air and gay bunting streamers formed a paper bridge between the ship and the hundreds who waited on the pier below. Paul's eyes scanned the sea of faces.

"I can't see anyone—"

"There's Dean!" Sloan shouted happily. "There's Dean and Kapiolani!"

"*A-lo-ha!*" Dean shouted at them, waving an armful of orchid leis. He was working his way through the crush of people moving up the gangplank to the ship. With him was Kapiolani Kahana, a tall, stately woman in her middle fifties, her dark wavy hair streaked with one white band, a red hibiscus behind her ear. When he saw his mother, Paul noticed a quick, strange expression in her eyes that disturbed him: that made him wonder, for the first time, what she would think of his plans for marrying Sloan Howland—what his own people would think. For the first time the thought flashed across his mind— Would they oppose it too?

He had long ago come to the conclusion that the marriage would come as a shock to everyone, and that unhappily, everyone would oppose it. But he realized now that he had been thinking solely in terms of the Howland family—haoles—never his own people.

This was a new twist. He had accepted the probability that Senator Howland would move heaven and hell to stop such a marriage. And he had not resented that probability. All his life, Paul Kahana had felt a deep affection and respect for the old man. Senator Howland had been a good boss to Paul's father, and he had fixed it so Paul could attend Kamehameha School after Doc had died. He had pulled the strings to get Paul's football scholarship to Stanford, and even now he was helping Dean through pre-med. No, no one had to tell Paul how much the old man loved the Kahana family. But there are degrees of love, and Paul was savagely aware that old Willard's feelings toward him would be shattered at the thought of having him for a son-in-law. And, Paul thought, I could never fight his reasons.

The same held true for Aaron and Garth, he thought. Especially Aaron, that screwed-up sonofabitch. Aaron will really hit the roof. Not because he gives a damn about Sloan, but because he's such a hot-shot Big Five social bastard that he'll consider it a slur against the Howland name. Well, the hell with Aaron and that fancy Howlands-of-Hawaii crap.

Garth probably won't care too much. Garth might even be all for the marriage if he was sure it meant Sloan's happiness. At least if Garth did oppose it, it would be for reasons other than color.

Paul knew that his mother might be against the idea because of her loyalty to the Howlands and the conflict her loyalty would have against the breaking of the old traditions. Traditions that are falling apart at the seams, Paul thought. Old rules that he saw no reason not to break. Well, the hell with all of them, he thought. Sloan and he were the ones who were getting married. It was their affair. If everyone in the immediate families objected to the marriage, then they could all go to hell. And thinking of the immediate families, the name was in his head before he could stop it: *Ward Akana.*

He almost laughed out loud. He chided himself for not thinking of Ward until now. He gazed down into the crowd on the pier to see if perhaps Ward had come to greet them. He grinned secretly at the thought: Ward Akana would be wholeheartedly in favor of Paul Kahana marrying Sloan Howland. Ward Akana would like nothing better.

Sloan tugged him away from the railing. He watched her speculatively as she hurried on ahead of him through the press of people and threw her arms about Dean.

"Gosh I've missed you so much!" he heard her say as she greeted Dean with a kiss. "We're home again, Dean!"

Chapter Four

FROM Punchbowl Cemetery, Ward Akana could not hear the band music being played at the harbor far below. He heard, instead, the clear sad notes of Taps as the Marine bugler in his full-dress blues paid Hawaii's final tribute to Delegate Joe Stinson. There is a way of playing Taps, Ward Akana thought, so that those plaintive notes bring every drop of emotion to the surface. And this bugler has mastered it.

Ward Akana was a squarely built young man with low, sloping shoulders that seemed somehow out of place beneath the white shirt, black silk tie and dark blue suit he was wearing. Although he had the slow powerful body of the Hawaiian, there was a stockiness to him, a bulkiness that suggested Japanese blood in his background. His hair was curly black, his skin a coppery lemon color. But his features were neither blunt and heavy like the Hawaiians, nor flat like the Japanese. He had a wise tough-nut face, a chiseled forehead, and a long aquiline nose. His mouth was thin and firm, breaking into a knife-blade smile. His clear hazel eyes were direct and challenging, intensely alert. Like a man who is seldom still, his present moment of immobility made him more taut and noticeable. There was an eager impatience about him, a restlessness of drive and dedication that was uncommon among his people. A year shy of his thirtieth birthday, he had already dedicated his life's work to the betterment of his people—the yellow-skinned, brown-skinned working people. He had long ago concluded that social and economic justice for all races in Hawaii would never prevail under the paternalistic benevolence of the Big Five and their white man's rule. To bring about that justice you had to break the back of the Big Five, he thought. Break the haole rule.

He glanced restlessly about at the crowd that had assembled at Punchbowl for the services. More than a thousand. At Hickam Field earlier that morning there were some two hundred of Joe Stinson's close friends talking gravely in little solemn groups while they waited for the C-54 transport from Washington to touch down on the landing strip with the Delegate's flag-draped coffin. There were two flags, the United States' and the Territory of Hawaii's. The same two that ruffled softly now at half-mast in the slated wind above Punchbowl.

Ward Akana had not joined in the talk. He had nodded politely to Governor Balter and Secretary of Hawaii Frank Lorrin. He had shaken hands with Johnny Wilson and Sheriff Duke Kahanamoku and nodded to leaders of the Big Five firms and to personal acquaintances among the military brass and newsmen: and he had walked over to the gleaming black Cadillac of Mrs. Martha Stinson and expressed his regret to the widow and her two grown sons. But for the most part, during the long wait while the rest spoke reverently about what a great man Delegate Stinson had been and what a loss his death would mean for the Territory, Ward Akana had moved off by himself, and, as was his habit, remained a little aloof from the crowd. Even at that early hour of the morning, he had put in a hard day.

Because of the funeral, his working day began an hour earlier than the usual six A.M. A cold shower tried to make up for the lack of sleep during the previous night. The conferences with the Big Five attorneys had lasted through the day and far into the night. Several of the men attending the funeral showed signs of wear from that conference. Two weeks of negotiations, and it was apparent now that nothing could ward off the strike. Cane and pineapple plantation workers and all the longshoremen. A crippler strike; tie up the lifeline of Hawaii. A strike that would cost millions, that no one wanted, yet seemed inevitable.

After the negotiations had failed, there had been two hours of phone calls to Union headquarters in San Francisco. The orders had been explicit. There was nothing else to be done. Slug the Big Five in the guts. Notify Union representatives on Oahu and all the Outer Islands—a general walkout on July first. And if this crippled the economy of the Territory, well, how else could you fight for fair wages in a feudal economic setup?

Tani was still up when he had finally gotten home. Little Barbara was teething. He went in to bed and was still half awake when the baby quieted down and Tani slipped into the sheets and moved close to him.

"How do you feel?" she asked.

"Tired."

"I know. How else?"

"Beat. Disappointed. All hollow inside."

"I listened to it on the midnight news. Isn't there any chance you won't have to strike?"

He shook his head. "Two weeks of talk and more talk and futile negotiations. And we're still where we were when we started. We were ready to drop the thirty-two-cent demand. We would have settled if they moved it up from twelve cents an hour to sixteen cents. But it wasn't in their thinking. They had to stand pat and we had to stand pat. So for four lousy cents an hour the Territory and the people will lose millions. Nothing's going to stop the strike now. Goddamn it, you work your head off—"

"I know, I know, Ward. Try to get some sleep."

He looked at her, warm beside him in the bed. She was the same as she had been that night so long ago when he had first looked at her and he had known that he would have to have her as his own or be haunted by loveliness unattainable for the rest of his life. Her black hair curled softly on the pillow, her darkly serious almond eyes, distinctly Japanese, looked into his with comfort and compassion that through the years he had come to rely more heavily upon, and had grown more and more thankful for. She lay on her side, her throat and shoulders lemon-gold above the lacy nightgown, the full mass of her hips curving the blanket, the flanks of her legs warm against his. As her fingers rubbed expertly and soothingly across his brow, he understood all over again the lovely enchantment about her that made everyone soften their voices when they spoke to her.

"Someday," he murmured, remembering the thousand hopes, "I'll make it all up to you."

"I told you over and over again never to speak like that. No matter how things get. It's been made up so many times, Ward. Every day makes it up. Every moment with you."

The distant lead-gray of dawn woke him. He showered and dressed hurriedly, taking care not to wake the baby or the boys, Matt and Mark. There was a light on in the kitchen and the smell of coffee filled the house. Tani grinned at him and burrowed into his arms like some warm, furry animal.

"Coffee and a good big breakfast."

"Just coffee, honey. I don't think I have time to—"

"You sit and eat." She placed a platterful of browned ham and eggs scrambled with cheddar cheese in front of him and poured the coffee. "Heaven knows when you ever find time to eat when I'm not around to see to it." She handed him the morning edition of the Honolulu *Advertiser*. "There's a big story about Aaron on the front page. He nearly got killed at the volcano eruption."

Ward's eyes skimmed down the story with slight interest. The reporter had termed the episode "cheating a fiery death" and recounted how Aaron had been trapped at the summit of Mauna Loa but managed to work his way down to the safety of the geophysical laboratory.

"What do you suppose he was doing up there all by himself?" Tani asked. She sat across from Ward at the breakfast counter, sleepily sipping her coffee.

"It doesn't say, and I'm sure I wouldn't have the slightest idea what Aaron does or why. I doubt if he does."

Ward had already dismissed the story. He was studying a one-column picture of Willard Howland that ran above a story stating that the Senator would deliver Stinson's eulogy at today's funeral and indicated that he would be named Republican nominee for the delegacy. It all made sense, Ward thought. Everything except that face. The nose, the set of the forehead, the strong mouth . . . How often had he seen a dark-skinned version of that face when he had glanced at himself in the mirror?

The paper's bannerline dealt with the failure of the new contract negotiations and the consequent probability of a major strike. The editorial page took the Union to task:

> Hawaii cannot afford another crippling strike like the waterfront and plantation strikes of 1946 and 1949. If such a strike is Mr. Ward Akana's intention, then it is fitting that he be reminded that his position with the Union is as a negotiating attorney, whose purpose it is to arbitrate and negotiate with management to a peaceful conclusion, not to bait management, nor to arrogantly demand that all Union requisites be met under threat of general strike. Mr. Akana's true position with labor is that of a trouble shooter, not a trouble maker. Hawaii cannot afford such a strike internally, and it certainly cannot afford to be portrayed on the Mainland and in Washington as a strike-troubled, Union-dominated area, if its dreams of statehood are to be realized.

Ward closed the paper. The same old line, he thought sourly. Press, radio and television, all controlled by the Big Five.

The Big Five, the germ of the Anglo traders and empire builders—the great positive force that built Hawaii: Castle & Cooke Ltd., Alexander & Baldwin Ltd., American Factors Ltd., C. Brewer & Company Ltd., and Theo. H. Davies & Company Ltd.

These five firms, established a little more than a century ago, developed this island kingdom. They were founded, Ward thought, on the surest combination ever known to mankind—money and God: in that order.

Over Hawaii's three supporting industries—sugar, pineapple and tourism—these Big Five firms brandish a hard, closed fist, virtually controlling $320 million of the Territory's economy.

This fist formed about 1820, when the traders and Congregational missioners from the American Missionary Society in Boston boarded the big Yankee Clipper ships and sailed around Cape Horn to the South Pacific. They found Hawaii an undeveloped island paradise peopled by some 200,000 carefree Polynesians, and they set about to take full control. They were hard-working, thrifty Anglos. While they preached the word of God to the natives, while they taught the natives to sing of love and some future world of them and Jesus, they also went about acquiring broad lands and establishing a powerful mercantile system. It was an old story: the arrival of the white man began an inevitable process of development. The traders and missionaries came to do good—and as the Island saying went they "did damned well." The natives were taught to bow their heads in prayer, another Island wisecrack had it, and when they looked up, everything they owned was gone. Well, a lot of that was true.

The founding fathers enthusiastically preached the Biblical law of rendering unto Caesar the things which are Caesar's and to God the things that are God's. Men like James B. Castle and Amos Starr Cooke, both missionaries, combined preaching the word of God with supplying the needs of man, thus establishing the multimillion-dollar firm of Castle & Cooke Ltd.—sugar factors, plantation agents, commission merchants, and parent company of the Matson Navigation Company, whose liners and freighters comprise a vital lifeline of the Islands' economy. The other Big Five firms originated in similar fashion.

These original developers of Hawaii formed corporations and pooled their talents, resources and energies. Since the Islands were a tight, remote, almost feudalistic region, the children of these founders invariably intermarried, establishing, perhaps, the world's last landed aristocracy. The presidents, vice-presidents and chairmen-of-the-boards of today's Big Five firms were in most cases direct descendants of the original founders.

The wealth of the Islands was derived from the pillars upon which the Islands were founded. First sugar, then pineapple, then tourism. The Big Five controls all three.

The twenty-seven separate cane sugar companies located on Oahu, Hawaii, Kauai and Maui, are either owned outright or controlled by the Big Five sugar factors. These companies produce more than a million tons of raw sugar each year, one-fourth the amount produced under the American flag. The annual crop amounts to $145 million. The plantations occupy 219,000 acres (about five and a half per cent of the land in the Territory). They provide year-round employment for some 19,000 workers, the highest paid sugar workers in the world, earning a total payroll of

$59 million. The companies have established refineries in Spreckles, California: and to their credit, established the Hawaiian Sugar Planters' Association, which hires scientists to develop better varieties of cane, more efficient machines, healthier conditions for its employees; though much of the latter was accomplished through constant prodding—and more than prodding, Ward reminded himself—by labor unions.

The pineapple industry was started in 1903 by a young Bostonian named James B. Dole, who listed his assets at the time as "my good name, a homestead, two horses, one plow, a harrow and a wagon." He bought sixty acres of red fields on the Wahiawa Plateau, some twenty-three miles from Honolulu. After scrapping variations of a native fruit called *Wild Kailua* he worked instead on developing Captain John Kidwell's *Smooth Cayenne* variety of the same fruit. In 1904, in a makeshift cannery he built with his own hands, Jim Dole produced 1,893 cases of Smooth Cayenne, and introduced canned pineapple to the world. In 1956, the Islands produced 18,464,061 cases of canned pineapple and 12,112,600 cases of canned pineapple juice—eighty-five per cent of the world's supply. Some 22,000 workers were employed at the summer peak of canning season and the crop was worth $110 million. Of the nine companies running the Territory's fourteen pine plantations, eight are controlled by the Big Five.

In 1956, more than 160,000 visitors came to Hawaii to satisfy a longing for Polynesia and enjoy the unmatched climate. They came, mostly, in Big Five ships, stayed at Big Five hotels, and spent their money at Waikiki Beach, a virtual Big Five gold coast. These tourists brought the Territory $60 million in revenue. To placate Islanders, the Big Five at one time coined a saying that every tourist dollar passes through ten hands before it finally comes to rest. The saying perhaps is true enough, but it is incomplete: for nine of those ten hands depend directly or indirectly upon the Big Five for sustenance; and the tenth hand, the one that finally put the dollar to rest, probably put it to rest in a Big Five bank. For the Big Five controls the banks, the insurance companies, the land, the contracting and building, the docks and the ships, the utilities, the power plants, the mills and canneries, the office buildings, the newspapers, the radio and television stations, the Police Commission, the Land Commission, and the Republican Party—which has ruled Hawaii for the half century of its inception.

But, Ward thought, the Big Five does not control me.

He did not believe he was unjustly critical of the Big Five. Perhaps no owning class in history ever was as conscious of its social responsibilities, but it had kept Hawaii distinctly feudal, not democratic. Ward also credited the sturdy individualism and thrifty pioneer blood of the New Englanders for transforming the lush idle valleys of Hawaii from a primitive paradise into a comfortable, healthy world where almost 600,000 people lived and worked. After all, everything suffers growing pains. It was just that Hawaii's pains lasted long after her growth. Had World War II not come along and brought military rule to disrupt Big Five rule and change the Territory's social-political standards, oppression and feudalism might still rule the Islands. It was, ironically, the Big Five's shortsighted, selfish opportunism that led to the cracking of its armor: that led to Ward Akana's power. Like the Frankenstein monster, the Big Five's creation would rise and destroy its creator, he thought. Because during its century of developing, during its century of reaping the spoils, the Big Five had had to import labor. The Hawaiian natives wouldn't work. They sang, danced, fished for dinner, ground taro root to poi, lived in coconut-frond shacks, made love, had babies—but they wouldn't work. So the great white fathers looked to Japan, China and the Philippines for their labor. They imported ruthlessly, blunderingly, bringing in coolie labor in lots of 250,000, continuing to bring them in long after the original labor forces had procreated and swelled, long after the labor force had become an oppressed majority, waiting to be organized. Men like George Hill moved in and despite police truncheons, marshaled these labor forces. Men like Ward Akana were making labor articulate.

There was, perhaps, another reason for Ward Akana's particular success and power within Hawaii's unions. The blood that flowed through his veins was part haole, part Japanese, part Hawaiian.

Since the dawn of Christianity, the white man has ruled the world. From Rome and Greece to Spain; from Spain to France and England, and then to America, it has been a haole's world. More precisely, during the last five or six centuries, an Anglo world, cradled in Britannia and spread from there to Plymouth Rock and Beretania Street, Honolulu. (Hawaii's flag is an Anglo flag, boasting a Union Jack and eight red-white-and-blue stripes representing the eight main islands.) The Anglo world conceived the steamship, the airplane and automobile; smashed the atom. The Anglo world conceived the thirteen colonies, defeated Napoleon, bled brother against brother because of the Negro world, opened up the West against the Indian world, developed Hawaii in the Polynesian world. Just as the North American Indian was looted of his continent by the white man, so was the Hawaiian looted of his islands. The facts are irrefutable. And morally indefensible. For five hundred years, the Anglos have been the master race of our time.

But now their days are limited, Ward thought. Their conquests have ended. The teeming populations of China, India, Africa and the East made it so obvious that he felt a vague contempt for the haoles who did not realize that their rule was soon to end. Who did not realize that they had to make way now for the yellow-skinned, the dark-skinned, the mixtures. The cycle was just about over: Colonialism, Big Five feudalism, the haole rule, all had to step aside now. Willard Howland and everything he stands for must give way.

He kissed Tani and walked out to the garage. There was a sweet morning wind. Below Wilhelmina Rise, the city was like a young girl stirring lazily from sleep. The sun was weak in the sky, moving up with dawn from behind the lovely Koolaus. Far out past Diamond Head, he could see the *Lurline* cut through the slick glistening waters toward the harbor. He remembered that Sloan was due to arrive today, she and young Paul Kahana. He made a mental note to call her and welcome her home.

He drove fast down the curves of Sierra Drive to Waialae Avenue. The streets had a freshly washed smell. There was a heady fragrance from the Peruvian pepper trees that lined the street. He cut across to Ala Moana Drive and drove past Kewalo Basin, watching the Japanese fishermen bring their sampans in from the Molokai Channel. The ships were not heavily loaded. The tuna have all but disappeared from local waters, the big schools ranging far south, around Samoa. He had met Tani at Kewalo. She had practically been raised there. Her father, Mitsu Kaizawa, was a shrewd old Japanese skipper who had invested what little money he owned in three sampans in the days when the tuna were still schooling in Hawaiian waters. Ward parked his car in his reserved slot behind the new Union headquarters building. When he had worked alone at his desk for more than an hour, George Hill came in.

"I can tell from your expression that you've already seen the morning paper," George Hill greeted him.

"Yes."

"They must be awful scared, to run an editorial like this." He folded the paper and sat down on the corner of Ward's desk.

He was a big man in his early fifties. Hard slabs of beef had larded the athlete's body. His hair was mouse-colored and balding, his nose had been broken in several places, and his eyes, beneath the folded, obviously stitched flesh of his eyelids, were a very pale gray, level, honest, unafraid. He had the battered look of an ex-professional football tackle who had grown accustomed to playing sixty minutes for the losing team. But Ward knew he had a mind so quick and so certain that, had he chosen private industry as a career, he could have carved himself a plush niche. His passion, however, had from childhood been for the downtrodden and the exploited. And it was to these that he had brought his administrative and organizational skills and his boundless energies. When he had first gathered Hawaii's labor force into the Union, during the depression, he had been the constant victim of police beatings, threats, deportations and jail sentences. He had been sent to prison as late as 1954, when the Big Five had ridden the crest of McCarthy's hysteria and denounced Hill and six others as Communists and perjurors in one of the Territory's more glaring examples of legal railroading. But neither the beatings nor the bars had deprived him of his energies, his bluff charm, or his dedication. And as he looked at Ward now, his eyes were bland and expressionless, but his tone had that combination of sincerity and calculating shrewdness that Ward knew so well from bargaining-table sessions. "What do you think about Willard Howland's candidacy?" he asked.

Ward glanced up at him. "I haven't had time to think anything about it. But that's a pretty shallow disguise to test my loyalties."

"I'm sorry," George Hill said with sincerity. "If it sounded that way, then I'm way off base. Forgive it."

"Forget it."

"I would, if I hadn't been deliberately off base and meant it to sound that way. This is our year, Ward. We're going to have to throw everything in to defeat Howland. And you're going to be quarterback."

"What makes you think I'd have loyalties to Willard Howland? Loyalties of any kind?"

George Hill moved away from the desk and averted Ward's stare. "I had to know, Ward."

"Okay," Ward said, getting up and putting on his jacket. "Now you know. And now that school's out for the day, we'd better start for Hickam."

They had driven out to the airfield in silence, and driven to Punchbowl in silence. And now, as the last brittle notes of Taps died out, and the Marine honor guard's rifles roared their twenty-one-gun salute, Ward shifted his weight easily to the balls of his feet, standing like a boxer stands, and his eyes moved slowly across the file of men who grouped around the Governor, until they came to rest at last on Willard Howland.

Old Willard had left the Governor's side and was crossing the little patch of nut grass behind the simple marble slab that marked Delegate Stinson's final resting place. There are no crosses for the fourteen thousand war dead buried at Punchbowl, the ancient Hawaiian "Hill of Sacrifice," now the site of the National Memorial Cemetery of the Pacific. Congress refused to appropriate money for crosses: just plain white slabs. Correspondent Ernie Pyle, and now Delegate Joe Stinson, lie among the dead.

An aged Hawaiian high priest stood at the foot of the grave, his golden-feathered cape stirring in the breeze. Two scarlet-cloaked Kahili bearers were at his side. They bowed their heads as the priest started his solemn chant.

When the native ritual was finished, Willard Howland walked heavily to the foot of the grave. He looked at the grave curiously for a moment, then raised his head quite solemnly and looked at the people.

"A man does not die, whose memory remains alive in the hearts of those he leaves behind," the Senator said. "And Joe Stinson will always remain in the hearts of all his peoples. In this earth he loved so well, beneath the two flags he served so well, Joe Stinson, in death, has rendered his final plea for his peoples' justice, his peoples' equality, his peoples' statehood . . ."

Ward found himself scrutinizing the Senator, studying his mannerisms, his way of talking, the words themselves, the feeling behind those words. He saw in the old man the unique gift of power over his fellow men. As he glanced about at the crowd, which was less than a third haole, the majority brown-skinned or coffee-skinned, and Oriental, he noticed that the Senator's direct, humble oratory, which combined power and restraint, moved the crowd. The Senator spoke for six minutes. As Ward listened, he had the feeling that the top politicos were also examining Howland—the Republicans to see the strength and charm of the man who would try to win Joe Stinson's post, the Democrats sifting through him for the flaw, the vulnerability, as a prizefighter measures his opponent in the ring. Press photographers crept up before him, popped their flashbulbs and retreated. Television and newsreel cameras hummed in the background.

"Joe Stinson died with a dream unfulfilled," old Howland said. "It is for us to fulfill that dream. It is for us to carry on without him now, as he would want us to carry on. Like Joe Stinson, we must work as if no amount of prayer could help, and pray as if no amount of work could help, until at last—as it must some day—the Nation sends us our star; the star for which Joe Stinson died.

"There is no life until one has loved and been loved in return, and then there is no death," Howland said. "And so for Joe Stinson, a loving man and a beloved man, there really has been no death."

He paused a moment, then he took an Old Testament from his coat pocket and thumbed through the pages. "This might be a little out of my jurisdiction," he said, nodding to the old Hawaiian high priest and a handful of other clergymen, priests, rabbis, Mormon doctors, Shinto priests and to the wrinkled ancient face of Bishop Iuwaki of the Hongwanji Buddhist Temple who had earlier officiated at the ceremony. "But if you gentlemen will permit me, Joe and I were quite fond of this. We learned it down the street there at Kawaiahao Church, and in a way, we grew up with it . . ."

He started reading:

> *"One generation passeth away and another generation cometh, but the earth abideth forever. The sun goeth down and the sun also riseth. All the rivers run into the sea and yet the sea is not full. To everything there is a season, and a time to*

every purpose under heaven. A time of war and a time of peace. A time to love and a time to hate. A time to live and a time to die . . ."

Afterwards, it seemed to Ward that when Willard Howland looked at him the old man's face darkened in a torrent of remembered futility, the eyes clouded for the moment with unspoken regret.

"We'd better be going," George Hill said to Ward.

"You go on ahead," Ward said, not turning to look at the Union chief, looking instead at the figure of Willard Howland, moving with utter dignity through the crowd toward him. Ward took a few tentative steps in the direction of the old man.

"Congratulations, Senator." Ward grasped Howland's extended hand. "That was an impressive speech."

"It's not difficult when you have an impressive man to talk about. Thank you, though."

"I should welcome you back to Honolulu. I understand from this morning's paper that you'll probably be here for quite some time. Until the elections."

Howland grinned sharply at the younger man. "You don't think I'll be around after the elections, eh?"

Ward smiled at the Senator's easy manner. "No, I didn't mean it that way—"

"Well—how about it? Think I'll be here after November? Or don't you see it that way?"

"I'm not sure I can say."

"Truthfully. Your honest opinion."

Ward studied the old man's eyes. "No, Senator, I don't see it that way."

George Hill and the other Union representatives backed discreetly away from Ward. At the same time, the group which had surrounded Howland—Governor Balter, Secretary Lorrin and other Republican leaders and several military chiefs—backed off, forming a speculative ring around the two.

"I appreciate your candidness," Howland said.

"I might be wrong."

Old Willard's head bobbed down and he peered at Ward from under his thick white brows. "I'd like to discuss the matter with you, Ward."

"No, I think that would be a waste of time."
"Maybe, maybe not."
"With all due respect, Senator, the picture is a little too obvious."
"Don't jump at conclusions."
"The whole setup is too obvious," Ward said. "The Governor and the rest of the big boys tap you to run for the delegacy. Well, I wish you luck. You'll need it. But I won't be a part of your luck."
"I hadn't exactly expected you to be."
"No, you hadn't exactly expected—but it would be nice for you."
"You're talking like a young damned fool."
"Am I?"
They kept their voices low. The two of them angled off a little from the ring of men who were trying not to stare at them. For Willard Howland and Ward Akana seldom appeared in public together, and the stragglers who had not yet left the cemetery were glancing self-consciously at them now, curious eyes studying the tall, erect old man with the shaggy white-gold mane and the dark son who stood beside him now; the son, they knew, who never bore the Howland name.
"You know damned well how foolish you're sounding."
"I don't agree with you, Senator. It's all very clear-cut. The Republican Party wants you as nominee because they think you're the best man to control—let's say to 'influence'—Island labor leaders. I'd be less than frank if I didn't make it clear to you right now that you'll have no persuasive powers over the Union."
Something seemed to move behind old Willard's eyes. His manner changed. An appeal came into his face. "You've changed an awful lot, Ward," he said quietly, but with great firmness and power.
"I'm sorry I disappoint you."
"You'll disappoint yourself with that kind of shoddy thinking. My nomination will not be based on any so-called persuasion I am thought to have with the Union. But because I may prove a good leader in Hawaii's battle for statehood."
"I'm sure you would, Senator. The best."
"Well?"
"I've changed even more than you've realized, Senator. I'm not

for statehood any more. I'm opposed to it. I think a commonwealth status would be better for Hawaii."

For an awkward moment their eyes met, but did not hold. They looked up at the sky together because it was the easiest thing to do.

"That's ridiculous," old Willard muttered.

"But true."

"Well, we're all entitled to our own opinions—"

"That's true."

"Just wait till I'm finished!" Willard snapped. "Stop interrupting me all the time!"

"I'm sorry, sir. I thought you had finished."

"The least you could do is hear an old man out!"

"Yes sir. I'm sorry."

"Goddamnedest thing I've ever heard," Willard muttered. "Commonwealth."

The funeral crowd was breaking up. The shining limousines were beginning to file slowly beneath the rainbow showers that lined Puowaina Drive, then down Fort Street into the heart of the city.

Old Willard made an indistinguishable noise in his throat. "Never turns out the way you plan it anyway," he muttered. "Fool to think it might." He glanced down at the parking area where Henry Alakea, the Governor's chauffeur, stood a little to the side of the high-ranking politicians who had gathered around the car. "I guess I should be going," Willard grumbled.

"Yes," Ward said dispassionately. In just a moment now, he thought, Henry Alakea would flip the siren on the black Cadillac and follow a police motorcycle escort down Punchbowl Hill through the rickety alleyways of Chinatown where the dilapidated wooden shanties crowd the streets, their porticos shading the sidewalk, softening the stench of urine in the alleys; and the ancient Chinamen sitting quietly and forgotten on the rotted squid barrels, their limbs warped with syphilis, their mustaches drooping like soiled feathers from faces dried out and furrowed as barren fields, would look up without expression as the shiny black car raced importantly by, then look inward again with that same blank expression that seemed like a caricature of futility, to their memories or lack of memories. Then the big important car would turn into Beretania Street, passing the Governor's mansion at Washington Place, the staid gray stone house almost hidden from view by banyan vines and shell ginger and pandanus, then finally into the wide palm-studded driveway of Iolani Palace.

The white-skinned rulers assembling in the palace that had been built for a brown-skinned king, Ward thought contemptuously. He pictured the vast gray cement face of the palace, the entire structure reflecting its intricately disproportioned European influence, its sharp central tower looming angularly and without grace above the sixteen colonnaded balconies. The only royal palace ever built in the United States, it was completed in 1881 for King David Kalakaua, the only Hawaiian king ever to occupy it. The first public festivity held within its walls was a formal dinner that Kalakaua, a 33rd degree Mason, gave in honor of a hundred fellow Masons. It was at that dinner that Kalakaua christened the palace "Iolani"—a sacred name of Old Hawaii, signifying the Bird of Heaven that is the supreme being above all gods. It remained the seat of government when Hawaii became an independent republic, and since has served as the executive offices of the Territory. The bandstand at the King Street entrance was originally Kalakaua's coronation stand. The giant banyan alongside it was planted by his wife, Queen Kapiolani; the kukui down the path toward Richards Street was planted by President Roosevelt in 1934. The fenced mound at the corner of the grounds is the site of the former royal crypt, and at one time was topped by a coral stone tomb. The royal dead, except Kamehameha I, were buried there until 1865, when all were transferred to the Royal Mausoleum in Nuuanu. At the site of the razed tomb, the king's representative transacted secret business with the English navy when the British occupied Hawaii in 1843.

Inside the palace, the main hallway is paneled with royal koa, ohia and kamani wood. It is dark and the wood has lost its gloss. The Governor's office upstairs used to be King Kalakaua's bedroom; the office now occupied by Secretary Lorrin was Queen Kapiolani's chambers. The state dining room is now the Senate chamber. And, Ward thought, when these powerful haole rulers meet in a little while to decide the political fate of Willard Howland, they will gather in the Throne Room, now used by the House of Representatives: the Governor probably will light one of those rank-smelling cigars of his, then take his place on the gilded koa and Oriental brocaded throne of Kalakaua, heave his cigar smoke up toward the red velvet canopy where it will cloud out the dedication carved plainly beneath the pointed taro leaves of Kalakaua's crown:

> *Ua mau ke ea o ka aina i ka pono.*
> THE LIFE OF THE LAND IS PERPETUATED
> BY RIGHTEOUSNESS.

The big boys, Ward thought, would crowd around Willard Howland, and with one voice, ask him: "How about it, Willard? Can you handle Ward Akana?"

And what would Willard Howland answer them? Ward wondered, turning his gaze upon the old man. What would old Willard, who has dreamed all his life of becoming delegate and leading his people to statehood, tell them? Yes, he'd say. I can control Ward Akana. I can control Ward Akana, Willard Howland would reason to himself, because Ward Akana is my flesh-and-blood son.

"You look like you're deep in thought, arguing with your conscience," Senator Howland said.

Ward smiled weakly. "No, nothing like that."

"What were you thinking about?"

"Nothing important."

"Tell me, boy."

"I was wondering what was going to happen when you and all the big shots got together."

"Ward," Willard said, his voice slow and somehow gray, his eyes watching the younger man with pained affection, "do you remember a night a long time back when you were a boy at Manoalani? It was a stormy night, and you and Garth and Dean were all in the playroom by the fire. And all of you got to talking about what you were going to be when you grew up?"

"Yes. Vaguely . . ."

"And you said how you were going to be president of Hawaii?"

"Yes, I remember."

"I told you then that there was no such thing as a president of Hawaii. That as a man born in Hawaii you could not become President of the United States; you did not even have the power to vote for the President of the United States."

"If I remember right," Ward said, "I felt cheated."

"You were perfectly justified in feeling cheated," the Senator said. "You'll remember that I told you the highest office a Hawaii-born person could reach was that of Delegate to Congress. And I pointed out that the Delegate's job was the most unfair, most heartbreaking task in the recent history of American politics. The Delegate represents almost six hundred thousand American people, yet when he sits in Washington's House of Representatives he has no power to vote. Neither he nor the people he represents has a voice. He cannot even vote on a bill that concerns Hawaii. It's a man-killing job, and as sure as I'm standing here, it's what killed Joe Stinson. But all my life," Willard said, looking into the strangely troubled eyes of Ward Akana, "I've wanted that job.

"I've wanted to go before Congress and tell them that the Territorial form of government in Hawaii is unmoral, undemocratic and essentially un-American. I've wanted to stand in Congress and remind the country that the American Revolution was based on opposition to taxation without representation, yet here in Hawaii we have federal taxation without representation. I've wanted to remind Congress that America was founded upon the idea that the government derived its powers from the consent of the governed, yet in Hawaii the government is appointed by the President, not through the consent of the governed. I've wanted to drill it through Congress that its failure to grant statehood to Hawaii is an unconstitutional abuse of power. That we should have statehood and equality or we should be set free to be governed by the wishes of our people."

Ward smiled at the old man. "A very nice speech, Senator. That part about being set free sounds good. A commonwealth form of government would set us free."

Howland looked curiously at Ward, as if trying to ascertain if the young man was serious. "No, commonwealth isn't a political reality," he said. "It would give us a semblance of self-government and it would relieve us of the obligation of paying federal taxes. But the end result, the moral and ethical result of commonwealth, would be the same as remaining a Territory. We'd be stepchildren of the nation, second-class citizens. No," he muttered, "you can't be serious about that commonwealth business."

Ward frowned. "Senator Howland," he said, "you and your dreams are the political unreality. Face the facts. We've petitioned for statehood for more than a hundred years, and Washington's leaders have always answered, *next year!* The hard political reality is that the big boys on Pennsylvania Avenue just don't want us to be a state. Isn't that clear by now? They've kicked us around long enough. The South is bigoted against our racial mixtures. The Democrats are afraid of new Republican representatives. The whole country is afraid of having a Japanese senator or governor. They just don't want us. Well, I say the hell with them. If they don't want Hawaii as a state, and it's perfectly clear they don't, then I say let's not want them. We don't have to beg. I say the hell with statehood. Give us autonomy and commonwealth, and keep the tax money here!"

"You don't really feel that way, Ward. You're just talking. You're sore and you're letting off steam."

"No, you're wrong. That's the way I honestly feel. And you can tell your pals at the palace that that's how I feel."

Howland looked at him sharply. "You wouldn't do anything to harm our statehood chances, would you?"

"No," Ward said, after a while. "No, of course not."

"If it was in your power to help the statehood cause, would you?"

"It's not in my power."

"Yes, it is."

"In what way?"

"Think about it, Ward."

A cold smile worked its way across Ward's face. "You mean like calling off the strike, Senator?"

"A strike at this time would kill the Territory."

"I doubt that."

"Can't anything be done?"

"It's out of my hands, Senator. Talk to your pals over there. Convince them to meet the Union's proposals halfway. If they're so interested in statehood and fair play—"

"They're going to ask me if I can help ward off this strike," Howland said.

"That's pretty obvious."

"Another major strike through the plantations and the docks will look very bad in Washington. Washington will say, as it has before, that we in Hawaii cannot manage our affairs as a Territory, so how can we expect to manage statehood?"

Ward spoke very evenly. "Senator," he said, "I don't care what they say or what they think in Washington. I only care that my people get a fair share of the pie."

A white hardness came into the Senator's face. He took his eyes away from Ward's, and glanced past his shoulder to where the flags rippled softly at half-mast against the blue curdling sky. *My people* Ward had said. And Willard Howland understood all too well the emphasis.

Still gazing past Ward, he said quietly, "When I get to the palace, they'll ask me if I believe this strike can be averted. If I believe labor and management can get along. And to a point, they will decide upon my nomination as Delegate on the answers I give." He paused for a moment, and Ward looked at him uneasily. "What do you think I should tell them, Ward?"

"It's your nomination, Senator," Ward said, his voice flat, void of emotion. "Tell them anything you think is right."

They stared at each other for a moment, then the old man turned and walked down the slope to the parking area, walking, Ward noted, with that old familiar stride of his, bent low with trouble, like some weary but undefeatable Jove. And for a moment, as he watched, Ward felt that brittle ache start working through him again, the pain that wanted to call out "Father," the word he had never used with Willard Howland, not even as a young boy riding the grazelands of Manoalani with Willard Howland riding alongside. *Dig in with your knees, Son, ride him with your knees. That's it, keep your shoulders straight, drop your heels and sit with him, that's the way, Son.*

He walked slowly down to the car where George Hill was waiting for him. He got in without a word and slammed the door shut. He stared with indiscriminate gloom out the window while the car tooled downhill following Willard Howland and the Governor. His eyes swung with the Governor's car as it turned into the driveway of Iolani Palace, and it was not until they had passed the palace and he could no longer see Willard Howland in that car that he became conscious of George Hill tapping him on the elbow.

"Ward? Are you listening?"

He turned and looked obliquely at the Union boss.

"You must have been in a dream world," George Hill said. "I was explaining how once we get back to the office, we'll have to finalize the strike plans. You'll have to work out the whole basic procedure for Oahu and the Outer Islands, okay?"

Ward nodded.

George Hill sat back comfortably in the car and glanced out the window. "And then we'll break 'em," he said. "You wait and see. We'll knock old Willie Howland and the whole bunch of 'em right out of the running."

Ward thought about the strike plans for a moment. Then that other thing moved slowly across the back of his mind and, as he knew it would, the pain started working through him again, *You're getting on to it much better now. Just sit with him easy and ride him with your knees. That's it, Son.*

Chapter Five

AARON studied the beaded glass pitcher of martinis he was mixing and decided to add another double jigger of gin. "It can't be too dry," he said. "One of the most pleasant truths of life is that a martini cannot be too dry. Painting, writing, all the treasured art forms of the world might pass on to oblivion," he said, handing Sloan a chilled glass and filling it. "Except two—copulation and martiniation, the anodynes against the wounds of time."

Sloan laughed. "I've never seen you in such a happy mood."

"My darling sister," he raised his glass and touched it to hers in a toast, "you're forgetting all the things we have to celebrate. Your return, your friend's first day in the Islands, the old man's being nominated for the delegacy, and—"

"Last but not least—"

"Yes. Last but certainly not least, my 'Cheating a fiery death on Mauna Loa,' " he ridiculed the newspapers' dramatics.

Sloan sipped her drink and beamed at her older brother. She had always been a little afraid of him. As a young girl she considered him a petty tyrant. She had feared his moods of black, violent depression. He had a gift for the savage phrase which he would lash her with to make her miserable. Then, when her eyes brimmed with tears, he would appear suddenly contrite. He would sit her on his lap and hug her. "Now, Sloan baby, no tears. Aaron loves you very much and that's why sometimes he has to scold you." But it was not scolding. It was something else, something willful and petulant; the cruelty of the insecure. He would pat her gently on the knee and his hand would slide up and cup her young thigh. "Aaron loves you, Sloan baby, so don't cry. Love Aaron back." And he would kiss her several times until she would squirm away, somehow hating the kiss more than the violence.

"You've changed a lot, Aaron," she said.

"How?"

"You seem gayer. You seem as if you're actually having a good time."

"How else could I feel when I'm with the most beautiful girl in the world?" He put his arm around her and kissed her. "Besides that, we have all these celebrations to be happy about."

She uncrossed her legs, noticing Aaron watching the flash of knee, and got up and walked over to him. Her skin was glowing against the rust-colored sheath dress. "We have something else to celebrate," she said.

"What?"

"I'll tell you later."

"A secret?"

She nodded.

"About who?"

"Me."

"Just you alone?"

She shook her head, gaminlike. "Me and Paul Kahana."

He set the pitcher and iced glasses on a silver tray and started carrying them from the kitchen.

"I'm not so sure I like any secret you might have with Paul Kahana," he said.

"You don't know what the secret is."
"Well, what is it?"
"You'll know later. Maybe when he gets over here."
"Is he coming over?"
"We're all going out later. Paul's picking me up about eight-thirty. Ramsey's going out with Peter Noa."
Aaron frowned. "Why with those two? You could have your pick of any fellow on the island."
Sloan looked sideways at her brother. "You like Paul, don't you, Aaron?"
"I've got nothing against him. Except that he's not for you."
"Why? I mean, how do you seem so sure?"
"Why? Goddamn it, Sloan, he's black, that's why," Aaron said irritably. "It's one thing being friendly and cordial with these people, to go out with them is another matter. You of all people. Be friendly with them, Sloan. But don't—well, never get too close."
"That might be a little late," Sloan said. "I'm very close to Paul Kahana, Aaron. Very close."
"I don't like it, Sloan. See to it during the next few weeks that you get away from him. I don't like it at all."
"Don't you think that I—"
"I don't want to discuss the matter, Sloan," Aaron snapped. "And I don't want to go into what kind of 'closeness' there is between you and that Kahana kid. It's childish and you're not thinking. I want it broken up and I want it broken up soon."
The house that Willard Howland had moved into for the interim of his campaign was part of the John Howland Estate, an old, three-floored, wood Victorian mansion on a hilltop above Manoa Valley. From the lanai in back of the house, northern vistas opened up to the brooding cliffs of Nuuanu Pali and beyond, to the slick hazy jewel of Kaneohe Bay.
Ramsey James, wearing tight white toreador pants and a black silk blouse, was chatting amiably with Willard Howland and Laura when Aaron and Sloan joined them. Aaron set the tray of drinks on the lanai table. They each took a glass.
"To the next Delegate to Congress," Sloan said, sitting on the arm of Willard's chair and raising her glass in a toast. "I'm so proud of you. You'll be the handsomest, most distinguished-looking man in Washington."

Howland beamed up at her, his thick white mustaches breaking like a bird in flight. "I'm not quite in Washington yet, Princess."

"All I know is what I read in the papers," Sloan said gaily. She reached for the copy of the evening *Star-Bulletin* that was lying on the table and she flicked it so the front page was firm. "Right here," she grinned, quoting the headline. "Senator Howland Named Republican Nominee For Delegacy."

"That's just a nomination, Princess."

"But a Republican nomination," Sloan said, tossing the newspaper back on the table. "And in Hawaii, a Republican nomination is as sure as a Democratic nomination in Dixie."

"Is that a fact?" Ramsey James asked.

"It's a fact so far in this century," Sloan said. "Republican through and through. Don't you think my father will look distinguished on Capitol Hill?" She kept it up, knowing the old man was enjoying it.

"It must be a wonderful feeling," Ramsey said, "to be leading the Islands to statehood. A kind of frontier feeling. That's all I've heard since I've been here. Statehood. We don't hear much about it in America—I mean, on the Mainland."

"That's been one of our troubles," Howland said. "Getting the story before the American people. Because in the final estimation, they will be the ones who will decide our fate."

"And they'll never decide for statehood," Aaron said, pulling up a lawn chair and joining the group. "Never, Old Man."

Ramsey, who was loosening up and enjoying herself more and more as she grew to know the Howlands, turned intently to Aaron. "Do you mean you don't think Congress will ever grant statehood?"

Aaron smiled. "Like everything else, it's a cold matter of business and politics, sugar quotas and the balance of power in Congress. It has nothing to do with emotions or moral justice."

"That's not entirely true," Senator Howland said. "Considering the history of Hawaii and its plea for statehood, we are closer to it today than at any time in our history."

He turned to Ramsey. "You know, Ramsey, that even before it became part of the United States, Hawaii asked for statehood. King Kamehameha the Third first proposed it in 1854. Then, after the revolution of 1893, when Queen Liliuokalani and the Hawaiian monarchy was overthrown and Sanford B. Dole became the first president of the Hawaiian Republic, we again tried to get statehood. Hawaii was never conquered or purchased by the United States. It was voluntarily annexed as a Territory in 1898, the year I was born. The people of Hawaii joined the United States after more than a century of their own independence. In doing so, they gave to the United States their public funds, their forts, their docks, and more than a million acres of public land. They also gave the United States the hearts, minds, and bodies of their peoples. Ever since then, the unwritten moral understanding was that the people of Hawaii were not to be kept in perpetual subjection to Congress. The Territorial form of government was simply to serve as preparation for full statehood.

"Way back in 1785, the United States granted Territories the right to graduate into states. At that time, Congress accepted the Northwest Territory and provided for its later subdivision into states when its population reached 60,000. Hawaii, now, has ten times that population. Eighty-five per cent of our population are American-born citizens, a proportion greater than New York's. Our real estate is valued at $600 million, higher than many states. Our taxes last year reached $230 million, more than eleven states. More than forty-five per cent of the adult population paid those taxes, a percentage larger than twenty-six states. No," Howland shook his head, "our necessary period of political tutelage has long passed. We are ready and eager for self-government."

Ramsey nodded. "It seems terribly unfair," she said. "My father, he's a lawyer and a long time ago he was an Assemblyman in Sacramento, he says it's because Hawaii's not connected to America by land. That Hawaii's so far away."

"That's one of the arguments against statehood," Senator Howland nodded. "But it doesn't make sense. Really, Hawaii is nearer in time to Washington than any except the original thirteen States when admitted to the Union. Hawaii is only fourteen hours from Washington today. We'll be about eight hours or less when the jets come in. When New Mexico was given statehood it was three weeks away from Washington."

He reached for the portfolio he had placed by his chair and searched through the various statehood documents he had filed away. "In this century alone," he said, "we have petitioned for statehood to nearly every Congress. Prince Kuhio Kalanianaole, who was delegate from 1902 to 1922, fought for statehood, as did Victor Houston after him. We have invited more than a dozen congressional investigating committees here, at our expense, to study Hawaii's adaptability for statehood. The Joint Congressional Committee in 1937 recognized the obvious facts that Hawaii was, and I quote from the Committee's report," he said, reading one of the documents he had taken from the portfolio: "'Hawaii is industrious, prosperous and progressive, and will not be content for long to be held in a subordinate position in comparison with other parts of the Union. It is inconceivable that the United States, dedicated to the very principle of self-government and equal treatment of its citizens, should long desire to impose any restrictions upon the full measure of self-government to be accorded to Hawaii.'

"In 1940, when Sam King was Delegate, a plebiscite held here showed the people favored statehood by a two-to-one majority. In 1946, a Gallup Poll on the Mainland found two-thirds of the people in favor of our becoming a state."

Senator Howland paused and sipped his martini. "It's a sad old story," he said. "President Roosevelt told me personally that we would soon be granted statehood. President Truman's 1946 State of the Union message asked for Hawaiian statehood. But, as Aaron said, we have become the victim of political skulduggery; the pawn in an unfortunate system of congressional checks and balances. Hawaii has come of age, politically, economically and culturally. It is inconceivable to all of us that the leaders of this country should continue to oppose our freedom. We are an integral and vital part of the United States, and we must be extended the same freedom, democracy and political equality that prevails throughout America."

He placed his glass on the table and reached into the pocket of his coat. He took his wallet out and unfolded a worn newspaper article. "Here." He handed the article to Ramsey.

Ramsey studied the newspaper clipping, then read it aloud: "'President Dwight D. Eisenhower said in his 1954 State of the Union message today that there is no justification for deferring the admission of Hawaii to statehood . . .'"

"Well," Aaron said, finishing his drink and pouring himself another, "that's all window dressing. Anyway, Old Man, congratulations on making the big-time political arena. And welcome to the delegacy. You can have it."

Laura looked at him nervously. She knew he had been drinking all afternoon. She hoped he wouldn't spoil the evening. "Maybe we had better keep away from politics tonight," she suggested.

"I agree," Aaron said. "It would be unfair to Miss James on her first night in Hawaii to get embroiled in politics. Especially the kind of politics we have here in the Islands."

"A continual circus," Willard admitted. "Ours is the only legislature in the world which convenes amid Hawaiian prayers, native chanting, torchbearers and hula dancers wiggling about the Senate floor."

"And it's senseless to talk about statehood," Aaron said, starting for the kitchen to mix another batch of drinks. "Hawaii will get statehood when hell freezes over."

"Oh Aaron, you're constantly throwing a wet blanket over everything," Laura said.

"And a false one," Willard said. "Hawaii will be granted statehood. Anything else would be a gross miscarriage of justice. The American people will demand fair play. As soon as the Mainlanders are fully aware of the situation here, they will demand that their Congressmen admit us."

"Don't hold your breath, Old Man," Aaron said.

"Do all the people in Hawaii want statehood?" Ramsey asked.

"Hardly," Aaron said, taking her by the arm and escorting her into the dining room. "There are a few things my illustrious father neglected to mention. First, we're not quite sure about our own feelings for statehood. Some people advocate commonwealth. Some say we're doing pretty damned good as we are, so why change?"

"Wrong!" Willard roared good-naturedly. "A poll now would show we are overwhelmingly and passionately for statehood."

"A consensus poll, like a set of figures, can be manipulated to prove anything the prover wishes," Aaron said. "For instance, the Senator mentioned the plebiscite that was held in 1940 which showed the people in favor of statehood two-to-one. That's just the way the newspapers hailed it as a victory for statehood. But on second glance, looking at it the other way around, it shows that a surprising one-third of the voters opposed statehood, while some 15,000 registered voters didn't even bother to mark that part of the ballot—in other words, a great proportion of our people are apathetic to statehood. They don't give a damn, one way or the other. While the newspapers hailed it as a statehood victory, it was, more truly, a defeat. And a house divided cannot stand."

"If a poll was taken now," Senator Howland said, "you would see that Hawaii is not a house divided."

"Hawaii is a house divided and will remain so as long as it permits situations in which a rabble-rousing Communist like Ward Akana can control the docks, the plantation workers and the vote of some 25,000 Union members!"

Sloan glanced harshly at her brother. "Aaron, please don't get like that. This is supposed to be a party."

"Ward Akana is neither a rabble-rouser nor a Communist!" Willard said angrily.

"What would you call him?"

"Let's drop it," Sloan said.

"I'd call him a—a sincere labor leader," Willard said.

"And since when has the Senior Senator from the Island of Hawaii spoken so well of Mr. Akana? Or of labor leaders?" Aaron asked. He was weaving a little, eying his father unsteadily. "Since he was nominated for the delegacy and figured he might have need of the—the prodigal's help?"

"Aaron!" Laura interrupted heatedly. "How can you say a thing like that?"

"Just a private citizen trying to find out what goes on behind the political smokescreens," he said. "How about it, Old Man? When did your side and Ward Akana's side get so palsy-walsy?"

Willard leaned forward, his eyes filled with unnamable things, like the eyes of an old tiger. "I don't want to discuss Ward Akana," he said, in a quiet, broken voice.

Watching her father, Sloan thought that she had never seen him looking so old. Only his fathomless pride held his head erect. He looked, she thought, like a statue of permanent defeat. She remembered Ernest Hemingway's handful of words, the words she had always considered to be among the finest ever written by man: *A man can be destroyed but not defeated.* Now she wondered about those words. Her father looked like a man who had endured many defeats and now awaited the final sweet destruction.

"Come with Ramsey and me, Daddy." She linked her arm through his. "Let's go inside."

When they had gone inside, Laura said, "Are you proud of yourself now, Aaron? Are you proud that you hit him so hard?"

He poured himself another drink, his sullen back to her.

"Why do you always do it?" She was close to tears at old Willard's grief. "What is so sick and twisted inside you that you have to destroy?"

"I did nothing. I merely—"

"You merely probed until you reopened an old wound. Why, Aaron? Why does your survival depend upon tearing through other people? Why do you—"

"Why do I insist upon showing up a pompous, proud old bastard so full of himself and his importance that he cringes when faced with the truth?"

"Aaron, your father has faced the fact of—of Ward Akana all his life. He's lived with it and he's overcome it as far as it's humanly possible for a man of conscience to overcome that sort of thing. He doesn't deserve to have it thrown up in his face by his son."

"That's just about enough, Laura. When I want your advice I'll ask for it."

Laura slumped dejectedly in her chair. "Please don't drink any more. It's when you drink that all that bitterness churns through you. Please don't, Aaron."

"And let's not talk about my drinking or the reasons I drink, either," Aaron said. "But if it will make you any easier, I'll finish this last one and call it quits."

"You don't need that one. That's precisely the one you don't need."

"No. I need this one more than I needed all the others. This is precisely the drink I do need. All the others were a waste without this one. All the others led up to this one."

Drunkenly, he saw her look at the glass in his hand as if it were her betrayer; look up at him with those pleading eyes of hers, those goddamned cocker spaniel eyes, the eyes of a person wronged, those turn-the-other-cheek eyes: and, as he expected, she buried her face in her fists and rubbed away the tears. Her words were mumbled but he knew them by heart now. "Why do you do it, Aaron?"

"I don't know," he said with the air of a man who has disgust for himself. "Maybe because I'm thirty-five years old and I don't know why I should want to become thirty-six. Maybe because I have to blame everyone close to me for my own disillusionments. I blame you for not becoming everything I hoped you'd become so long ago. As you blame me."

"I don't—"

"Oh, cut it out, Laura. Why deny it? It's the fable of American love and we're both caught up in it. Every American boy grows up with his dream of Cinderella; every girl with her dream of Prince Charming. Then the boy and girl meet and they're goggle-eyed by the great myth. They think they've found their Prince Charming and Cinderella, although in reality, nothing could be further from the truth. And in time, they see it. In time, they realize how different is their real love from their dreamed-of love. And instead of blaming themselves and their need and foolishness, they blame each other. So the dream crumbles and the marriage filters down to a mutual contempt. And it's too late to start to dream again."

Slowly, Laura raised her eyes to his. "How did you become so bitter, Aaron?"

"Practice, my dear. I've made a science of it."

"And so clever."

"Why should we pretend, Laura? Why play the jolly husband-and-wife bit? It doesn't fool anyone, it's too off-key. There's a distinct, unfakable flavor to a good marriage. Call it warmth, call it magic, call it luck. And there's also an unmistakable twist to a bad marriage that no amount of pretense, public affection or nesty enthusiasm can do away with. Unhappily, that's what we've got."

"Why, Aaron?" A tear fell like hot wax to her cheek.

He finished his drink and put down the glass. "I don't know," he said.

The dinner was awkward; the conversation forced. Aaron picked at his food with little appetite. He started drinking again halfway through the meal. It was, he reasoned, the only way he could get through it. He slipped his fingers about the keychain in his pocket and separated the key to Lei Villanueva's apartment from the rest. It gave him an obscure thrill, feeling the key. He should be able to get there by nine. That beef with Laura made everything easier. He would not have to keep up the shabby pretense. That resolution he made at the volcano about quitting the affair was inane. He would never give her up. Why should he? He needed her now more than ever. He would get her to have the abortion, but he would not give her up. The key felt warm in his fingers. In a little while he would be with her again.

"Well, we'd better be getting ready," Sloan said, finishing her coffee and getting up from the table. "They should be here any minute."

Aaron raised his head from the table, an odd, slanting flatness in his eyes. It was almost as if he had been hoping for the opportunity. "Who'll be here," he sneered, "the black boys?"

"Please, Aaron," Laura said.

"Amos an' Andy a-comin' up t'pay a call on us white folk?"

Sloan's face was a white, frigid mask. "Aaron!"

"Shut ma' mouf, honey-chile, ah jes' wuz askin'—"

"You're drunk," Sloan said. "You're contemptible and disgusting."

"I'm saying this for your own good, you little fool!"

"I don't want to hear anything you have to say."

"It's about time you listened to someone!" Aaron roared. He got to his feet and staggered around the table toward her. "Awright awright—pardon my crudeness. But it occurred to me that you'd have more respect for the family than to run around with these goddamned gooks!"

"Don't use that term, Aaron."

"Why whassamatta, honey-chile, does da trouf hurt?"

Sloan whirled and flung a glass of icewater into his face. It sobered him and enraged him and his fingers gripped her arm like a vise. "Listen to me, you—"

"I don't ever want to listen to you and your filthy mind again. You and your cheap talk about respect. You don't even have enough respect for yourself to—"

"Sit down, Aaron." Old Willard had stepped between them and broken Aaron's grip on her arm. "Sit down."

"Awright awright." He planted his feet and stared into Sloan's face. "Look, kid, I'm saying this for your own good."

"There's something you should know, Aaron."

"There are a few things you should know, young lady, and one of them is your place in—"

"I'm going to marry Paul Kahana."

The words hit him with an almost physical force. He stepped back, then slumped down into a chair by the dining room wall. "Say that again."

"No," old Willard said. "We've had enough—"

Sloan stepped in front of him and stood looking down at her brother. "Paul Kahana and I are in love with each other. Can you understand two people loving each other, Aaron? We're going to get married. At Manoalani."

"Oh my God," Aaron groaned. He looked helplessly to Laura, then to Willard. They both averted their eyes.

"You knew about this?" he said weakly, accusing them. "Everyone knew about this but me? You, Old Man—you knew?"

Willard sat down heavily at the head of the table. Laura looked curiously at her husband, as if trying to figure out if he was being sincere or leaning on theatrics. She did not indulge in pseudo-psychiatry; she hated it as a parlor game with its terms being bandied about by the inept. But she was certain there was something warped in Aaron that made him destroy things. And she admitted to herself, with sad wisdom, that he would go on like that, soiling things: the party tonight, Willard's dreams, Sloan's love, their own marriage. And looking at him now, slumped in the chair, his face in his hands, she felt that she had failed him. She had failed him as a woman, and she had lost him that way. She failed him as a wife, and could give him no more children. As she walked over to him, hoping that it was not a cheap theatrical gesture, she decided that she didn't have to fail him as a human being—she would stay with him.

"C'mon, Aaron. Let's go home."

As he stood up, his total dejection struck Sloan.

"I'm—I'm sorry, Aaron," she said softly.

"Forget it. It's your life."

"Aaron, I've known Paul since I've been a baby. I'm not crossing color lines. I'm not trying to parade as some avant-garde Bohemian, making speeches for brotherhood or the equality of races or any of that. I'm in love with Paul. And there's nothing anybody can say or do that can change my love for him, or change the color of his skin."

Aaron looked at her dully. "My God—"

"Won't you even try to understand?"

"I understand one thing. That marriage will never take place. Not while there's breath in my body. And if the old man—or anyone else here—had the guts to be truthful, they'd say the same thing. Cause that's how they feel about it."

Sloan turned and walked out of the dining room. She stopped and stared hopefully at the front door. Ring, she prayed, ring. And the doorbell chimed.

"Oh, I'm so glad it's you," she said. "Hold me tight."

"This is quite a welcome." Paul grinned.

They walked down the front steps to the garden.

"I've missed you."

"How did you find the time? It's only been—"

"It's been five long whole hours."

"Will I always get this kind of a welcome? What if we were apart a whole day?"

"I'd smother you. I couldn't stand it."

He held her face in his hands and studied her. "Is there anything wrong? You look as though you've been cryin'."

"Nothing's wrong now. No tears in me."

"But something was wrong."

"Yes, but it's over. Forget it."

She looked over his shoulder and saw Peter Noa standing by the car. "Hi, Peter! I didn't see you there at first."

"It's pretty hard to miss all of me," he laughed. He was about Paul's height but perhaps fifty pounds heavier; a beefy, jovial youngster in his middle twenties. His features were rounder and thicker than Paul's, and his skin was considerably darker. Like Paul, he wore a dark blue blazer with brass buttons, white duck trousers and loafer shoes, and a soft white sport shirt open at the throat.

"Aloha, welcome home!" He placed a pikaki lei over Sloan and kissed her. "I hear this wahine you lined up for me is a numbarh one wahine!" He stopped as he saw Ramsey James come to the front door and walk down the steps to meet them.

"Yeah man!" Peter's face broke into a wide grin. "Numbarh one!"

When Sloan introduced them, Ramsey hesitated for a moment. What struck her, aside from his immense darkness, was his extreme homeliness. He had something of a clown's homeliness, almost to the point where it was definitely appealing. His smile saved him, she thought. It was an engagingly crooked grin in the middle of that funny, clownlike face. She shook hands with him and Peter was aware of her hesitancy.

"Here," he said, placing a lei over her head. *"Aloha."* There was an awkward moment when Ramsey feared she would have to go through the custom of the kiss. But she thanked him inwardly for sensing her recoil. He merely settled the lei across her shoulders, smiled at her and turned to Paul.

"Let's make tracks," Paul said, taking both girls by their elbows and leading them to the car. "We've got a big night ahead of us."

"Where to?"

"The Broiler. Don the Beachcomber's. Let's do the whole Waikiki strip."

"Including the Royal. I've told Ramsey how beautiful it is there dancing at night."

Ramsey felt no strangeness at the touch of Peter's hand helping her into the car. She had imagined there would be a different feel to it, a graininess, something alien. But it felt just like anybody else's hand.

As Peter backed the car around the driveway, Sloan caught a glimpse of her father, stooped and silhouetted in the doorway.

"Wait just a second," she said.

She got out of the car and walked over to him.

"Daddy?" she whispered tentatively.

"Hello, Princess."

She placed her hand on his. "I'm so sorry that had to happen."

"It's over now. Don't take anything Aaron says too seriously. There's something wrong inside him." He smiled at her in a sad defensive way. They strolled along the driveway to a Roman stone bench arched with bougainvillaea.

"I don't want to detain you."

"No."

"Maybe you're not too interested in the mutterings of an old man."

"I am, Daddy."

"Well," Howland conceded, "I was hoping to have a chance to talk with you before anything was settled."

"It seems settled now, Daddy. But . . ."

"But what?"

The glow of his cigar etched his face and she could see into the trouble of his eyes. "I'd like to hear what you have to say about it."

Willard sighed heavily. "I'm not sure how to go about it, Princess. You know, never in my life have I ever talked to you about your—your romances. That subject seemed to paralyze me."

"Daddy," she opened his hands and traced her fingernail down the creased lifeline of his palm, "this isn't a 'romance.' I'm deeply in love with Paul."

"And he's in love with you?"

She nodded.

"There couldn't be any question about it?"

"No."

"I wonder if you kids know what love is. Or what it does to you—good and bad."

"Maybe not. But we've got to learn."

"A marriage like this could be a terrible way to learn. Princess, I should have talked to you more often when you were growing up. I should have taken more of an interest in your doings, but it's difficult for a father to talk to his daughter. Perhaps if your mother had . . ."

"Daddy, you've been the most wonderful father a girl could have. I hate to see you sad this way. I wouldn't make you sad for the world. You know that."

"This marriage would make me sad, Sloan."

"Why? Why should it?"

"Because it's not right. Somewhere along the line I've missed out with you. And this is the result."

"This isn't a bad result, Daddy. I'm a girl in love and I want to marry the man I love."

"You're not a girl, Princess. You're a woman now. I always meant to sit down and talk with you, but the years raced by before I had time to turn around and you're no longer a little girl but a grown woman. I've lost touch with you. You've got the body of a woman and the emotions of a child, and it's the worst combination possible."

"Daddy—was what Aaron said true? About your feelings?"

He waited a moment. "I don't want you to marry Paul Kahana."

Sloan slumped back on her hips as though the wind had been knocked out of her. "It seems like everyone feels that way."

"In this case, everyone's right." He turned to her. "You're

twenty-one years old, Princess. When a girl is that age, she's perpetually in love. And the more obstacles, the more important the love seems. You'll fall in love a dozen more times before you really know what it means. This thing with Paul is—"

"Because of his color, Daddy?"

Her words stopped him. But after a minute, he nodded his head slowly. "Color does a lot of things to a person. Race and heredity and color are deeper than just the surface."

"I don't see his color. I just see him. Color isn't important. I see inside it."

"What is important, Sloan?"

"Love is important. Happiness in a home. Children."

"You've discussed children with Paul?"

"Certainly. We're not going into this blind. We want children. We know they'll be of mixed blood. We've talked about it many times. We're going to have as many as we can afford. Not right at first."

"People in love should have children. They're the only thing in life that stands up, in the long run." He looked at her. "What do you think is in store for your children?"

The question gave her a nervous little throb. "The same thing that's in store for all children. I'm not afraid for them. Their mixed blood won't be a disgrace. The things that will go against them in life are the same things that are going against our marriage now: bigotry, smallness, fear, prejudice. Paul and I are ready to stand up to those things now. And I have faith that our children will be able to stand up to them."

"I see." Old Willard stared moodily at the high white bulk of clouds damming up behind the pali. Sloan cupped his head in her hands and turned it to face her.

"Daddy, please pull with me in this. Don't kill it."

"You're making a mistake—"

"Then let me find it out for myself, Daddy. Please."

"I have to tell you how I feel. I'm against the marriage. It's unwise. Be sure of what you're doing. Don't rush into anything. This thing with Paul Kahana is no good. You'll regret it. We'll all be hurt by it."

He continued talking for a few minutes. Sloan bowed her head helplessly. Well, that's it, she thought. As I always knew it would be. It was all so much easier in California. Two thousand miles across the sea, Paul and I could talk about it, dream about it, plan for it. But here at home, face to face with everyone, I have to sit by and watch it hurt the people I love. Why should my love hurt other people? "You know I wouldn't hurt you for anything in the world, Daddy," she said quietly.

Old Willard nodded.

"Then why does it have to work out this way?"

"Because it's no good," Willard muttered.

They stood up. He could feel her young smooth hand cover his. Her hand trembled at first, then held firm. "Despite what anybody says, I love him with all my heart. And I'm going to marry him." She pressed her cheek to his. He could feel the tears on her cheek. She kissed him. "Please forgive me."

She was gone suddenly. He could hear the nervous clicking of her heels across the driveway. For a moment he was lost in thoughts of the things he wished he had said.

Later he heard the clatter of the screen door and saw Aaron stomp angrily to his car.

"Can I speak to you a moment, Aaron?"

"Later, Old Man." Aaron piled into his Jaguar and raced out of the driveway.

In a little while a taxicab tooled up to the front entrance and Laura walked down the steps and got into it. Willard leaned against the cab window. "Where are you going?"

"I'm not sure," she said. He could tell from the sound of her voice that they had had a row again and she had been crying. "Somewhere, Willard. I don't know yet."

He watched the taillights disappear.

In a few minutes Coyama padded out and put a shawl about old Willard's shoulders. "You catch-a co'd, you catch-a co'd out here."

"Just for a little while longer," Willard grumbled, dismissing the old Japanese.

Alone again, he tramped to the end of the driveway. A dark tumbling wind moved through the garden. He stared up at the moon, in whose mottled face he had, on other nights, so often found solace.

Chapter Six

LEI VILLANUEVA studied the reflection of her naked body in the bathroom mirror. Lately she had been trying to see herself through Aaron's eyes. This is the body that delights him, this is the skin he calls palomino silk, these are the hands he loves to caress him. She raised her hands behind her head to remove her shower cap, arching her breasts. They were heavy, high-hung breasts, the ebony-dark nipples erect from the shower sting. They swelled with milk. But that was the only sign.

She sucked in her stomach, inspecting the slender line of her torso. No swelling there yet. She was anxious for it to show. Like all Hawaiians, she loved babies and wanted one of her own. It was one of the factors that made Hawaiian children probably the happiest on earth, she thought. They were loved, they were secure, they were prized. She pressed the palm of her hand to her stomach and felt the little lump of hardness. It felt good. She smiled secretly. She hoped it would start to show soon. She would carry it proudly.

Her hair tumbled from the shower cap to her shoulders and she rubbed it vigorously with the towel. She wrapped another towel about her hips, below the smooth curve of her belly. She thrust out her hips and grinned happily in the mirror. Island girl, she thought. Happy love-making little palomino savage.

She wondered how long her face and body would last. At twenty-two, she was precariously overripe. There were times when she had caught Aaron looking at her with that remote, calculating stare, as if he was trying to decide if her body would spread and soften, her features sag. He had looked at her that way one afternoon when they had finished making love and the oblique cast of his eyes had surprised her. But when she had understood what it meant, she smiled to herself and walked over to him quite deliberately, her body full of rich promises, and when she reached him the physical impact of her made him dizzy and crazy with need all over again.

She had laughed softly at his eagerness. At his driving, unthinking blindness, at his insatiable lust for her. He used her with deadly persistency. The times in between were a vacuum, a nothingness, an impatient, almost irritable waiting. She did not worry about his remoteness during those times. She was certain that her body and its love-making had drugged him beyond his own realization; that she was both a need and a habit he would find impossible to break.

Besides, she reasoned, he was a man, and much of being a woman was to understand a man. Understand his need for her; understand the craziness as well as the nothingness, the waiting until the craziness began again. He was a man who was good to her and she loved him.

She slipped into the pale blue silk lounging robe Aaron had given her and walked into the living room. The sliding glass doors to the lanai were open. A warm breeze stirred the drapes. She selected a few of her favorite Frank Sinatra longplays and set them on the hi-fi. Then she took her brush and comb and went out to the small lanai.

The ocean was dark and at high tide. Wavelets sloshed leisurely against the seawall beneath the lanai. Next to her apartment house, the bachelors who lived at Red Hale at the foot of Diamond Head were having a party. She listened as they harmonized on some barbershop songs. The murmur of their voices sounded pleasant in the warm night. About seventy yards out on the reef, two spearfishermen waded noiselessly through the waist-deep water. They carried torches and a small wooden box with a glass bottom, and now and then they bobbed under with the box, probing the coral for morays or squid.

She liked to watch the spearfishers. When she was a little girl her grandfather showed her how to clear the surface of the water with a spread of kukui nut oil and catch the squid with bright cowrie shells tied to a piece of string. In those days the fishermen would dive down into the caves of coral cliffs after the giant octopuses. They would wrestle the monsters and bite them to death by sinking their teeth into the soft bone between the eyes. She watched as one of the fishermen aimed his spear gun and she heard the thick twang of the rubber before the spear cut through the water. He dove after the spear, surfaced, and unhinged the squid from the barb. He pinned the squid to the wire length that held his other trophies and moved on again, his eyes scanning the shallows of the reef for more.

Lei stretched out on the punee in the corner of the lanai and brushed her hair. The brushing, the sloughing of the surf, the music, combined to relax her. She was, as a general rule, an easy, relaxed, happy person. Nothing troubled her. She had the Hawaiian attitude that life was too short to worry. Live for today and let tomorrow take care of itself. And if tomorrow could be even half as good as today . . . She wondered idly why Aaron could not be that way. He was always so tense, so wrought-up over things. Her pregnancy, for example. She had been so happy and proud when she found that a human life grew within her.

Marriage would make everything perfect. But that is not the main thing. Happiness is the main thing. And happiness through love is the best. Now, motherhood through love will mean greater happiness.

She had been in love many times. She had been quite a worry to her father, Danny Villanueva, one of the harbor pilots at Aloha Tower. A widower for ten years, he had had quite a time of it keeping all the boys away from her. A lot of silliness, she thought.

Love is good and love makes happiness. Marriage is another thing altogether.

In a way, she would like to be married to Aaron Howland. She was certain that she loved him. And part of that love was her realization of his need of her. He was troubled and unhappy, and at night he would twist and turn nervously in his sleep, his teeth grinding against each other until she slipped her hand across his chest and kissed him, half waking him, and whispered to him that she was there and she loved him and everything would be all right.

But those things that made him so dear to her were the very reasons why she was not sure that she would be happy married to him. He was fundamentally a troubled person, and some mechanism in the back of her mind rang a warning gong against troubled people. When she was with them, she became a little troubled herself. She was sensitive to other people's emotions. With happy people, she was happy. When she was with sad people, she tried to make them happy, but usually it wound up with them making her sad. She gave to people unfailingly, with whole heart. She longed to give Aaron all her happiness, but she was wary of having to shoulder his troubles because they were never defined, and consequently impossible for her to cope with. Anyway, she thought, he is already married so it's out of the question. She did not believe in divorce. Just live and enjoy everything while you can. Dream, don't analyze. She would have to tell that to Aaron when he arrived. Aaron always analyzed, never dreamed. Maybe that was his trouble. He was so busy regretting yesterday and worrying about tomorrow that he had no ability to enjoy today. She had known a yachtsman similar to that. He was so frustrated lusting for the next woman that he was incapable of understanding or enjoying the woman he was with. She had left him within a week.

Haoles, she thought, with a trace of contempt, didn't show anything. They didn't know anything. Did they really know sorrow? Or love? Or the hot crazy throwing away of everything when a man and a woman were together? They don't know how to cry even, and their laughter is thin and tinny unless they're drunk. And the haole women were even worse than the men. They didn't think, say or do anything except what they thought they were supposed to think, say or do. Women like Aaron's wife; brittle, nervous, insecure women with laughter like the cracking of glass.

Their love-making, she'd bet, was some ridiculous composite of the movies they had seen, the bad books they had read.

"You and Laura," she had asked him one evening. "Do you have a good marriage?"

"Yes, we have an all-right marriage."

"All-right marriage?"

"It's average, I guess," he lied. "Why?"

"I was curious. If you and she have a good marriage, then where do you and I fit in?"

He felt a sudden alarm. "Do we have to fit in somewhere?"

After a moment she had said, "No, I guess not. It was just something I was wondering about."

"Why do people feel they have to fit somewhere?"

"I don't know. It was silly of me to bring it up."

No, she was not at all sure she'd marry a haole. Her kid brother Bobby had married one of those coast haole girls who hang around the beachboys. It hadn't worked out. What was it that Bobby had told her yesterday? Oh yes, she remembered. Paul Kahana was planning to marry one. Lei hoped he wouldn't. Paul was too swell a guy to get mixed up with one of those haole girls.

She felt a little sorry for the haole race as a whole, and a little sorry for Aaron as an individual. He was always so worried. Like now, that she was pregnant with his child. He had been stunned when she told him. Instead of making him happy it filled him with anxiety. He had raved and carried on, saying how impossible it was. How was it so impossible after all the nights? After all the drowsy, lusty afternoons? He had complained bitterly that it was just his lousy luck. How could her pregnancy be lousy luck? It was the most wonderful piece of luck in the world. Then all Aaron's ranting and raving about an abortion was the silliest thing she had ever heard. Maybe now, after what almost happened to him at the volcano, he'll have changed.

She smiled at the thought of his changing. Maybe he'll be happier, easier, at home inside his skin, and forget all that ridiculous talk about an abortion. She wouldn't have one anyway. Maybe he'll want the baby now.

Thinking that way about Aaron, she hungered to be in his arms again. The ring of the doorbell was like an explosion of joy in her heart.

Sloan toyed nervously with the stirrer in her Collins glass. "Well, it looks as if we're batting just about a hundred per cent. Everybody's against us. Including Daddy."

"Was that what that long talk was about?"

Sloan nodded. "Trouble. It's going to be a tough game, coach."

"How tough?"

"I'm not sure yet. It's hard to tell."

"What did he say?"

"Well, he's against our getting married."

A wave of caution swept over Paul. "It doesn't sound like there's anything unsure or hard to tell about that."

From their green leather booth in the corner of the Monarch Bar at the Royal Hawaiian Hotel they could see past the glass partitioning to the crowded dance floor outside. Beyond the dance floor was the curve of Waikiki Beach. At the end of the beach, Diamond Head rose in silhouette against the wide white moon.

"I think Daddy might get used to the idea. He might accept it in time."

"I thought you were goin' to wait until we could talk to him together."

"I intended to. But it just came up this way. It started at dinner." She told him about the row with Aaron, then detailed her conversation with her father.

"I'm not worried about Aaron," Paul said.

"Neither am I. He's against everything and everybody. But Daddy's feelings upset me."

He held her glance for a quarter beat, then looked away. "What do we do now?"

"We wait," Sloan said. "And hope Daddy changes his mind."

"And if he doesn't?"

"Then I guess we'll just have to get married without his blessings." She tried to make a joke of it but it didn't come off.

"I wonder if you're as brave as you sound."

"Try me." She grinned.

"No, I'm serious, Sloan. It's a little tougher here than it was in California, isn't it?"

She nodded thoughtfully. "Yes. But it's not too tough. And it never will be. You'll see."

They both stared down at their interlocked hands. After a while,

Sloan said, "There's nothing really to talk about. Our skin's not the same color. So what? We've lived with it all our lives. I don't see the difference any more."

"That's good to say. But does it really work out that way?"

"Why shouldn't it? People get married with different backgrounds, different religions, different desires, even with different hearts and souls. Compared to those, color of skin isn't important."

"You sound awfully smart tonight." Paul managed a weak grin. "Very akamai."

"Neither of us is blind, Paul. We can see the difference if we want to. But we've gone above that."

"Not according to my mother."

Sloan looked at him curiously. "Your mother—?"

"She says we're both blind."

"I don't understand."

Paul took her hand in his and gestured with it.

"Maw and me had a long talk, just before I came over to pick you up. Maw was nearly in tears. She took my hand in hers, just like I've got yours now. And she raised it right in front of my eyes. 'This is why you can't marry Miss Sloan!' she said. 'Now look close. If you can't see the difference—the reason—then you ain't lookin', Son. You're refusin' to see. You and Miss Sloan ain't the same color, Paul,' she said. 'That's why you can't marry her. Now or never.' "

He released Sloan's hand and they sat quietly brooding. The story caught Sloan off balance. She admitted, with not a little surprise, that as far as the marriage was concerned, she had never given any thought to the Kahana family. She never dreamed that opposition might come from Kapiolani Kahana. The thought just never occurred to her that the Kahanas would be anything but pleased.

"What does Dean think?"

Paul sipped his drink. "You know Dean. Quiet, keeps his opinions to himself."

"Didn't he say anything?"

"Nothing I could really pin down. Somehow I got the feelin' that he felt kind of betrayed. That he nevah figured on someone like you marryin' someone like me."

"It's strange," Sloan said, "but I never expected Kapiolani to object to our wedding. She's been just like a mother to me."

"Maybe that's part of it."

"But I thought she'd be overjoyed. I never thought she'd have —well, racial feelings. When she nursed me she couldn't have had any feelings like that. She couldn't have thought one skin better than another, or haole's blood better than Hawaiian blood."

"You've got it backwards."

"What do you mean?"

"Maw doesn't feel inferior at all. Quite the contrary. She's a proud old Hawaiian, you know."

"I still don't get . . ."

"What I mean is, she thinks I shouldn't marry you because a Hawaiian would be steppin' down by marryin' a haole. Just like your old man feels, only in reverse. I guess all races feel that way."

For a moment, Sloan was stunned. And strangely angry. She turned the matter over in her head several times, until it came sharply, impersonally in focus, and her practical mind started working on it.

"Judas Priest, this is almost slapstick!" She turned to Paul and started laughing. "If only parents could forget their prejudices, maybe their children would have a better chance of getting along in the world. I say damn the parents and full speed ahead—to the altar."

But her gaiety failed to reach Paul. He remained broodingly serious. "It's not that easy."

"I was only joking, Paul."

"Maw talked about children, and all that."

"So did my father. I'm not worried about our children. Are you?"

"I guess not."

"Then what is worrying you?"

"You. I'm worryin' if I'm bein' fair to you. I didn't think of it that way before. Not until Maw brought it up. But now I'm wonderin' if the changes you'd have to make would be fair."

"Everyone makes changes when they get married."

"These are bigger ones, added ones." He looked at her levelly. "Does the fact that I'm worried about them indicate that there's something wrong?"

"Darling, nothing's wrong. Not with us."

"You've grown up with the world at your feet, Sloan. You've grown up with the certain knowledge that if you wanted something badly enough, it would be given to you. Me—if I wanted anything, I'd have to go out and get it. Go out and fight for it."

"I'd rather be with you, fighting for them, than have them given to me. Damn—now I'm mad! I'm not a dewy-eyed teen-ager with a crush. I'm a woman in love with you!" She took his hands in hers and leaned close to him. "Paul, there's only one thing we've got to do. We've got to love each other more than any two people ever loved before. We've got to accept as an irrevocable fact the difference that color has made between us. We've got to accept that fact, then forget about it."

Something seemed to move behind Paul's eyes. Sloan's gutty spirit, her total love, never ceased to amaze him. "Do you think it might be easier some place else? California, for instance?"

"No." Sloan shook her head. "As far as racial tolerance and equality, there's probably more of it in Hawaii than any place in the world."

"It's harder with our families here."

"I know. But basically we're not fighting our families. We're fighting prejudice. Moving to California would be like running away and prejudice is the same all over. You can't run away from it. You must live with it until someday it destroys itself."

"You suah talk like you know a lot about it," he said lightly.

"I'm learning. The more we find out about it the better we'll be able to fight it."

"Right now, how do we fight it?"

"By being together. Our love will defeat all our troubles." She looked up at him gravely. "Do I sound awfully awfully young and naïve? Do I sound like a child?"

Despite himself, Paul shook away his gloomy mood. He grinned at her. "You're sayin' just what I want to hear, so I guess you're soundin' like a very wise person. You amaze me. You're such a hell of a girl."

"You bet I am!" she laughed. "A hell of a girl to handle!"

"A delightful girl to handle."

"Now after all that deep discussion," she said, joining his happier mood, "can a girl get a drink?"

He signaled the waiter and ordered another round.

"Do you still love me after all that?" she teased. "Do you still want to marry me? Or am I too much trouble?"

"Shut up." He leaned over and kissed her.

"Always necking. What does it take to get you to ask a girl to dance?"

They danced very close. Paul felt that he was the luckiest man on earth. Folded in his arms was the rich beautiful haole girl, Sloan Howland, with her body warm against his, graceful and supple as a young tree; and a face of everything he had ever dreamed—the awakening child, the reckless girl, the compassionate woman. And she loved him. My child, my girl, my woman now, he thought. And she had never belonged to anyone else.

"I wonder where Pete and Ramsey have disappeared to?"

"I haven't seen them for a long time."

"They probably went for a stroll down the beach. They seem to have hit it off real good, don't you think?"

Paul nodded. "Pete's crazy about her. She was shy at first, but she loosened up a lot."

"I'm glad they're getting along so well together."

Ramsey swung as hard as she could and the flat of her palm smacked against Peter Noa's cheek.

"Now wait a minute—"

"You wait a minute! Who do you think you are?"

"I was just tryin' to—"

"I know damn well what you were trying!" Ramsey said, furious at him. "Now just get me back to the dance floor."

"That'll spoil everything."

"You've just spoiled the evening."

"I was just tryin' to make it interestin'."

"You mean you were dreaming. Now let's get back."

"I'm sorry. No hu-hu."

"And what does *that* mean?"

"No hu-hu . . . Don't get mad."

"I'm plenty mad. Plenty hu-hu."

"Auwe!" Peter exclaimed. "All I did was kiss you. You make it sound like I tried to rape you or something!"

"You were on your way."

"Auwe! I kiss her so I'm on my way!"

"Isn't that the standard operating procedure between the beachboys and the girl tourists—malihinis? Always trying to—to get somewhere?"

"I kissed you because I like you. I wasn't tryin' to get anywhere."

"You weren't, huh?"

Peter shrugged. "Well—okay. Maybe a little bit. Us beachboys, we're kind of—kind of overfriendly."

"I'll bet."

He waited until she calmed down, then he said, "Did it hurt your face much? When I kissed you?"

Her eyes flared angrily for a moment, then they crinkled at the corners and she could not help laughing. "You're impossible," she said. "No, I guess I couldn't say your kiss hurt. How about my right cross?"

"Like Bobo Olson's," he said, rubbing his cheek. "Tell me something else. You didn't mean it when you said the evening's spoiled?"

"I guess not. I guess really I've been having a wonderful time."

She had been hesitant, shy, obviously ill at ease during the early part of the evening. When they entered the porticoes of the Royal Hawaiian, she had felt so conspicuously uncomfortable that she wanted to shrink from sight. They had had a few drinks and tried to make a party out of it with bright but completely artificial smiles and an inundation of puerile chatter. Their dancing was graceful and correct. Without hurting his feelings, she had tried to stay as far away from him as possible. Her eyes kept weaving and darting about the crowded dance floor, afraid she might recognize someone she knew.

A Charleston number broke the ice. Peter was a good dancer. They danced so well together now that the crowd formed a ring around them and applauded heartily when they finished. It seemed to break some kind of a barrier in Ramsey. There she was, dancing, laughing and having a wonderful time with an Hawaiian boy, and nobody considered it out of place; everyone accepted it as the most natural thing in the world.

They strolled along the beach and talked about all the things they liked to do, the wonders they wanted out of life. Soon she began to see a generous charm in Peter Noa. She liked his wide, engagingly ugly face with its crooked, disarming grin. They began to make plans for surfing picnics and moonlight catamaran rides and skindiving at a special beach he knew over past Aina Haina.

They sat down against a coconut tree and she leaned back against him, her eyes closed tranquilly to the moonlight and the sea and the warm, tropical night.

"Have you always lived here, Peter?"
"Wouldn't live anywhere else."
"Have you ever been any place else?"
"Suah. Korea, Tokyo. I been up to California, too," he said. "It's pretty good up there. But travelin' around all the time is for *lolos,* fools. If you are happy where you are, why move?"
"You talk as if you've always been happy."
"Suah. That's the only way to be. Why not?"
"Well, I never knew you could just be happy if you wanted to."
"Maybe. Me, I think a man's as happy as he wants to be."
"Sometimes I get very sad," Ramsey said. "I don't know why. I just do."
"How about now?"
She looked up at him and laughed softly, deep in her throat. "Now I'm very happy."
So he had leaned over and kissed her and she had not minded the kiss as much as the feeling of black on white and she had stiffened with indignation and slapped him. Now that he had kidded her out of it, she realized her indignation was shallow.
They walked back to the hotel and sat on the low stone wall and watched the dancers.
"They make a great couple, don't they?" Peter nodded toward Sloan and Paul.
Ramsey nodded. "What's in store for them?"
"Only good things," Peter said. "Sloan's a terrific wahine, Paul's a numbarh one guy."
"But what about—" She hesitated, a little embarrassed.
"What about the color difference?" Peter asked easily. "That's no sweat out here. Maybe on the Mainland it would cause trouble, but not here."
Ramsey remembered one night aboard ship when she and Sloan had been discussing all the things they would do in Hawaii and Sloan had told her about Peter Noa. "Is this Peter Noa *very* dark?" she had asked. She remembered the way Sloan had stiffened. After a moment, Sloan had shaken her head and there had been a definite contempt in her voice. "No," she had said. "Not very."
It was, after all, a ridiculous question, Ramsey realized. *Very* dark. As if it were a matter of shade, not race.
She glanced at Sloan, dancing gracefully in Paul's arms, and

was struck once again with the full, vibrant beauty of her friend. Sloan had had every guy at Stanford after her. Just the way every man aboard ship kept staring at her speculatively, and the men here on the dance floor were having a hard time keeping their eyes away from her. And Sloan just didn't give a damn. Cool and aloof and regal. As if there were a brand on her marked Paul Kahana and she flaunted that brand in every man's face. Well, Ramsey thought, still frowning, there's an awful lot to Paul Kahana. He's one of the best fellows I've ever known. But face it, he's black.

Maybe, as Peter says, that sort of thing can work out in Hawaii, where Caucasians—haoles—are outnumbered six-to-one. Maybe a girl like Sloan can brazen it out and get away with it. She's never let anything interfere with what she's believed right. No taboos, no social pressure, nothing. She's in love with him and she's got the guts it takes for that kind of love. I guess that's one reason I idolize her so much, Ramsey thought. But I wonder how Mom and Daddy would take it if I ever decided to snuggle down in Hawaii with a nice big native. With Peter Noa, for instance. That would make a nice little conversation tidbit for the social set around Burlingame and San Francisco. Something to top the Top of the Mark. *You haven't heard about Ramsey James? Why darling, you won't believe it, but the girl's gone native. She's found herself some aborigine and they've settled down in a grass shack off Waikiki, raising a passel of brown-fannied savages.*

"Peter," she said, "do you think that kind of love is right?"

"Love is always right."

"I mean, do you think it's good for them? And their children?"

"Yes. You see, out here we got da kine polyglot. A mixture. You gotta remembah one thing. The Hawaiians are *the* people around here. This used to be our kingdom. We've had interracial marriages out here for more than a century. About two-thirds of the marriages in Hawaii are interracial. Islanders accept it."

"Do you think Sloan's family will accept it?"

"Yeah, byanby. The Howlands are pretty high up there with the foundin' fathers. The social haole set. And Paul's family is—well, da kine, the other end of the ladder. There haven't been many marriages of that type. If Paul was a descendant of the old alii—the Hawaiian nobility—then it would be easy. This way, they're kind of breakin' new ground."

"For a girl like Sloan, with her family background and upbringing, to stand up and defy traditions takes an awful lot of courage."

Peter looked curiously at her. "Love takes courage."

The offhanded yet misty way he said it surprised her. She turned and looked into his eyes. What a funny face, she thought. What a homely but kind face. "I guess I've been kind of—of distant," she said softly. "I'm sorry."

Peter smiled shyly. When he had seen her standing in the driveway of the Howland house earlier that night, the moonlight bright on her hair, he had felt a quick and warm stir of pleasure. She was a cute little wahine, all right, with that sweet face and that look of hers, wide-eyed and serious like a little kid, and yet with a hint of the adult woman. Her hair was a crisp dark sheaf, and the beige taffeta dress was a showpiece for her figure, deftly accenting the curve of her hips and the sharp rise of her breasts. Here was a rare young girl whose beauty was at once lusty and pixie, a lovely little piece with sensitivity and intelligence, and a sense of humor that would make her laughter seem like bells. He figured that he might just as well admit it, watching her smooth delicate profile as she sat next to him on the wall, that she was just too close to the image he had been carrying around in his heart of a girl he had never met, of a girl made up of bits and pieces and attitudes of girls he had met, combined with the one he had always hoped of meeting. Buster, he thought, you're hooked.

She leaned close to him. He placed his hands on either side of her face, his thumbs near the corners of her eyes, his fingers curled in her crisp brown hair. He looked down at her quiet face, but her eyes were unreadable. Then her eyes closed and he kissed her on the mouth. She did not break away this time, but neither was she responsive. It was as if she was trying to prove something to herself.

Tani Akana had always felt a deep warmth for Willard. She considered this affection peculiar. She felt somehow that she should resent him. But it was not in her to do so. Although she was, as always, glad to see him, she wished he had not come to call this late. His visit, she knew, would upset Ward. Long after the Senator had left, Ward would still be awake, brooding, searching for all the answers the old man had never given him.

She unplugged the coffeemaker and wrapped the soft gray kimono tight about her body, knotting the enormous maroon sash loosely at her hip, and, carrying the coffee and cups on a tray, walked pin-toed on her white cork zoris out to the living room. One thing's for certain, she thought, I don't want to take any part in this conversation tonight. I don't even want to hear it.

"Fresh coffee." Ward grinned at her. *"Ichi ban."*

Old Willard smiled at her. "I hope you'll forgive this late call."

"Nonsense, it's not late at all, Senator. I wish I had known you were coming over. I would have kept the boys up. They would have loved to see you again."

"We'll have to have them over to Manoalani soon. This Christmas. Would they like that?"

"They'd love it." She set the tray on the table between the straightbacked chair Willard was occupying and the tatami mat propped with pillows that Ward was sitting on. Ward had a dark blue kimono wrapped about him. He was barefoot, save for white tabi socks, and he sat cross-legged at the table.

"I'll leave you gentlemen-of-the-world to your business," Tani said, after she had poured the coffee. Willard's eyes followed her as she left the room. There was an utter charm about her that he had always found appealing. Probably the combination, he thought—the serene wisdom of Japan mixing with the flowing gaiety of Hawaii. She seemed completely comfortable within herself, a compassionate and stable woman who had succeeded in finding her man and being happy and contented with him.

When she had closed the sliding sojhi screens behind her, Ward said, "I more or less expected you to come up. When I read that you got the nomination, I figured you'd be around."

"I had to come to see you," Willard said. "I had to talk with you alone. I want to know definitely where you stand, Ward."

"You know where I stand."

"I know where you claim to stand."

"You haven't accepted that?"

"No. I can't believe you'll go against me, Ward. I can't believe you'll go against the Islands."

"Just a moment, Senator. There's something you've got to learn. Going against you is not the same as going against the Islands. Quite the opposite."

"Going against statehood is going against the Islands."

Ward stood up and paced quietly across the room. It was an intimate room, decorated in simple Japanese style. He glanced out the picture window. Below the sweep of Wilhelmina Rise, the lights of the city glittered like spilled jewels beneath the moon.

"Let's look at this statehood thing accurately," Ward said. "I remember a time when you were strongly opposed to statehood."

"Not me," Willard muttered. "Maybe some of my—"

"Okay, not you. But the people you represent."

"They've learned. They've progressed with the times."

"They haven't progressed, they've just changed," Ward said, coolly unimpressed. "Today, the big cry is for statehood, with both an emotional and economic basis. But let's look at it without emotion. Let's go back a few years to when the sugar and pineapple people and the Big Five agencies, the people you represent, were opposed to statehood. Hawaii is doing damn well as she is, why change? That was their feelings. Two things made your boys change their minds, and neither of them had anything to do with patriotic emotions.

"One," Ward said. "In 1933 Congress almost pushed through Rankin's bill which would take away the three-year residency requirement for Hawaii's Governor. If the bill had passed, Hawaii's governorship would have been reduced to a plum of political patronage, Presidential spoils available to anyone who had made a sizable campaign contribution. Hawaii got up in arms against this bill, and for the first time, the powers here realized just how subject we were to the will and whims of Congress.

"The next year, when the Jones-Costigan amendment was tacked on to the Agricultural Adjustment Act, then the Big Five really went to work for statehood. Why? Not because of patriotism. Because of sugar quotas. Because the act stipulated that Hawaii, like Cuba, Puerto Rico and the Philippines, was to be designated as a 'foreign country,' and the big sugar quotas must go to the Mainland plantations. If that act had passed, Hawaii would have just about lost its livelihood. So the Big Five decided that as a full state we could circumvent that kind of legislation. So the big drive started. It was a pocketbook matter, not an emotional one."

"So what?" Willard said. "It was a true enough cause."

"Yes, but not an emotional one."

"You're the only one talking about emotional causes. No great cause in history—not even the slavery issue of the Civil War—was pure emotion. There's economics behind every cause. But it doesn't make that cause a bad one. Or any the less just."

"True," Ward said. "But we should not look at statehood now as an emotional cause. And that's what you're asking for.

"What happened when the Big Five decided to back statehood? They hired a public relations firm. Public relations," he said with contempt, "the big panacea of modern America. The most cynical and potentially dangerous business in the world: telling people what to think and what to believe. Its power is frightening. And the Big Five decided that that was what Hawaii needed to sell itself to Congress. So the Hawaii Visitors Bureau was formed, to sell Hawaii to the Mainland and sell statehood to Washington. And what was the big result of their first campaign? When they brought writers from *Fortune* magazine out here to conduct a poll on statehood? The magazine listed Hawaii as a foreign country. The writers polled the Mainland and discovered that seventy-four per cent of the people favored protecting Canada more than Hawaii. Twenty-eight per cent favored abandoning Hawaii if it was attacked!"

"The next year changed all that," Willard muttered.

"The next year a war came along and all things change in war. Here's my point." Ward leaned close to his father. "Hawaii's statehood has been, and will continue to be, the victim of a political theory that has not yet matured, as no political theory or political system can ever really mature. I'm for the betterment of my people, Hawaii's people. Not the few, but the many. And I don't give a damn what name that betterment goes under . . . territory, state or commonwealth.

"After all the years of petitions and promises, I honestly believe it's time we put our cards on the table and call Washington's bluff. If we're going to be treated as second-class citizens, then let's stop footing the bill for it. At least with commonwealth, we'd have the pride of self-government. At least we could insist upon commonwealth as an interim form of government until the big shots on Capitol Hill got off their duffs and decided upon statehood. That way, we'd have something. We wouldn't be patsies, we wouldn't be pawns to a handful of lying Congressmen's chess game.

"I don't know how you feel, Senator, but I'm tired of being

kicked around with a lot of phony promises. Especially when I'm paying the bills. We petition for commonwealth, raise a stink about it, and we'll get some action. As a matter of fact, if we set up a howl for commonwealth, they'd probably give us statehood pretty damned quick."

Old Willard scowled. "You can't expect to blackmail the nation into granting us statehood."

"It's not blackmail at all. It's a straightforward presentation of the facts. On an either/or basis. Either give us statehood or set us free. Washington should not be permitted to deny us our equality. America is supposed to be a land with liberty, justice and equality for all. Yet in maintaining Hawaii as a territory, it denies Hawaii her liberty, denies her equality and denies her justice."

"Yes," Willard said, "I agree. On that point you're correct. But you're wrong on commonwealth. It's a boneless substitute. It would be a heartache and it would mean that Hawaii's people had settled for second place; that we'd be content to be second-class citizens. People want what they want, they don't want a substitute. You can't get what you really want by going after something you don't want. Commonwealth would be prostituting a fine moral cause. A cause I've been working for all my life. More than a half century. That's a long time in labor, Ward. A long time sweating out this baby. It's been my life."

"It was Joe Stinson's life too," Ward said dispassionately. "And you buried him today." Ward poured fresh coffee for the two of them. "Naw—it all sounds grandly patriotic, 'Hawaii, the Fiftieth State!' But you can remember when the battle cry was 'Hawaii, the Thirty-second State.' There's nothing as hopeless as a dead cause. And that moral justice folderol just doesn't hold water."

He stared at Willard, sensing again, as he had so often, the old man's peculiar discomfort with him. He wondered if that discomfort was caused by any resentment within himself. He did not believe that he harbored any resentment toward his father. Nor, he admitted, had he felt any love. There was a yearning within him, a nostalgia for those moments he remembered out of the lost gentle time when he and the old man and maybe Dean Kahana would rein the horses along the wooded green shoreline of Manoalani and watch silently as the ocean blacked out with rain squalls or glittered with dawn, the surf piling in against the shore like cream. *You boys want to run the horses through the surf you be sure to keep their heads up. Don't swim them out too far. Ward, you stick close to little Dean. Keep a good eye on him, Son.*

Afterwards they would ride home late and tired, the horses lathered, crossing beaten range trails and finally trotting up the macadam, little red wings from the poincianas crunching under the horses' hoofs like soft broken pieces of flame, and in the distance ahead of them, sundown tinting the old weathered face of Manoalani with a deep peace like gold wine. He had ridden, in that lost time, with wild and beautiful boyhood dreams, as mysterious as the echo of the rainbow, with Willard Howland riding alongside like God ranging heaven, until that terrible night when he knew he would dream no more. . . .

It was the Christmas Eve of his twelfth birthday. That Thanksgiving, his mother and the man she had married had been killed in an automobile crash over the Pali road. He was at Manoalani, on Christmas vacation from Kamehameha School.

Silver bells and a streamer of red crepe paper proclaiming Mele Kelikimaka. Carol-singing by the tree. A bright mountain of presents wrapped in ribbons more beautiful than a rainbow.

You can open one present tonight, the rest in the morning, Garth Howland said. Go ahead, Ward. Pick out one of yours and open it up.

The red one! The red one with the wide green ribbon.

Garth selected it from the heap and handed it to him.

The children gathered around him. Only the children were in the playroom—Garth, Steven, Dean, Paul, Sloan—the parents were in the living room. Aaron, home from his freshman year at Yale, had been with the older folk, but now he leaned against the playroom door, a Scotch and water in his hand. He was drunk.

Go ahead, Ward, Garth said. Open it up!

He yanked the ribbon and scraped away the paper.

Pin the tail! he said, showing them all the present. Pin the tail on the donkey!

Garth took the papier-mâché cutout of the donkey and placed it against the wall. We've got time for one game, he said. He tied the blindfold about Ward's head, spun him around three times and placed the nailed tail in his hand. Go pin it on the donkey, he said.

Ward wove cautiously about the room, searching. He stumbled into Paul, who pushed him away. Sloan shrieked with glee when Ward pushed up against her. Then Ward bumped into Aaron.

Get the hell away from me, Aaron said. I'm no donkey.

Play with us, Aaron! Ward happily handed Aaron the tail. Daddy Will gimme this for Sannaclaus. You wanna play, huh?

Aaron sneered. Don't call my father Daddy Will.

He arranged the blindfold across his head so that he could see out of one eye. I've got a better game, Aaron said, finishing his drink and setting it on the mantelpiece. I've got a much better game!

He started after Ward, jabbing the nailed tail through the air. My game is called Pin-the-tail-on-the-bastard!

The children became very quiet. The fun had gone out of the evening.

Ward backed away. His eyes were black saucers staring uncomprehendingly at Aaron. Bastard, Ward thought, feeling funny at the word. Bastard . . .

C'mon, Ward!

No. I no wanna play.

You got to play, Ward. You're the only real live little bastard around.

No. No, I no wanna.

But you're going to. I'm going to make you.

Cut it out Aaron, Garth said.

Aaron reached out and grabbed Ward. He knocked him down to the floor, straddled him and jabbed the nail into his behind. You're a little bastard and now I've got you pinned, Aaron said.

Ward twisted, his eyes filled with tears of rage. I'm not! he screamed. I'm not a bastah!

What is a bastard? Aaron teased.

Ward squirmed away from him. You! he shouted, pointing at Aaron. You're a bastah!

Aaron lunged for him again but Ward punched him as hard as he could, his tiny fist catching Aaron's jaw. Aaron angrily pushed him down and cuffed him several times.

Leave him alone!

It was a high, thin, boyish voice, but the tone was hard. Aaron turned and glared at Dean Kahana.

Don't tell me what to do in my house!

Then I'll tell you, Garth said. He walked straight over to Aaron and looked up into his older brother's eyes. Leave the kid alone.

Aaron towered over all the other children. He looked down at Garth, then at the rest. Am I right or wrong? he demanded. Isn't he a bastard?

Ward was crying now, off in a corner of the room.

I'm not a bastah. I'm not.

Garth and Dean crowded around Aaron. Very slowly Garth said, Get out of here, Aaron.

Aaron looked around the room contemptuously. Sloan began to bawl. Paul picked up something and threw it at Aaron, but missed. Aaron dropped the tail and started out of the playroom. At the doorway, he turned to face Ward.

You don't like my little game, eh, Ward? Well, you'd better learn to like it. Because you're going to have to live with it all your life.

And, Ward thought, he had learned to live with it. After that shocking, wrenching first knowledge, he had learned, in time, to accept it. The wisdom of life is not merely to endure, but to prevail.

In our ways, both he and I have prevailed, Ward thought, studying his father. Although he had never felt an active resentment towards his father, he wondered at times whether his entire life had not been cast to oppose the old man.

Willard had sent him to Kamehameha School, the University of Hawaii, then to law school at the University of Southern California. Did it really surprise the Senator when Ward declined to join Case, Conklin and MacDaniels, the Island's leading law firm and the one to which Willard had secured him a junior partnership, and took his law diploma over to the Union and became a negotiating attorney instead? Two years with the Union headquarters in San Francisco had taught him just how much power the Union could swing in the Territory. And the Union learned just how much power Ward Akana could swing with his own people. He returned to the Islands where he could rise with the Union to break the grip of the Big Five, break the grip of Willard Howland's class, break now the Republican Party's stranglehold on Hawaii. Ward wondered now why he had been chosen to break his father. Had every step he had taken through life led to this end? Deep within him, was there the seed of resentment and bitterness, or something very close to it, just as there was the seed of something close to love?

"About the elections, Ward," he heard the Senator say, "just what kind of a chance do you think I have?"

"Any year but this year, you'd have an excellent chance," Ward said. "You'd be a sure thing. All you'd need would be the Republican nomination. But now, after a half century, the common people are beginning to flex their muscles. They've found their political voice. They've found their true strength, and they're not going to release it until they've been given a fair share of the opportunities in these islands. You're part of the old guard, Senator. Part of the theory of protective benevolence in government: give the workers just enough so they can work another day, then just enough for one more day and so on. Your time is finished, your world is dying. You're sitting on the wrong side of the political fence. For the first time in history, Hawaii will have a democratic rule."

"And that kind of rule," Willard said tautly, "means strikes in which everyone loses. Strikes which lead Mainlanders and Washington to believe, wrongly, that Hawaii is Union controlled, and that the Union can cut off our lifeline as it wishes. Strikes that give Hawaii's statehood chances a punch below the belt."

Ward grinned slowly, and Howland noticed with a start how identical was his son's smile to his own. "Those strikes gave the workers more money to buy more food," Ward said. "I don't care what Washington or the Mainlanders think as long as the people here are better off."

"Could more sincere negotiations between yourself and management stave off this coming strike?"

"More sincere negotiations between labor and management could stave off any strike."

"And do you agree that such a strike now would be a black eye to our statehood chances?"

"That doesn't interest me. I don't intend to sacrifice the welfare of the working people because of a statehood chance that we've been missing since the last century. And I'm not worried about what Washington might think of a strike out here. It's not, after all, a case of statehood right or wrong."

"I want to ask a favor of you, Ward."

"Go ahead."

"I want you to try as hard as you can to negotiate this trouble without calling a strike."

"You'd like us to keep the negotiations rolling until after the elections?"

"No. You know that that's not it."

"And you know that I can't hold off a strike. I haven't got the power, and I'm not sure that I'd use it if I had."

"If the strike is held off, it will give me a chance to go to Washington and convince Congress that Hawaii is ready for statehood."

"Hawaii's been ready for statehood for years and Washington knows it."

"Will you try to negotiate as hard as you can?"

Ward regarded the older man coolly. "I always try that, Senator."

Howland accepted the sarcasm, nodding to himself several times. Somehow it always goes wrong, he thought. Somehow, there's always that gulf between us that's impossible to cross.

He stood up and walked heavily to the door. Ward opened it for him. They walked outside and for a while they looked up at the clouds furling silver-white against the violet sky.

Howland grinned a little self-consciously. "You don't give me any chance at all of winning a single labor vote, do you?"

"I might be wrong, sir."

"You don't think I have a chance in the world of winning your Union's support?"

"No, Senator. Not a chance in the world."

"Do you, or don't you, control that vote?"

"The only vote I control is my own."

"This might be a terrible thing to ask," Howland said, looking off into the sky. "But from a grown son to his ancient father, would you be proud of me, if I won, and brought Hawaii statehood?"

"I'd be very proud of you, sir," Ward said simply.

Ward's answer seemed to pick the old man up a bit. His voice came out weak and dry, like a voice that had not been used lately, but he managed to ask: "Could I win *your* vote, Son?"

It took a hell of a lot out of him, Ward thought. That cost the old man a great deal.

Long ago, he remembered, there had been a moment like this. A moment of utter candor; a moment when old Willard's eyes burned with the flint of some forgotten sun as he looked at Ward the night before Ward was to leave for the South Pacific with the First Marine Division. And that night Ward waited, hoping to hear the whole true story from his father's lips. Is he afraid to tell me? Is he afraid to admit it out loud to himself? And as he waited, Ward knew that the old man had to tell the story. That the old man's heart was weighted down with the need to tell it truly. But the moment passed with awkward, troubled falterings. The story remained locked in old Willard's heart. And as he left the house for the troopship that night, Ward Akana was not sure whether to thank the old man or to curse him. Someday, Ward knew, the old man would have to tell.

"Can I, Son?" He heard Willard's soft but hopeless question. "Can I win your vote? Can I earn it?"

Ward fought back an impulse to place his hand on his father's shoulder. In the leafy shadows Ward contemplated the fierce, unyielding eyes, the tortured solidity of his father's head.

Abruptly, Willard turned and tramped down the steps.

"Never mind, Ward."

Ward watched him go. "I'm sorry," he said.

Chapter Seven

WILLARD stalked along the shores of Makapuu Point, staring out at the wide flat face of the sea, which shone sad now like whores' eyes at morning.

How can I reach across the years and explain it to you, Ward? How can a father face his grown son?

To the hum and lull of the surf, Willard dreamed back across the years to the moony bohemia that was Old Hawaii: to the time when pagan drums throbbed through the tropic nights like oil dropping on a leaf, and he heard his mother's voice, the soft velvety side of the leaf:

"Don't you be listening to those drums, Son. Drums of sin. Pagans, all of them." She turned her sweet-stern face toward Kailua town. "Sailors and their heathen women, drinking and soiling themselves straight out from the grace of the Lord. Sinning themselves to eternal damnation. Your father saddled-up and rode into town a while ago. He'll run them out, you'll see." There was a sweet sureness to her touch as she led him to the stairs. But her face seemed to tighten. "John Howland will run them out of Kailua town, mark my words, just as the Good Shepherd chased evil from His flock. Now off to bed, Willard. A kiss first, that's a good boy. And pray to Jesus."

The edge of the summer moon poured in through his bedroom window. The four-poster creaked as he twisted beneath the netting. He listened to the pagan drum, the musky-throated chant, the jonquil notes of bamboo shafts being beaten on hollow logs, the easy rum laughter of the whalers and the singing of the women, far away and lovely—*Maluna, malalo, mawaena*. And, as he had expected, he heard John Howland's rich laughter echoing through the night. Father would chase the sinners out of Kailua town . . . sure he would.

Later, the moon wasted out of the sky and the drumming stopped. He heard the lusty clatter of hoofs on the macadam, then nervous thunder against the wood of the stairs, and finally on the veranda, the crashing of a door, the sound of breaking glass and mellow curses, and he knew that his father had failed again in one of his fond drunken attempts to canter the mare into the living room.

"A man of God!" Martha Howland's voice rang out in rage. "A Christian man of the Bible, falling with those pagans to the depths of degradation! May the kind, forgiving Lord have mercy on your soul!"

"No, Martha, not a man of God! Not a man of the Bible!" John Howland roared drunkenly. He paused, listening as the mare trotted back down the macadam and cut across the turf, cantering now back to the stables. "Put God away long ago, Martha. Put man up instead of God. Let man be God—"

"Quiet! You'll wake Willard with all that vile blasphemy."

Their argument became a mumble, stale, indeterminate, and without passion. Finally Willard heard his mother's tired sobbing as she padded upstairs, passed his room, and closed the door to her bedroom. And from the stairwell he heard the hollow pounding gloom of John Howland's voice: "I'm sorry, Martha. I've been sorry for so long now . . ."

Then the slow, heavy cadence of his bootsteps on the stairs; his door being opened.

"You awake, Son?"

"Yes," Willard whispered.

John Howland wavered at the door.

"Mother was crying," Willard said.

"Grown people cry, Son. Mothers more than most."

John Howland sat down on the edge of the bed. Willard liked the whisky and leather and horsy smell about him.

"Mother told me you rode down to stop the luau. But I knew better. I knew you wouldn't—"

"Damn it, I did ride down there, and rode back," John Howland said, a little puzzled. "I wonder where I left that mare. I remember riding back—"

"I heard you trying to get her into the house."

"That's right. Just about got into the living room when your mother . . . Yes, she must have run back to the stables."

"Why was Mother crying?"

"I don't know. It's hard to explain, Son."

"Is it because you're a heathen?"

Old Howland wrinkled his face. "Where'd you get that idea?"

"Mother said so. She said you got to be a heathen when you started running around with that writer."

"Sam? Mark Twain?"

Willard nodded.

John Howland chuckled. "Son, what's happened to me is—well, it's just something that happens to a man. It's got nothing to do with Mark Twain. He wasn't even Mark Twain then. Just a roving newspaper guy writing travel pieces for a Sacramento paper. Sam Clemens. One of the finest men ever to come to Manoalani. Slept right here in your bed. Maybe tomorrow you and I can saddle-up early, before your mother gets up, and we'll ride out past Naalehu and I'll show you the spot where that crazy wildhead planted the banyan. You know, the big one with—"

"I've seen it, Father. You took me, remember?"

John Howland laughed softly. "Never do pass that place without remembering Sam.

"Reason he came here was because he'd heard how your grandfather and Melville were old cronies. He thought he'd do a story on Melville's getting thrown off ship at Lahaina. You remember

—I showed you the place. Your granddad brought Melville back to the old house and put him up until he could get another ship back to Honolulu. Mark Twain thought maybe your grandfather or me could give him a pretty good story. But the old man was too far gone by then, and I didn't remember much of Melville except for that beard of his and his ravings about Typee Valley in the Marquesas. I didn't remember anything clear enough to give Twain a decent story. So I rode him up to the volcanoes and he did a piece on that instead."

He got up from the bed and walked to the corner bookcase and selected the volume of letters by Mark Twain. He struck a match to the kerosene lamp and placed it at the head of Willard's bed. Then he sat down and thumbed through the volume until he found what he wanted to read. "Listen," he told Willard, and started reading:

"Hawaii is the loveliest fleet of islands that lies anchored in any ocean.

"No alien land in all the world has any deep strong charm for me but that one; no other land could so longingly and beseechingly haunt me sleeping and waking through half a lifetime, as that one has done. Other things leave me, but it abides. For me its balmy airs are always blowing, its summer seas flashing in the sun; the pulsing of its surf-beat is in my ear; I can see its garlanded crags, its leaping cascades, its plumy palms drowsing by the shore; its remote summits floating above the cloud rack; I can feel the spirit of its woodland solitude, I can hear the plash of its brooks, in my nostrils still lives the breath of flowers that perished twenty years ago."

John Howland closed the book and blew out the light. He was quiet for a long time, gazing out the window to where the Pacific lay like a sheet of stained glass beneath the dark sky. "These islands . . ." he muttered.

There were other moments. There were afternoons on that island ranch when the sky was soft brass and the wind rumbled with the bawing of a thousand head being driven out of the Humuula grazelands to headquarters post. A sea of dust rose above headquarters post where young Willard and the paniolos worked the calves away from the marketable stock and rode herd on these down into lower pastures where the yearlings waxed sleek and indolent in the sun. They would ride the stock straight through Kailua town, down along the leafy green tunnel of Alii Drive where the wahines carrying their baskets of wash would curse the paniolos for the dust and the children would race through the dung-steamed road after the herd; past Ahuena Heiau, where Kamehameha the Great died in 1819, and down across the lava flats where the petroglyphs had been carved into the rock, toward Kailua wharf where young Willard would join his father and watch the cattle bobbing through the water to the steamer that would carry them to Oahu's markets.

Longhorns founded Hawaii's cattle kingdom. They were brought in by George Vancouver from Santa Barbara in 1793 as a gift to the king. Cattle raising was a major industry in Hawaii long before it was in the American West, just as Hawaii was publishing newspapers before print was introduced in California, and children of affluent families in Western states were being sent to Hawaii for schooling.

The Longhorns were protected by the King's kapu, and they multiplied until they roamed the Big Island as far as stock could roam.

William Howland, Willard's grandfather, founded the Howland ranch. He came to the Islands in 1820 as a member of the American Missionary Society of Boston, and after a few years, combined his preaching with a little ranching. Along with John Palmer Parker, the elder Howland set up ranch headquarters at Waimea in the saddleback between Mauna Kea and Mt. Kohala, their job to shoot cattle for King Liholiho and later Kamehameha, prepare the cattle hides and salt the beef for visiting schooners. Later, John Howland moved the ranch site to the Kona Coast, sharing the cattleland with the fabled Parker Ranch, which grew to 300,000 acres, and which, except for the King Ranch of Texas, was the largest cattle ranch in the world. Aberdeen Angus were imported, and then Herefords and Durham bulls and Dexter and Shorthorn; and the Hawaiian cowboys—the paniolos—who worked the Howland Ranch with Willard were the sons of the grizzled veterans who were taught to ride and rope by the Spanish *vaqueros* that Parker and John Howland brought in from California.

"C'mon, get 'em moving," John Howland shouted from the pier. "Keep 'em moving fast through that water."

The steamer was anchored just beyond the breakwater of Kailua Bay. Sailors rowed a whaleboat in from the steamer.

Willard maneuvered his little sorrel gelding through the corals. He dropped the noose of a seven-fathom lasso about the head of a steer and worked him out of the coral.

"Aea aea!"

He spurred the sorrel, and with the steer in tow, galloped across the flat beach into the surf for the long swim out to the whaleboat.

"Shark! Auwe, shark!"

Willard tightened the slack of lasso. He pulled the steer alongside his horse. He turned toward the sunlight and he could see the dorsal fin cut sleekly through the surface. He heard three quick rifle shots and saw his father on the edge of the pier, firing at the shark. The dorsal fin vanished.

Two paniolos rushed an outrigger into the surf and started out toward Willard. Willard hurried his horse through the water. His eyes scanned the surface for the fin, then turned to the pier where his father waited.

"I don't see him," John Howland called.

But as he spoke, Willard felt the rush of water next to him. The sorrel screeched in terror. Willard could see the dark bulk circle and come in again. He shoved his boot as hard as he could into the monster's nose. The kick diverted his attack and again the shark dove deep, swimming very strong now, bullets spattering in his wake.

"I don't think we got him," John Howland called out. "Keep the rigger after him!"

Willard reached the whaleboat, keeping his horse close to the stern so the sailors could bat the shark away with their oars if he attacked again. The steer was secured to the side of the boat, eight head making a load, and the sailors rowed out to the steamer where the crew would cinch slings about the bellies of the cattle and hoist them aboard. Willard swam his horse back to shore, the outrigger alongside the paddlers watching for the shark. But the shark did not return.

It was twilight before the steamer was loaded and Willard and his father mounted and rode tiredly home. When they reached the rise of Manoalani's land, John Howland turned in his saddle and watched the steamer plow its way toward Oahu. "All yours, someday, Willard," he said. "This land is my legacy to you." And beyond the steamer, the Southern Cross moved up into the sky.

Sometimes at night when kona storms battered against the south face of Manoalani young Willard would lean back against the warmed lava rock of the fireplace, listening to the flames lick into the wood while his father recalled the days of King Kalakaua's court.

"Days of glory," John Howland would say. He would have been at the bottle for some time by then, and his burned-out eyes would gaze hypnotically into the flames, almost as if he could see, on the stage of the hearth, the setting of the palace, the people, the way it was. "Days of miracles, when your old father put behind him the cloth of God for the wine of man. I can only see those days now as if they were something from a Gauguin canvas, with all the colors bright, with all the riotous glitter, and Kalakaua himself bellowing through the palace, pumping champagne and okolehau into everyone and when the party started to lag the poker games would start and I'm telling you, the money in those poker games could have papered every wall at Iolani. If the King had a stroke of bad luck you could hear him laughing as he sent a runner to the royal treasury to bring back a couple of thousand in cash or a few choice deeds of land in lieu of cash.

"Those days Kalakaua could leave the palace in the morning with forty thousand dollars in his huge fists and come home broke before sundown. I remember one night in particular when we were all down at the summer palace at Waikiki and a big game got started between the King and myself and Henry Adams, the writer, and Claus Spreckles, the California sugar man. The betting got too heavy and I dropped out, and then Adams had to fold. There must have been more than five thousand dollars in that pot. Spreckles and big Kalakaua, sitting cross-legged on the floor, splits of champagne at their side, stared over the rim of their cards into each other's eyes. Finally David calls and Spreckles grins so you'd think his mouth was a rubber band being stretched and comes up with four aces. Kalakaua flinched for a second, then started roaring with laughter and telling Spreckles how four aces couldn't beat five kings. And with this he shows the four kings in his hand and jabs his thumb into his chest. 'I'm the fifth king!' he roared, and he scooped up the pot and left Spreckles sitting there with egg on his face." Howland laughed softly to himself and tumbled whisky into his glass. "And all that time," he continued, "while the hell-raisers among us were roistering around that beach palace, Stevenson would be lounging out on the sand, beneath the sky he loved so well, talking with Princess Kaiulani—Lord she was a beautiful young girl in those days, I've never seen a more beautiful girl—and she'd sit close to Stevenson, loving him, while he read poetry to her, while he wrote poetry about her. Kind, troubled, dying R.L.S., may God be tender with his sweet soul," John Howland muttered, shaking his head with ancient sadness sharp as the woodsmoke from the fire, wondering, for the moment, where his friends had all gone, why all the gold grew dim, why time had broken down upon him as if from the youth of yesterday, so quickly, with such ruthless surprise, to cripple him, slowly, inevitably, clogging the flow to his heart, knotting his once fluent hands.

He staggered to his feet and over to the bookcase, returned to his chair and thumbed through a slim volume of poems by Robert Louis Stevenson, and from the volume extracted a letter written in ink and bearing Stevenson's initials. He read aloud clearly, distantly, with the ancient sadness still heavy in his throat:

"Written in April to Kaiulani in the April of her age: and at Waikiki, within easy walk to Kaiulani's banyan! When she comes to my land, and the rain beats upon the window (as I fear it will), let her look at this page; it will be like a weed gathered and pressed at home; and she will remember her own islands, and the shadow of that mighty tree; and she will hear the peacocks screaming in the dusk and the wind blowing in the palms; and she will think of her father sitting there alone.—R.L.S.

"Forth from her land to mine she goes,
The island maid, the island rose,
Light of heart and bright of face:
The daughter of a double race.

"Her islands here in southern sun,
Shall mourn their Kaiulani gone;
And I in her dear banyan shade,
Look vainly for my little maid.

"But our Scots islands far away
Shall glitter with unwonted day,
And cast for once their tempests by
To smile in Kaiulani's eye."

The letter fell from John Howland's hands. He made no effort to retrieve it. His eyes glazed flatly as he stared into the fire, seeing again the tortured wreck of his dear friend, Robert Louis Stevenson, the way he looked that day when he waved farewell and set sail to roam the South Seas. "He nearly died here that winter," John Howland said. "Over at Brown's house. His tuberculosis got so bad that weekend that everyone gave up on him, Doc Wilson and Captain Brown himself. Everyone but little Kaiulani."

Willard picked up the letter, placed it back in the book and laid the book on the table by his father's chair. The old man nodded vacantly. Then, as he would often do when he was truly drunk and lost in the sweet-sad orgy of nostalgia, he began murmuring to himself in dreary incantations the epitaph that marks Stevenson's simple grave at Vailima in the Samoas, the words John Howland insisted Stevenson wrote that winter in Honolulu when he was so ill: *"Home is the hunter, home from the hill; And the sailor, home from the sea."*

Exactly how John Howland became confidant and court advisor to Kalakaua had always remained a mystery to Willard. The appointment came about somehow because of the King's plans to expand his island empire by annexing Samoa, the Gilberts, Tonga, the Carolines, and eventually Tahiti and the Society Island group to his Hawaiian kingdom. The King believed he needed a warship to complete the dream, and somehow John Howland arranged for the acquisition of a heavy cruiser from France. The warship would enhance Kalakaua's prestige among his fellow Pacific Islanders and persuade them to join his empire. But Kalakaua used the warship solely to host his parties and the scheme never came off. In later years, John Howland was in such good favor with Kalakaua that he accompanied the monarch on his royal visit to the United States, where he was the guest of the nation as the first ruling king ever to visit America. In 1881, John Howland again accompanied the monarch on his royal tour of the world, a tour in which Kalakaua was received in every throneroom of Europe.

John Howland stood by the King when the Chinese opium license scandals erupted in Honolulu, and he rallied with Kalakaua to overthrow the bloody Wilcox revolt of 1889, when Iolani Palace was captured by the revolutionists. He remained close to the monarch during the last troubled years of his reign, and it was this friendship, Willard knew, that enabled John Howland to amass so much cane and cattleland on the Big Island.

After the King's sudden death in San Francisco's Palace Hotel, John Howland drifted away from the royal court. Queen Liliuokalani brought him back, but only on rare occasions. They both realized that the era was closing.

John Howland once wrote:

> She might have been a difficult woman to understand, especially in her later years after her monarchy was overthrown by Sanford Dole, after the kingdom was replaced by the Republic of Hawaii. Because by that time, her hatred for America and all Americans was implacable and savage. And she had her reasons. But to me, as to all who knew her, she was one of the finest women on earth.
>
> Her face wasn't coarse or heavy as the pictures show her to be. It was a thin, strong face, with narrow black eyes set close, blazing with her hatred for America. It was a face of European feature, pervaded by an elusive refinement, and there was always, in the early days, that charm and gaiety about her; the charm that kept the Kaiser smitten with her as he took his place at her right hand as German courtier at her royal banquets; the charm that, no doubt, was the reason why she became Queen Victoria's specially favored guest at the Golden Jubilee in London. Except for a very few, that charm faded in her later years, the years which brought her downfall from the throne. Her fault was that there was too much Hawaiian alii in her. She was ruined by her damnably stubborn determination to rule instead of reign.
>
> But I am talking about the earlier days, the days of her untouchable charm and warmth.
>
> One afternoon, when David Kalakaua was still alive and I was his palace advisor, he asked me to escort his young sister to a party at Ed Boyd's home. Boyd was the King's chamberlain and he owned a ranch at Maunawili, on the windward

side of the pali. On our ride back from the party Miss Lydia, who was soon to become Queen, grew very pensive. She trotted on ahead to be by herself. There was, as I remember, some wordless glamour to that tropic night. It seemed that the very air was blue. After a while I rode up to her.

"Are you feeling all right?" I asked.

She smiled gravely at me. "Do you want me to tell you a secret, Mistah John?" she asked. "Well, I will. I'll surprise you.

"I have always envied my brother, not because of his being King, oh no. But because he composed 'Hawaii Ponoi,' the song that has since become our national anthem. And all my life, I have wanted to compose some beautiful song, a hymn to my land! And I think I have."

She pulled her horse to a stop and looked solemnly at me. "It is based on an old English ballad that Mr. Stevenson, your friend, would hum, 'The Lone Rock by the Sea.' Would you like to hear it?"

"I would love to, Your Grace."

Our horses stood very still. Miss Lydia rested her hand on mine. She looked deep into my eyes, and in that heavy, sweet voice of hers, started humming a hauntingly beautiful theme. Then, I believe I became the first person in the world, except Liliuokalani herself, who wrote it, to ever hear the words and the exquisite strains of her hymn to her land, for she started singing:

"Aloha Oe, Aloha Oe,
"One fond embrace,
"Aloha e-a
"Until, we meet again."

Willard knew the rest of the story by heart. The final disintegration of the palace and the monarchy; the revolution which overthrew Queen Liliuokalani and proclaimed Sanford Ballard Dole as the first President of the Hawaiian Republic on July 4, 1894; and, in time, the celebrations of August 12, 1898, that ushered in Hawaii's annexation to the United States, the cheering for President McKinley, the parades, the skyrockets, the ceremonious raisings of the American flag high above Iolani Palace, and high above the small wood courthouse in Kailua town, while at the moment, six miles away, Martha Howland was giving birth to her only child and heir in the high-ceilinged back bedroom of Manoalani.

As a young boy, Willard lived in awe of his father, and of what his mother termed "the moral disintegration of John Howland." Liquor and gentle nights and pleasant brown-skinned women. As Martha Howland became more drab and faded, more emotionally obsessed with her relationships with Jesus and the Church, John Howland, it seemed to Willard, became more and more obsessed with his riotous relationships with liquor and life and women.

"Don't you look at me like you were the Great God Almighty ready to pronounce my eternal damnation," John Howland told Willard one night, when the former was recovering from a three-day debauch. "And don't worry too much how me and Jesus are getting along. I didn't just drift away from the cloth, Son. I turned and fled from it.

"Son," John Howland continued, "the cloth of God and the purse of the merchant might well have been the backbones that built these islands, but along the way they ruined something. When your grandfather first came here, when I was growing up here, to a point when you were a younger boy, these Island people were the finest creatures God ever placed on earth. See them while you can, hold them, love them while you can. For they won't survive. The merchants exploit them; the humorless missionaries go forth with ice in their hearts and cheese in their brains and look at these wonderful natives like a ring of jackals leering at a fawn. They outlawed the pareus and sarongs and forced them to wear those goddamned Mother Hubbard muumuus, like their spinster aunts wore in Boston. They tabooed the dancing and the wonderful drums and singing and taught them to sing about some dull future world of them and Jesus. They whipped the loveliness, bruted the warmth and almost castrated the bright silver purity of feeling these natives abounded with.

"These islands," he muttered, staring out across the green earth. "Hawaii is a woman beautiful and utterly seductive. These islands can seduce a man with such charm and grace . . . Take it while it's still here, Son."

On his deathbed, John Howland prayed feverishly for forgiveness. Watching his father die, Willard vowed that he would never fall victim to the fabled disease of Polynesia. He left that year for the Yale School of Divinity.

It was while he was at New Haven that he first met Grace Caldwell, a slender, dark, tragic beauty, who was attending Vassar at the time and frequented the Yale dances. By the end of his first year at Yale, he was deeply in love with her.

He returned to the Islands that summer, remaining in Honolulu where he took a summer job as a reporter on the Honolulu *Star-Bulletin.* It was in his capacity as a newspaperman that he met Jack London.

The writer and his wife, Charmian, were spending the summer in Honolulu aboard the iron-hulled, pine-planked *Snark* which London had sailed down from San Francisco. In the late afternoons, when Willard had completed his stint at the paper and the novelist was through his day's work, they would meet out at Waikiki with Duke Kahanamoku and surf in on the waves, using those eighty-pound koa boards they do not make any more. London took a fancy to young Willard, and often at night they would dine aboard the *Snark* and drink okolehau, and London would expound his views on the Pan-Pacific Union he was attempting to establish.

"The Pacific is a very personal thing to me," the writer said one night. "I love its lands; I love its peoples. The kind of a war that's going on in Europe right now, and in which we'll be involved pretty soon, need never come to the Pacific peoples. Not if a union between these peoples is formed. A brotherhood across the sea of all nations, all islands, all peoples, regardless of race or color. The world is getting too small for people to allow themselves racial prejudice and intolerance. Any time I hear the word 'gook' or 'chink' or 'nigger' or 'kike' it's a personal offense to me, and it hurts me; because, as Donne said, I am involved in mankind. And, if 'every man's death diminishes me,' so every man's loss of human dignity diminishes me: and these words chop away at the base of man's dignity.

"You, Will," he said, brushing a lock of dark hair from his forehead with his hand, "are in a perfect position to work for the brotherhood of our Pacific peoples."

"As a minister?" Willard asked.

London got up and paced the cabin. "I'm not sure," he said. "A man's got to taste and smell and feel and know life to guide another man's soul. I'm not sure that the ministry develops any true understanding of man. It develops a misty understanding of dogma; of cluttered history. I'm not sure at all," he said. "But it seems to me that if God was all He's cracked up to be, the world would be a better place. I believe in Cardinal Newman's prayer for the agnostic: 'Oh God if there is a God, save my soul if I have a soul.' I'll tell you how I think you can best serve, Will. Serve mankind. That's the best way to serve God. It's got to be."

When Willard returned to Yale that autumn, he transferred to the School of Law. Four years later, he returned to Manoalani with honors from Yale and with the fragile grave beauty, Grace Caldwell, who had become his bride.

At first, the pleasure they had taken in each other was intense. But after that first flush, Island life churned through Grace Howland with slack disappointment. It was, after all, a barbaric land of savages, with little refinement and an appalling lack of conveniences. The birth of Aaron, and then the twins, Garth and Steven, eased some of this disappointment, but sapped nearly all her strength. The cheeks became more famished; the large, soulful eyes darkened. Her face, which was once so lovely, became set not in the sharp quick lines of bitterness, but in a mask of continual sadness. When the twins were a year old, she took them and Aaron for a summer cruise to her home in Virginia.

It's just something that happens to a man in these islands.

Willard remembered his father's words as he watched the Matson freighter pull away from Hilo. Three weeks later, it happened to him.

Her name was Kalea Hirozowa Akana. He met her at a roundup luau at the Parker Ranch. Later, a group of them continued the luau down at Keawaiki Bay. It was, Willard thought, the lost beautiful world again: the world of the drumming and wild dancing. He understood, now, how his father had been seduced by this world.

She danced for him, and there was, in her dance, the promise of everything Grace could never offer. The glow of the dull gold moon caught on her breasts. Her knees flashed to the rhythm of the drums. As the drums quickened, her body twisted with violent yet curiously tender passion, and her promise became a need. He took her that first night, down the beach past Keawaiki; the two of them locked in lust and a vague spiritual coarseness, locked perhaps in loneliness beneath the high, impassioned grief of the stars.

She became a need to him, an anodyne against the disappointment of Grace. And he kept her always close to him, even after Grace's spiritless return. And although they understood that marriage between them was an impossibility, she bore him happily a son named Ward.

How can I reach through the curtain of the years and explain it all to you, Ward? Willard Howland thought, staring moodily out at the black drawn sea. How can I say it so it will all make sense?

Beyond Makapuu Point, the endless sea was a thing for poets and fools to gawk at. Ward stood there, at the edge of the beach, the wind blowing his hair and the open shirt about his throat. His fists dug hard into his hips and his head was cocked to one side, his eyes grave with all the unanswered questions.

Willard did not seem surprised to see him there.

"Did you love her?" Ward said quietly.

"I've seen that question in your eyes a million times."

"Why didn't you ever answer me?"

Willard shook his head, slack with regret. "There are no answers."

"You're lying."

"I've tried to tell you, Ward. I've tried to tell you so many times. Earlier tonight—" Old Willard stopped. There was a weight in his heart like a cold stone: a feeling of emptiness when love is withheld. "You're not really there, Ward. Only my conscience is there. My guilt."

"Yes, Old Man," Ward laughed. "Your guilt is here. Your guilt will always be with you. Wherever you go in this world, you have to take yourself. But I'm here too. Look."

Howland glanced up and saw him.

"Now tell me, Old Man. Once and for all. Did you love her?"

"Yes," Willard said. "I loved her very much. You must believe that. I would have married her if I could. I've always wanted to tell you. God, it's hurt me not to have been able to explain."

Ward looked at him without emotion. "What happened to that love?"

What happens to many loves? Willard wondered. Wine sours and love, like gold, grows dim with a sudden brutality that must amuse worms. But he said nothing. He looked up, hoping that Ward would be gone.

"Was the love a lie?" Ward asked. "The love from which I came?"

"No," Willard said. "I loved her with everything in me. And we wanted you. Please believe me."

But Ward was gone.

Willard tramped up the shallow sand dune to where he had left his car, stumbling through some wild eternal pilgrimage as if he were trying to walk through pain to come out on the other side. He paused by the car. He raised his head and his old burned-out eyes seemed to stare out from deep in his skull where hope had taken a final stand. But he could not see Ward. And suddenly, just for that moment, he was overwhelmed with the strange heartache of being alone on a dark beach and remembering with a start all the things that might have been but never were.

Chapter Eight

A YEAR after her husband's death, Kapiolani Kahana had taken what money she had saved, and, with a loan from Willard Howland, purchased a small bungalow-type beach house at Nanakuli, on the western shores of Oahu. It was a square wood-frame structure set far back from the beach and sunned and faded to the dull color of guava ice cream. The shutters were open to a lanai which ran along the front of the house, facing grassy sand dunes and the ocean. There was a chipped red table on the lanai, surrounded by four straight-backed Queen Emma chairs woven of pandanus and looking elegantly uncomfortable. Across the wooden railing of the lanai, a fishnet had been hung to dry in the sun. Two of the wood steps leading from the dunes to the lanai had split and caved in. Bougainvillaea vines tangled about the broken steps and climbed up along the north wall of the house. A grove of lahala shaded this wall, and from the grove came the rich shrill sound of a hundred birds. The house had a flavor of pleasant comfort.

An outrigger canoe was beached at the edge of the water and two old rowboats lay like overturned shells on the dunes. As she walked past the rowboats, Kapiolani Kahana was beginning to realize that what was happening was not part of a dream; that it was all true. That she was, in fact, being hostess to more than one hundred friends, including the Howland family, at a luau celebrating her son's engagement to Sloan Howland. She smiled at her guests and walked to a little rise of sand and stood there solemnly, waiting for the luau to begin. She was nearly six feet tall, sumptuous, bearing her splendid proportions with the remarkable poise and grace of her people. There was about her a resemblance to the old Alii, the Hawaiian nobility; a queen without a trace of humility, but rather with those qualities of sweet frankness, gentlehood and dignity that had for centuries been the mark of her people. She stood straight, her back arched, the pose of her head majestic, piled with heavy fine hair, the ringlets brushed until they shone like dark carved wood against her shoulders. Her full black, calm eyes were striking against her tawny skin. The tropic wine in her veins gave her face a look of humid passions and warmth. She wore crude sharktooth earrings of a barbaric design, an hibiscus in her hair, and a lei of pikaki twined with maile about her shoulders. She was gowned in a white silk holoku, its square neck set in ivory lace. The light breeze snapped her hair against her cheek and molded her dress against her high breasts and against her thighs. She looked past the semicircle of guests to her son Paul.

He stood beneath an arbor of palm and lahala trees, a long wooden spade in his hands. He wore a blue and white print lavalava, a male-type sarong hitched securely about his waist and falling in folds to his knees. He was naked from the waist up, except for a lei of twined fern and Island rose about his shoulders. With the wooden spade, he described an arc in the sand, thus selecting the site for the imu—the underground earth oven in which the luau food would be cooked. Then he signaled his mother.

Kapiolani clasped her hands together. She raised her face to the sky and began the low, throaty incantation:

"Ke kuahiwi i ke kua Lono, O Laka e"

It was a primeval chant, a savage ritual to Laka, deity of nature. Translated, it was both pious and practical:

> O god of the heavens above, look down
> favorably upon our endeavors:
> Assure the members of this family that
> the animal to be prepared will be
> delectable from one end to the other.

The men wore lava-lavas, or beach clothes, or bright aloha shirts with white duck trousers. The older women wore muumuus or colorfully printed holokus; the younger girls wore the enticing Tahitian sarongs called pareus. The women wore flowers in their hair and both men and women wore leis.

Tradewinds washed the sky blue and the sunshine lay like a golden shawl across the land. The sea was coming up in risings of sun-washed liquid silk. The screech of sea gulls mingled with the sound of the surf. Somewhere behind the house a peacock screamed.

Bobby Villanueva moved into the half-circle by the imu. He raised a heavy Hawaiian conch shell to his lips and blew a single, haunting note. Then Kapiolani's simple, two-beat chant was punctuated by the rhythm of hollow ipu gourd drums. Two beachboys sitting cross-legged in the sand started beating their sharkskin drums, while a third kept time with the pahu-niu coconut shell half-drum. A group of boys rattled feathered gourds about two strapping women who snapped ili-ilis, the lava rock castanets. Hardwood sticks were beaten against la-au hollow blocks. A dozen girls clad in red and white pareu halters and ti-leaf skirts moved into the center of the crowd, their hips and shoulders swaying as they beat split bamboo reeds against their wrists in tempo with the chanting.

Dean, Peter Noa, Bobby Villanueva and several other young men started digging deep into the sand, preparing the five-foot-wide kapuahi ditch for the imu. Dry kiawe branches were placed in the pit and Paul lit these with a flaming torch. Then a mound of volcanic stones was placed on the fire to heat.

Three hundred-pound kalua pigs, their skins scrubbed pink, were placed at the edge of the imu. Dean wrapped strips of wet canvas about his hands and reached in and selected several red-hot stones from the pit. These he forced steaming into the hollowed shoulder and hip sockets of the pigs. The carcasses were then wrapped tightly with ti leaves and banana leaves, finally with canvas, and lowered into the smoldering pit—not to be roasted, but to be steamed in a natural pressure cooker which would preserve all the essential flavor and succulence of the pigs. Other delicacies which were to be similarly cooked—Maia wild bananas, Uwala yams, Lawalu whole raw fish—were also wrapped in puolo bundles of leaves and placed into the imu alongside the pigs. Then the imu was covered with many layers of leaves, canvas and sand, and Kapiolani sang the closing chant.

She joined the crowd in a kava toast to Paul and Sloan, and watched with mixed emotions as the couple led a group of the younger dancers in a hula to "Melanai Oe." Then she walked thoughtfully back to her house.

The house had acted as a buffer against the shock of Doc's death. Death was always such a faraway thing until it struck home that night with that shamefully insulting suddenness: the twist of a pony's foreleg on a trail that he had ridden ten thousand times and knew by heart.

She had remained at Manoalani that first year after Doc's death. She had wondered just how long it took the human constitution to tune itself to the final acceptance of death. Even after that first year, she had not been able to dull the sharp newness of the pain that seemed to insist that death came yesterday. She decided that as long as she remained at Manoalani, with the old sweet haunts that had been her home and her life for more than a quarter of a century, she would never free herself of this grief. There were too many memories at Manoalani; too much love and laughter that she knew would never come again.

"Perhaps you're living in the past," old Willard had said to her one day. And she nodded her agreement. "That's not wise," Howland continued. "The past plays tricks on us, fooling us with its nostalgia into accepting a life of memories alone. Doc wouldn't want it that way."

She had decided then that a person could not truly live in the past. It was worse than a half-life. It was an emotional narcotic; a semicatatonic state in which the edges and outlines of things were softened and bearable, from morning till night. And, she agreed with Willard, Doc would want her to live fully in the present. The present is the only time, the only reality. Past and future are illusions, imaginative gymnastics. Doc would want her to continue alone on the same plane of happiness that they had shared together. She could best do that by leaving Manoalani, by leaving the Island of Hawaii. The boys were grown up and away at school, and there was nothing left to tie her to Manoalani but lingering memories. She moved to Honolulu and lived with relatives for a while, and as life seeped back into her, she had found the old small house at Nanakuli. Moving into it was like learning to live again, and she proved a good student.

She paused at the steps of the lanai and looked over her shoulder at Paul and Sloan dancing in the sand. She still found it hard to believe. The idea of her son marrying Sloan Howland was incredible!

She had struggled and cajoled and argued against their marriage. But that was in the days when she had felt, because of some intuitive yet inexplicable reason, that such a marriage was wrong. During the past month, Paul and Sloan had convinced her that it was right. They had convinced her not through logistics, not through any inundation of reasoned arguments, but just by being together; the way they looked at each other, the way they touched. They had convinced her not merely that their marriage was right, but that anything less would be wrong.

Where had all the years gone? she wondered. Yesterday they were crawling around on their hands and knees, screaming at each other in the playpen at Manoalani. And now . . .

"I hope I'm not intruding," Willard Howland said quietly. "You look as though you might want to be alone for a while."

She smiled at him. "I guess I'm trying to reassure myself that I'm not dreaming. That all this is real."

"It's too real," Willard said. He stood beside her gravely for a moment, watching his daughter. "They give you a strange feeling, don't they? Those kids of ours aren't babies any more. They make you feel as if life is hurrying on to some bright, gay, loving place, while you stand still and watch it go by."

She nodded, then turned and smiled. He bowed, and with a flourish of old-world courtliness that was habit with him he extended his arm and escorted her up the rickety steps, and for the moment there was about them an aura of that same oddness of being out of their proper place and time, perhaps from a more graceful time, and yet the look of being at peace within themselves in their kind and fading world. They crossed the lanai and he seated her in the tattered Queen Emma much in the same manner as John Howland had escorted Liliuokalani to her throne, and she sat that beat-up chair as though it were a throne. "It seems that byanby you and me will be in-laws, Senatah."

"Stranger things have happened."

"Do you think it very strange?"

"I've not really pondered the—the strangeness of it."

She studied him with mild amusement. She had always had a good instinct about people, and with that instinct she probed through the façade of old Willard, sitting stolidly beside her, no emotion marking the unchanging gray stone of his face. "I'm not so suah that you're telling the truth," she said. "Knowing you as I do, I'd say you've given this wedding plenty of deep thought. And I don't think you've accepted it yet."

Willard shifted in his chair.

"Have you?" she asked.

"Yes, I've accepted it. As a fact. As something Sloan thinks will mean her happiness."

"Deep in your heart, you've accepted it?"

Howland nodded. "Yes, I guess so. It's inevitable."

"You're resigned to it," she corrected.

"That's right."

"That's different from accepting it."

"What am I expected to do, stand up and applaud? I can't accept it fully until I know whether it's right or wrong."

"I tell you something, Senatah: any old fool can tell the difference between good and evil. But it takes a special kine of person to tell the difference between right and wrong. I don't pretend to be that kine of person, but I say this: when love comes so strong, like it is between your daughter and my boy, then there is no right or wrong. Their love is their life."

"Have you never considered the fact that they might be making a mistake?"

"Auwe—love is never a mistake! The trouble is that there's not enough of it to go around. Everyone in the world wants to be loved, but there just aren't enough lovers any more."

He could see again in her dark eyes what to him had always been the epitome of the Hawaiian heart—all softness, bigness, gentleness, sweetness. "I understand how you feel, Senatah. A man's love for his daughter is probably the purest of all love. When a man loves his woman, there's desire and passion. When he loves his son, there's pride and ambition. But in the love for his daughter, there's something so fine and pure it's beyond expression. Perhaps it's the same as a mother's love for her son. You see, frankly, it had always been my hope that Paul would marry a nice Hawaiian wahine. I never dreamed that it could be any other way. Just as you never dreamed that Sloan would marry anyone but a haole boy.

"But they're surprising us. And maybe we deserve the surprise. After all, Senatah, you and me, we are very proud people. And with pride comes prejudice. They go hand in hand, and one cannot be without the other."

"Paul and Sloan have pride. Can you believe that they're without prejudice?"

"No," she said mildly. "No people are without prejudice. But remember this: of all kines of love, the kine that begins between two children is the strongest. When two children who have been friends grow up to be sweethearts and then man and wife lovers, it's part of the miracle of this world.

"When they were children they had no prejudice. They had to be taught. And the only ones to teach them were the adults, including you and me. When they moved into the fear and insecurity of the adult world, maybe they realized what a small thing prejudice is. And maybe they decided that their heart and their intelligence could carry them above it."

"And maybe you're talking with a lot more confidence than you really feel," Willard muttered.

Kapiolani remained quite solemn for a moment. Then she said, "Yes, that's a habit of mine. I like to look at things and people the way I'd like them to be instead of the way they are."

"Well, forget for a minute the way you'd like the marriage to be and tell me what you really think."

"I have told you. Really. I was against it at first. I talked with Paul several times, trying to show him why such a marriage could never be. But lately, he's proven to me—both he and Sloan have proven to me—that it can and should be. They've put away my fears, schooled me away from my prejudices. Now I see no reason to oppose their marriage. It would be like opposing their happiness.

"Look, Senatah." She turned to him with fresh enthusiasm. "You and I can't analyze their love. Love has nothing to do with wisdom or logic or experience. Love is the prevailing wind across the island of youth. There's an enormous amount of people in this world who are incapable of true love. We should be happy for Sloan and Paul. They are capable."

He looked at her with remote curiosity and she leaned over and covered his gnarled hands with hers. "Do you understand me, old Willard?" She smiled. "Love is a gift."

He escorted her to the foot of the stairs. "I hope someday I'll understand that," he said. "I hope you're right."

"When the day comes that you do understand, when you realize that I'm right and they're right, then maybe we'll all learn from them. And be able to help them."

"You think they'll need help?"

"Yes. Everyone needs help. Especially two young people in love."

As he watched her walk down the beach, he noticed again the innate grace and stateliness of her that was the most perfect example of a proud race of people doomed to extinction. Except for a few families like the Kahanas, the representatives of the Hawaiian stock are half caste or less, the bloodline weakening with each generation. Willard's professor at Yale had claimed that "The Hawaiians soon will no longer exist. Their own development brought them to a dead end. They had some fatal flaw which made it impossible for them to survive in a changing environment. They could not adapt. It is an oversimplification to call them nature's mistakes. They were merely dead ends in nature's endless experiments."

Willard had argued then, as he would now, that the flaw was not with the Hawaiian people, but with the mold of the world. There is a twist of history that cannot be stemmed nor denied, and it has almost turned now on these fine and noble people. The Hawaiians have never really changed. They were not strong enough to endure as a race, but their blood, their character, their features, endure mixed with other strains, to the betterment of those strains. The pure-bred Hawaiian has become very rare, dying off each year with none to fill his gracious place. Their page of history has almost turned, and, Willard thought, it is a pity, a flaw of nature, a poorly balanced book of God, for the world can ill afford to lose so splendid and lovable a race. And as he walked down the sand dunes, he felt strangely proud that his grandchildren from Sloan would be a part of this race.

Peter Noa was lying back against a koa log, his hands folded beneath his head, a coconut frond beach hat cocked over his face. For the first time in his life, he felt vaguely discontented. Ramsey James was the source of his discontent.

The loaf life at Waikiki Beach might not be the greatest thing in the world, but it was pretty damn nice. In a good summer season he averaged about a thousand dollars a month, most of it in tips and consequently tax free. He never saved any of it. Money was to spend. Loaf on the beach all day, teaching pretty malihini wahines how to swim or surf or take canoe rides. Then at night, teach them other things. Better things. That's what they came to Hawaii for in the first place. It was a jeweled life, a phallic galaxy. What was the sense of working hard to become a lawyer or a businessman when all the lawyers and businessmen worked hard all year round to come to Waikiki for a two-week vacation in order to do what the beachboys did all year round? Besides, he reasoned, the haoles got all the good jobs. Or else the buddha-heads—the Japanese. The only thing a Kanaka boy could do was stay on the beach and look picturesque, or get a job singing or playing the uke. If he had gone on to the University after graduating from Kamehameha School, he would have his degree now and Ramsey would have more respect for him because he would be headed somewhere. But on the other hand, chances are that he would never have met Ramsey in the first place and wouldn't have the time or the money to take her out.

He heard a noise behind him and thought it was Ramsey returning from the house, but he looked up and saw Bobby Villanueva.

"Eah, howzit?" Bobby said. He sat down and handed Peter a can of beer. "Where's your coast haole wahine?"

"She's up talkin' with the Howlands."

"You all lined up for tonight?"

"I guess so. Why?"

"We got some hot ones all ready to go."

"Auwe—moah bettah count me out."

"You pretty stuck on this wahine?" Bobby asked curiously.

Peter shrugged. "You know how it is. Nevah do I meet a wahine like her. She's something special. Yeah, I guess I'm real stuck on her."

"You two getting along pretty good, huh?"

"So-so, I guess. I don't know, she's kinda funny."

"She's a good-looking wahine, that Ramsey. How does she go, pretty good?"

"Balls! She don't go at all. You know da kine. She does everything but. She gets all hot working up to it, then chickens out."

"Damn!" Bobby shook his head. "That ain't no good."

"You bet it ain't no good. Been a whole month now I been taking her out. Alla time she yaks about how us guys—beachboys—got no da kine morals. All we want, she says, is a piece of malihini tail. So she says no, not from her."

Bobby Villanueva seemed to sit and brood for a moment. He was a lean-hipped, fine-featured youngster in his early twenties, his skin darker than his sister Lei's. His eyes were restless and intense, the same jet color as his hair. A chain with a slender gold cross hung about his neck. He had a reputation as a vicious and merciless brawler, and had twice been in Oahu prison—once when he was sixteen and convicted to statutory rape, and again for knifing a Pearl Harbor sailor.

He pulled on his beer. "Take my advice and watch yourself with these coast haole broads," he told Peter. "They can't stay away from us guys. But after it's all over, they go back an' marry their haole boy friends. Best thing is not to fall for any of them but screw 'em all. They're no good. Screw 'em all."

"Yeah—I guess yoah right," Peter said.

"We're moah bettah off," Bobby said, "if we stick to our own kine."

Peter remembered a night three weeks before when Ramsey James had told him that she loved him with all her heart. It was the same thing he had been telling her ever since that first night at the Royal. So he asked her to marry him, and he watched the glow of her face become sodden and her eyes fill with tears. "Oh Peter, that's impossible," she had said, and her voice was like a whimper. "You and I could never get married, no matter how much we loved each other."

He finished his beer and looked up at Bobby. "Is yoah sister comin' tonight?" he asked, wanting to change the subject.

"No. She can't."

"Too bad. Man—there's a wahine for you! Yoah sister, I mean."

"Yeah," Bobby muttered. He turned abruptly and stared at Peter. "Can you keep your mouth shut about something?"

"Me? Suah."

Bobby's eyes flashed with hatred. "Lemme tell you something, Pete, but you gotta swear you'll keep your mouth shut about it. Don't tell no one."

"Yeah—I swear."

"This mornin' I go over to Lei's apartment to see if she's comin' to the luau, huh? An' she wants to know if all the Howlands will be there, so I say, yeah, probably, and she says how it's moah bettah that she don't come."

"How come? She don't like the Howlands?"

"Naw—that ain't it. You swear you keep your mouth shut?"

"Honest."

"Lei's hapai."

"Goddamn!"

"Yeah—an' she's showin'."

"You know who did it?"

"I'm pretty goddamned sure."

"Who?"

Bobby Villanueva's eyes glowed like coal fires. "Aaron Howland."

Peter remained silent.

"He fixed her up with that swanky apartment down by Sans Souci," Bobby said. "I seen his car there plenty of nights. It's got to be him."

"What you gonna do?"

"When I'm sure—dead sure that it's Aaron who got her hapai, I'm gonna kill the sonofabitch!"

As she walked down from the lanai, Ramsey studied the complexion of the party. Less than a fifth of the guests were haoles. There was every possible shading of skin from her own ivory through all the yellows, tans and coppers to Peter Noa's chocolate-brown. Yet everyone mixed quite naturally. Perhaps, she thought, this land in the middle of the vast sea was a real racial paradise. Or as close to one as could be fashioned. There were thirty different racial groups in the Territory, and never a race riot. She wondered why she had become so acutely aware of racial groups since her arrival in the Islands. Could it be because in America all the do-gooders bleat about racial tolerance and it still ends up in hatred and violence, while here no one seems to talk much about it and there is harmony? Or, she wondered, could it be because of her feelings toward Peter Noa? She smiled at her absolute enjoyment of herself. Here I am, the coast haole girl from Burlingame society, in the midst of dark-skinned friends, having the most glorious time of my life. It's not only possible, but it's wonderfully true. Damn your foolish heart, Ramsey James, you're in love.

Futilely in love, a voice in the back of her brain taunted her.

Oh shut up, she told the voice.

She recalled a conversation she had with Peter one night as they were leaving the Kuhio Theatre. They had seen a romantically technicolored South Seas movie. While Ramsey was not too impressed by the story, Peter was openly antagonistic to it.

"It's the same old Hollywood junk," he told her. "All the South Sea stories are the same. Always about some haole guy who comes to the island and falls in love with a beautiful island girl and marries her. They nevah do it the other way around. They nevah show a haole girl falling for an island guy. An' that's what really happens most of the time."

It was what happened in her case anyway, Ramsey thought. She had dated all the haole young men, the fellows from the Outrigger Club, the tourists, even a few servicemen, but she always found time to spend with Peter, and that had become the best part of the day. Being with him this evening at a real Hawaiian luau somehow made her feel more native, almost a kamaaina. She was joining into the real native life, not the Waikiki tourist folderol. But how seriously could she join in with that life? the voice baited her again.

She joined Peter at the sand dune and curled her bare feet beneath her legs and leaned back against him. "Did you miss me?"

"Auwe—were you gone?" he grinned.

"Fine thing. Anyway, I missed you. I didn't mean to be gone so long. I was up on the lanai chatting with Mrs. Kahana and Ward and Tani. Gosh, I sure love Ward and Tani. They're so darn nice! And Mrs. Kahana—did you ever see a more gorgeous woman?"

"Yes—you."

"We were having so much fun, just yakking and getting to know each other better. Then Aaron came along. God, he's a case. I mean, straight out of a psycho ward. He was lushing it up like it might go out of style tomorrow and he started making a lot of, well, real cheap remarks about Paul. You know what I mean."

"That sounds like Aaron, all right."

"I mean, honestly. He was vile! I thought there was going to be a fight or something. Until Ward practically booted him down the stairs."

"It's a good thing Bobby Villanueva wasn't around."

"Why?"

"Well—nevah mind."

"I saw you and Bobby talking together. Was he trying to get you to join all of them?"

"All of who?"

"All of them." She pointed down the beach where Bobby Villanueva and three other young beachboys, King Mud Akapai, Blackout Kekai and Rabbit Kealoha, were disappearing behind a cove with four hula dancers. Bobby and Blackout were each carrying a case of beer, and Rabbit had several rolls of blankets beneath his arm. One of the girls was exceptionally striking. She wore a brief halter of jade green and a Tahitian grass skirt set astonishingly low on her hips. As she walked off with the group she shimmied suggestively.

"Well," Ramsey said, "were you supposed to go off with Bobby and his harem? Stop ogling that girl."

"What wahine?"

"You know darn well what wahine. The shimmy dancer."

"That's a Tahitian mating dance. Verra authentic."

"Put your eyes back into their sockets. You're drooling."

"Naw. I'm da kine conosoore of folk dancing. I was just checking to see if she had the keerect rhythm."

"She's got the right rhythm all right. Is she one of your old girls?"

"Auwe," Peter laughed, "if she was one of my old girls, she'd still be my—erh—well, ah, no; I don't really know her."

"She's sure fabulous-looking. I mean, hot and sexy."

"You can say that again."

Ramsey frowned. "No, once was enough." She looked impishly at him. "Do you think she's sexy?"

"Numbarh one!"

"Umm. What number am I?"
"What?"
"Don't you think I'm sexy?"
"Suah. But you keep it all to yourself."
"I guess you'd rather I just tossed it all around?"
"Naw, I didn't say that. But if you don't use it, it might fade away. You know, the law of evolution."
"Well," Ramsey pouted, "I plan to use it. And I bet I'll be just as sexy as that little Tahitian hotbox. But I'm going to save it all for my husband. I mean, really. He'll be the first and only man to have me, and he'll be getting something untouched. And I'm pretty damn sure that's the way he'll want me."
"I want you every way."
"You wouldn't want me—soiled. By other men."
"I'm in love with you and I want to marry you. What you did with other men before you met me is no concern of mine."
"That's what you say now. But if I were going to be your wife you wouldn't feel that way. You wouldn't want to know all about my other—affairs."
"I wouldn't want to know about them, no. But it wouldn't make any difference in my love for you."
"Yes it would. If I were like that—you know, free—you wouldn't really care for me. You'd use me, but you wouldn't truly care. You'd want a virgin. All men do."
"Yoah livin' in a dream world. Until I met you, I didn't think there were any virgins left. Look—sex is overrated, huh? Everyone alla time talkin' about it and readin' about it. People should quit talkin' about it and—"
"And do more of it, I suppose? Action speaks louder."
"Auwe—sex is almost a—how you say?—a fetish. Who says yoah not supposed to shack-up until yoah married?"
"God."
"Show me."
"And society."
"Society—auwe! Society is the biggest liar, the biggest lotta crap in the world. Figger it out," he said patiently. "If you was gonna hire an engineer, you wouldn't hire one without schoolin' and experience. Because he wouldn't be a good engineer. If you was gonna hire an architect, you wouldn't hire one without schoolin' and experience. Because without 'em, he wouldn't be a good archi-

tect. Everybody either goes to school or gets trainin' before they can do a job good. Everybody except women. A wahine, accordin' to society, is supposed to get married as a virgin, without trainin' or experience or nothin', and still do a good job. It don't make sense. Bein' a wife is the only job in the world where a wahine is supposed to start off without no practice or experience, and be perfect the first night. Auwe—maybe that's why we got so many divorces. Everything works moah bettah after a little experience, a little breakin'-in. Even my surfboard had to be broken-in a little before it was any good."

Ramsey twisted around to face him, her eyes bright with argument. "Listen, buster," she said, her face livid, "a man doesn't hire a wife. It's not exactly a 'job.' Some men treat it as a job, as some flunky hired hand, and maybe *that's* why we have so many unhappy marriages and divorces. So stop fiddling around with a lot of things you don't know about. Stop trying to kick the facts to Molokai. And as far as your surfboard is concerned, I noticed that you did all the breaking-in by yourself. No one else got to try it out!"

She sat back, pleased with herself and her reasoning. But Peter's eyes twinkled with mirth. "Okeh—yoah a numbarh one akamai wahine," he said. "No one else got to ride my surfboard and I did all the breakin'-in myself. But I'll tell you one thing, for suah, you smug akamai little wahine: I rode plenty of waves in on that surfboard, trying it out—*before* I bought it."

"Humph," Ramsey muttered, coolly unimpressed. "If you were a little smarter, a little more discerning, you wouldn't have had to try it out. You could tell just by looking at it that it was a damn good board."

Peter slumped back against the koa log. "Auwe." He shrugged. "I can't top you."

"Because I make sense."

"In a kine of illogical female way."

"You're just mad because I'm right. Anyway," she added, "I don't want to spend the whole night talking about sex."

"I thought we were talkin' about surfboards."

"You know damn well what we were talking about. Sex."

"Well," he said easily, "we might just as well talk about it, since it don't look like we'll evah get around to doin' anything about it—"

"Okay, let's drop it. I'm having too nice a time to argue."

"Okeh, we'll drop it. No hu-hu."

They gave each other a big chunk of silence to mull over until finally, Ramsey said, "Is that why they went up to the cove?"

"Is what why who went up to the cove?"

"You know perfectly well what I'm talking about. And I'll bet Bobby was trying to talk you into going with them."

"With who?"

"With Bobby and Blackout and the rest. Those girls. That belly-dancing sexpot."

"I thought we weren't gonna talk about sex?"

"I just asked you a civil question. You needn't get snippy about it."

"Now wait a minute—who's gettin' snippy?"

"Well—were you?"

"Was I what?"

"Supposed to go with that sexpot?"

"Auwe," Peter groaned. He pulled her close to him. "No," he said, kissing her nose. "I was supposed to stay right here with this sexpot."

"Oh damn you, I love you."

He settled her back against his chest, one arm around her, and he reached for his ukulele. He strummed a sentimental ballad, his fingers moving with a surprising dexterity across the strings.

"Play a love song," she murmured.

"That's the only kine of song there is." He started playing "Ka-lua." "Incidentally," he grinned, "before I bought this ukulele, the man let me try it out."

"Oh hush."

He laughed. "I couldn't resist that."

"Ukulele," she murmured, listening to the sound of the word. "That's another of those funny-sounding Hawaiian names."

"It means 'jumping louse,' but it's not Hawaiian. It's really an old Portuguese instrument. The old Hawaiians had something like it. A funny-lookin' deal made out of ulei wood, a piece about a foot and a half long and half a foot wide, strung across with gut. They'd hold it in their teeth and sweep the gut with straw. Lovers would whisper through their teeth, and the tuneful wood vibrated their voices so they'd carry through the night to their wahines."

Ramsey smiled up at him. "What did they whisper?"

"I love you. Aloha."

She closed her eyes. "Hawaii is so wonderful," she sighed. "Aloha . . . say it loud, and it sounds like a band playing; say it soft and it's almost like a prayer. All the other peoples in the world greet each other so coldly and impersonally, like 'Good morning,' or 'How are you?' Only in Hawaii do they greet each other with Aloha—love, I love you, my love to you. Aloha . . . It's wonderful!"

"You're wonderful," Peter said. And he could feel a wild warm rocket burst in his heart. I've got to figure something out, he thought. I don't want to turn around when I'm fifty or fifty-five and be like Whalebone Charley or Long Blue Brown. The beachboy life isn't enough for me; isn't enough for her. I've got to figure out something to do with myself, so I can offer her something worth while.

"Hey you," she said quietly. "Alo-ha," and she lifted her face and kissed his lips.

Paul had slipped off by himself. There are moments, he considered, when a man just has to be by himself, because he can just about see his dream coming true and a rich sweet scream tries to explode from his throat and the only thing to do is to go off somewhere alone and savor the moment as it hums, sings and glitters inside him. He leaned back against one of the rowboats, his feet stretched out in front of him, his toes wrestling the sun-bleached weeds. He flipped the small alligator box in his hands several times. He studied the box curiously, then opened it. The rings winked at him from their bed of dark blue velvet. They were a matched pair in white gold, the wedding ring plain, the engagement ring set with a large rose-cut diamond. He grinned at them, turning the box so that the diamond caught the last rays of the sun and blazed like a match.

"They're beauties."

Surprised at the voice, he looked around and saw Dean. "They're unpaid-for beauties. You think she'll like 'em?"

"I know she will." Dean straddled the rowboat and handed Paul a beer. *"Mahalo nui."*

"Like Maw says, all you need to get married is the down payment on the ring and ten bucks for the preacher."

"Plus a girl and a lotta love."

"I got that. I'm workin' on a plan to raise the ten bucks." Paul grinned, "You know, Dean, I got a feelin' there's a miracle due, comin' to me."

"Sloan's the miracle."

"Yeah. I guess I'm the luckiest guy in the whole wide mother-lovin' world."

"It's good you feel that way. Take care of that luck. Cause when luck goes, everything else goes with it. You are the luckiest guy in the world, gettin' a girl like Sloan."

Paul drank his beer quietly and looked up at the sky. The sun was gone now and the first colors of evening came into pale existence over the sea.

"What are you gonna do for Sloan?" Dean said mildly. "I don't want to butt in, but I was curious just what kind of plans you had."

"I'll do my best for her, so she'll be happy." Paul looked seriously at his older brother. "Our weddin' plans came as a surprise to you, like they did to everyone else. But you know, Dean, all along, evah since I was a little kid, I knew someday I'd marry Sloan. Don't worry, sport, I won't let her down. Here," he said, reaching into the fold of his lava-lava and handing Dean a thick envelope. "Read this."

It was a contract from the San Francisco Forty-Niners offering him a salary of ten thousand dollars a year plus a three-thousand-dollar bonus for signing.

"Man, you can buy a lotta poi with this," Dean said.

"And I would have gotten more later on," Paul said. "We suah could use that kind of dough, but Sloan wants to stay in Hawaii. She doesn't want to live in San Fran."

"What are you gonna do?"

Paul took the letter back and solemnly tore it up. "I had a talk with Moose Pawaiki. He offered me a job as backfield coach at Kamehameha. It won't be even half as much dough, but we'll be livin' in Hawaii. And, as Sloan said, I'll be comin' home every night and she won't have to worry about my gettin' all busted up playin' pro ball."

Dean's face was passive. Paul stood up and put his arm around his shoulder. "C'mon, sport, I know what you're thinkin'. You're wonderin' how a waste-time Kanaka boy like me can sweep the prize of the Islands and make her happy, huh? Well, you bet on me, sport. I might not be able to make anything too valuable out of my life, like a doctor or something like that. I've got plenty of enthusiasm, I just haven't got a cause; no real dedication, like you have. So the best I can do is get along, have fun, and make a buck with the least possible fuss."

"But you should have some ambition for Sloan's sake."

"Ambition? Hell—I've gotten along without it for twenty-two years. I don't see why I need it now. Ambition is okeh, so is work okeh, as a way to kill time. But it's a hell of a way to make a livin'," Paul grinned. "Look, sport—maybe I'm talkin' like there's a hurdy-gurdy clown in my head, but for the first time, Sloan and I got smooth sailing. The opposition to our marriage has petered out. Even old flint-face seems resigned to it. All my life, up until now, I've been waitin' for things to happen; now they're happening. Lovin' Sloan makes me love everybody and everything."

Dean grinned at him. "You're suah a lucky guy."

"Suah, love's a little bit of luck. But you can't wait to find luck. You gotta go out and get it and tear it out of God's hands."

They drank their beer silently. Then Paul glanced up at his brother and there was an odd flat quality to his voice. "Dean, what do you really, deep down, think of our gettin' married?"

Dean stared at his brother with frank surprise. There was a dividing line between them, a certain indifference. They had always been comrades, but they had never been close. They had gone their separate ways with a strong measure of aloofness. They had never confided in each other and never sought each other's advice. Dean had always considered himself to be the one at fault. He was the oldest, the one to give counsel, but he had never been able to penetrate Paul's cocksure, glib, devil-may-care attitude. Dean came to the conclusion that Paul was the happy animal Hawaiian, sensitive, kind, lazy, openhearted, and full of warmth and song—but without a single idea in his head. Now he realized that there was a probing going on inside Paul, a sensitively objective rationalization of what would soon take place. But Dean would not enter into it. To act as a catalyst or a mental irritant is not something to be lightly assumed. To probe other persons, to stir them into examining their own deeds, to plug them into an introspective current and introduce them to self-doubt, is too great a responsibility.

"C'mon, sport." Paul grinned. "You've always been able to level with me. Give it to me straight."

"No, that's just it. We've nevah leveled with each other. Not about important things. We've nevah even talked seriously before."

"Well, we nevah had anything real serious to talk about before."

"Didn't we?"

Paul cocked his head, his eyes puzzled, as though he were listening to a distant sound he could not identify. In a way, Dean thought, he looked like a man who was acquiring his first true awareness of his own responsibility.

"Okeh—have it your way," Paul said. "Maybe I don't talk serious alla time. But I'm serious about this, Dean. You've always been a good guy with your head. You could always think deep and come up with the right answer. What do you think about us?"

Dean finished his beer and stared solemnly into the empty can, as if to see the answer written on the bottom. At last he said, "Sloan is a great girl. Most wonderful girl I've evah known."

"Best girl in the whole world, huh? And me—I'm the luckiest guy in the world."

"You oughta stop and figger out just how lucky you are."

"I have, sport. Really. That's why I'm so happy. You think it's a good thing then, huh? Our gettin' married?"

"I think it's the best thing that could evah happen to you."

"How about Sloan? You think it's good for her?"

Dean clamped down hard on his teeth, the ridge of muscle switching in his jaw. "Yeah, I think it's good for her. I think yoah both doin' the right thing. You'll be good for each other. You've got to make it work out that way. Be good to each other and treat each other kindly, and it will work out. Promise me one thing, Paul." Dean turned to face his brother and there was a heaviness in his eyes, a stain of autumn. "Promise me you'll take good care of Sloan."

"I will," Paul said seriously.

"Don't evah break that promise."

"I won't, Dean."

Watching his brother rejoin the party, Dean felt oddly disorientated, as if he was almost a stranger at this house, among all these people he had known all his life. How could Paul have lived with the giddy dream that someday he would wed Sloan Howland when to Dean, the poignant futility of the very same dream had haunted his life? He had chased the dream away with a feeling of shame.

He walked to the edge of the beach and waded into the warm water. He speared the luau torches into the wet sand, spacing them ten yards from each other along the curve of the beach. Then he lit a match to the last torch and watched as it flared brilliantly against the warm purple dusk. He listened to the strumming of a steel guitar and several ukuleles; then the sound of the drums, the moonharp, and the bamboo flutes. And from the lanai, his mother's clear lovely voice rose in the night:

"This is the night of love,
The shining hour of Kalua . . ."

The rich voices of the men blended with hers:

"Who will her lover be?
O nei a ka po?"

And his mother's voice again, like a stringed instrument, with falls and slurs that were pure and incredibly musical and human:

"Before the night is old
Some arms will hold Kalua;
And now the tradewinds blow, soft and low,
Her love will blossom bright in the night,
And stars will sing above
The love song of Ka-lu-a."

The moment gripped Dean with an almost intolerable beauty, a sense of loveliness and loss, of somehow balancing joy in his hands but never grasping it; and when he looked into the darkening water, he saw, next to the reflection of the torchlight, not his own face, but the face of Sloan Howland, a weak and irregular remembrance in the sloughing tide, but very much her face, always hers, and his brain filled once more with the thousand promises of her unattainable loveliness.

All the bright days by the sea with the gulls flashing white against the turning sky were Sloan Howland; and all the nights when they swam naked beneath the high sweet stars, and the lazy afternoons when they drifted in the yawl far out along Kailua

Bay while the sails hung limp in the windless air and the sea was a sheet of coppery glass, the sun blazing down on it like a cane fire from the western horizon, those too were Sloan Howland. That summer had been Sloan Howland. She was the secret, furious joy in his throat. She was the sharp, quick pain of unfulfillment. The stories started about her that summer, as she rode like a wild queen across ranchland where before no woman rode, the new stallion creamed with sweat, responding like a bronze explosion to the flick of her spurs while old Willard roared ceaseless curses after her and the paniolos stopped their work and eyed her with frank speculation.

"Damn fool girl's going to bring trouble down on our heads, galloping across here like a bitch in heat," old Willard muttered. "Soon'll have every sonofabitch ranch hand between here and Parker's riding trail after her.

"Dean," he said, "go out and bring that crazy daughter of mine back before she breaks her goddamned neck and the stud's too."

Dean loped his pony a mile behind her, following the dust of the stallion's sabering hoofs. When the afternoon showers broke over Mauna Loa she turned and rode through a dark forest of pine and he trailed her down to Kapela Falls. The rain stopped and when he rode into the clearing the sun poured down from a washed sky making steam rise from the rocks, and the pool glistened like a slab of jade. He did not see her at first, but as his eyes followed the graceful arc of the waterfall he spotted her lying on one of the ferny boulders near the falls, grinning down at him.

"If it isn't Sherlock Holmes." She had to shout to be heard above the roar of the cascades.

"Can I join you?"

"Be my guest. Although I must admit I'd feel more complimented if you followed me down here on your own accord instead of at my father's bidding."

He dismounted and crawled over the rocks and sat down beside her. She wore a bikini suit improvised from two bright red bandanas. There was a knot between her full, rising breasts, and a knot at each side below where her waist curved out to form the line of her hip. The taut red fabric bisected the satin flatness of her stomach. She was all of a piece, flawless and tightly curved, a perfect even shade of light copper, and the texture of her was like cream. Her hair was swept up from her temples and he could see the sweet little beads of perspiration nestling there. He felt a stir of blood as he looked at the curve of her throat, the dusky separation of her breasts, the slow, even lift of her breathing. She was lying on her back, her oiled body soaking in the sun. He watched a clear bead of perspiration river its way from between her breasts down along the velvety decline between the two columns of stomach muscle and slide into her navel. She was, he thought, just naked enough so that it was embarrassing to stare at her and impossible to look away.

"Do you approve?"

He laughed self-consciously. "I'm sorry. I didn't mean to stare."

"Don't be sorry. I like it. You've never stared at me like that before. Not even when we've gone swimming in the buff at night."

"That's kinda like playin'."

"Ooh?"

"This is—kinda different." He looked down at his hands. She slid her hand into his and pulled him close to her. "Why is it different, Dean?"

"I—I don't know. Look, Sloan, yoah father said—"

"Who cares what he said? I know what he's worried about."

"What?"

"This." Her fingers curled into his dark hair and she kissed him, pressing into him with a kind of tortured despair, thrusting her body insolently against his, her mouth wild and hungry on his. She stopped abruptly and stood up. "It's no different from the nighttime, Dean," she said. "Look."

Her fingers tugged at one of the bandana knots and the halter fell to the ground. Her face was calm and her smile measured but her clear gray-gold eyes were bright with excitement. Quite deliberately, she untied the knots at her hips and balled the bikini panties in her fist. "See?" She stood for a moment at the edge of the cliff, like an oiled bronze goddess, then she dove in a graceful arc into the lagoon.

The coursing of the blood in his ears was like the roar of the waterfall. He watched her race through the water, swimming very strong, as though she was deliberately tiring herself, deliberately trying to dull the shifting subtle torments of her body's demands. He stripped off his clothes and plunged in after her. She saw him coming and laughed. At the last moment, she dove deeply and swam half the length of the lagoon underwater, avoiding him. They made a game out of it for a few minutes. Then he caught her. His arms wound tightly about her. Their bodies locked together and he kissed her and they drifted underwater, turning slowly, his body like brown stone against hers, the water folding secretly and noiselessly above them. She could feel the long pull of his muscles as he held her and swam easily to the shore. He carried her in his arms through the shallows and set her down slowly against the sandbank, water whispering about their hips, and he was over her, his hands and mouth learning her body. At the first thrust of invasion, her fingernails raked across his shoulders, she made a crazy whimpering sound, and, as realization and shame exploded inside her, she twisted suddenly and summoning all her strength, kneed him away from her. They fought almost without sound. The water splashed about their writhing hips. Somewhere a jungle bird screeched. At the edge of the forest, the tethered pony cropped its teeth on fern. The stallion gleamed like burnished flame against the dark trees, his eyes quietly and arrogantly sweeping across the struggling man and woman with regal disdain.

Dean pinned her wrists with one hand. His body was like a gigantic boulder on top of hers, pinning her hips against the sand. His breath came in savage bursts. His strength was frightening with its demand. He forced open her quaking thighs and again moved toward invasion. When she thought she could struggle no more she found that final surprising strength and rammed her knee into his groin. She freed her right hand and it found stone and with all her strength she smashed the stone into his skull. She hit him again and a third time, and she felt him go slack on top of her and her nails tore furiously through his flesh and when he slid off her she turned on him and beat her small fists into his chest until exhaustion dulled her fury and she slumped suddenly and put her head down against his chest and cried.

"I'm sorry, Sloan."

"No no, I'm the one who should be sorry. It was my fault. I'm such a bitch."

"Don't say that. Yoah everything in the world, Sloan. And I love you. I always have loved you."

"And I've always known it. God—I'm such a bitch for doing this to you."

He watched her walk down to the pool and slide into it, staying underwater a long time. She bobbed up to the surface, scooping water in her palms and washing her face. He joined her and she bathed the grainy sand from the gash in his cheek. They waded across the lagoon quite solemnly, like scolded children, and climbed back up to the rock by the falls.

"Don't get dressed, not yet, Dean. Come sit by me." She was sitting at the edge of the rock, her chin resting on her drawn-up knees, her fingers laced about her ankles.

"I don't know what's gotten into me," she said. "I feel restless all the time. Wild and hungry and savage. That's probably why I'm always on that stallion, galloping all over the place. I can feel all that muscle and heart and power and plain maleness beneath me, and I guess I respond to it. It's physical, I know, but it's something else too. It's as though there's a tiny evil inside me that's got to be fed or else be killed. I know I should kill it, but I don't want to, because there's a beautiful madness about it, an anticipation of fulfillment, of what it would be like to yield to it. I was a little crazy wanting unknown things."

"Are you a virgin, Sloan?"

"Yes." She grinned at him. "That's probably my real trouble. I guess I wanted you to rape me. Like a savage."

"I didn't want to rape you, Sloan. I'm in love with you. I wanted to make love to you."

"I know." She turned and her breast brushed his shoulder and he could see the muscles pull like silk ropes in her thighs. "I was unfair," she said. "I wanted excitement and you wanted love and I denied both. You're so damn kind and good and I'm such a bitch. I don't want to be bitchy; I don't want to cheat you, Dean." She leaned over and kissed him gently on the mouth. "Take me, Dean."

But the surge died inside him. He did not reach for her. She seemed a thousand miles away. "That wouldn't be love, Sloan," he said, standing up and pulling her to her feet. "Do you know what an affair like that would be founded on? Pity! We got sorry for each other."

"No, it wouldn't. It would be true. I want to give myself to you. All of me."

"With love?"

"Yes—with a certain kind of love. I love you, Dean. I'm—I'm not in love with you, but I love you."

"Thanks."

"Dean, don't—"

He held her shoulders tightly. "Sloan, could you evah fall in love with me? Completely?"

"I don't know." She shook her head. "I don't know, Dean, maybe I'm just a scatterbrained little bitch, but I'm pretty sure I'm already in love with someone."

"Who?"

"If I told you, you'd laugh."

"No I wouldn't. Who?"

"Paul," she said quietly. After a moment he released her and he stared dumbly as the white imprint of his fingers on her shoulders filled slowly back with color. He turned and started getting dressed. "How long has this been goin' on?"

"Nothing's been going on," she said. "It's just that for the past year our emotions have been on a joy ride. That's why Paul took that summer job on the Mainland instead of coming home. So we could be apart for a while and see how we felt."

"How do you feel?"

She waited until he turned to look into her eyes. "I'm in love with him, Dean." She reached up and kissed him. Then she dressed hurriedly and ran ahead of him into the forest, mounted, and galloped away.

Fallen needles matted the floor of the forest and he rode along soundlessly as smoke. Sloan Howland had offered herself to him and he had rejected her. Sloan Howland, who was everything in the world he dared not touch, dared not hope for.

That summer, Sloan Howland had brought to him his time of gold. She had brought a strange warmth like the slant of a sunray through a kona storm, and she had made all the colors loom brighter. Sloan Howland had been love, and she had changed from one beauty to a different beauty as a white mango blossom changes to the golden fruit, and at the close of the summer, before she returned to Stanford, he had told her of his plans to become a doctor, and it was almost as if he had concluded the search for his own identity and established himself—without her—in his sphere of reference in time and place and need. And as that summer faded, so did the dream of Sloan fade, and so did the sadness fade. He no longer had the feeling of being lost, of having lost out somehow, with only Sloan to point the way, only Sloan to find him, for he had understood, by that time, that while she could show him a place where he had never been, it was also a place that he could never reach.

As the memory of that summer faded, so did the face of Sloan Howland fade from the water as a wave sloshed gently into shore, and his mother's voice faded with the closing notes of "Kalua," and above the applause he heard Sloan's rich wonderful laughter —the kind of laughter that can only come from a woman in love. Then he turned toward the laughter and saw her on the lanai. Their glances locked for a moment before she waved to him.

He hurried toward her, and he knew again, as he watched her walk down the sand to meet him, that there was inside her too much for any one girl to contain, to hold: too much of life, too much of love, too much of maybe just glory, he was not sure; but he knew, looking at her, that the thrill inside him was a scream of thanks just for being alive and being Dean Kahana at that same moment with her in space and time, and he knew he would admit in the next moment and for all times thereafter, a vague despair because she was not his and he knew he would carry this sense of loss for the rest of his life, because for the rest of his life nothing less would do.

A soft darkness fell upon the Island. The luau torches flared brightly. Thin wisps of smoke curled up from the imu and the scents of the cooking pigs fanned out from under the scorched leaves, bringing a flood of water to everyone's mouth. The crowd separated, making an aisle of sand for Kapiolani Kahana, as she and Paul walked solemnly to the imu, chanting an old Hawaiian blessing. Kapiolani sprinkled the path with ti leaves. Paul carried a cornucopia shell filled with salmon-pink crystals of paakai, the fabulous rock salt. He sprinkled the imu area with the crystals. Behind them, the old men rattled feathered gourds and the girls beat bamboo shafts in rhythm to the chanting. When the sand was dug away from the imu and they cut away the canvas, smoke wooshed through the night carrying the sweet roasting scent of the meat. The banana leaves and ti leaves were scorched black and the skins of the pigs were steamed a crispy sizzling brown. Each pig was hoisted on to a papapuaa, a huge koa wood platter. Paul sliced off the ears and tails as the ritual came to an end.

"Hea—kaukau!" Peter yelled.

"Haiaena hau!"

The guests sat cross-legged in the sand, or on woven mats of pandanus. Two large boards had been placed side by side along the shore as tables. Sloan, wearing the palest of blue silk pareus and a lei of white rose, sat next to Paul at the center of the table. Willard and Kapiolani sat across from them. Willard leaned across the table and held his daughter's hands. "Looking at you now, I'm ashamed of what I said before," he whispered. "Since you love him so much that he means all this happiness to you, the marriage won't hurt me. I'll be happy for you. And I'm sure your mother would be too."

"*Kamau,* Senatah!" Paul toasted.

Willard raised his glass. *"Kamau."*

Ramsey took her place next to Paul, and Peter Noa wedged his bulk in alongside her. "Now you'll eat real luau food."

"It smells fabulous," she laughed. *"Lu-aww!"*

"The word means 'leaf of the taro.' " Peter explained.

The table was covered with tapa cloth and layers of fern and ti leaves. Jacaranda and shell ginger vines laced about the table. Floral displays of orchid and plumeria sprays wound about bird-of-paradise were spaced at intervals along the table. At each setting was a red hibiscus, the official flower of Hawaii.

The center of the table was piled with fruit: tender, milk-filled coconuts, sweet-meated papayas, avocados from Hana Maui, malala peels of raw sugar cane, slices of watermelon, Isabella grapes bunched in high glossy clusters, mangoes, alligator pears, juicy rose-colored guavas, wild bananas and halakahiki—standing pineapples which appeared whole and uncut but which had been hollowed, corded and cut into long spears and reassembled with the top as a lid. Long slivers of wood had been stuck into the tops of the pineapples, and on these were speared the pupu—Hawaiian hors d'oeuvres—including succulent pieces of marianated Terayaki steak, raw mullet cut in tempting cubes and dusted with paakai salt, chunks of tiny parboiled lobsters fresh out of Kalama Bay, small alemihi crabs with their shells pierced so that the sweet meat could be filled with coconut pudding.

While the men quartered and sliced the three pigs, the young girls brought to the table big calabash bowls of jumbo shrimp, sushi and saimin, and relish bowls of ake raw liver mixed with chili peppers, kukui nuts crushed and baked with paakai salt, and limu, strips of dried kelp and opihi seaweed. On koa wood platters the girls brought marinated slices of moray eel, and pinkish tidbits of barbecued squid tentacles, and stewed fern stalks served hot and covered with a melted butter and honey sauce and tasting something like asparagus. Coconut half shells filled with Chinese crackseed and roasted macadamia nuts supplanted the pupu. For liquid refreshments there was pineapple juice, chilled and poured into hollowed husks, guava juice, coconut milk straight from the shell, and beer, whisky, okolehao, and Mai Tai, a heady mixture of rums sipped with straws from pineapple husks.

As the pupu was being devoured, the girls brought in platters of lomilomi—fresh raw king salmon mixed with chopped onions and tomatoes and minced with the fingers; moa—tender white meat of chicken mixed with the Hawaiian spinach called taro roots and coconut cream and served in coconut half shells; boned chicken baked in coconut shells with wild rice and pineapple and served in koa wood calabashes floated with mint-flavored spun sugar; breadfruit roasted over kiawe coals so a crust formed about the succulent inner meat; thick rare slices of pipioma roast beef; heikaukau rock crab with tartar sauce sprinkled with paakai salt, and the all-inclusive welakaukau Hawaiian hot stew.

There was fried butterfish with garlic sauce, i-a paakai salt fish, uahi smoked fish, maloo dried fish, slabs of the wonderfully fresh ahi tuna, boneless chunks of ono which is something like swordfish but tastier, kawelea fish, barracuda, barbecued black sea bass, and finally, as it was taken from the imu and the scorched leaves unwrapped from it, the sizzling lime-white mahimahi dolphin, the most glorious-tasting fish in the sea.

It took six men to carry the three platters of puaa kalua pigs to the table, the meat still steaming, the pink-scrubbed skin turned a crispy brown, the platters surrounded by the yams and wild bananas that had been cooked with the meat for the last five hours in the underground oven.

At every place there was a large goblet carved from a coconut shell that had been thinned and polished and scalloped around the brim, and in the goblet was a quart of that most mystifying of food, the mainstay of the Hawaiian luau—poi.

Ramsey watched those around her dip two fingers into the bowls, twirl a little poi about their fingers, and scoop it into their mouths. Without much enthusiasm, she tried it.

"Uugh!" She made a disagreeable face and pushed the bowl of

pinkish-gray paste away from her. "I've tried and tried to like it, but I can't. It's like eating paste."

"You gotta develop a taste for it," Peter said. "It's numbarh one pink Kona poi."

"What's it made out of, glue?"

"Naw, it's the staple food all through Polynesia. Now it's made in poi factories, but in the old days the natives would take the tuber of the taro plant, wrap it in leaves and roast it on hot rocks. Then they pounded it with stones until the root broke up and then they massaged it with their hands—you know, a lomilomi. When it became pasty, like clay, they diluted it with water or coconut milk and rock salt. It's verra good for you."

"Why does everything that's good for you have to taste so flat? Like fermented starch."

"Don't eat it by itself. Eat it this way," Peter said, dipping into the poi and getting a twist of it wrapped like taffy about his fingers and conveying it into his mouth. He followed it quickly with a pinch of salmon and a slice of kalua pig and chewed it all together, smacking his lips and grinning at her when he had finished. "C'mon, try it!"

Hesitantly, she dipped a finger into the bowl. "One finger?" she asked suspiciously.

"Suah. This is thick one-finger poi. Two-finger poi is thinner."

"Ye gods, three-finger poi must be like soup."

"A real Hawaiian likes to push his whole fist into the bowl and get a numbarh one scoopful!"

She managed to twist a little on her forefinger and suck it off. She followed it with a big piece of meat. "Uh-uh," she said. "Still no sale."

Peter grinned, handing her a coconut shell filled with kava. "Here, wash it down."

Ramsey sipped the kava, coughed, but managed to swallow it. "My God, what's that stuff?"

"Kava. It's the traditional Polynesian drink."

"It tastes almost as bad as the poi."

"It's made the same way, crushing taro roots to powder, then mixing it with other crushed roots and adding water."

"I'm not cut out to be a Polynesian," she said. "Can you get drunk on it?"

"Auwe—drink a little moah and see."

"No thanks. No more mud water," she said, reaching for a shell of pure coconut milk.

A group of beachboys started working over the sharkskin drums with their hands, elbows and knees until a soft thunder filled the air. Bobby Villanueva seized an old guitar and, sweeping the strings masterfully with the back of his hand, started singing a wanton Tahitian melody, repeating each phrase in a fainting, tremulous falsetto as Paul and two other young men joined him on the chorus. A row of girls danced into the clearing, their bamboo shafts keeping rhythm with the simple two-beat melody. Soon they were joined by men dancers, the group swaying and undulating like mad sweet nymphs and fauns, their bronze limbs catching the flicker of firelight, their shoulders garlanded with flowers, the girls telling the story with the movements of their hands, while from the throats of the men came an old barbaric chant that had never seen the printed page. Then the dancing and the music ended, and only the drumming continued, becoming louder and more savage.

A wild scream pierced the night. As Ramsey turned, she caught a glimpse of the Tahitian girl she had seen earlier on the beach, racing toward the table.

"It's that shimmy-dancer!"

"This is no shimmy-dancin'," Peter said. "This is the real thing."

The girl leaped upon the table like a wild thing possessed. She danced with a surging, wanton, barbaric splendor; her undulations were flashes of tremendous mad music, coarse yet violently beautiful. She was a hard young animal, dark as mahogany, her teeth flashing in her face, her lips Burgundy red. Her breasts were sharp against the brief halter, her hips rocking suggestively beneath the swirl of grass skirt. She stood braced in the center of the table, her arms extended, her eyes half shut, a film of sweat glistening on her quivering thighs. Her mouth twisted, and as the rich flood of drumming rushed like a fluid through her nerves she started working with unbridled fury, twisting and contorting her body with an astonishing rhythm, almost as if she were in a spasm, except that the smooth muscles bunching and trembling through her torso were always under complete control. When the drumming reached its wildest pitch, a male dancer joined her, wielding his Samoan sword in a flashing arc about her. They danced together with an evil pride, with a lithe yet savagely powerful grace, a sheen of sweat rivering down the columns of their bare backs. As the arc of the sword closed in on her, she threw her head back, her eyes squeezed tight against the sword, against the surging drums, her face corroded with passion. Her spread palms brushed upward along the satin hardness of her thighs, then moved with obvious sexual eagerness across the intricate curves of her body until they cupped her own rigid breasts, and something inside her was making a screaming animal sound as the knife dancer lifted her to his shoulders and carried her away.

Ramsey's breath exploded as the cheering started.

"Wow, was that terrific! Who was that guy?"

"Auwe—I mighta known you'd be watchin' the guy. That was Bobby Villanueva. See?"

She hadn't recognized him while he was dancing, but now, as he and the girl bowed to the applause, she looked at him with awe. "I had no idea he could be so violently savage," she said.

"Aw, he's okeh. But you should really see me do my dance."

Peter disappeared for a moment, then he burst through the crowd and leaped into the center of the table. There was a roar of laughter. Somehow, he had obtained a yellow and red muumuu from one of the fatter women and slipped it tentlike over his lava-lava. Long Blue Brown tossed him two coconuts, and these he fixed into the bodice of the muumuu and wiggled them around like the breasts of an improbably gross wahine. Blue then handed him a flaming red T-shirt, and he shimmied this to and fro along his backside as he started a riotously burlesqued hula, some of the boys joining him with ukuleles as he sang in a raspy voice:

"Princess Papule got plenty papaya
She love to give it away,
All of the beachboys they say,
Oh me-a, oh my-a
You really oughta try-a
A piece of the Princess Papule's papaya . . ."

Ward Akana laughed heartily at Peter's antics. He realized, with not a little surprise, just how much he was enjoying himself. It's been a long time between parties, he thought. It's been a hell of a long time since he and Tani had kicked their heels at a real go-to-hell fun-time party. Fun equals luxury equals time to waste.

Why couldn't he manage to find some time somewhere, and sit around and watch it go by? Why couldn't he take just an afternoon and lie on some hillside the way he did when he was a boy and watch the clouds change shape as they drifted across the sky? When a man can't find the time to look at clouds, then something's wrong.

"That's a pretty profound chunk of silence you're working over, pal," Tani said.

"I've been wondering why I can't just sit down and watch clouds roll by."

"Because it's dark out. And there aren't any clouds."

"Let me put it this way: I'm trying to figure out why I find myself putting in a tough sixteen-hour day at not too hot a wage so a lot of other people can put in a soft eight-hour day at a pretty damn good wage."

"Because that's the hand you dealt yourself. And I don't believe you'd have it any other way."

He pushed back from the table, leaning his elbows in the sand, his head back against Tani's shoulder. "I guess the luxury of wasting time belongs to the very young. Shaw was right. Youth is a wonderful thing."

"Ah-so. 'Tis pity honorable youth must be wasted on honorable young." She bent down and kissed his ear.

"Having a good time?" he asked.

"Ah-so. Honorable ichi ban wife having ichi ban good time."

He grinned at her with quick pleasure. "My God, you're as tight as a tick."

"Ah-so, number one wife tight as ticky." She bowed mockingly. "If pleases honorable husband, lowly wife like go home now, make lovey."

"Hush, woman. Someone'll hear you."

"Good," she bowed again, "then maybe they'll take me home make lovey."

He leaned up and kissed her throat. "No, only me."

"Number one husband lousy sport."

"No. Number one husband very akamai. Won't risk lowly wife to other men." He pulled her close to him and kissed her. "Have I told you lately how very much I love you?"

"I forget."

"I love you very much."

"Yes, you told me this morning. And last night. And the night before. And—"
"Okay, okay."
"Don't you remember? You tell me every night."
"Good. I didn't want you to think I took your love for granted."
"You can, truly. But I don't believe you ever would."
"Don't ever let me. The surest way to kill love is to take it for granted. Your love should be treasured."
She looked tenderly at him with her warm, slanted eyes. "I've wondered about you. You've been so quiet and lost in thought I was worried that you weren't having a good time."
"Just the opposite. I've been having such a good time that the party has kicked all that strike mess clear out of my thoughts. But it's made me think about us. How we haven't had a chance to have fun in such a long time."
"Don't be silly; and don't get gloomy on me. It's been wonderful. Twelve years of something wonderful."
"The lady is easily pleased." He grinned. "But seriously, there's been too much work and not enough of those lovely moments we used to have when we had time to dream."
"There's been a lot of work, sure. But it's the work that makes the dreams come true. With a little bit of luck," she added.
"Luck is for fools to believe in."
"No, luck is a very intangible but productive element. It's a very real thing. There's an old Hawaiian proverb that claims if you throw a lucky man into a tidal wave, he'll come up with a fish in his mouth."
"Proverbs are only so many homespun inanities," Ward said. "Only fools hope and wait for luck, while luck itself waits around for the hard-working man to come pick it up. Luck is nothing but a tricky name for hard work. The only good luck most great men have had was the ability and determination to overcome bad luck."
"I'm lucky," she said, kissing him. "I'm married to you."
It ended the discussion for a moment, then he turned to her and said, "Tani, it's just that I want to have more time for fun with you. Without you there's no purpose in anything I do. I stop at times and catch myself remembering all the days with you, and all the nights when we were young. It seems changed, somehow. It's like that cotton candy at the circus, all fluffy and wonderful and pink, and you take a few bites and suddenly it's all gone. With

too little of that sweet taste left on your tongue. The old days seemed so much more fun, somehow. Like tonight."

"We'll have time, darling."

He rested his arm on her leg and caressed her knee.

"When this goddamned strike mess is settled, we'll go away for a couple of weeks. Just the two of us. Alone. It's been a thousand years since we've been alone with each other. We'll park the kids with your mother and we'll get away from everything and spend all our time making love, and actually wasting the time in between, and then making love again. Maybe we'll go to Hana, or some place on Kauai," he added, listening to his own voice trail off and wondering if it would ever come true; if they would ever get a chance to go away by themselves and learn to dream again. The thought somehow made him feel like an old child. Someday, he promised himself, I'll repay her for all the goodness she's brought to me. Someday I'll give her what she deserves.

His thoughts were interrupted by the clamor of tin pails being crashed together. He looked up and saw Long Blue Brown bellowing for attention.

"Ladies and gennelmun, can we git yoah kokua ovah hear? How bout shuttin' up fer a minute, ladies and gennelmun, please?" Blue yelled. He looked around as the crowd quieted. "We got any gennelmun here? Yeah—I see one. And if dis ain't too disawkward a time, howzit we git Senadah Will Howland to yak a minute er two bout da kine campaign, huh?"

Blue led the applause himself, then quieted the crowd for the Senator.

"I don't think this is the right time or place for a political speech," Willard said.

"Dere ain't no right time for a political speech," roared Blue, "but you go on anyway, Senadah."

"Tell us about the strike!" someone yelled. "When will it be over?"

Willard stood up and looked around until he met Ward's hard glance, then he smiled at the crowd. "When the strike started a couple of weeks ago, I made a speech at Honolulu Stadium which pretty much covered my feelings about the situation. There's not much left to be said, except that we should all hope and pray that the strike will be over soon, settled by the good will of both factions.

"And I don't want to talk about the campaign either, because it's a partisan campaign, and what we in Hawaii seek should be above political parties. I want to talk about something else," he said.

"A couple of days ago, people in Hawaii and all over America were celebrating July fourth, Independence Day. I didn't celebrate it. While the firecrackers were exploding and the flags were waving and the military bands marched down Bishop Street, I asked myself just what kind of independence we had to celebrate?

"Are we in Hawaii independent? No, we are not. Can we in Hawaii celebrate the abolishment of what Patrick Henry termed the tyranny of taxation without representation? No, we cannot. Can we in Hawaii celebrate this Nation's claim of granting freedom and justice for all? No, we cannot. Can we in Hawaii celebrate this Nation's claim that all of its men are equal? No, we cannot, for this Nation has refused to grant us our equality!"

He leaned forward into the crowd, his shaggy mane spilling across his forehead, catching the pale red blaze of the torches. "No, I didn't celebrate July fourth. I was a little hurt, a little disappointed, and pretty damned mad.

"And I got to wondering how the Mainlanders, how the Government and Congress of the United States, could justifiably celebrate Independence Day throughout the land, knowing that the independence, liberty, equality and justice of six hundred thousand of its citizens had yet to be established! I got to wondering just how in the name of a righteous God the leaders of this Nation could hold their heads high, knowing in their hearts that they were denying to six hundred thousand citizens the very same goals for which that original Independence Day was fought!

"So . . . I tried to put myself in the Mainlander's boots. I tried to jump the fence and look at it from his point of view. For in the final analysis, despite all our parades and slogans and newspaper editorials and congressional pressuring, it will not be the people of Hawaii but the citizens of the Mainland and their Congressmen who will determine the fate of Hawaii as the fiftieth state. So the Mainlander is justified in asking:

" 'What is Hawaii like? It's all very nice that the people of Hawaii want to join us and become a state, but do we want them? What kind of people live in the Territory? Is the Big Five a monopoly group and the Union Communistic—or did we get that story wrong? How about the Chinese, and the Hawaiians, and the Portuguese and Filipinos and the Caucasians out there? Do they get along well together? And how about the Japanese who make up more than half the population—will they run the Territory? If Hawaii becomes a state, will there be a Japanese governor? What kind of Americans will all these peoples make? How will Hawaii's becoming a state benefit this Nation?'

"That's how the Mainlanders are figuring," Willard said, brushing a lock of hair from his forehead. "And with the grace of God and your votes, when I get to Washington this is what I'll tell them:

" 'The people of Hawaii are among the finest in the world, by any standard of civilized humanity you care to measure them. They want and deserve to move deeper into the American community. By admitting Hawaii to statehood, the United States would reaffirm before the entire world its great moral policy that all people deserve the highest degree of self-government for which they are prepared. It would reaffirm that policy especially insofar as Asia is concerned—Asia, headed for a position of unprecedented importance in world affairs, perhaps would look with more confidence toward American democracy once Hawaii with its vast Oriental background was accepted on a basis of full equality.

" 'The Senators and Representatives Hawaii would send to Washington would contribute substantially to Congress, particularly in handling of Pacific and Asiatic problems, and in dealing with all other races in general. For in the melting pot of Hawaii, more than any other land in the world, racial harmony has prevailed; and perhaps our representatives could bring this unique and special kind of talent to bear on national and international problems.

" 'No place or people stand still,' " old Willard said. " 'They move forward. Since annexation, the hope of Hawaii for equality has grown stronger as its population, industry, economy, and cultural and moral level have grown stronger. We have moved forward on our own. The time has come now for the rest of America to invite us to move forward as an equal, with full political participation in American affairs.

" 'Statehood is a matter of heart. We in Hawaii have demonstrated that we have the heart. It is for the Nation now to welcome that heart. I call upon this Nation, conceived in liberty and dedicated to the proposition that all men are created equal, to prove now that dedication!' "

The crowd started standing up and cheering, and old Willard's voice roared above it. " 'I call upon this Nation to abolish second-class citizenry and grant us our due equality—to send us our star! We don't claim we're better than anybody else,' " he roared above the cheering crowd, " 'but we'll be damned if we're not just as good!' "

"It's about what I expected it to be," Aaron said sourly, "a drunken brawl."

Laura looked at him with bemusement. "You're a fine one to talk about drunken brawls; a man who won't buy an aloha shirt unless he's sure that spilled gin won't run the colors."

"Very funny."

"Oh Aaron, don't lose your sense of humor. When that goes, everything goes."

"Okay, I'll keep my sense of humor and sit back and laugh while my sister throws her life away with that damned gook."

"Calling names won't help."

"It won't harm," he snapped at her. "Don't you understand? There's something screwy inside Sloan."

"She's young."

"Don't try to defend her, for God's sake! Sloan just doesn't give a good goddamn! She's in high gear racing toward a dead end and she refuses to see the light. I'm supposed to sit back and watch her destroy herself and the family name. Well, I can't do that," he said, feeling the inevitable anger coming on. "I've got to fight them, right down to the altar."

Laura studied his eyes, gauging the degree of his intoxication. His kind of drinking started with a gentle cocktail. Innocent enough, until the wrong word that always was said was said, and then, while the dull repetitive arguments droned on, the tempo of the drinking increased. Now he was at that point where the liquor blackened his emotions and honed his tensions to a slender edge.

"Aaron," she said, "I have one small forlorn little point, and I'd like to try once more and make it clear to you. I am not trying to defend Sloan. And I haven't implied that you should sit back and do nothing. I agree with you that the marriage isn't the best for Sloan. But I can't agree to condemning her for marrying a boy you and I don't approve of. It's their affair. With or without your approval they're going through with it. It's out of your hands and there's nothing you can do but accept it and wish them well. We should try to help them instead of trying to destroy what chances of happiness they might have. God knows, marriage is tough enough under normal conditions without having to face the problems that they'll face."

"And just what kind of a crack was that?"

Laura turned away. "Nothing," she said faintly. "Just don't let their marriage become an obsession with you. Don't destroy them."

"Why did you have to come out with that?"

"With what?" Laura said.

"That remark about my destroying them?"

Laura bit her lip. "I'm sorry. It was just an expression."

"You're lying. It was more than just an expression."

"Well—I don't know now just why I said it. Let's drop it. Let's have fun. We're at a party, remember?"

He looked at her accusingly. "Do you honestly believe that I destroy things?"

She turned away, staring out at the black sea. "It was nothing more than a slip of the tongue. Let's forget it, Aaron, please."

"I've asked you a question."

She still did not answer him.

"Goddamn it, I'd like to know!" he persisted.

She knew now that he would stay with it until she answered. He was always like that. Clever and bright and argumentatively opportunistic. If she made a slip during a discussion he'd pounce upon it, rolling the argument along like a snowball going downhill; a snowball that never stopped of its own accord and melted, but always smashed to pieces against something. Against herself, she thought, wondering, for the moment, why she always had to pick up the pieces, then lie in an effort to appease.

"Are you going to answer me? Or are you just going to sit there with that whimpering look on your face?"

Her mouth trembled and her pink tongue licked across the dryness of her lips. But she spoke evenly: "Yes, you do destroy things, Aaron. You have a talent for destruction." She stood up and started walking down the beach.

"Where are you going?"

She did not turn. "I don't know, Aaron. Just for a little walk."

"Why?"

He could see her back tremble. "I just want to get away for a minute," she whispered. "I want to get out from under your cloud of gloom."

He watched her disappear into the crowd. Beachboy gooks, old-timers and a couple of tourists, no one he could join. Why was it that he always had to make the effort to join a group? No one ever came to him. But there was no group he could truly join, anyway. What was he supposed to do, be a good-time Charlie and join Laura and Tani and Dean? They were probably laughing at him anyway. If he went over and joined them, he thought sourly, they'd probably split up and drift away. To hell with all of them.

He slumped down against the trunk of a palm tree and poured himself another drink. *You have a talent for destruction.* Stupid wife, stupid words. But they had hit him where it counted. He had heard them before, from Sloan, from the old man, even from Lei Villanueva, although she had cloaked them kindlier.

It had happened on an afternoon when he and Lei had driven up Nuuanu Avenue past the city streets and along the hilltop where the vast stone-faced mansions overlook the town like stoic dowagers peering out from their fans of fern and tangled hau and ivy climbers, and they had raced past upside-down falls, where after a rain, if the wind is strong enough, the falling water is blown back over the cliff, and they had parked at the pali lookout. From the lookout they could see one of the most spectacular views in the world—the emerald abyss of Windward Oahu, stretched out beneath its flanking cliffs across a varishaded plain of green past Kailua and Kaneohe to the shimmering wash of the sea. Over the pali's awful pitch a century ago King Kamehameha forced the warriors of Kalanikupule, then King of Oahu, and thus brought all the Islands into his reign. The skulls of the doomed warriors who had to leap to their deaths became souvenirs for strong climbers of succeeding generations, and, gazing down the steep gorge, Aaron remembered when he and Garth had climbed down past the ferny bower just below the highway where once Prince Kalanianaole had kept a hunting cabin, to retrieve one of those skulls. Beyond the pali the Koolaus rose in green majestic grandeur to form the valley, and far off, Aaron could make out Olomana Peak separating the Waimanalo and Maunawili ridges.

"What are you so deep in thought about?" Lei had asked.

"I'm contemplating jumping over."

"Oh, cut it out, things aren't that bad."

"They will be if you don't go through with the abortion."

Lei slipped her arms about him and hugged him. "Oh Aaron, you know I can't. This is a life inside me. This is a life that's part of you and part of me. Please don't ask me to destroy it, Aaron!"

Are certain people born to destroy? Or is it, he wondered, some dirty, bitter frustration in the bottom of my soul that swells up inside me, pouring across every decent niche of me, demanding the destruction of other people's dreams; seeking failure and unhappiness for others because of a morbid quirk that such failure would make my own lot seem more bearable? Destruction certainly prompted that idea of suicide when he was at the summit of Mauna Loa. His drinking was a symptom of self-destruction. Perhaps even his seeking for the subtle depravities, the almost degenerate lust of his affair with Lei Villanueva, was a form of destruction. Or was it the result of his being driven and harried by an almost unbearable consciousness of the passing of time and the delusion that there was only one fundamental way of making time stand still for a little while? In a country ruled by advertising slogans which claim youth is synonymous with happiness, proving that the hands of the clock can lie has become the grand obsession of a million men and women.

When he got to his feet, the beach was a tilting place. Reality came in weird blurred flashes. Where in hell was Laura? That was a shoddy thing for Laura to say, he thought. It was not true that he had a talent for destruction. It was not true that he destroyed things. He was merely involved somehow with things and people cast for destruction.

Nausea rolled up toward his throat. He closed his eyes and shook it away. A blinding, battering pain hammered inside his forehead. He pulled himself together and focused on a noisy group on the lanai. His father and Ward Akana seemed to be arguing about something. The goddamned old man thinks more of his bastard son than he does of me, Aaron thought. Ward Akana ought to be got rid of, the ingrate, the muckraking Commie sonofabitch.

As he started across the sand dune toward the lanai, someone deliberately blocked his way.

"Can I talk to you, Mistah Aaron?"

"Who are you?"

"Bobby. Bobby Villanueva. I want to talk to you about my sister."

Aaron scowled at him. "Get the hell outta my way!"

Bobby smashed his beer bottle against a tree. He wrapped his hand about the neck of it and jabbed the splintered edges into Aaron's stomach. "You and me are going to talk, Howland."

A star fell.

"Did you make a wish?" Sloan asked.

"I've got nothin' left to wish for. I've got you. I've got everything wonderful in the world."

"I made a wish," Sloan said. "I wished that we'd always be happy like this. I wished that we'd always remember that life is too short and love too strong not to be in each other's arms every moment, close, like we are now. And I wished that I'd grow to be everything you could ever want me to be."

"You are everything I want you to be," Paul said. "You're more than I evah dreamed could come to me. And it's almost midnight now, and we haven't kissed."

They had walked down the beach to a cove sheltered by sand dunes and a grove of guava trees. The breeze was soft and sweetened by the trees. She stirred in his arms, her face very young and sweet. Her lips brushed across his face, his eyes, his throat, with warm, fluttering kisses.

"I want this to last forever," she said, her voice faint as a whisper. "Is that silly of me? Is that naïve? Tell me that lasting love isn't a myth."

"We'll prove it isn't a myth."

"And I'll try so hard to be all you want me to be. I'll be tender when you want me to be tender and I'll be wild when you want me to be wild, and I'll love you both ways—by God, I'll be loving when you want me loving."

"Sloan, no guy has evah been happier than I am this moment. I just want to lie here with you in my arms and listen to your heart beat next to mine and freeze time, so we're like this forevah. I'll wait on you and bring you happiness and love you all the days of my life."

"And I'll help you."

"Yes—help me because I'll need your help."

"It *will* last forever, Paul. This is the most wonderful love of all and we'll help each other so we can keep it all our lives."

He kissed her nose. "This bein' in love is great! Everybody smiles at you and says nice things and you're happy all the time and pretty soon you start believin' that you're a specially wonderful guy."

"You are. We'll be wonderful together. We'll take our love to a secret place where the years won't be able to get at it; where the years won't be able to get at either of us."

"Because we'll be part of each other. We are now."

"Whatever you do, I'm going to be part of it. Oh God, Paul, do you realize that we're free? That there's nobody standing in our way? Has it actually dawned on you yet that nobody's going to stop our getting married? Not Daddy, or Kapiolani, or—anybody! We're free, Paul! We can hold each other and kiss each other and say I love you to each other in front of everyone; in front of the whole world; in front of all the zillion stars!" She took his hand and placed it against her heart. "Can you feel it beat? Like it's getting ready to explode out of my chest and go into orbit. Man—my heart's in orbit!"

And, she thought, it needn't ever stop spinning. Love had come to her and it deepened her emotional scale: love that was a mixture of need and timing and the right person and luck—a giddy, elusive formula. She could not convince herself that such love came to other people. No, most people settled for a compromise without ever finding the formula. They rode the pink horses of the carousel and hummed along with the nostalgic pipings of the calliope, but they dared not grab for the golden ring. She had, and she would hold on to it.

There was a time when she did not think she would be able to hold on. During those first few weeks after she had returned home, while everyone was taking turns trying to prove to her what a great damn fool she was, a voice inside her kept warning her to cherish as much of the love as she could, for it soon would be ripped apart. Those nights when she knew Paul would be coming to her she would ready herself for bed with great haste, wanting to hold to her mood of glowing passion. Yet when in bed, in the darkness, waiting, all the carefully compartmented nagging fear would start eating away at her heart.

But then he would come and the fear took wings. He would sneak into the big Manoa Valley house through the kitchen door, ease up the long flight of stairs and into her room, and they would embrace with all the heat and heart and courage of their need. With him she felt warm and good and oddly virginal, full of sweet stupor. And during the eternal seconds, she realized with a sense of miracle that each time could be better than the last. Afterwards, as they lay side by side in the dark room, murmuring the sounds of love, her eyes would sting as she remembered with her shy, gentle fury all those who were trying to stop her. Selfish, self-righteous and utterly stupid people. Always pushing at you, they constantly tried to impress you with their shallow inanities and tell you how to live your life, while their own tight little lost lives moved toward their own tight little lost tragedies.

"You on cloud nine?"

"No." She grinned. "I was just thinking how we could have lost each other if we weren't the kind of people we are. If we didn't fight city hall and all the red tape they tried to wrap us in."

"You were the one who did our fightin' for us. It was your family—"

"I know. And family quarrels are such terribly bitter things. They don't go according to any rules. They're not like a broken bone that can be mended—they're more like a skin burn that won't heal because there's not enough to go around, so grafting must be done and the skin is left permanently scarred."

"Look." He pointed. Behind them, in the grove of trees, night-blooming cereus opened, their petals glowing milky white against the trees. "Now look back," he said. And he had opened the box and she could see the soft gleam of the rings in their velvet bed.

"Oh Paul . . ."

"Here." He slipped the engagement ring on her finger and she held it up so the diamond winked.

"Oh Paul, it's so beautiful." She sobbed softly in his arms and ducked her face into the hollow of his shoulder. "I don't mean to cry," she murmured. "It's so damned corny. And it would sound even cornier if I told you that I was crying because I'm so happy."

He kissed the smooth gloss of her hair. "Here," he said, bringing her chin up to his. "Don't take your sweet face from me."

"I love you so much, Paul."

"C'mon, slip on the wedding ring. See how it looks." He took her finger and moved the plain gold band along its length, setting it next to the engagement ring.

"But isn't that supposed to be bad luck?" Sloan asked, withdrawing her finger. "I mean, trying on the wedding ring before—"

"Auwe—how can you and I have bad luck? Look!"

The matched rings curled together and gleamed in the night. "Paul, I—"

He gathered her in his arms. "I love you, Sloan. You are love. Love is your face and your body and your wonderful heart and the way you're lookin' at me now, and love is your touch, and love is the way you wear those rings."

They kissed quietly and he could taste the salt on her lips. After a moment she slipped the wedding band from her finger and handed it to him and he placed it back in the box. "Let's not tempt bad luck," she said, smiling, fanning her left hand in front of her so she could contemplate the engagement ring. "Yep," she grinned, "it's just what I've always wanted."

"And it's just what I always wanted to give you." He swept her up in his arms and spun around with her and just as he was going to kiss her, Peter Noa appeared on the rise of the sand dune and called to him.

"Hea, Paul—I been lookin' all over hell for you!"

"I've been right here in heaven."

"There's a little trouble. C'mon!"

The fights flared up in rapid succession, first in one section of the crowd, then in another. A holler of pain came from the lahala grove by the house. In the next instant, out from the grove raced King Mud Akapai, a tall, ropy-muscled young beachboy. His hands were at his face, trying to stop the flow of blood from his nose. As he ran, he ducked a flurry of beer cans and coconuts thrown at him in a black fury by the Tahitian dancing girl. Her halter had been torn from her shoulder, exposing one breast. She raced after him, spewing out a stream of curses. Blackout Kekai stumbled out of the grove after them, doubled-up in pain, his hands supporting his groin. Rabbit Kealoha saw them and exploded with laughter.

"I warned you, Mud," he called out. "Dat's why dey call her de iron virgin!"

In his bumbling eagerness to get away from her, King Mud leaped over the outrigger canoe—almost. His foot caught on the gunwhale and he fell heavily to the ground.

"Hea—you crazy wahine, please, please! Ah jes losted my—"

The girl had taken the paddle from the canoe and bashed away at him, swinging the paddle like a baseball bat. When the paddle split in two across his shoulder, she straddled him, pummeling the back of his head with the broken half.

"Here, baby." Rabbit handed her another paddle. He was still in stitches over the scene. "Bust 'im wit dis."

But all men had become one to her. She grabbed the paddle from Rabbit's hands, and with one tremendous swing, clouted Rabbit on the side of the head. He slumped down on the beach next to King Mud, and the girl looked about savagely for her next opponent. But it was difficult to locate anybody free. Most of the beachboys were busy in various brawls along the beach. She gripped the paddle tightly in her fists and waded into the brawl nearest her.

From the lanai, Willard Howland scowled down at the scene. "Hawaii—land of the morning calm, the afternoon shower, the evening tranquillity," he muttered. "I'm going."

Tani Akana cocked her head, listening to the singular whir of police sirens as the patrol cars started out from the Nanakuli station. She tugged at Ward's sleeve. "We'd better go, too."

But Ward was smiling broadly down at the melee. "Go? I haven't seen anything like this since Kamehameha upset Iolani High for the championship!" He trotted down the steps with a vividness that Tani had not seen in him for years, and moved down along the beach, circling about the different brawls.

"Oh my God!" Sloan screamed. "Stop them!"

Paul raced across the beach and threw a flying tackle into Bobby Villanueva. He wrestled him down, pinning his arm and forcing him to drop the jagged-edged bottle.

"For Christ's sake, Bobby! You wanna be back behind bars for good?"

"I'm gonna kill the sonofabitch!" Bobby hissed between clenched teeth.

Peter Noa, Whalebone Charley and Long Blue Brown stepped in front of Aaron and stopped him from going after Bobby. Bobby had caught him with the bottle at least once, and there was a scrape of blood along Aaron's shoulder.

Bobby got to his feet, but Paul kept his arms pinned.

"He tried to kill me!" Aaron swore, trying to push his way through the three men blocking him. "That goddamn gook kid tried to shiv me—"

"And I'm gonna! I'm gonna finish the job!" Bobby yelled back at him.

Peter had to help Paul holding Bobby back. The sirens screamed louder as the patrol cars neared the beach.

"C'mon, Bobby, cool off," Paul said. "Cops."

"You'd moah bettah get outta here, Bobby."

Paul released him.

"I'll catch up with you later, Howland," Bobby shot at him, with a wild, glaring look. Then he darted through the crowd and disappeared.

"Get your gook hands offa me," Aaron said, pushing his way past Blue and Charley to Paul.

"It's okeh, Aaron," Paul said. "He's gone. We can all relax now. Simmer down."

"Don't you tell me what to do, you lousy nigger!"

Paul turned swiftly. "Look, Mistah Aaron, I don't call you no names—"

"Aaron, please don't start anything," Sloan said.

He turned on her. "You afraid I'm going to mess up that kanaky face of his? That face you love so much? Are you going to stand in front of me and call it love? Your big glorious hearts are in tune or something like that?"

"Paul didn't start anything—"

"I don't want any rumble with you, Aaron," Paul said, backing away.

But Aaron kept after him. "Look, boy, maybe my bird-brained sister turned out a nigger-lover, but that doesn't mean the whole Howland family can be pushed around and degraded!"

"Come off it, man," Paul said. "You're drunk and you don't know what you're sayin'."

Paul saw the flash of motion, but he did not have time to duck before Aaron's thick fist smashed into his face. He fell across the luau table into the sand. He could feel the sick-sweet flood in his throat. He tried to get up, but Aaron's great force caved-in over him. Aaron's hard fists exploded against his face and body with violent, punishing precision. He tried to roll to his feet but Aaron bulled him down again, kneeing him, crashing his fists into his heart. A pain like fire roared through him. He caught a glimpse of shoulder shifting, of fist flashing down at him again. He tried to cover it. The blow missed his jaw, exploded instead against his throat. He felt Aaron's great bulk straddling him, fingers tightening, thumbs pressing into the gristle of his throat until his own breath came rattling and gasping. Dimly, he heard Aaron curse, "Gook bastard—!"

He felt all the strength drain out of him. But from somewhere, from some ultimate reserve, he found the power to break Aaron's grip. He shot one fist into Aaron's mouth, not a punishing blow, but one with enough sting to buy time with. When Aaron charged again, Paul eeled away from him and caught him with another blow. He stepped back and shook his head, trying to clear away the images so there would be only one Aaron. But four images charged him and he swung blindly with a stone fist and caught the right one. Aaron spun and buckled to the sand. He braced himself on his hands and knees, shaking his head, surprised that one blow could so sicken him. He stood up slowly, glaring at Paul with hatred, and went in again. But this time he went into a flurry of viciously aimed fists that seemed never to stop. He leaned back against the trunk of a palm tree, refusing to go down. His face was hideously slack; a dead face, the skin sagging down from the eyes in bloodless folds as if all the muscles had been removed. But the eyes were utterly bright with malice. And the malice made him charge once more. He wrenched a luau torch free from the sand and swung it at Paul like a club. The torch hammered the air beside Paul's face, the blast of flame searing his shoulder. He ducked low beneath the arc of the torch and caught Aaron flush in the stomach. Aaron doubled over, dropping the torch. Paul came up with an uppercut into Aaron's jaw. The blow straightened Aaron, but he was staggering like a rag doll, his fists flailing the air like drifting paper bags. Paul moved in again, hammering him back against the tree, until one last blow crushed Aaron's nose and he started down through a long tunnel of roaring, final blackness.

Paul turned and left him there and walked painfully to the edge of the beach and washed his face in the water. Sloan came to his side and walked up the beach with him wordlessly.

The beach was practically empty of people. Most of the crowd had vanished with the approach of the patrol cars. When Police Sergeant Barney Wong led a handful of officers up to the lanai, Kapiolani Kahana greeted him with a subdued grace and offered each of them a beer. She glanced stoically out across the scene, the mounds of beer cans and overturned beer kegs, the empty okolehao jugs, tattered flags of torn clothing, the split outrigger paddle, Big Splash Papele sleeping it off against a palm tree, a ukulele crashed over his head. The luau table had been split down the center and overturned, the tapa cloth and flowers drifting along the debris of the beach. A pack of poi dogs had appeared from nowhere and was busily yipping at each other while devouring what was left of the food.

Sergeant Barney Wong scratched his head as he looked over the scene. "You gave a luau, Kapi?" he said, a note of awe in his voice.

"Yes," she told him. "I gave a little luau." She walked across the lanai and sat down in the regal Queen Emma chair and stared dully across the beach. "My son and Sloan Howland became engaged."

Barney Wong finished his beer and set the can neatly at the end of a row of cans that had been placed on the railing of the lanai. "Well," he said, "it looks like it was a verra nice luau, Mrs. Kahana."

"It was," she smiled. "I'm sorry you couldn't have gotten here sooner."

Chapter Nine

GEORGE HILL punched his index finger into the palm of his left hand and folded it until the knuckle cracked sharply. He repeated the ritual until the knuckles of all his fingers had been popped. Then he propped one hand on Ward's shoulder. "That's a mighty pretty sight," he said, gazing out the window of the Union headquarters to the harbor below. "That's the kind of a sight that makes me glad to be alive."

The harbor seemed deathly still. Spread out below the chalky gleam of Aloha Tower, five Matson freighters were idle in their slips, neither loading nor discharging. The *President Wilson* was like a ghost ship locked at Pier 8. The *Oronsay,* which had come into port three days before, appeared helpless in her berth at Pier 10, the great liner and its passengers virtually stranded. There were a dozen other freighters, American and foreign, idle at their docks. Across the channel at Sand Island, Coast Guardsmen were unloading a hospital emergency ship, but that was the only activity in the great harbor. Union pickets leaned against the walls of the piers and warehouses, smoking quietly in the shade, their strike placards at their feet. A file of Hawaii National Guardsmen ringed the harbor. They were armed with rifles and bayonets. They stood with a patient military bearing beneath the hot glare of the sun, watching the pickets.

"I don't think it's pretty," Ward said. "I think it's a stinking sight. I think it's a damned shame."

George Hill eyed him curiously. "You talk like a man who's in the wrong business."

"Maybe I am."

"Maybe you're forgetting that you had quite a part in arranging that little scene down there."

"Don't worry, George. I'll never forget that."

"Take it easy, fella. I'm sorry, I used the wrong tactic. If you've got a bitch, spell it out. I can read."

Ward pointed to the harbor. "There's my bitch, George. Idle ships, idle docks, idle men. I've never called a strike before, and I'm wondering now if I have the right. I'm wondering if any of us has the moral right to prevent a man from going to work and earning his daily bread; from serving himself and his family the best way he knows how. And if I do have that right, am I using it justly? Who gave me that right? Certainly those pickets down there didn't. They don't have the slightest conception of why this strike was called."

"They have faith in us, Ward. They trust you and me. They believe we're doing the right thing for them, and so help me God, we are doing the right thing. I know how you feel, Ward. The only trouble with you is that you're beginning to believe what you read in the newspapers, especially the editorials. Well, don't read 'em. And don't forget which corner you're in—the right corner."

"How are you so sure, George?"

"I've been in this corner all my life, fella. I agree with you that a strike like this is shameful and wasteful. But it's our only weapon, Ward. And it's a just one. It wasn't too long ago when there was no such thing as a strike in Hawaii, because there were no labor unions to call a strike: because the Honolulu Police Department was nothing more than a Big Five Gestapo outfit hired to break the skull of anyone who tried to form a labor union. But I formed one, Ward. Three nights a week the cops would send their experts to give me a good working over, to scramble up my brains and my insides, and they hit me with everything a man could invent to hit another man with, and I took it all and the harder they beat me the harder I got. Despite the Gestapo boys, despite the Big Five, despite the big landowning robber barons—Willard Howland included, and if that treads on sensitive toes you'll have to forgive me, because he was with them all right, he sure as hell was—but despite all of them, I got the Union started. I tried to convince the big boys to give the little guys a better break in life.

"We'd meet secretly at night, in hidden little coves all over the Islands, a handful at a time, and soon we built a little muscle; we signed them all up in the Union—Japanese, Chinese, Filipinos, Portagee, Kanakas, it didn't matter whether they worked on the docks or in the fields—and soon they started coming to me and I got things for them. I put a little bread in their stomachs and told them tomorrow would be better; a little more bread.

"The big boys, Willard Howland included, tried first to buy me out. When they couldn't buy me out they tried to ship me out, and when they couldn't ship me out they called the Gestapo boys again, and they called the FBI and they called G-2, and they beat me till I wished I was dead. They crushed the maleness out of me, can you figure out what that does to a man? They said I was a hoodlum, a Mafia bum, a Communist, and they beat me some more, but all the while we kept growing. We grew because we were right, and they could not beat that; they could not defeat our right.

"That strike out there is right," George Hill said, shaking his heavy finger at the window. "That strike out there is one of the prettiest goddamned things in the world, Ward, because like every other strike in these Islands, it will help the people get a little more food in their stomachs, a doctor for their children, some kind of a home to go to at night, and maybe a few dollars in the bank so they won't be so terribly afraid of tomorrow.

"Don't worry about this strike, Ward. Don't let your conscience work overtime on it. We're justified." He walked angrily to his desk and showed Ward the headline of the morning *Advertiser:*

HOWLAND CALLS UNION LEADERS SLUR AGAINST HAWAII!

"This is what grinds against an honest man's conscience," George Hill said, rumpling up the paper and fireballing it into his wastebasket, "because it's such an outrageous lie! It's not you and me who are slurs against Hawaii. Willard Howland and everything he stands for, that's the slur against Hawaii!"

Ward pressed his forehead against the window and closed his eyes for a moment, letting the swirl of fatigue flow over him. Sleep was getting to be such a precious thing lately. Last night it had eluded him completely. Just a long black tunnel with a few restless winks at the early-morning end of it. He wondered if the strike was acting upon him like some chronic disease that left his energies at a low ebb, burned down to raw nerves. The last few days had seemed that way. Endless meetings to present testimony to the Governor's fact-finding committee. A complete overhaul of the two thousand and fourteen pages of Union transcript to be presented at the special session of the Legislature which Governor Balter had called to meet the strike crisis. And on top of all the work, there was learning to live with acrimony. With the constant damning editorials of both dailies. The grim bunch of vinegar-voiced television newscasters pricked into him on all channels. How do you learn to live with that? How do you learn to live with yourself when your ten-year-old son comes back from school with a bloody nose because he defended you? Is there a Do-It-Yourself book that tells you how to look into your son's eyes and explain that you are not an anti-American rabble-rouser when that's all they hear all day long? He was busting one nut to bring 25,000 workers four extra cents an hour, an absolute cost-of-living necessity, so it made him anti-American. And they were calling him worse things, he knew. They were calling him a Red.

"You win, George," he said. "I'm sorry I blew up."

"This is a blow-up business," George Hill said, walking over to him. "Don't take this strike as a personal defeat, Ward. Trying to negotiate the Big Five into paying labor a decent scale is like taking a swing at a puff of meringue. That harbor down there will be just as idle tomorrow and the next day and the day after that. Just like all the plantations will be idle. Until an agreement can be reached. An agreement between you and the combined powers of the strongest men in Hawaii. You'll reach that agreement, Ward. And the people will be better off because of it."

"But when? It's been eight weeks now."

"And we're getting stronger every day. We're not doing the bleating, industry is!"

"The Governor said yesterday that if the strike goes into September he'll ask for a Taft-Hartley injunction."

"The Governor is full of pixie shit!" Hill roared. "First, Taft-Hartley cannot be invoked unless Congress declares Hawaii to be in a state of national emergency. Second, Congress cannot declare this, because Hawaii is without a Delegate in Congress to beef it up. We'll be without a Delegate until November, and the Delegate will be Judge Blanding, and he'll call the tune our way."

"Supposing Willard Howland becomes Delegate?"

"If Howland becomes Delegate, the first thing he'll do is throw a Taft-Hartley against us. But he's not going to become Delegate. You and I will see to that. We're going to knock the dream out of the old man."

And, Ward thought, they could just about do it. It's a hell of a thing to wake up to every morning. But the old man could hit back. The old man was scheduled to hit back in one hour. Right down on those docks there. Well, luck to him.

The office buzzer sounded on George Hill's desk. He talked into the squawk-box for a moment, then flipped the switch off and looked up at Ward. "Speaking of our next Delegate to Congress, our illustrious candidate is on his way in."

"Then I'm on my way out," Ward said, starting toward the door. "I'll be in my office if you want me."

As he reached the door, Judge Adam A. Blanding entered the room. He was a large pasty man with an open face and a bloated look. He sauntered across the room with all the preposterous elegance of one of the larger water birds, and shook hands with George Hill. "Excellent, excellent to see you again, Mr. Hill, sir," he bawled. "Are we all prepared to watch the circus? Hah-hah, it won't be long now. How are you, Ward, young fellow?" As he shook hands, Ward noted the bright and completely artificial campaign-poster smile snap on and off like a neon sign. The Judge seemed always out of breath and he had the irritating habit of wiping his lips every few seconds with a handkerchief. When he spoke he flailed the air about him with outdated theatrical gestures, proclaiming inanities in a rich, affected voice, trying to make each banal comment sound like Biblical wisdom.

He was not, and never had been, a judge. He was an attorney whose talents were almost up to mediocrity, a member of that strange inexplicable cigar-juice-spitting crew of hangers-on around city hall. However, he had, Ward knew, the strangest of all political talents: his mediocrity was of such a low level that he went about unnoticed, and consequently he had no enemies. It was because of this fact that he had, to his utter surprise, been selected as the Democratic nominee for the delegacy. He was a most affable nonentity, Ward thought with distaste. This was the man selected by a great political party, by my own political party, to represent Hawaii before the United States Congress. Well, it's bad enough that the Union is committed to him, I don't have to take him personally.

Several of the Judge's campaign workers had followed him into the room and they gathered about him now at the window, looking down into the harbor. "Ah-ha-ha, a perfect view of the slaughter!" Judge Blanding said, patting his stomach. "When Willard Howland walks into that harbor to make his speech, I'll feel like a Roman emperor watching the Christians enter the Colosseum."

"You just better pray to God it'll be a slaughter," George Hill said.

"And just what else could it be, sir? No one but a madman like Willard Howland would go into that lion's den down there to berate the Union! I tell you, gentlemen, that's what's wrong with my illustrious opponent! Too much pride, no humility. That's what will cause his final fall, while I, on the other hand—"

"Save all that pap for your speeches," George Hill told him. "I've heard enough of your speeches and they certainly need something—pap or otherwise. That's why I wanted you over here today, Judge. To listen to Howland, not to hoot at him from our windows. It seems that every time you open your mouth you lose a couple of hundred voters, and every time Howland opens his mouth he gains a couple of hundred. Most politicians have a way of saying nothing graciously, but you seem to have mastered your own knack of letting the voters form the idea that the only thing you're competent at is incompetency."

"Now just one moment, Mr. Hill, sir, I must beg your pardon but I will not stand—"

"Sit down, Judge. And don't worry about begging my pardon about anything. I'm in trouble enough over you as it is." George Hill placed his hands on the Judge's shoulders and gently eased him into a chair. Hill sat on the corner of his desk, looking down at the Judge.

"Judge Blanding, do you know how much money the Union has contributed to your campaign? Not the Democratic Party campaign, but your individual campaign? Almost thirty thousand dollars, Judge, and it's only the end of August! We've taken money from our strike fund to back your campaign, Judge. We're your very loyal supporters, Judge. We want you to win very much. And by the great god Pele, you'd better win!"

"Ah-hah! Mr. Hill, I might remind you, sir, that Willard Howland was beaten before he started."

"That's true. Before he got started he didn't have a chance. A clean Democratic sweep. But every single speech since he got started has upset the applecart. When he speaks, people listen. He's worked statehood to a fever pitch, making a *cause célèbre* of it so that a vote against him seems tantamount to a vote against Hawaii. If he wasn't walking all over your fat behind do you think I'd have been forced to pull this stunt on him today? Do you think we'd have to stoop to—"

"What stunt?" Ward asked.

The Judge turned to him, his beady little eyes wide with glee. "Fireworks," the Judge roared. "Political fireworks!"

"What the hell is he talking about?" Ward asked George Hill.

Hill shrugged his ponderous shoulders. "Some of the boys worked up a surprise for Howland. Too many people listen to him, and too many voters are leaning over to him, so the boys worked up a couple of tricks, that's all."

"I figured that, but what kind of tricks?"

George Hill threw his hands in the air. "Tricky tricks, for Christ's sake! What do you think, we're playing a game of marbles or something? We're playing for keeps and my team is up against Willard Howland's team, and since the Judge here can't seem to go out and whip Howland, then I'm going out and whip him myself!"

From the street below they could hear a sound truck tool its way into the harbor. They went to the window. The truck was decorated with bunting and posters of Willard Howland and a hula troupe performed in the rear of the truck. Ward noticed Willard's black limousine following the truck.

"All hail the conquering hero," Judge Blanding said.

"You'll be the conquering hero, Judge," George Hill said, resting his hand on the Judge's shoulder. "I didn't mean to sound harsh with you. I just want to needle you into putting up a better fight. Stop grinning into those television cameras and go out and speak to the people. That's where Howland's gaining all his popularity. In the grass roots. The people are going for him."

"Not these people," the Judge said, indicating the crowd that was assembling in the park across from the harbor. As Ward opened the window, the hula troupe was stepping from the platform in back of the truck and Willard Howland was introduced. A segment of the crowd booed his introduction.

Senator Howland moved up to the microphone. "Many of you here today might well ask yourselves what this strike will mean to you. What it will mean to your families. What it will mean to the greater family of Hawaii as a whole." The booing died away. "You good men have been idle and without pay for almost two months now. If this strike continues, it will render you helpless to survive.

"This strike, brought about by the greed of your Union leaders, has brought hardship to everyone in the Territory. Two large-scale strike riots have already broken out on these piers. You are almost without funds to buy food, and the stores are almost without foods to sell. And the stores will not have food or other necessary supplies until this strike is settled. Do you know the price of blood plasma at the hospitals, now that it must be flown in on emergency? How much are you paying now for a pack of cigarettes—fifty cents? More? Are you able to buy them? If an epidemic were to break out and medical supplies, already low throughout the Territory, had to be flown in, who would be able to pay the price for them? Certainly not you good workers. You workers are not at fault, we all know that. Neither will you be the beneficiaries of this strike! For even if you get this raise which your leaders demand, it will take each and every one of you at least ten years to make up, with the raise, the wages you're losing with the strike. No, gentlemen, you will win nothing with this strike. The men who caused the strike—those bosses of yours sitting right up in their plush offices in that building over there—they're the ones who'll win in this strike! The George Hills, the Ward Akanas, they're the ones who'll benefit, not you good workers! You're pawns!"

A man roared through the crowd, "Hea, Senatah, how much da Big Five pay you to make dis kine talk?"

Willard seemed caught off balance, but in a second he managed to grin wryly at the man and raise his hands to quiet the snickering crowd. "I'm sorry to disappoint you fellows, but I'm not on their payroll. And those of you who know me know I'm not on anyone's payroll."

"It's okeh, Willie," someone else shouted. "We like you okeh, we just don't like yoah bosses."

"He's a tool!" another shouted, working up the handful of Union goons around him. "A rich man's tool! A Big Five tool!"

Anger flashed in old Willard's eyes. He shook a finger at the Union goons. "Now wait a minute! Hold on before it gets too rough," he said, his voice rising. "I didn't come down here for a fight. I came to speak to you men about your future. Let's not look for a fight," he said, as the crowd quieted. "Two people preparing for a fight will sure as shooting find their fight. Just like two countries arming themselves and stockpiling hydrogen bombs will sure as shooting find their war, sooner or later. No country prepares an army for peace. Maybe that's what caused our strike here. Two different sides ready and looking for a fight. Well, they've got their fight, and we're all the losers. You workers could do this great land a service by going to your bosses and telling them that they should take stock of themselves. Union leaders cannot continue to force wages to a point where it kills industry's profit, because that will kill industry itself, and when industry is dead, so are your unions. If these leaders of yours were honest men, they'd realize that they're twisting a tiger by its tail, but they don't give a tinker's damn about the future of you, the workers; they only care about getting their own share while it's handy—"

The goons started the booing again. One of them yelled, "Go back to the Big Five and tell 'em you can't bust organized labor!"

"I'm not trying to break organized labor!" Willard shouted above the hooting of the crowd. "I am in full agreement with the right of the workingman to organize his ranks and demand a fair shake at the contract table. What I am against is one powerful labor union dictating—yes, dictating—terms to Hawaii's industry and economy! Dictating unfair terms, and threatening to paralyze Hawaii by a strike if its terms are not met. I am against what they all stand for—Hill, Akana, all of them. They stand for unadulterated Union domination of Hawaii—total control, economically, politically and socially! I stand before you unopposed to the basic theory that organized labor should become strong in unification, but I must oppose the racketeering among the Union leadership. I am against the wrongs and injustices within the Union, and I believe you should clean house!"

The jeering became louder and a barrage of eggs splattered across the platform. One of the eggs smashed on Willard's shoulder. He shook his fist at the crowd but the jeering mounted. Fruit cascaded down on the platform, tomatoes squished all over the truck. A ring of National Guardsmen formed about the truck, pushing the crowd away. Another platoon milled through the crowd, trying to quiet it.

"Why don't you clean up yoah own house, Senatah?" one of the goons yelled at him. "Why do you point to the Union an' say, Clean it up! while industry, specially the scummy Big Fivers, has been filthy an' corrupt an' exploitating us for sevendy years?"

"Yeassuh! Clean up the Big Five and the robber barons!"

The crowd, growing larger now, whooped it up. The goons continued heaving things at Howland. Several police cars raced to the harbor. Ward turned away from the window. "Are those your little tricks?" he said, twisting George Hill about and glaring at him. "Is that the kind of circus you've planned?"

"Now hold on, Ward! I told you we're not playing for marbles. What do you suggest we do? Let him walk all over us? Throw in the towel?"

"I didn't expect you to hire goons to—"

"You didn't expect to barge into politics and keep your hands clean, either!" George Hill roared at him. "You want a brick house, you got to go paddle in the mud to make the bricks! You want to eat steak, you got to kill cows! We want to beat Howland, and we're starting right now."

Ward turned angrily and stormed over to the door.

"Where do you think you're going?"

"Down there," Ward said. "I'm going down to stop that mob. Do you have any idea of what's going to happen down there? If those soldier boys start playing rough? You'll have a nice bloody riot on your hands. And that old man—whether you agree with him or not—will be torn apart by the mob. Haven't you ever seen a mob at work? They don't play for marbles! You guys should be."

When he reached the outer fringes of the mob, the Guardsmen were busy running the goons out. Police were locking them into paddywagons.

"Let those men stay!" Willard roared at the police. He raised his hands, and for a moment the crowd quieted down. "Boo and holler and whimper all you want," Willard roared, his face black with outrage, "but we vowed—the decent people of this Territory —that never again would such a paralyzing strike as the 1949 one cripple these Islands. I am here before you now to reassert that vow! We will not be subjugated to Union domination! We will not give up our lifeline, the harbor at which our necessities arrive at our shores, to Union hoodlums! We will not let our homes, our children's bread, come under Union control!"

The hooting and jeering became thunderous. The crowd's resentment against the Guardsmen and the police was hurled at Howland. Ward elbowed his way to the platform. He found the sergeant of the Guardsmen.

"If you can let me through, I can stop this crowd," he said.

"Just shove off, buddy. Just move along and don't cause any ruckus."

"Look, damn it, I can—"

"I said move, buddy! Now move!"

Ward broke through the Guardsmen and got up on the platform next to Willard Howland. He held his hands high to quiet the crowd. "Now you men, listen to me, please listen to me!" he shouted. "You know me. Now let's knock off this display of—"

But Guardsmen mounted the truck and rushed him off to the rim of the crowd. Willard pointed angrily to him. He grabbed the microphone and roared at the crowd, "We will break the Union's control of Hawaii's lifeline! We will break the Union's stranglehold on our economy! We will break the Union and its leaders—the George Hills, the Ward Akanas!"

A cordon of police escorted Howland to his car. His white linen coat had been smeared with tomatoes and he was wiping the splatter of an egg from his forehead. Ward elbowed his way close to him.

"Senator, I'm ashamed of what's happened, sir. Please believe me, I had nothing to do with it. I'm very much ashamed, Senator."

Old Willard stopped and stared at him with eyes hard and bright as topaz. "So this is what you represent," Willard said, looking at Ward with disgust. "This is the way you plan to lead Hawaii."

"No no, please, Senator—"

"I'm going to break you, Ward. I'm going to break you down into the gutter where you and all your pals belong. I'll break you for this if it's the last thing I do."

The old man walked through the police cordon and got into his car.

"Senator Howland—" Ward tried to follow him but the police pushed him away. Old Willard had rolled up the car windows. The color had drained from his face and he was staring stolidly, bleakly ahead. The car pulled out of the square and Ward trotted after it several yards. Then he stood still and watched it round a corner. Eggs were still splattering on the sidewalk and the crowd was still booing, not at anything in particular, just loud, constant jeering.

Chapter Ten

THE second week of September brought a big surf to Waikiki. The combers started about a mile out, at a fissure in the reef called "first break." They rolled in some twenty yards apart from each other, seven waves to a set, sweeping in clear and green and swelling to heights of twenty feet. They are fast and dangerous green cliffs with bowers of crumbling white foam at their crests. Once he has caught the wave, the rider slides left down across the moving sheer green face of the wave, balancing precariously just in front of the breaking curl, guiding his twenty-pound balsa wood board with the weight of his feet. The coral reef is so formed that the wave will break, rebuild and break again three times before it eddies into the shore; and the rider, by turning the direction of his board as a skier christies down a mountainside, keeps to the same wave, catching all three breaks at speeds greater than thirty miles an hour, until the giant comber expends its once tremendous energy in broken wavelets against the shore of the Moana or the Outrigger Club. Riding these giant waves is one of the most incomparable thrills in the world, Paul Kahana thought. It gives a man a rare taste of almost pure freedom.

He and Sloan had paddled out together on a long, hollow tandem board. They had let one set of waves roll past, gauging the height and speed of the crests.

"It looks like a real boneyard surf," Sloan said. "Do you think they're too big?"

Paul sat up, his legs straddling the board. "No. All summer long we've had a lousy malihini surf. These big boys are long overdue."

Sloan was lying on her tummy, leaning up on her elbows. "They're sure late in coming. I wonder what brought them."

"Maybe a quake near Japan."

"Or an H-bomb at Bikini. When they test those things it really brings up the waves. Like Makaha surf."

Paul paddled easily out just beyond first break. A dozen surfers sat straddling their boards, their heads turned seaward, quietly waiting the next set. The water was clear jade. They could look down into the depths and see the craggy coral caves where the squid and the moray battled for survival. The late afternoon sun burned like a branding iron against their backs. A mile-long mauka, Waikiki Beach was a curve of stained gold. The hotels rose in clean-colored, clean-lined, honeycombed slabs against the rich green loam of the mountains. The beach was lined with the crowds watching the giant combers roll in. The tourists and the servicemen and all the inexperienced surfers were on shore. Only expert surfers could handle first break. The outrigger canoes also had been brought to shore. Several of them had already been swamped and capsized by the surf. These were finally bailed out and righted by the beachboys, and the tourists piled back in and taken to shore, half laughing, half panicky. Paul could make out little groups of people on the upper balconies of the Moana and SurfRider, and he remembered with a grin the day back in 1951 when those same balconies were crammed with fear-struck tourists who watched in awe as he and several other beachboys surfed in on the tidal wave that had erupted near Midway four hours before.

"They're coming up outside!" Sloan said.

Paul turned the board around and watched the approaching set. Bobby Villanueva paddled close to him and tossed him a cube of wax. "This might help with these buggers," Bobby said.

Paul rubbed the wax over the upper surface of the board. The wax would make his and Sloan's footing surer.

The first wave of the set reached its peak and glistened with sunlight. Paul studied it, then decided to pass it up. Because of the long, shoulder-breaking paddle back from the shore to first break, it was only possible to catch one wave out of a set. Paul knew that the fifth and sixth waves were always the largest of a set, and he wanted to wait for them. He watched Bobby and several other surfers paddle with the wave, catch it, stand up quickly and begin sliding their boards left across the face of the wave. One of the surfers lost balance. His board did a pearl dive, the nose going underwater, then shot up spinning and gyrating six feet into the air. The rest of them made it.

"How do you feel?"

"Good." Sloan grinned. "As long as I'm with you. They look awfully big though."

Paul laughed. "They are awful big."

He let two more waves roll by underneath him. He looked around and saw that they were alone at first break. "We've got this next one all to ourselves," he said. "You game?"

Sloan looked at the wave. It was huge. It was about ten yards behind them and she could feel Paul lie down, his chest against the back of her hips, and start paddling into position to catch it. It looked as though the wave would be a twenty-footer. "Yep, I'm game."

"Let's go!"

He pointed the board toward the shore. He paddled easily, staying a few yards ahead of the still-building wave. He turned his head once to gauge the advance of the wave. Then he nudged Sloan and they both paddled hard, working with the wave now, feeling it beginning to pull on the board.

The wave moved in with a great rush. They could feel the water fall beneath the board as the wave rose to its peak. It was a smooth, pure wave, not a trace of foam on it. The tide moving out against it was as even and flat as a parade ground. Suddenly the board shot out ahead, its nose way out of the water. The wave, at its peak, began to curl. Paul heard the earsplitting buzz in his head. He sprang to his feet, guiding the board as it zoomed down across the face of the wave. The board seemed to drop away from Sloan's stomach. She could hear the rush of the water hissing by, then the noise of the wave starting to crumble to her right and the chittering of the board as it slid down the unbroken face.

As the nose of the board slanted downwards in that familiar angle, Sloan jumped to her feet. Paul crouched behind her and moved his head between her legs, lifting her to his shoulders. Then he straightened, and they raced down across the moving hill of water, turning at Blowhole Break and racing across the second build of the wave, turning for the third time closer into shore, and riding the last final break of the comber into shore.

They toppled off the board in the waist-deep water.

"Try another?" Paul grinned at her.

"Sure. I'll stay with it all day long."

Ramsey was stretched out on a beach blanket outside the Moana when Peter joined her. He looked down at her firm, tanned body and grinned. "Yoah almost as brown as me," he said.

She stretched her arm along his and compared the color. "I'm afraid I'll never be that brown," she said. "But at least I'll be going home with a good tan."

"Yoah still plannin' on leavin' tomorrow?" he asked seriously.

"Yes. I have to. It's best anyway, Peter."

They were quiet for a moment. Peter glanced idly at the book alongside her. It was a copy of Peter Buck's *Vikings of the Sun*.

"How do you like it?" he said.

"I've got to confess I just started it today. I thought I should learn something about the Islands before I left. But I haven't been able to concentrate." She looked at him. "Have you read it?"

"Suah. In high school. Out here we study about the history of Polynesia, just like you study the history of California."

"Exactly where is Polynesia? Who are the real Polynesians?"

He leaned back on his elbows. "Well, the name comes from two Greek words: *polys*—meanin' many, and *nesos*—meanin' islands. Simple, huh? The Polynesians are membahs of the brown races of Oceania. Like me. Anthropoligists say the Polynesians came from the southeastern tip of Asia, gradually spreadin' throughout the islands of the South Pacific."

"I thought the voyage of the *Kon-Tiki* a few years ago showed that the South Pacific was populated by people who sailed west from South America."

"No, it showed only that that was possible. I don't think that was the case. Because pioneerin' is caused by overpopulation—lack of land and lack of food. These conditions didn't exist in South America, but they did in southeast Asia.

"Anyway, the Polynesians, my people, discovered Hawaii more than a thousand years ago. Sometime durin' the tenth century, a Polynesian named Kure sailed from Tahiti and discovered New Zealand and formed the Maori branch of the Polynesian family. Later, a second branch of the Polynesian family was formed the same way in the Samoan Islands. And a third branch in the Hawaiian Islands. Anthropologists aren't suah just when the Hawaiian branch was established. Some say durin' the sixth century, some say as late as the thirteenth."

"What made them leave their home islands?" Ramsey asked.

"The need for land and food. The whole land area of the Society Islands is about five hundred square miles. Not even as big as Oahu. There wasn't enough land to farm taro or yams to feed the people. So they set sail to find moah land. You got to remembah that these Polynesian voyages took place a couple of hundred years befoah Columbus. The Polynesians were bold adventurers whose trips were moah darin' and moah dangerous than any other seamen in history. They'd make the Vikings and Columbus look like kids sailin' over to Molokai. They were proud people, and they cut down hundred-foot koa logs and hollowed them out into canoes; then lashed planks between two canoes, loaded their women and children and plants and animals on to the planks, rigged up a sheet of pandanus to catch the wind, and set sail across moah than two thousand miles of unknown ocean. When the wind stopped, they'd paddle for days on end. They didn't have a compass or a sextant; they navigated by the sun and the stars. They fixed their course by the first bright star of the evenin', and when it sank, they'd pick a star followin' it. They had to know all the currents and the winds. They had to study and understand the movements of fish or what a certain flight of birds meant, so that they wouldn't miss their mark when they neared land. It's awful easy to miss a speck of an island in the Pacific. Their probable course was straight east from Tahiti to Easter Island, where they would have run into the heavy swells that roll across the Pacific from South

America. From Easter Island, they could have seen the flight of the kolea bird—the golden plover—from its summer home in Alaska. Land, they figured, must lie to the north.

"And all this happened some five or six hundred years befoah Columbus," Peter said proudly. "Oahu was pretty heavily settled as far back as one thousand A.D."

"When did the first white man come?" Ramsey asked.

"A Spanish boat—a galleon—was shipwrecked off Kauai in 1527. And another Spanish ship visited Hawaii in 1555, but for some reason they kept the discovery a secret. Then Cook—Captain James Cook—sighted the islands of Oahu and Kauai on January 18, 1778. Two days later he sailed into Waimea Bay and named the islands in honor of his sponsor, the Earl of Sandwich. But the name 'Sandwich Islands' didn't stick; our name did," he said.

"And the Hawaiians killed Captain Cook, is that right?"

"He was a numbarh one cocky guy. The natives thought he was their god Lono who had returned to fulfill an old legend. The same thing happened the next year, when he anchored in Kealakekua Bay in Hawaii—that's where his monument is. The natives bowed down to him when he came on shore. They gave him presents and he gave them a boar and a sow and some melon and pumpkin and onion seeds. They started tradin' and Cook was worshiped as a god for a while. Then the trouble started. Cook's men broke into a Hawaiian temple and cut up some wooden idols for fuel for their ship. Us Hawaiians got back at him by stealing the cutter boat from his ship. Cook really blew his top at this—which was sad for him. He and ten of his marines marched to King Kalaniopuu's hut to take him prisoner until the cutter boat was returned. A fight developed and one of the marines shot down one of the King's guards. That was it for Captain Cook. The natives charged and killed four of the marines, then beat Cook to death with stones. The great explorer, circumnavigator of the globe and discoverer of Hawaii, was dead. In keepin' with native custom, Cook's body was carried to a small temple where the flesh was removed from his bones by the high priests. His flesh was burned and his bones became sacred. There is a legend that claims some of the bones were kept in the Temple of Lono until 1819, when King Kamehameha ordered the taboos overthrown and the temples and idols destroyed, and that they were taken away and hidden somewhere. But no one's evah found 'em. Some of Cook's bones were returned by the natives to his ship. These were buried at sea with full military honors."

Ramsey was silent for a while; then she said, "Quite a story."

"Yeah," Peter grinned, "those haole guys couldn't fool around with us."

"How many Hawaiians were there then?"

"No one's suah. Between 200,000 and 400,000. Disease—the white man's diseases—killed many of them. Intermarriage led to a decline of the race. Today, there are only about thirteen thousand full-blooded Hawaiians like me and Paul; about eighty thousand hapa-Hawaiians."

"Now that I've got that history, I don't need to read the book," Ramsey said. "But tell me just one more thing. Tell me about Kamehameha. King Kamehameha the Great, conqueror of the Islands."

Peter grinned. "He was the 'Napoleon of the Pacific.' About the time Cook discovered Hawaii, each island was ruled by a separate king. The Island of Hawaii, for example, was ruled by King Kalaniopuu, whose men killed Captain Cook. Before he died in 1782, Kalaniopuu named his nephew, Kamehameha, a high chief. But Kamehameha had bigger ambitions. By 1790, he had an army built up and started conquering the Island of Hawaii in a series of spectacular battles. He established Kailua—right near the Howlands' home at Manoalani—as his capital. The opposing army was marching from Hilo for an all-out battle, but as they crossed Kilauea, the volcano erupted, killing half the warriors, and Kamehameha became King of Hawaii. The Englishman, Captain George Vancouver, became an advisor to Kamehameha, and the King thought so much of him that he placed his entire island under Great Britain's rule. In 1794, the British flag was hoisted over Hawaii, and one of Vancouver's lieutenants took possession of the island in the name of the King of England. But the possession was nevah confirmed by Great Britain. In February 1795, Kamehameha set sail in a thousand war canoes and conquered the Island of Maui, then Molokai. In April that same year, he landed at Waialae Bay on Oahu, marched his army up the plains of Nuuanu to the pali, where the greatest battle that evah took place in the islands was fought. Kamehameha won, his warriors celebratin' by pitchin' the losing army over the pali cliffs, and Kamehameha united all the islands under his rule; all except Kauai, which came in later anyway." Peter grinned sadly at her. "I feel like a numbarh one palolo," he said. "Here it is, yoah last day in Hawaii, and we're talkin' about history."

"Okay," Ramsey grinned, "no more questions."

"No, it's my turn to ask questions." He held her hand and looked down at it. "Why can't you stay, Ramsey?"

"I can't, Peter," she spoke very softly, "I just can't."

"You mean you won't," he said angrily. "You don't want to."

She turned away and closed her eyes. "Oh please, let's not get into a big hassle about it again."

"Did you call yoah folks?"

She frowned, remembering her promise to him that she would call her mother to try to postpone her return home. Once she had tried to write her parents a letter about Peter:

> *Dear Mother and Dad;*
>
> *I know this will come as a surprise to you, so pour yourselves an old-fashioned and make for the easy chairs. It's a happy surprise! I've fallen in love! Really, wonderfully, head-over-heels in love! His name is Peter Noa . . .*

She could never get any further than that. She tried half a dozen times, but each time the wretched battle started inside her and she tried to fight it with all the wisdom of her twenty-one years. She told herself that she was not afraid of the facts, but she wished desperately that the facts were different. She was deeply in love, she knew that. In Hawaii, that love could work out. But her life was not in Hawaii and that love was so totally opposed to everything in her life, her background, her home, her friends and especially her parents, that it could never be reconciled. The part of her that fought the love was rooted deep inside herself. To lose that fight would mean a total divorce from all the strong blooded roots from which she was not at all sure that she should—or could—cut herself away. The mental image of her mother and father reading such a letter broke down all her desire to write it, and broke down all her courage to love.

She had decided to flee from love. She admitted to herself that that was precisely what she was doing. She refused to fool herself with any notions that it was, after all, a summer romance and the summer was over. No, she was leaving because here in this island country she had fallen deeply in love and she knew the love could not work out. Staying on any longer would lead only to a deeper hurt, to herself and Peter. Falling in love with Peter was one thing, but marrying him was something else indeed. It was something that a girl like herself just could not do. Call it cowardice, call it breeding, she thought, frowning at the words. Call it impossible. The quicker she got away from the Islands the better it would be for both of them.

"Well," Peter repeated. "Did you call 'em?"

"Yes."

"You really did?"

"About coming home, Peter. Not about us."

"Oh."

"Peter, believe me, I couldn't call them about us! I just couldn't! I don't see what good it would do. It would only upset them, and there's no reason for it, since nothing's going to come of—of us."

"Even though we love each other."

"Yes, even though we love each other. Love isn't the answer to everything. It's not a cure-all."

Peter turned away resentfully. "Why is this thing between us? Why is it so unfair and why can't we do anything about it? Are we too young or too scared or too prejudiced to buck it?"

"Oh, please don't get like that, Peter. It hurts both of us."

"It hurts both of us because you're scared, that's why! It doesn't hurt Paul and Sloan 'cause they aren't scared. What do you think I am, some sort of caricature? A comic? A dumb happy Hawaiian? I might have been born with this face, but goddamn it, I've got bone and blood and heart and feelin's! I've got blood that can be just as proud as haole blood and I've got feelin's that can be hurt just as easily as anyone else's—"

"Oh please, please stop!"

"You're scared."

"All right, I'm scared. I'm scared of love and I'm scared of sex and I'm scared of life! But I can't change it. I wish I could. I wish with all my heart that things were different. But they're not. And the whole thing rubs me wrong. It's against everything I ever learned."

"You learned wrong," Peter said. "It's not against everything Sloan's learned."

"How can I impress you with the fact that I am not Sloan Howland! What would do for her would not do for me. She's rebellious, I'm not. Maybe I'm one of those lily-livered conformists you hear about. I don't think like Sloan and I don't act like Sloan, I never have and I probably never will! I'm me, and I act like me and I think like me and I decide like me, and you should understand that!"

"Okay, have it yoah way," Peter said. He walked down to the water, took his surfboard and plowed angrily into the surf. Ramsey cried quietly for a long time after he had gone. Later she walked the length of Waikiki. Her eyes were still stinging. At Waikiki, there was no sensible way of looking at life, she thought. The magic of Waikiki had worn thin. Not the magic of the Islands, that was still strong, but Waikiki, after all, was nothing more than a barnyard: a quarter-mile strip of coarse sand converted by the Hawaii Visitors Bureau into a sunny Sodom. She must have been delirious when she had first seen it, because now it seemed nothing but something cheap and phony, reeking with sex and decaying morals and squirming, searching bodies: the fat tourists and their everlasting coy games, the servicemen obscenely on the prowl, the beachboys with their flourishing adulteries, everybody lusty-eyed for scraps of desire, openly contemptuous of all the worth-while, solemn things in life. At first, she admitted, she had wanted desperately to be one of them and be accepted as one. But she discovered to her dismay that the only way this would be possible was for her to act like one of them, and this she refused to do. Now, Waikiki and the affairs of everyone on or about Waikiki seemed to be nothing more than a coarse, obscene grasping for cheap fleshy pleasures; sex above all and let love come last. She felt genuinely sorry, realizing that most people who come to visit Hawaii see only Waikiki.

As she walked up to the Hau Terrace at the Outrigger, her back stiffened. The love between herself and Peter Noa had been doomed from the start, and now it was all but over, she thought. Well, love was one thing, obligation another. She had her obligations to her parents and to herself and to everything that they and she held dear. And, she thought, she had an obligation to her children—yet unborn. And all those obligations called upon her to give up love. This particular love, at any rate. Some things, she thought, are stronger than love.

Early that evening Sloan sat at a bridge table in the living room of the great Manoa Valley house, busily addressing her own wedding invitations. She had a cocktail beside her, and every once in a while she would look up from her wedding list, sip the cocktail, and watch the image of her father on the television screen.

"If we are to achieve our dream of statehood," Senator Howland was saying, "we must impress upon the Nation and Congress that we are not the foils of Union terrorists. We must evict these terrorists from power. We must throw out the Ward Akanas! We must defeat the political party supporting the Ward Akana elements!"

Sloan walked over to the television set and turned the volume down low. She studied the black and white electronic image of her father. He looked old and haggard beneath the glare of the television lights. Lately, his speeches seemed to have lost sight of his goal, she thought. His campaign seemed not as much pro-statehood as it did a personal vendetta to destroy Ward Akana. On the six o'clock television news report, she had watched Whitney K. Frazer of the *Star-Bulletin* interview Ward concerning the growing animosity between himself and Senator Howland. Ward had said that the bitterness had developed on Howland's part because the Union would deliver a solid hundred-thousand-block vote to defeat him in the November election. And when Mr. Frazer asked why, Ward had said simply, "We don't think Senator Howland is the man for the job."

"Who doesn't think he's the man for the job?" Mr. Frazer had asked.

"The Union membership."

"And yourself, Mr. Akana? How do you feel?"

"I don't think Senator Howland is the man for the job," Ward had said.

Now, listening to her father revile Ward, his eyes cold and watchful on the screen, Sloan wondered about her wedding invitations. She walked back to the bridge table and scanned her list. Ward and Tani Akana were right up on top. Their envelope had been addressed already. And Aaron, of course, had to be invited. And Bobby Villanueva, too. It might be quite a wild wedding reception.

Ramsey wheeled into the living room. "Snap me up?"

Sloan worked the hooks on the back of Ramsey's beige silk brocade evening gown. "All set to rip up the town on your last night here? You look beautiful," Sloan told her.

"I don't feel too beautiful."

"Why?"

"Because it's my last night in Hawaii. Because I had something of a scene with Peter."

"Maybe this will cheer you up," Sloan handed her her invitation. "Maybe you can fly back for the wedding."

Ramsey read the gold-printed card. "I wish I could."

Sloan went to the liquor cabinet and poured Ramsey a cocktail. "I thought maybe we could have a few drinks by ourselves before the fellows got here, so I chilled these earlier." She raised her own glass to Ramsey. "Aloha."

Ramsey managed a faint grin. "Do you think I'm being a coward, Sloan? Do you think I'm running away?"

"Yes."

Ramsey slumped down into the chaise longue. "You don't have to sound so cool and predatory about it," she said.

"I was just being frank."

"I shudder when people say they're being frank. It always means that they're going to say something bad. You don't think too much of me for running away, do you?"

"I didn't think anything about it at all, until you brought it up. But it does kind of put me on edge. The reasons that make you believe that you and Peter couldn't work out hold true for Paul and myself. And I hate to have them thrown in my face."

"Then maybe you're the one who's running away."

"From what?"

"From the facts. From the way things are."

"That kind of a crack isn't worthy of you."

Ramsey bit her lip. Her wide green eyes stared frightenedly at Sloan. "I know it wasn't, and I'm sorry I said it. Really. I'm just so mixed-up. There's no one else I can talk to about it, and you're so damned honest you refuse to make it easy for me and I guess I wanted to hurt you back. I'm sorry, Sloan."

"Do you really think you're in love with Peter?"

Ramsey nodded. "I know I am."

"I think you're full of saccharin. I think you're in love with him as a symbol of Hawaii. You love your dewy-eyed idea of the way you'd like him to be more than you love him as a person."

"Maybe . . ." Ramsey whispered.

"There's no maybe about it, Ramsey, hon. If you loved him you'd marry him. You couldn't dream of going away."

"If I ever married Peter it would kill my mother and dad."

Sloan stalked away stiff-legged, her high, delicate head rigid. Damn her, she thought. Damn her for bringing that up. Of all the things to bring up . . . "Parents always say that," she whispered, "no matter whom you plan to marry. And I don't want to get on that subject. It strikes too close to home."

"But I thought your father—"

"My father hasn't changed his feelings one bit. He's been too busy to sit down and become fully aware of the fact that I'm getting married next month. And I hope he stays too busy until it's too late for him to do anything about it."

"That's too calculating for me." Ramsey shrugged. "I don't know, maybe I'm still a babe in the woods. Do you know I've never even made love to a man?"

"Yes, baby doll, you've made me painfully aware of that sterling little niche in your character."

"Do you think I'm a prude?"

"No. I just think you have your ideas and I have mine."

"We sure do. We're sure different about—about morals."

"Everyone's different about morals."

"Way down deep inside you, Sloan, do you think it's right—morally right—to sleep with a man you're not married to?"

"Yes, absolutely right. Providing you're sincere and you're in love and neither of you is married to anyone else. If I didn't think that way I wouldn't sleep with Paul."

"All my life," Ramsey said, her eyes serious, "I've been brought up to believe that love was right but sex was wrong. It's always confused me. My parents were demons on the subject. They kept telling me to keep myself pure for my husband. I guess that sounds corny."

"No, it doesn't."

"My mother kept drilling it into my head that a good man wouldn't want a girl who wasn't pure. That it would cheapen my marriage. I always went along with her, but I'm not so sure now. Peter is always bugging me to prove my love for him—you know. But I don't think you can prove love that way. I can't believe that love needs proof. All a girl has to do is prove it that way a couple of times and she's promiscuous."

Sloan lit a cigarette. "I guess I'm promiscuous," she said quietly.

"What does it feel like?"

"Being promiscuous?"

"No. Making love. What does it feel like, Sloan?"

"I can't explain it," Sloan said. "If love is deep and sincere, then making love puts glory into it. Makes two people one in a happy explosion."

"Does it happen every time?"

"No, but no woman expects it to, unless she's out of her mind. With Paul, it's a matter of caring. He knows me now. He works until I do explode, and he does with me. He makes love with me, not to me. Anyway, this is a crazy thing to be talking about."

"But I want to talk about it. Tonight especially. Sloan, did you ever regret—"

"No! I've never regretted anything I've ever done."

"Sloan, if you were me, would you let Peter make love to you?"

"If we were in love?"

"Yes. Very much in love."

"If I loved him, I'd make love with him."

"That's what I knew you'd say! Sloan, you've got so much guts and spirits and you're full of beans, but you've got no sense."

"I've got love."

After a moment, Sloan looked speculatively at Ramsey. "But you're not going to let him, are you?"

"No," Ramsey said flatly. "No, I'm not. I'm going to wait. But good God, Sloan, sometimes I wish to heaven I could be like you. Things would be so much easier."

Sloan's eyes rolled inward and she seemed distracted, as though she had moved a little apart from herself. "Sometimes," she said softly, "I wish I was more like you."

At three o'clock the following morning, Ramsey suffered a change of heart. She had just kissed Peter good night and good-by. She entered the vast dark gloom of the house, shut the door behind her and slumped back against it. Then the tears came, like warm wax falling to her cheeks. She opened the door and ran out of the house, down the driveway into his arms. "I love you, I love you, I can't leave you."

It was a warm, soft morning, the dead quiet time of morning, the time when love died; and against the dark sky, high, fat clouds floated lightly like burls of cream, and the scent of plumeria and fallen ginger drifted through the garden along the soft breeze. Peter held her close and kissed her and they leaned against the trunk of an old leafy tree and kissed again.

"I love you," she whispered.

"Tell me yoah not afraid of our love. Our particular love."

"I'm not, I'm not."

"All night long I was makin' up a thousand things to say. A thousand new ways to tell you how much I love you. A thousand new reasons why you shouldn't leave. Now I've forgotten them all."

"Oh Peter, I'm sorry I hurt you."

"You didn't hurt me, you taught me how to dream. All my life I had the feelin', like most Hawaiian guys, that the future was limited to me. How maybe it's moah bettah for a Kanaka guy to stick to the beach. Moah bettah to forget about big things. Big things and dreams—they're for haoles, I thought. But you came along and suddenly with you I wanted to dream. About the future. I want to quit the beach and become something. I don't know how to yet, but I'll learn. I've nevah had any reason to befoah."

She walked away from him and stood beneath a dark cluster of leaves. She made no sound, but he knew she was crying. She had her arms folded across her stomach and she was bent forward slightly from the waist, standing in a strange, stricken way. He walked over to her. "Don't feel sad," he said.

"I can't help it. I've never taught anyone to dream before. And I want you to dream. That's how everything starts. A person has to have a dream."

"Youh my dream, Ramsey. I love you with everything in me."

"Even though you know I'm going away from you?"

"I've known all along that you'd go away."

"I just don't see how it could work, Peter. No matter how much we love each other."

"Because of this, huh?" He kissed her and released her. "Because when you kiss me, when you touch my skin, you know it's dark, huh?"

"No no no—"

They had both had a considerable amount to drink during the evening, and they were feeling it.

"My dark skin has nevah hurt me befoah, but right now it hurts me down through all the layers to the bone. But tomorrow, I won't give a damn."

She kissed him, to quiet him. Her kiss started demurely enough, then her arms wound tightly about him, and after fulfilling her concessions to convention and her picture about herself, her kiss became a wild, wanton embrace. The meticulously constructed dam within her burst, flooding him in a torrent of abandon, her breasts thrust against him, her hips and belly writhing into him, her mouth a gash of hunger on his. He lost his balance and thumped back against the tree and she was on him in the shadows like an awakened animal. "I want you," she murmured, "I swear I've wanted you all along. I want you to make love to me now, slowly, sweetly, right here, darling, right here and now, and at least we can have this to remember."

He tried to push her away. "No, cut it out."

"Yes yes yes, I'm being honest and unafraid for the first time in my life! Take me, please take me now!"

He lifted her and pinned her against the tree. "No, it wouldn't be any good now. Yoah drunk now, and someday you'd sober up and you'd remembah it, and you'd resent yoahself and hate me for the rest of yoah life."

She slumped bonelessly to the grass beneath the tree and sat there solemnly with her legs pressed tight together, a handkerchief balled and pressed to her lips. The slant of moonlight against her face made her look wan and fragile, like a discontented child. "I didn't think you had it in you," she said. "I'm sorry."

"You've got a lot to learn."

"The only thing I've learned this summer is that I love you; I've learned love and I've learned it doesn't always work out."

"Suah."

She heard the bitterness in his tone but she was too weary, too emotionally exhausted, to convince him otherwise. She looked up at him through the leafy darkness and she realized again that she could see no difference between them. "I love you with all my heart. I think I'll always love you."

After a moment, he said, "I'd moah bettah be goin'. Aloha, Ramsey."

Try not to think about the people until tonight, Ramsey said to herself. If you think about them now you'll start to cry all over again. You can save all of tonight to think about them. And tomorrow night. And all the rest of the nights. Right now just think about the Island and the way it's growing smaller and smaller and watch it until it disappears beyond the horizon, and if the people keep interfering you can close your eyes and remember that you promised them you would return. If things get too bad, you can keep telling yourself that until you actually start believing it: someday you'll return.

She was leaning against the railing of the promenade deck of the *Lurline*. It was the sort of late afternoon when the water is very blue. On shore straight ahead of her she could pick out Nuuanu Avenue winding its way like a slick black ribbon toward the pali, then Roundtop and Tantalus and the house in Upper Manoa, and down the ferny slopes to Kewalo Basin, and then Ala Wai where the fleet of slender yachts rode the tide with quiet dignity and finally the curve of Waikiki and she remembered her first night out with Peter Noa and the way she had slapped him when he had kissed her. Peter Noa, she reasoned, will never change. He will always be on the beach, because that is the life he truly loves, and it would have been wrong for me to stir him with discontent, to try and change him. But you were not supposed to think of the people yet, she told herself; think of the place, think of Honolulu.

Far to her left, Honolulu lay under its warm glory, the cloud rack high above the Koolaus. Honolulu, she thought, is a belled, honey-throated city in the middle of a country of sea. It is a tattered poem, a teahouse on a hill, a path lined with shower trees and fallen pikaki, a cannery stink, a quality of heat, a slant of moonlight, a valley where warm rain falls and opens orchids, a melody that Menotti has yet to compose, a season of firecrackers and Polynesian drums and China bells when the trailing Bon dances of Japan and the dragon rites of China compete with the fawn-graceful hula; Honolulu is the drift of plumeria across the marbled gardens of Blackpoint and the drift of gutter smells through the alleyways of Kalihi where slum kids like Bobby Villanueva and Bobo Olson have to fight their way to survival. It is the city where they do not celebrate Lincoln's birthday, but Kamehameha's, where no billboards mar the scenery and no snakes or poisonous insects mar the lush gardens; it is the city where the districts bear the strange-sounding names like Kaimuki, Kapahulu, Kalanianiole, Waimanalo, Moiliili and Palolo; the air is sweet and filled with varied tongues—the clipped gravity of the Japanese, the robust guttural of the Hawaiian, the lusty bellow of the Portuguese, the delighted screams of the Filipinos betting at some secret cockfight in Wahiawa, the brittle pidgin gaiety of pretty Chinese girls leaving Iolani School, their voices like the falling of coral petals in some giddy, far-off land. Honolulu is the crossroads city of East and West and North and South, where foreign correspondents arrive at dusk, lonely and scarred from covering the Asian wars, and talk with admirals and generals about the ever-coming East; it is a statehood torch that will burn atop Punchbowl until the star is granted; a new beach hotel; a fat, ridiculously dressed sunburned tourist; a gull passing lovely white against a green mountain; a ship leaving port and a sailor getting drunk, walking down the canal along River Street with his arm about the expansive waist of a dark-skinned, pleasant whore, she barefoot, big sausage calves, laughing, wearing the sailor's cap jauntily on the back of her head; it is a Kewalo Basin fisherman teaching his son how to make a strong net and it is a pretty girl making love. And, Ramsey James thought, it is all over. Those moments when time stood still and the stars flashed brighter than diamonds against the dark sky and she and Peter Noa would walk along the beach hand-in-hand until they came to the exact center of the night where everything ugly and brutal and cold seemed far away and here kiss and speak of love—all that was over; pau, finished. Because it would never have worked out, and it's silly, now, to keep thinking about the one, small, grave, lovely chance it did have of working out.

As the ship purled past Diamond Head, it issued from its funnels two long, familiar blasts, the same as she had heard so often from the beach, the four o'clock in the afternoon farewell to the Islands, and she knew, finally, that she was leaving the Islands behind. Hawaii, most generous in her loving, most warm in her hospitality, her welcome had been impartial. To her great heart she had enfolded all, some alien and good, some alien and bad, all embraced and cherished by Hawaii. As, Ramsey liked to think, I too have been loved by this land, and I too am alien.

She squeezed her eyes shut. She tried to keep Peter Noa tightly sealed in some hidden compartment of her mind. Later, she knew, she would have to let him out. But not now. Now it was all over. Let the ship sail.

"That's an awful big cry you're working up," a man's voice said to her.

She turned to find a tall, blond, collegiate man leaning against the railing next to her. He was neatly dressed, tan, with clear wide-set blue eyes and brush-cut hair, grinning at her from a face cast in the traditional mold of the American athlete. He reminded her of the men in Jon Whitcomb's illustrations. She had seen the face a thousand times before, at the Stanford beer-busts, at Burlingame cocktail parties, at the "hungry i" and the Top of the Mark. "I hope I'm not out of line," he said pleasantly.

"No. You just surprised me." She dabbed a tear from her cheek. "I'm just having one of my silly moments."

"Sentimental, not silly," he said. He flipped his cigarette overboard and crossed his ankles, half slouching against the railing. "I know how you feel. It seems too beautiful a place to leave."

"I was crying because I hated so to leave. Yet I know I had to."

"We all have to leave sometime," he said. "Maybe you'll come back someday." He looked at the collar of leis about her throat. "May I?" he said, and he slipped the top lei over her head and placed it in her hands.

"They say that as you sail past Diamond Head you should toss your lei overboard, and if it floats in toward land, then you'll return."

"And if it floats out to sea?"

"Then you and everything in Hawaii are finished, over with."

"I'll take a chance," she said, throwing the orchid lei as far as she could. They watched it disappear in the wake of the ship.

"Name's Blake," the young man said, lazily extending his hand to her. "Jim Blake."

She hesitated, then smiled at him, liking him. He was, after all, so clean-cut and charming. So like home and all the things she had grown up with and become part of. "My name's Ramsey James."

"Pretty name—pretty girl."

"Pretty line," she grinned, "pretty old familiar line."

"Will the pretty girl with the pretty name forgive my pretty line and permit me a question?"

"Shoot."

"Will you join me for dinner? It's not a line."
"It sounds like a nice invitation."
"How about a nice answer?"
"Okay, you're on, Jim Blake."

He took her by the arm and started leading her to the bar when she remembered about the lei. She took a last glimpse over the railing, but she could not see it.

"The legend isn't true anyway," he said lightly, waiting for her.

"I—I guess not."

"If you really want to go back, throw the rest of them over. You've got a wreath around your neck that would make Silky Sullivan jealous."

"You mean throw them all overboard?"

"Why not? One of them is bound to float into Waikiki and some beachboy will pick it out of the water and that'll mean that someday you'll return to him."

She looked curiously at him a moment, wondering if he knew anything about her. But she decided he was just being glib and making a guess. "No," she said, keeping the leis. "I guess that's not for me."

"Good." He took her hand. "We have time for two drinks before dinner." She smiled at him and linked her arm through his as they walked down the deck to the bar.

Peter Noa sat quietly on his surfboard out at first break, watching the *Lurline* fade into the horizon. Several of the leis that the passengers had tossed overboard were drifting in now, but he didn't pay any attention to them. He paid no attention to the waves, either. Surfing didn't seem to be any fun today. He just sat on his board, watching the *Lurline* finally disappear over the horizon.

The trouble with you and me, Ramsey James, he thought, is that we didn't meet when we should have met. When we were both ripe to meet; when it was scheduled. That kind of a time rolls by and nothing you can do can bring it back. You can cry and you can whimper and you can beg and you can pray but you can't bring time back, and you can't travel backwards over your own road to try another turn instead of the one you took.

Aloha, Ramsey.

Chapter Eleven

IT WAS a young girl of a morning, soft and almost wanton, filled with the radiant promise of Island October. The sky was bright as glass above the coral singing sea. Yet there were strange nuances sweeping across the sky, vague, barely perceptible, bringing with them the fine filaments of storm. Early in the afternoon, clouds started scudding along the Kona Coast with a curious absence of plan or destination. They swooped with all the erratic indecision of gulls over Kailua town and over the white-washed steeple of St. Peter's Church. The church was a box of charm no larger than a bungalow, built of wood and volcanic rock on a promontory at the edge of Kailua Bay. Along the mauka wall of the church was a grove of poinciana and old palms, and a low hedge of cape plumbago choked by weeds. There was a small green lawn in front of the church with a shell path curving to the entrance and a file of young colvillea on either side of the path. At intervals a shaft of sunlight would move through the unpredictable clouds and through the colvillea and waver upon the path and the church itself with a graceless quality, with a final saffron-colored light which made Sloan seem unduly somber as she stood at the end of the path, proud and impatient and discreet, waiting for the wedding to start.

All morning long she had moved through a misted world, delicately responsive to the lift and float and flow of love that closed around her. She had never felt more alive and restless, as though life was burning high within her, scorching her remotest nerves. Her cheeks were flushed, her eyes brilliant with high enthusiasm, her smile full of warm secrets. She had whirled through the giddy rhythm of the morning with unceasing heartbeat, humming some vague melody she could not identify, her clear voice like some incredibly sweet and lilting bell rising above the confusion of Manoalani as it was being prepared for the reception. Early in the afternoon she leaned out of the window in her room, looking doubtfully beyond the leafy treetops of Kailua town to the white spire of the church. Ragged clouds had started coming in, and she hoped desperately that it would not rain. It couldn't rain!

"Good gracious, honey, you're supposed to be taking a nap," Laura said, entering the room.

"I can't! Sleep is for babies and old folk, not for a girl about to be married." She danced across the floor of the room as if it were water and gave Laura a kiss.

The melody she had been humming all morning popped back into her head as Laura was buttoning her into her bridal gown. The dress was of very soft white silk brocade, elegant in its simplicity, molded to her hips and waist and flowing from the backs of her calves in a slender train. Laura adjusted the train. "Do you feel able to walk in it?"

"No." Sloan grinned. "That's the only thing I'm afraid of, that I'll get all tangled up in the train and sprawl down the aisle."

Laura laughed with her. "Every bride who ever walked down an aisle has been afraid of the same thing. And I've never heard of it happening."

There was a knock on the door and Tani Akana came in.

"Sloan honey, you're going to be late for your own wedding," she said. She walked over and kissed Sloan lightly on the cheek, stepped back and inspected her with admiration. "But then, no groom would mind waiting for all of this!"

"I'm so glad you're here, Tani. I was afraid for a while. You know, what with Ward and Daddy blasting each other all the time."

Tani smiled. "Darling, you know nothing could keep me away from your wedding. And Ward too."

"Is Ward downstairs?"

"No. He thought it would be better to wait at the church. He'll be here for the reception though. Maybe he and your father can patch things up then."

Sloan frowned. "I've decided, this last day under his reign, to give my father a wide berth. I haven't seen him all day long."

"I know," Laura said, helping Sloan adjust the ivory lace veil. "He's waiting for you downstairs."

For the first time that day, Sloan became aware of increasing nervous tension. She swallowed hard, clutched her little bouquet of pikaki and white orchids tightly to her midriff.

"Be careful, you'll crush them," Tani said.

Sloan wet her lips. "I guess—finally—I'm a little scared."

Tani winked at her. "Don't be too scared. People always say that the bride looks beautiful, but in your case it's an understatement. I've never seen anyone lovelier, Sloan darling."

Sloan paused before the full-length mirror of her room, pinned back her veil, lifted her head in a slight feminine gesture, her face young and white with emotion. She studied herself candidly for a moment, and the feeling that in one hour she would belong completely and openly to Paul Kahana coursed through her and spread over her like her wedding gown going on. She replaced the veil, and still looking at her reflection in the mirror, thought: Well, Sloan Howland, you're starting off on your one big turn around the track—so run a good race.

Slowly, and with a sense of pageantry, she descended the long curving stairway of Manoalani, the light filtering through the leaded glass windows framing her in rich solemnity. She saw Aaron at the foot of the stairs, a drink in his hand. His expression was oblique, almost baffled. His mouth hung slightly open; his eyes seemed glazed. At the police investigation afterwards, all she could remember about Aaron that day was the way he had looked at her as she descended the stairs. That plus the fact that he was drunk.

At the bottom of the stairwell old Willard waited, rigidly erect and implacable in his tailed white linen suit, his boots shined to a dark gloss. A lock of hair stirred restlessly across his high skull, and she realized with a renewing sense of loss how old, how utterly weathered he had become, his head like a fierce bust of veined granite. The eyes in that face of his turned toward her with awed and unmeasurable affection, and with pain. The slow color rose in his leathery cheeks and he sucked in his breath sharply as if he had seen a ghost, but he recovered quickly and his face grew incommunicable; and if, as Sloan feared, each second of her wedding was a secret wound in his heart, he fought against giving any indication of it. Sloan's eyes, soft beneath the veil, glanced expectantly into his, but he chose to ignore them. He crossed the stairwell, walking slowly, grayly, in his struggled erectness, bowed charmingly to her and extended his arm. She turned her grave smile full upon him, and he spoke with unfailing courtliness about her beauty and how he wished her well. Then he escorted her with terrific slowness down the steps of Manoalani and into the limousine, his old hand trembling as he opened the door, and together they drove silently through town to the church, where she stood now alone at the end of the path, her shoulders at a defiant angle, her delicate face thrown up, her gloved hand pushing a strand of indefinite hair back in place.

The guests had all filed inside the church now. Only Peter Noa and Bobby Villanueva remained outside, as Kahili bearers, one at each side of the church entrance, their golden-feathered capes whirling in the ocean breeze. From inside the church she heard the organ being played, the Wedding March, and a choir of young Hawaiian boys lifting their bell-like voices to the music. She saw Ward and Tani hurry into the church, Ward turning to wink at her. She caught a glimpse of Laura, her matron-of-honor, standing nervously just inside the church, waiting for the procession. Then she saw old Willard walk gravely up the path toward her.

She could feel the whipping of blood in her throat. Her fingers clutched the bridal bouquet damply. She felt her mouth tremble and she closed her eyes for a moment. It had been such a long time since she had prayed, since she had even considered God. She bowed her head in concentration and tried to pray, but she could not remember any of the dun, desperate, chaotic, chattering words of formal prayer. She felt awkward and self-conscious for a second, then decided to talk to God in her own words:

Dear God, please let me thank you for all the gifts you have bestowed upon me; and especially for this gift of love. Please help me treasure it and protect it. And especially, too, for the gift of the child that is within me now; the child you have given me and of which only you and I are aware; I have not yet told Paul. Please send me the grace to bear and love and cherish and guide this child, and become a good woman, a good wife, a good mother, Amen.

As her prayer ended, so did the organ music and the choir singing. She knew then that everything was ready, everyone in place; the minister before the altar, the guests jammed solid in the pews of the tiny church, craning their necks as they watched the entrance; Paul waiting for her, quietly; Dean, his best man, at his side.

At the entrance to the church, she looked up at Peter Noa and saw a tear well in his eyes. She leaned her head to one side, as if listening to distant thunder, but the thunder did not come. From just inside the church, she heard Kapiolani Kahana's rich, lovely voice begin the hauntingly beautiful Hawaiian wedding song, "Ke Kali Nei Au."

Her young live arm tightened about old Willard's like a warm wand. Slowly, and with regal splendor, she started down the aisle, hesitating on each step, in time with the strains of the music. And there was something more than glory, something unforgettable in the slender way she walked; a fine-fibered creature, her breathing very young and eager and exciting as she came closer to Paul; when she pinned back her veil, her sensitive face was higher and cut finer and more articulate than ever before, and as she became Mrs. Paul Kahana, all the hopes and glories and wishes in the world glistened in her eyes.

From his vantage point by the grand piano, Willard watched his guests file in from the main entrance of Manoalani, pass noisily through the living room and out into the banyan garden. The French windows by the piano had been opened and he could look down into the garden at what appeared to him to be half the population of Hawaii swarming insatiably about the two twenty-foot-long buffet tables crowded with platters of sliced ham, turkey and beef, chicken salad, tuna salad, potato salad, terayaki steak, chopped mahimahi, half a dozen kinds of fish and fruit, all manner of vegetables, bread, rolls and pastries. The Filipino waiters in their white mess jackets were having a difficult time replenishing the platters. The circular bar around the giant banyan tree already was three deep, the four bartenders working it harried. Willard noticed with mild distaste that the bandstand should not have been placed in such proximity to the bar. Two members of the eight-man orchestra hired to play at the reception were already drunk. If they start to dance with the guests I'll have them thrown out, Willard thought, union cards or no union cards. The dance floor, which seemed so spacious an hour ago, now seemed insufficient for the crowd. Champagne corks popped with total disregard for the tempo of the music and the champagne flowed and foamed, and Willard noted with something akin to dismay that it was only six o'clock in the evening. The party was only an hour old and already, he guessed, a thousand dollars' worth of food and drink had vanished. Plans called for a midnight supper featuring rare prime ribs of beef and baked Alaska, more champagne, and dancing until dawn. He should have opposed the marriage more strenuously and forced Sloan to elope, he thought wryly, watching the scene in the garden. Except for one thing—Manoalani was alive again, as it hadn't been for years. Old houses, like old men, should be granted one last proud gallop at their close.

"Feeling nostalgic?" a voice behind him said quietly. "Or are you just down in the dumps because all the loot that went into this party could just as well have gone into your campaign fund?"

Willard turned to see the familiar, rumpled form of Dr. Earl Judd at his side. "Hello, you sweet old degenerate," Willard said fondly. "Pour yourself a drink."

"I have," Dr. Judd said, exhibiting a glass of dark amber-colored whisky. "A triple, with a piece of ice. Sorry I can't professionally suggest the same for you." He was a thick-set, shambling man in his late fifties; the only man Willard ever knew who could manage to look unkempt even in the white dinner jacket, black tie and tuxedo trousers he was wearing. It was obvious from the thick unruly shock of gray on his skull that he regarded the combing of hair as a fad that had never caught his fancy and would soon fade from fashion. Occasionally his thick, stubby fingers would brush up through his hair, but it would repeatedly fall again across his forehead. His eyes were small and bright blue, judicious, objective, slightly scornful. His wide mouth was carved with cynical amusement. He had an acid edge to his tongue and delighted in his quick-witted facility of saying exactly what he thought, no matter where he was, no matter whom he spoke to. He had once been a brilliant neurosurgeon, destined for a success of almost classic dimensions; but he had suffered the bad luck of a scalpel slip during a thousand-to-one operation and the worse luck of an acid-tongue slip before the executive committee of the American Medical Association, and he had come to Hawaii thirty-one years ago as a general practitioner, working mostly among the plantation laborers and the natives, accepting as his fee anything they were able to offer. He had accepted an outrigger canoe for an emergency appendectomy and a crate of pineapples for delivering twins. Almost a quarter of a century before, he had saved the life of a Howland Ranch cowboy after the regular ranch doctor had given up, and since then had been Senator Howland's personal physician and one of his few truly close friends.

"How are things at the abortion mill, Doc?" Willard said.

"Fine," Dr. Judd said, circling his fingers about Willard's wrist, taking count. "I've been working on a secret remedy to prevent all young children from pain. Hold still."

Willard shook his wrist free. "This is a goddamn wedding reception, not a clinic."

"You look like you might be better off in a clinic," Dr. Judd said, his clear, bleak eyes studying Willard. "If you had had to pump one more handshake on that reception line you'd have ended up handshaking with the Great Boss Himself. That is, if you're headed in that direction, which I doubt. I don't know whether you're popping heroin or triple TNT pills into that system of yours, but you better come see me someday this week."

"I'll come see you after the elections," Willard said. "Have another drink."

"I will, but you'd better not. And you'd better not wait until after the elections. You come in this week, or I'll hold a press conference and show the news guys your latest cardiograph."

Sloan and Paul worked their way through the press of people and joined them at the piano. Dr. Judd kissed Sloan on the cheek and shook hands with Paul. "The reason I like to look at these kids is because they seem so much more alive than the rest of the world," Dr. Judd said. "Sloan baby, if I had known when I slapped your fanny and ushered you into the world that you'd grow up with all this radiance, I'd have married you myself. As for you, young fellow," he said to Paul, "keep the dream in your eye. As long as a man can hold on to just one dream he can stay undefeated and he can still love." He turned to Willard. "I guess now you think you're going to dance with the bride?"

"Damn right I am," Willard answered gruffly, walking past the doctor and taking Sloan into his arms.

"No Fred Astaire stuff." Dr. Judd winked at Sloan. "And make it this week," he said to Willard's back as the old man and his daughter descended into the garden, into a wavering band of gold that had slipped through the clouds and etched the fierce rutted profile of Senator Howland and the sweet beauty of Sloan as they moved together slowly and with utter grace to an old kind waltz.

Dr. Judd watched them for a moment. Then he put down his drink, and without looking at him, patted Paul on the back of the shoulder and said, "Luck, boy," and worked his shambling frame through the crowd to the bar, thinking, as he did so, that he had never seen a more sumptuous feast in all his life. Let's see, he thought, taking his position at the bar and looking over the crowd, the church holds about a hundred people. And there's at least three, or probably four times that many people here now; a regular four hundred party. He grinned, and remembered the figure the following morning, when the newspapers claimed that never before in the history of Hawaii had there been so many witnesses to murder.

"What time is it?"

"Nine o'clock," Sloan said. "We've been married four hours. Two hundred and forty minutes. Fourteen thousand four hundred seconds. And our marriage hasn't been consummated yet. Are you sure you're still in love with me?"

"Very suah." He kissed her. "And we've got a suite with a huge bed waiting for us at Volcano House."

"Are we going to stay in bed for our whole honeymoon?"

"Why not? Do you have a bettah suggestion?"

"No," she said. "What if the volcano erupts?"

"We'll make our own eruption. My things are in the stationwagon, all ready to go."

"My God," Sloan said, "I haven't even packed!"

"Well hurry, honey."

"It'll take me twenty minutes to change and pack. Don't be impatient, darling. We have the rest of our lives."

She kissed him softly. They made their way to the stairs, and as she mounted the first few steps, many of the guests jammed excitedly into the stairwell. She tossed her bouquet high into the air. And as she watched it arc just beneath the chandelier and hang suspended for a second before it started falling, the thought flashed through her mind: I am the happiest girl in the world. Then she hurried up to her room.

Aaron could not enjoy one bit of it. He had attended the wedding through a sense of family obligation. But he had not wanted to attend the reception. He did not want to see Sloan, the Howland name, Manoalani itself, disgraced. When he had looked at Sloan on the staircase a moment before, he had thought that there was a wonderful sauciness about her; a look of emotional competence and fulfillment, as though she were completely alive and at home in her skin. Then Paul had joined her for the photographers and the sight of it made him want to vomit. That dark hand on his sister's pure skin.

He made his way over to the bar and ordered a double martini. He downed it quickly and ordered another.

"Are you trying to blot yourself out?" Dr. Judd asked him.

Aaron grinned and took a stool next to him. "Why not? Lose my identity, lose all the mangled pieces of myself. You've been doing it for years, Doc."

Dr. Judd shook his head. "No, it's too dangerous a compulsion for me to try it. Besides, it can't work. Next morning you wake up and you're all there together again with all your own juices and bones and torments."

"Drink up, Doc," Aaron said. All evening long he had been at the bar, drinking with remote efficiency, watching the party. Aaron ordered another drink, but Dr. Judd declined. "To tell you the truth," Aaron said, "I'm not trying to blot myself out. I'm on my best behavior tonight. Truth is, the whole family thinks I'm some sort of an alcoholic; an embryo candidate for the psycho ward. So I'm playing it cagey. Show 'em how wrong they are."

"You're doing a great job of it." Doc frowned. "Almost spectacular."

Aaron pushed his drink away. "What do you expect me to do, Doc, while that damn fool hoyden of a sister of mine ruins her life with that gook—"

"Oh come off it, Aaron, you're just using that as an excuse for your drinking and your own disintegration," Dr. Judd said. "You're using Sloan's wedding as moral fodder. A target for all your torments. And you think it gives your drinking validity as flight from indignation and grief. But a blind man could see through it."

Aaron turned and stared at him with calculated arrogance. "Why is it that all the broken-down GPs feel they've got to talk like head-shrinkers?"

"Okay," Dr. Judd said without taking offense. "Have it your way. But just one word of caution, Aaron: your drinking is down-drinking, unhealthy; it's almost an hysterical compulsion with you. A man can thump his chest and flex his biceps all he wants, but inside, emotionally, he's a pretty delicate organism. And an emotional crack-up can come when he least expects it. It's like a roller coaster—you're up one second on top of the world, and the next second you've slid down into the pits. And the coaster can be women or horses or money or booze, or just the utter frustration of trying to accomplish something worth while in life."

"You know what my coaster is, Doc?"

Dr. Judd looked at him curiously. "What?"

"Trying to beat time."

"There's no way to stop the clock, Aaron. No way to turn it back. But there is a way to beat it."

"How?"

"By doing something of value."

Aaron grinned shrewdly. "That's a mouthful of limp philosophy."

"Well, starch it up and try it sometime," Dr. Judd said. He finished his drink and walked away.

Aaron leaned back against the bar, nursing his dogged gloom. He lost track of his drinks. He knew he was tight, and he could sense the gin beginning to depress him, but he had another anyway, and in the midst of the gay crowd he stood alone and angry, giving way to the dissatisfactions of subjective thought. Plumeria blossoms slanted across the bar and dropped without concern about his shoulders, down to his feet. Japanese lanterns rode like rocking moons in the soft breeze that drew across the dance floor.

This has been the goddamnedest year for me, Aaron thought, his brain wandering back through the alleyways of memory, peering into closets, looking under the rugs of his heart, searching for some unknown grail that he admitted he needed desperately, that he hoped he would recognize once he came upon it. Ever since that damned birthday party I seem to have lost track of myself; I seem to spend the day wondering where I've been and where I might be going and why the hell I've been where I've been and why the hell I'm going where I seem to be going. Which is nowhere. Lei Villanueva put it so perfectly one night:

"I'm going to have your baby, Aaron," she had said. "I'm going to have your baby and love your baby because I want it and it will need love. But you and I are through. You and I are going nowhere," she had said. "I want a bright future. Yours will be dark, because you hate everything."

"That's not true," he had said. "I just hate your being all ballooned out like—I just hate your being pregnant."

Her face was without expression, but he had the vivid impression that she had grown contemptuous of him. Almost disgusted. "I've noticed that, Aaron," she said.

She was sitting in front of her dressing table. She had just stepped out of the shower and the ends of her hair were damp and she was rubbing them vigorously with a towel. She wore a pair of flimsy flesh-colored nylon panties and that was all. Aaron was sitting back on the vast bed, seeing her reflection tripled in the three sided mirror. From every angle, he saw that she was still the taut, vital, exotic woman, despite the swollen breasts, the obviousness of her stomach. She stood up and slipped on a maternity bra, her arms craning awkwardly behind her, hammocking her breasts, and when she sat next to him and he adjusted the clips for her he could feel the sudden dryness under his tongue, the tremble and arch of desire. When he reached for her she tried to block him. "Is that all you want, Aaron?" she said. "Is that all you've ever wanted of me?"

He forced her down and he heard her mutter something like "All right then, take it," as she lay motionless beneath him and afterwards he realized that it was no good. It was worse than no good. It left him with an aftertaste of emptiness and shame and a slow steady increase of gloom. He poured each of them a drink and when he placed hers on the bedside table he saw that she was crying, soundlessly, as if from a private pain. He sat on the edge of the bed.

"I'm sorry, Lei."

"It doesn't matter."

"I don't know what's wrong with me lately. It's like I'm not wearing my own body or something. Like there was a big vacuum in time. Jesus Christ, I don't understand it. I'm twenty-two, just like you, and the next second I'm damn near forty and I'm wondering where the hell I've been, and what the hell I've been doing and where the hell all the years went. I keep chasing after something, I don't know what—but every time I get close enough to catch it, it flies away. And I've used up half my time already. Doing what? Nothing: like a tin man clanking down the path to Oz and when the path ends he falls over the edge of the world because there is no Oz." He sipped his drink. He seemed bleak and contemplative for a while, thinking over what he had said, what there was left to say, and he started to cry. "I thought maybe having you would be having the answer."

"I'm sorry," she said quietly. "Maybe it could have been." She got up from the bed and walked to the lanai and leaned against the door, her face to the sea. "When you came to me," she said, "I thought you wanted my love. And I gave you my love. I wanted to. You seemed to need it so badly. But I never meant love to you. Flesh, lust maybe, but not love. I was nothing more to you than a cushion to soften the sharp knocks of your anxieties and frustrations.

"But all this fuss over the abortion destroyed my love for you. It made me feel used. Now I guess I just feel sorry for you. You're an emotional cripple. You spit on dreams."

After a while Aaron said, "Can we have a drink together?"

"Yes." Lei went to the liquor cabinet and poured two fresh drinks. "That's one thing we can still do."

Aaron gazed slackly into his drink. "At first," he said, "I wanted to have you so I could conquer time."

Lei nodded. She avoided looking into his eyes. "When you destroyed our love, Aaron, you destroyed your victory over time."

Lei had put it so perfectly that night, Aaron thought, leaning against the bar in the banyan garden. But he did not want to think of Lei, or of her love-making, or of the end of her love-making, or of the baby that was almost due now, or of himself, or of Dr. Judd's innuendoes that perhaps he needed psychiatric care, or of that stupid wet remark of Judd's about doing something of value. Just what could he do that would be of value? he asked himself. He shrugged his shoulders. Nothing. Then, like a door being opened, like a road where before there had been jungle, he knew what he could do. He looked up along the wall of Manoalani until he saw Sloan's bedroom window. The light was on. Maybe he could still catch her. Apologize. Wish her well. He put his drink down on the bar. Maybe he could find that Kahana kid too, he thought, cutting across the dance floor to the veranda. Shake hands with him. Wish him good luck.

He hurried up the side stairs to the veranda and Bobby Villanueva moved out of the shadows.

"Remember me?"

"What do you want?"

"I'm goin' to kill you," Bobby said. He was drunk. Sweat beaded on his forehead.

"C'mon, kid, you're flying. I'll talk to you some other time." He tried to walk around him but Bobby blocked his way.

"I said I'd get you and I meant it," Bobby said. His hand slipped from his pocket. Aaron heard the oiled click of the switch-blade knife.

"Now wait a minute, kid, what the hell do you want to cause this kind of trouble for?" Aaron cried, knowing that his voice was whimpering, like a petulant child's.

The blade came up to his throat, glinting clean and silvery. "Cut it out, goddamn it!" Aaron said. He felt his knees tremble, then his whole body shook. His lips felt thick, but he managed to get it out: "You're drunk, kid, you don't know what you're doing." He swung ponderously with heavy, wooden muscles, trying to push Bobby out of the way. Bobby reeled back against the railing of the veranda. Then he swept in low, the knife poised in his hand. He slashed with the expertness of the street fighter, but Aaron had rocked down to his knees. Bobby spilled over him and into the wall. He crouched there for a second, nostrils wide, neck swollen. "You sonofabitch, I'm going to get you this time!"

He slashed wildly. Aaron blocked it and smashed a roundhouse into the side of his head. Then he rammed his fingers into his throat as hard as he could. Bobby gagged. Aaron kicked him in the knee, and when Bobby started going down, Aaron brought his knee up brutally into his face. He could feel the nose go in a sickening looseness. Bobby moaned, but the pain only made him wilder. He got to his feet and backed off into the shadows. When Aaron moved in on him he raised the knife and slashed, but Aaron caught his wrist and wrestled the knife from his grasp.

Paul and Dean and several other people ran toward the muted scuffling. "Good Christ, what's wrong with you guys!" Paul said. He moved in between them, trying to separate them. The three of them struggled for a moment in the shadows. Aaron felt a knee race painfully to his groin. He had the knife in his own right hand now, and he tried to lunge at Bobby. He could feel a strong hand gripping his right wrist. Then he raised his wrist and broke free of the grip and he brought the knife down hard. He could feel it go in deep, missing all bone. The point of the blade must have slipped in, downwards, at a slight angle, just inside the collarbone, very deep.

When Aaron looked up, Bobby Villanueva was leaning back against the shadowy wall, his face a wash of terror. Aaron could not tell how long Bobby had been leaning there. Paul took an involuntary step backwards. His hand was at his chest where the knife was buried and he looked up at Aaron with an expression of bafflement. But the backward step he took apparently upset his balance, for his body turned slowly to the left and fell heavily to the floor of the veranda. For a moment he shuddered on the floor. His legs writhed in a hesitant motion as though he were trying to run. Then he lay perfectly still.

Sloan screwed the lipstick back down into the gold-plated container and tightened the cap over it. She dropped it in her handbag. She inspected herself in the mirror of her dressing table. She had changed into a new black sheath cotton dress with a smart white jacket over it and she wore a single strand of pearls to set it off. She decided not to wear earrings. For some reason, she winked at herself in the mirror. Then she stood up and looked about her room. At the head of her bed, a row of stuffed toy animals—two tigers, a giant panda, a sleeping kitten and a floppy-eared puppy—seemed to stare happily at her from their glass button eyes. Her suitcase was in the center of the bed, all packed and ready to go. She looked for a warm, curious moment at her bridal gown, hanging in its serene splendor over the chair by her bed. She closed her eyes. Night of my nights, she thought.

There was a knock on her door. She rushed to it and flung it open. But it was not Paul. It was Dean.

"I have to talk to you, Sloan."

Part Two

Chapter Twelve

KAILUA BAY was a flat meadow, pale as absinthe and tiger-striped by rags of cloud shifting across the wearier greens of the sky. Ocean mists drifted somberly as smoke along the beach. It began to rain suddenly; a soft warm rain like tears that blew in gentle gusts from the Kona hills.

Dean walked gravely to the water's edge. He wore a cloak of golden feathers about his shoulders. He carried the ritual urn containing Paul's ashes. He placed the urn on the floor of his canoe. It was a small outrigger, garlanded with flowers. One huge carnation lei wound about the gunwhales from the bow to the stern. Dean wondered a moment about the flowers and the ashes. They did not mix. Flowers were full of color, and young and alive. Ashes were soft and gray and always very old. They seemed to have nothing to do with Paul.

He stepped into the canoe and pushed off from shore through the small crests. His was the third outrigger in the processional. Ahead of him were the two great double war canoes, sailing with ponderous grace toward the reef. Beachboys who had flown over from Waikiki for the services paddled the lead canoe—Long Blue Brown, Rabbit Kealoha, NipNip Rose, Whalebone Charley Akoni, Big Splash Papele, Blackout Kekai—all wearing the traditional vermilion feathered capes. The Reverend Moke Kamuela stood on the koawood platform which had been lashed between the hulls of the canoes. He wore the barbaric headdress and furling golden cloak of the Hawaiian high priest. He stood alongside the crowned savage image of the god Kukailimoku, its head flushed with feathers of the iiwi and oo birds, its mouth grim with the fangs of dogs, its eyes flashing with pearl shells. Peter Noa and King Mud Akapai stood just behind him, bearing the torchlike Kahili staffs of hibiscus blossoms and croton leaves. Manoalani ranch hands paddled the second canoe. On its platform Kapiolani Kahana stood, stiffly indomitable, her head high yet solemn and strangely humble. Torchbearers stood as an honor guard at each corner of her platform. Flanking her canoe were two sixty-foot outriggers in which rode the members of Kamehameha School's *a cappella* choir, dressed in long flowing black funeral robes. Then came Dean's canoe. Behind him were the garlanded outriggers carrying the old Hawaiian priests with their feathered gourds, and finally the drum canoes, silent now, waiting for the ritual to begin.

When they reached the edge of the coral reef, the paddlers turned the canoes in a long slow arc. A man stood up in the bow of each canoe and raised a black orchid lei to the sky, then cast it upon the waters of the reef. The voices of the choir rose in a haunting litany. The soft beat of the sharkskin drums punctuated the Reverend Kamuela's murmurous chanting. As he chanted, he accepted from his torchbearers four leis of black orchids, and these he raised to each wind, blessing the wind, and then cast into the sea. Dean watched the leis separate and begin to drift slowly across the bay. Then he rose solemnly, and with a nod from the Reverend Kamuela, he lifted the urn toward heaven and sprinkled his brother's ashes over the pale absinthe-colored tide.

And in a few shockingly swift moments, Sloan thought, it will be all over. Love and glory and the reason for living will be all over; a handful of gray dust drifting among the flowers out to sea beyond the Kona Coast.

Paul is dead. He will never come to you again. He will never hold you or kiss you again. He will never love you again. You must try to understand that, she told herself. You must learn to accept that, even though it is the most unacceptable thing in the world. You do not have to understand it all at once. Try to understand it in parts. Try to forget him in parts. Try to forget the touch of his hand, or his smile, or the way he laughed. No, those things are impossible to forget. Everything about him is impossible to forget. But you must try, because your survival now depends upon your ability to forget, to accept. Well, what good is survival? By itself it means nothing. It is the things you survive with that count. How do you learn to forget? If you could forget just one thing about him, then maybe, in time, you could forget other things, and slowly he would fade away. But you cannot forget even the slightest detail, and maybe it is because deep down in your secret heart you do not want to forget. You refuse to forget. Forget the death, yes; but not the life.

For a moment, Paul, we shut out the world. We loved in a way no two people on earth ever loved before or will again. I am sure of that. I do not ever want to forget you. I promise I will never forget you. I want only to forget the pain of your not being here with me. I want to forget the pain of remaining alive without you. Oh Paul, I wish I had told you. You're not dead, Paul. You'll never be completely dead. Do you understand what I am trying to tell you, Paul? There is a part of you living and growing within me.

She stood absolutely alone, in a little grove of poincianas, from whose lower branches drooped the sad poetic festoons of island moss. The wind drew through the moss with a lost, murmurous sound. From the reef she could hear the choir's hymn.

She closed her eyes, feeling a little dizzy. Her knees trembled. She flexed the muscles in her thighs and stiffened her knees, being careful to keep her back arched, her body rigid. If she slumped, if she showed the least sign of buckling, she knew her father and Dr. Judd would leave the group of mourners down the beach to come and stand by her side. And she wanted to be alone.

She shook her head to clear away the dizziness. She knew she had been pretty strongly drugged for the services. She had the vague impression of being doped-up all week long, ever since the killing. She felt sodden and glassy from it. She felt abused. It seemed to her now that Dean had knocked on her bedroom door and told her of Paul's death, and the next instant the needle was going into her. And each time she drifted aimlessly up from sleep and tried to collect her shattered passions, tried to understand and cope with what had happened, she could feel the needle again and the fluid coursing through her, making her vague. Death had turned her vague; sick and drained of feelings. She needed no sedatives. The great gray weight of death had numbed her with a brutality far more efficient than any medical fluid. Yet there had been nights when she woke up screaming, and on those occasions the needle brought something close to peace: a semicatatonic state during which she would lie in her bed without emotion, sensing the worn security of walls, listening to the dark rain against the roof.

Once she had been awakened by the tolling of bells. She got out of bed, her eyes a little blind, a little lost. She walked unsteadily past her dressing table, past the watchful but unseeing eyes of a row of bedroom animals which had been arranged precisely along the top of the bookcase. She caught a glimpse of herself in the mirror, like a thin gray ghost. I do not want to live, I want to die, she told the ghost. She walked to the window. The curtains drifted wearily with faint, almost fluted sounds. It was later than the time of golden dusk, and not yet twilight. The bells were ringing from the steeple of St. Peter's Church. Sloan thought: The last time I heard those bells . . .

She parted the curtains and leaned across the windowsill.

There was a knock on her door and Sloan turned, white-faced, to see Kapiolani Kahana enter the room. Kapiolani drew in her breath. "Oh good lawrd, baby, what are you thinkin' of!"

Sloan bolted back into bed, hurling the covers over her head. She lay there in a tight motionless knot until she could no longer breathe. When she looked up she saw Kapiolani sitting calmly on the edge of the bed, looking down at her with her dark limpid eyes, her face stained with tears. Kapiolani shook her head. "No, baby, that ain't no answer."

Sloan did not move. She lay rigid in the bed, her body straight and her legs pressed close together, the covers drawn to her chin.

Her face was small and wan against the pillow, framed by the rich sprawl of her hair. Kapiolani sought her hand and held it. "Sloan dahlin', tryin' something like that won't help. Paul would be grievin' if he thought you'd evah try anything like that. You got to go on now, foah both you and Paul. It's God's will, dahlin'," Kapiolani said. "The Good Lawrd called Paul foah reasons of His own, and it's not foah us to question."

Just to grieve, Sloan thought. She wished she believed more fully in God. In the utterly blind consolation of prayer. God's will: what a relief to be honestly able to accept such a balm. But how could a person truly accept it? What kind of a God would will such sorrow and pain? And how could you be expected to love such a God? Earlier, she had considered prayer. But now the idea repelled her. It would be nothing more than a whimpering, half-hearted, perhaps even resentful gesture, and if there was a God, He had long ago stopped paying any attention to her. After perpetrating a horror like this, God should be the one to pray.

The dizziness left her. She stood erect and still beneath the moss-garlanded trees, and yet there was about her the look of a person oddly broken, as though the life cord within her had been snapped. The beautiful bones of her face showed prominently under the thin ashen flesh. As the canoes started the long solemn pull toward the shore, she stared at them with a certain withdrawn curiosity, her deep, gray-gold eyes so lifeless that the pupils seemed covered with dust. It was as if she had been trapped into observing a scene she did not want to see: something happening in a movie, or a tragedy she had read about in the newspapers; or as if, in her inarticulate grief, she had become a little witless, a remote stranger gazing with mild, confused incredulousness upon the funeral of another stranger.

"Do you feel all right, Sloan?"

"Yes," she said, without turning.

"You frightened me. I thought you were going to faint."

"I'm all right."

Willard placed his hand lightly beneath her bent elbow. Her hands were clenched at her breasts. She was shivering.

"Would you like to go now, Sloan?" he said.

"Go where?"

"Home."

"No."

Earl Judd came up alongside Willard and looked at her doubtfully. "Do you feel tired, Sloan?"

"No." She did not look at either of them. She stared vacantly out across the green bay, hard and old-looking beneath the frail October light. The rain felt sweet against her face.

"Sloan, Doc Judd thinks you should come home now and get some rest. It's been a difficult—"

"I just want to be left alone," she said.

She walked away from them. In sudden restlessness she hurried to the edge of the water and started walking up along the beach, indifferent to the curious glances of the beachboys who were pulling the canoes up along the shore. She heard Dean call out to her but she ignored him. From the corner of her eye she caught a glimpse of him trotting across the sand toward her. She quickened her pace, and after a while, sensed that he no longer followed. She did not look back. She walked a mile up the beach, letting the pain flow heavily through her veins until it turned to weariness; until she felt strangely old and somber. As she walked she tried, for the first time since the raw horror of Paul's death, to rationalize. Paul is dead, but I am alive, she thought. Somehow I must find a way to cross out the hours, and the days, and the years. I must endure, because that is what people do. If I believed in prayer, that would help. But I do not believe in prayer. If I had a career, if I had some work to plunge into, that would help too. But Paul was my life; that is how great my love was, and loving him was to be my career. Perhaps when the baby comes . . .

But I don't want to think about the baby now. I can't think about the baby now. Not yet. I'll think about the baby tomorrow. If I thought about it now, I'd . . .

She shuddered with a sudden attack of weakness and nausea. She leaned back against the trunk of a palm tree. Rain still fell from the green sky. She watched the funeral cars moving slowly along the sea road back to Manoalani.

Toward evening the seas began to thunder into the shore. She saw Dean far up along the beach, coming toward her, tracing her footprints, and she walked out to meet him.

She had reached for love with all the courage and impotency of her need and it had been violently wrenched from her. Well, she would endure. But she would never love again. She had lost confidence in her strength, her sense of survival, her affinity with luck. Luck was riding on your shoulder. Luck was your best friend, because it brought you love. Until one bright day it pulled the rug out from under you.

Paul is dead. What's going to become of me now?

For a moment, Paul Kahana and Sloan Howland loved each other in a way that made each other forget the utter loneliness of the human soul.

Now the moment was over. There once were bells within me, now there is thunder. She did not want to think about it, but her mind kept returning to it the way a child will persist in picking at a scabbed elbow: Paul is dead—what will become of me? I have outlived love.

Chapter Thirteen

AT TEN MINUTES before nine o'clock the following Monday morning, Hawaii County Attorney Al Murakami left the Hilo Hotel and walked down Waianuenue Street to the courthouse. The steady drizzle gave the gray concrete Federal Building a clean look. A row of myna birds cawed and feathered beneath the eaves. Beyond the courthouse, the Wailuku River was running fast and bank-full. The sky was the color of oatmeal. In the distance, a mantle of snow covered the summit of Mauna Loa.

Al Murakami entered the Federal Building and walked in his slow, lumbering gait through the post office and up the polished koa stairway to the second-floor courtrooms. He swung open the door and descended the aisle past the crowded press and spectators' benches to the prosecution counsel's table. He slapped his briefcase disconsolately on the table. He had slept poorly and his digestion was bothering him more than usual. With the palm of his hands, he pressed against the area of stomach cramp. The bacon and greasy fried eggs at the hotel had been a mistake. The breakfast was a sodden, indigestible lump in his stomach. The trial would be a similar mistake, he thought: sodden and completely indigestible.

"Wha s'mattah, Al, you don't look too happy. I thought a man in your position would be verra happy today of all days."

Al looked up into the grinning lemon-colored face of Richie Wong, chairman of the Hawaii County Democratic Central Committee. "How did you get in here, Richie?"

"It's a public court. I thought you'd be happy to see me."

"You've never had one complete correct thought in that thin brain of yours ever since I've known you."

"Okay, so no sweat." Richie Wong moved sleekly around the table and sat on one edge of it. "Say, how come you're so grumbling today? I thought you'd be a verra happy man today."

"You did, huh?"

"Sure. All of us—us Democrats—thought you'd be happy today."

Al looked at him heavily. "Okay, Richie. Why should I be so happy today?"

Richie Wong's lips spread out above his teeth. "Because things are going so unnaturally fast," he said. "Let's see, the Kahana kid was killed eight days ago. And here you are—already in court for trial. The police investigation must have taken all of five hours, the preliminary hearing was waived by the District Magistrate; and I don't know how many scheduled cases were set back in order to get this one heard so quick. You know what I mean: aired-out, heard and over and done with before the elections."

"Don't you fret about it, Richie."

"Okay, so no sweat. I'm not worried. It's just that I always thought that justice never liked to be rushed, ain't that right?"

Al Murakami looked up at him with obvious distaste. "Richie," he said, "I'll bet you know of one political party in this Territory that would offer a fat disgruntled county attorney like me everything in the world to keep this trial and all its publicity rolling right on through till election day, don't you?"

"Yeah, you're sure as hell right. And I'll bet you sure as hell know of another political party that wants this trial over and done with as fast as possible. And me and a lot of other people—you know: voters—are kind of curious how you're going to serve justice when you're speeding things up so quick."

"Don't you worry your thin little brain about justice."

"Okay, Al, okay. But I tell you this, like a friend, huh. Lots of people are going around saying lots of funny things: like the whole trial is rigged."

Al reached into the breast pocket of his seersucker jacket and took out a roll of Tums. He unwound the wrapper, fingered loose the top tablet, and placed it on the tip of his tongue. He looked up, seemingly surprised that Richie Wong was still sitting on the table. "Get out of here, Richie," he said.

Then he sat down in his chair behind the prosecution counsel's table and gazed moodily out the window. He was a blunt, energetic man in his middle forties. His expression was placid, but he had more than his quota of restless mannerisms: he tugged at his ear lobe; he scratched at a bald spot the size of a silver dollar at the back of his skull. His hair surrounding the bald spot was gingery gray. His lips were wide and fleshy and he had very bad teeth. He wore square-cut glasses with heavy tortoise-shell rims, and the glasses were always slipping a little way down his blunt nose and he had a way of looking up over his glasses and grinning wryly at the judge or jury or witness and no one ever noticed that the grin never reached his eyes. His eyes always remained small and dark and watchful, and there was a cold detachment about them, like the noses of two bullets seen down the cylinder of a gun.

He was an amiable man. He had the knack of telling a good story. He had practiced fifteen years before the bar and accumulated a reputation for reliability. Four years ago, his amiability and his reliability won him enough votes to become County Attorney. And he had served the voters with credit. But now, as he sat in the courtroom in his damp nylon shirt, his red figured tie and his seersucker suit, staring out the window, he knew he would not serve creditably today. It had been made very plain to him: he could not convict a Howland in Hawaii.

He turned from the window and gazed down at the polished tabletop. He started playing a mental game that was new to him: a game that had begun shortly after the killing of Paul Kahana. He divided his mind into two sections, like a big white balance sheet with a line down the center. On one side he listed all the things which, as prosecuting attorney for the Island of Hawaii, he could and should do according to the meaning and essence of the law as he interpreted the law: namely—charge Aaron Howland with first-degree murder and win a conviction.

Two days after the abortive police investigation into the killing, he had driven up along the Kona Coast to Earl Judd's office and home at Keauhou. He pulled into the driveway just as the doctor was walking up from the beach, his fishing tackle slung across his shoulder.

"How'd they bite, Doc?"

"Not good not bad." Dr. Judd eyed him speculatively. He had always harbored a deep-seated, humane mistrust of civil law. "What are you doing way up in this country? Trying a little fishing on your own?"

"Yeah, Doc, a little fishing."

They went into the office and Dr. Judd mixed two gin and tonics.

"I've just spent the last two days reading over the sworn statements by the people who witnessed this Kahana killing," Al Murakami said. "None of them are much use. But your statement really throws me, Doc."

"How so?"

"Because it's twenty-two typewritten pages. And it doesn't say a goddamn thing."

Doc Judd shrugged his shoulders. "Well, maybe your cops went about the whole thing the way I went about this afternoon's fishing. Using the wrong bait."

"We don't need any bait for you, Doc. We just want complete answers."

"What kind of answers?"

"Honest answers."

"You got honest answers from me. If you couldn't use them, it's your fault."

"I know they were honest, Doc. I just can't shake this feeling that everything doesn't fit right."

"Like what?"

"Doc, you were the last person to have spoken with Aaron Howland before the fight took place, isn't that right?"

"Yes. I think so."

"Was he drunk?"

"I'm not sure I can answer that. You'd take my opinion as a man and twist it into a medical opinion and pump it up in court—"

"Forget the medical aspects of it, Doc. Did he look or act as if he had been drinking?"

"Yes."

"Heavily?"

"I'd say so."

"But you wouldn't give an opinion on whether he was drunk or not, huh Doc?"

"No, I wouldn't."

"Was he—morose? Depressed in any way?"

Dr. Judd frowned. "Aaron is a strange duck. He's often depressed. I would say yes, he was depressed that night."

"Why?"

"He didn't want Sloan to marry that kid."

"No, I mean why do you say he's often depressed?"

Dr. Judd brushed his hand through the tangled gray mass of his hair. "Al, I'm not a psychiatrist. My opinions concerning the man's depression couldn't hold up in court and I wouldn't want them introduced in court."

"I understand, Doc. But this isn't for the courtroom. This is just for me."

"Why?"

Al got up and paced slowly about the office. "Doc, I'm not on any crusade. I'm just a guy with a job trying to get that job done. Neither you nor me would want to see a murder grease its way through court under a different name. No matter how accidental, no matter how spontaneous that murder seemed. I've got a file of sworn statements two feet thick concerning Aaron Howland, defendant: Aaron Howland drank to excess and became violent; Aaron Howland swore to stop the marriage of his sister, Sloan, to the deceased, Paul Kahana; Aaron Howland had previously threatened the life of the deceased. I've got all that and more, much more. But I can't bring any of it into court. I can't even bring it up before the Grand Jury for a decent indictment. They'd throw it out. It's not enough."

"Do you think there's any more, Al?"

"There might be, and there might not be. I've gone over Aaron Howland's statement with a fine-tooth comb. I've talked with him.

It might all have been accidental, the way he claims, then again it might not have been. It might have been a case of Aaron Howland seeing a perfect opportunity and making use of it."

"If that might be the case, you'd better get your coppers hopping."

"My coppers don't hop," Al sighed. "Not in a case like this. They salute."

"Then maybe you don't have a case, Al," Doc Judd told him.

Al sprawled comfortably into the worn leather chair in the office. He hooked the back of his knee over the arm of the chair. Then he reached into his coat pocket and extracted a notebook. He started turning over the flyleaf pages, one by one, lackadaisically reviewing his notations. "What was this all about? Your telling Aaron Howland to do something of value?"

Doc Judd leaned against the edge of his desk and folded his arms across his chest. "Aaron is an extreme example of a manic-depressive. He's either on top of the world or down in the dumps. For some time now, he's constantly been down. He's fallen into an even, almost psychotic, pattern of depression."

"Would you say he was psychotic?"

"I wouldn't say it in court, no. It wouldn't make any difference anyway: being psychotic isn't a criminal offense. But just between you and me, I'd say he was. He certainly borders on it. He's a complex and massively frustrated creature, goaded by relentless guilt complexes—"

"What kind of guilt?"

Doc Judd shrugged. "It could be caused by any number of things, or a combination of any number of things—furtive childhood habits, resentment of his father, all those Freudian soliloquies."

"Could his guilt be caused by cheating?"

"It could be. But I doubt it. Are you referring to this Villanueva girl?"

"Yes. I talked with her for two hours yesterday. She and her brother Bobby. He started the fight, apparently."

"I know. Aaron had me bring the girl over here from Honolulu to have the baby. She's staying at a private home with some friends in Kailua. No," Doc Judd said, "I don't think his guilt complexes are caused by his affair with that girl. You've got to be careful about that, Al. Suspicion creates the wrong impression of each symbol, each act a man commits. I don't think Aaron's guilt is caused by his affair with Lei Villanueva in the least. I think on the contrary, it might have prompted the affair. He's something of a neurotic erotic. He's obsessed by the passing of time. Many people are, although God knows why we worry about time, since it seems to take care of itself so well. Aaron, like so many of us, is obsessed by this need to get his share before the clock runs out. Life is too short and death too long. He's in a mad headlong race toward nowhere or less. He's a victim of a peculiarly widespread American anxiety: a greed for more lives than one.

"That night at the wedding reception, he started talking about it. So I told him that one way he could beat the clock was by accomplishing something of value."

Al Murakami gazed thoughtfully at his drink. "Do you suppose that he could figure he'd accomplish something of value if he stopped his sister's marriage by killing Paul Kahana?"

Doc Judd nodded. "He could. But I doubt it. He isn't that unstable—mentally or emotionally."

"A man like Aaron Howland seems extremely capable of committing murder, doesn't he, Doc?"

"That's kind of a naïve statement. Especially coming from a county attorney. Murder is within all of us. We're all capable of committing it."

"Doc," Al said, studying his notebook, "do you know how tall Paul Kahana was?"

"About six-three, I'd guess."

"He was exactly six-three. Two hundred pounds. And Bobby Villanueva stands five-feet-seven; one hundred and sixty-seven pounds."

"So what?"

"So I don't think a man could mistake them. Even in the dark."

"Well, put it to a jury."

"Tell me, Doc," Al said quietly. "Is it easy to plunge a knife into a man's heart?"

"No."

"Is it hard?"

"Very hard."

"That's what I thought. During the war, I was with the 442nd Regimental Combat Team: the 'Go For Broke' outfit. I learned a lot about hand-to-hand combat. I learned that you practically had to be an expert to sink a knife into a man's heart."

Doc Judd walked over to a corner of his office where a medical chart depicting the anatomy of man hung from the wall. He pointed to the heart, and indicated vaguely the bones surrounding it. "There is a lot of armor about the heart, protecting it. It's guarded by an intricate arrangement of heavy bones: the ribcage, the breastbone, backbone, others. Unless a man knows exactly what he's doing, and has an expert aim, the blade won't slip through these bones. A man would need a long-bladed knife, a lot of power, a damn good aim—and luck."

"I have a hunch that Aaron Howland had it all," Al said. "Including the luck."

"Bad luck."

"It's a pretty damn tough thing to do, isn't it, Doc?"

"Yes. I'd say it was almost—" He stopped abruptly.

Al Murakami looked up at him over the rims of his glasses. "Almost what, Doc?"

"Nothing."

"Almost impossible, Doc? Almost impossible to do it accidentally?"

Doc Judd's heavy eyebrows curved upward. "Quit playing Scrabble, for Christ's sakes! 'Almost impossible' is a screwy phrase for a county attorney to try to use, especially in a courtroom. There is nothing impossible—accidentally. If you want a straight honest answer you've got to ask a straight honest question."

"Okay, Doc, I get the message," Al said, standing up and placing his empty glass upon the desk. "If I ever want the answer in a courtroom, I'll straighten out the question for you."

Driving back to Hilo that night, he added three more items down the same section of his mental list: motive, disposition, opportunity. Aaron Howland had all three. Bringing a first-degree murder charge would be an ambitious project. It would take some time and a lot of doing. But he believed he could make it stick.

Except for one thing, he told himself: the other section of that mental balance sheet. On the other side of the big dividing line was one singularly brief item—the political future of Alan K. Murakami. If he brought a murder charge, he could rip off that section of the balance sheet and throw it in the wastebasket. Because there would not be any political future. Unless . . .

Unless he decided to buck the Republican brass, step up to the plate by himself and swing for the bleacher seats. And, he reminded himself, connect. There was a chance he could connect. He had the evidence, and he could build a bonfire under the police department and get more evidence. Better evidence. Then he could go before the Grand Jury and somehow convince the members to bring in the indictment. And a conviction in such a widely publicized trial would unfailingly hang his political star high in the heavens. Not as a Republican, of course; but it was a two-party system. He was a politician with no pretenses of statesmanship. This certainly could turn out to be the opportunity he had been waiting for for so long.

But if he gambled and lost? Then he would be all finished. Pau. He had spent his public life within the confines and dictates of the Republican Party. The Republican Party, with Senator Willard Howland's endorsement, named him nominee for County Attorney, with the election assured. If he was to go gung-ho for a murder charge against Aaron Howland at this time, two brief weeks prior to the general elections in which Willard Howland was campaigning for the highest office in the Territory, those same Republican kingpins who had tossed him the County Attorney plum would cut him off at the knees. And they'd fix it so he would never get up again. He was like a crapshooter who had won an enormous amount of money on one roll and it had come time to decide whether to bet again and try for even more money or quit with the amount already won. It was safer, even wiser, to quit and keep what you had. Because the longer you gambled, the more you tried to win, the greater the risk. He needed no initiation into those less public aspects of politics. He did not have to be told; but they told him just the same. They made it clear to him that very night. At Manoalani:

"Hello, Al," Willard had greeted him at the door. "Come in, come in. I'm sorry we found it necessary to make you drive all the way out here on a night like this. Come on in by the fire and maybe we can dry some of that rain off you. What will it be? A couple of inches of Jack Daniels and ice can do wonders for the insides."

"That will do fine, Senator. Or should I say, Delegate Howland?"

Old Willard fixed the drink and handed it to him. "Whether it's to be Senator or Delegate might well depend on you, Al. That's why we had to drag you out here in this storm. To see if you can help pull us out of this mess. And there's no point in kidding you, Al. It's a hell of a mess."

They sat down by the fireplace. There were two other men in the room. One was a tall, wide-shouldered haole named Dwight Candles. He was vice-president of Theo. H. Davies, and Chairman of the Territorial Republican Central Committee. He was impeccably dressed in a dark suit, soft white shirt and black knit tie. His manner was abrupt, his speech clipped as if he regretted having to part with the words. His hair was theatrically gray at the temples, and his forehead was creased in a permanent frown. Al knew him only by reputation. The second man was Mickey Shigita, a wiry, affable Nisei, Chairman of the Hawaii County Republican Central Committee. He and Al were old friends. Mickey Shigita waited for Al to take a couple of good swallows from his drink, then he said:

"Senator Howland and Mr. Candles thought it would be best if I told you straight from the shoulder what the situation looks like, Al."

Al nodded and waited.

"It could look worse," Mickey Shigita continued, "but no one knows how. The Senator and Mr. Candles have just flown back from Honolulu after an all-day conference with Governor Balter and the executive committee. Something has to be done, and it's got to be done immediately if we want to elect a Republican delegate."

"What Mickey is trying to say," Willard muttered, "is that what the Democrats weren't able to do to me, my own family was. Ever since this—this tragedy—I've been losing voters by the hundreds. They attach a stigma to me. They still come out for my speeches, but it's more out of curiosity to stare at Aaron Howland's father than it is to hear what I might have to say concerning statehood. And statehood is my only interest in this matter, Al."

"Yes, I understand, Senator."

"First, Al," Mickey Shigita said, leaning forward on his chair, counting on his fingers, "we have to know if this—this mess—is going to get any messier when you go before the Grand Jury for an indictment."

Al loosened his collar. He wanted another drink. "Well, gentlemen," he said, "we haven't exactly formulated any plans as yet. It looks like it was a case of—"

"May I interrupt?"

Al looked up into the big frowning face of Dwight Candles. "Yes, of course, Mr. Candles."

Dwight Candles stood with his back to the fireplace, his face in shadows. "We might just as well come to the point as quickly as possible. There's much work to be done.

"First, it's quite obvious that no murder charge can be brought up. It was an accidental killing, perhaps committed in self-defense, although I agree, against the wrong person. But I am sure the Grand Jury would never bring in a murder indictment based on any evidence you happen to have, is that not right, Mr. Murakami?"

"I'm—I'm not sure yet. We haven't completed our investigation."

"I am sure. And if you think about it, you will be equally sure. Now—whereas from the facts and the evidence we all know that a murder charge cannot be issued, it is also unwise—politically unwise—to let the whole affair blow over as an accident. It was an accident, we all are aware of that. But the public is not aware of it, and we must convince the public. Therefore, it is absolutely necessary that we have a trial."

"On what charges, Mr. Candles?"

"You think up the charges, you're County Attorney. It's imperative that Aaron Howland stand trial in a public court and be acquitted and it must be done immediately."

Mickey Shigita looked questioningly at Al. "You don't have any real stuff you could convict him with, do you, Al?"

Al slowly shook his head. "No."

"Good. Then there are no legal or moral difficulties. All that must be done is a little red-tape cutting. Speed up the proceedings. We've arranged, with your permission, to eliminate the preliminary hearing. The District Magistrate has okayed it, pending your consent, Al. What we have to do is get the whole thing off the front pages. We've got to get the whole incident fully aired and explained to the public at a public trial, get Aaron exonerated, get the whole mess finished and forgotten by November second."

"Can you arrange that, Mr. Murakami?" Dwight Candles asked.

"I believe so, Mr. Candles. There are a few things we can straighten out in the morning and—"

"It would help if you straightened them out tonight."

Al nodded. "Yeah, that's right. Tonight."

"Al," Willard said quietly, "what charges will you bring against Aaron?"

Al twisted on his lip for a moment. "Manslaughter," he said, not looking at Willard. "Involuntary manslaughter. That's what it seems to have been."

"Thank you, Al," Willard said.

So with gentleness, with firmness, they had put the blocks to him, Al Murakami thought, sitting in the courtroom waiting for the trial to get underway. He could have shoved the blocks down their throats, but why run the risk when the percentage was against you? This way there was no risk. His future was assured. Dwight Candles went back to the executive committee with the quiet but so important message that Al Murakami played ball on the right team. Why try and make a name for yourself when you can get just as far without the risk? The big shots in the Republican Party now owed Al Murakami a favor. And old Willard Howland had said Thank you, Al. Well, Willard Howland could goddamn well say thank you. Because he, Al Murakami, was just about to save Willard Howland's goddamn chances. Jesus Christ, he thought, the biggest opportunity of my life comes around, and it knocks on my door with a gloved fist.

The judge entered the courtroom. The bailiff pounded his mallet.

"Ladies and gentlemen, please rise, huh? The Third Judicial Circuit of the Circuit Court of the Territory of Hawaii, Hilo, Hawaii, is now in session: Judge James J. Ewing presiding. No smokin' while the court is in session, huh? Criminal courts case number five-five-eight-nine-five; the Territory of Hawaii, plaintiff, versus Aaron Howland, defendant."

When the judge took his chair and the courtroom was seated, Al Murakami selected from his briefcase the few papers he would need for the trial. Hell, it's probably all for the best, he consoled himself. It probably was accidental.

"The court will hear the opening statements by the prosecution," the judge said.

Al stood up and hooked his thumbs inside his belt.

"Your honor, if it pleases the court: the prosecution is desirous of saving the court's time and expense. In lieu of opening statements, we would like to call only one witness: the defendant, Aaron Howland."

"You wish to place Aaron Howland on the stand as a prosecution witness?"

"That is correct, your honor."

As Aaron was being sworn in, Al Murakami lumbered like a surly bear to the witness stand. His whole investigation of the case seemed now like a voyage that could never be relaxing to him because his hands had been tied. There was constantly in the back of his brain the certainty that he had left something unanswered. There was some essential factor that had not been satisfactorily cleared away: a question that Aaron had not been able to answer, a line of investigation that he himself had not completely developed; an unlocked door somewhere. How could Aaron Howland have mistaken Paul Kahana for Bobby Villanueva? How could it have been accidental?

He stopped a few feet from the witness stand and studied Aaron with a look of both anger and disgust. As he looked into Aaron's sunken eyes, he was certain that Aaron had not mistaken the men: he was certain, too, that he could have proven it.

He leaned very close to the witness stand. He caught the faint, stale, whisky flavor of Aaron's breath. "Mr. Howland," he said quietly, "the Territory of Hawaii is charging you with the felony crime of involuntary manslaughter: the accidental fatal stabbing of Paul Kahana. You have pleaded not guilty to the charge. Quite possibly, within an hour after the conclusion of this trial, you will walk out of this courtroom a free man. Yet I notice that you have had a few drinks already this morning, and I want you to know—you should know by now—that drinking will never be able to do you any good any more—"

Aaron's counsel was on his feet: "Your honor, I object to the prosecution's line of—"

"Whatever you have on your conscience you have for good now; for all time." Al Murakami continued talking to Aaron, ignoring the defense counsel. "It will be a part of you from now on. And if you drink yourself unconscious every night for the rest of your life, when you wake up in the morning it will still be there with you. You will never be able to forget," Al Murakami said, "that you have killed a man."

Chapter Fourteen

"THE crooked sonofabitch threw the case! Can you imagine that? He threw the goddamned case!"

George Hill cracked his knuckles slowly one by one and looked up from his desk. "What did you expect him to do, Judge?"

"What did I expect?" Judge Blanding rattled the newspaper excitedly and slammed it down on the desk. "What does any law-abiding God-fearing citizen in this Territory have the right to expect?"

"I don't know, Judge. You tell me."

Judge Blanding paused to suck in some wind. His cheeks and his whole frame were bloated out like a pigeon's. "I expected the County Attorney of Hawaii to fulfill his office, that's what! To prosecute! To uphold his public trust, the no-good corrupt sonofabitch! I expected him to—"

"Relax, Judge," George Hill said easily. "What have you got against Aaron Howland that you're so hot to see him hung?"

"Now wait, sir! Now wait," Judge Blanding said, waving his hand in Hill's face. "I am not speaking out against Aaron Howland, nor am I implying that he is guilty of any crime. But a two-day trial! Two days! After what? After a half-hour police investigation and a waived preliminary! God in heaven! That damn island over there has one law for the people and another law for the Howland clan. That trial should have lasted right on through till election day, costing old Willard five hundred votes a day! That's what I expected! The man stabbed another man to death and by God he should have been prosecuted to the full extent of the law, and I speak, gentlemen, from my knowledge of the law!"

"Which is questionable at best, isn't it, Judge?" Ward said. He walked over and grinned harshly at the Judge. "Lots of people around town have been trying to figure out just what you know about the law. Or anything else, for that matter."

The Judge hesitated, then smiled without confidence. He leaned forward, his eyes eager, his whole attitude one of being anxious to please. He tried to rest his hand on Ward's shoulder but Ward shook it away. "I'm sorry I spoke that way, Ward. I know it was unpardonable of me, but for a moment I forgot that this whole matter has some, well, some personal aspects for you."

"Shove it, Judge."

Judge Blanding's lower lip dropped and he took a step backward. "You needn't be rude, Mr. Akana!"

"No, I needn't be rude. And I needn't have to sit here and listen to an incompetent, bought-paid-and-delivered fraud of a politician make remarks about the corruption of other—"

"I've never been addressed in this manner in my whole life, Mr. Akana! And I certainly don't believe it's in keeping with the dignity of my office or your position to speak to me in such an—"

"Oh Christ, come off it, Judge," George Hill said. He walked over and put his arm around the Judge's quaking shoulders. "Relax, Judge. You're a shoo-in candidate now. Aaron Howland's midnight dueling has just about tolled the funeral bells for his old man. And you'll be in Washington next month as our Delegate to Congress. Ward didn't mean anything. He's your number one booster. I've had him beating the bushes in Maui for the last three days and he's forgotten how to act in civilization." He grinned over at Ward. "Why don't you shake hands and congratulate our new Delegate, Ward?"

"Congratulations, Delegate," Ward said. He was angry and surprised at himself for having lost his temper. He had always considered the Judge a contemptible hypocrite. But it was childish to blow up at him like that.

He realized that he had become much too quick tempered these last few weeks. He felt sometimes that he was continually wet-nursing a dogged anger. There was a raw, irritable edge inside his brain fraying the emotions that rubbed up against it. Nerves, perhaps. Or maybe too much work, he thought. Maybe that was why George Hill had sent him over to Maui for the last three days to settle a few inconsequential disputes. Any of a dozen staff members could have gone over, but maybe Hill had decided that Ward Akana needed a rest. But it hadn't been an emotional rest. Everywhere he went on Maui—the various plantations, the docks at Wailuku and Kahului—he had witnessed the waste and desolation of the continued strike. All the workers he had spoken to wanted to get back to their jobs. Management wanted their industries to get back into gear. Then why in the name of heaven was the strike continuing? Because of something he had said or done or not said and not done? Was there an avenue of settlement he had not explored? Four and a half months now of stymied negotiations.

Before he had left for Maui, he had felt certain that the strike would be over when he returned. Management had raised its hourly wage increase offer to the sixteen cents he knew the Union would accept. Everybody had shaken hands at the end of that meeting and a bottle had been opened and even the Governor had made a brief appearance to thank both Union and management negotiators for their diligence. Now it was all stalemated again. Something must have gone haywire. As soon as Judge Blanding left the office he would get George Hill to fill him in on the facts.

"Would you like to join the Judge and me across the street for an afternoon snort?" George Hill asked Ward. "We're going to celebrate his delegacy with one short one before the Judge returns to the campaign trail."

"No thanks."

"Okay. Be back in five, ten minutes." George Hill put his arm around the Judge's shoulders and started for the door. "Yessir,

Judge," he said jovially, "you can relax now. It's in the proverbial burlap."

"There's a rumor they might not even hold the delegacy election," Judge Blanding said, going out the door. "Old Howland might just concede. Hah-haw!"

Ward looked up. "Don't hold your breath, Judge. You'll explode."

George Hill closed the door.

Ward glanced at the newspaper the Judge had thrown on the desk. The first few paragraphs of the Hilo-datelined story told of Aaron's acquittal. The jury had been out thirty-seven minutes. It must have been a hell of a trial, all right. He looked at the newsphotos taken after the trial. They showed Aaron, weakly jubilant, with Laura at his side. Willard was not in any of the photos and Ward felt glad that the old man had been spared that. He turned to the jump page and read quickly the continued report of the trial. There was a bold-print paragraph at the end which stated that Willard Howland had "no comment concerning the trial or its effect upon his campaign."

That makes sense, Ward thought. The newspaper would not have been able to print the comment old Willard would have made. Willard's comment would have been succinctly encased in three words, only one of which would be printable.

As he was folding the paper closed, he was startled by a boldfaced headline which read:

AKANA BLASTS HOWLAND
FOR BACKING BIG FIVE,
NOT ISLAND STATEHOOD

He stared at the headline incredulously; then, reading slowly down the story, his hand began to tremble:

> Union Attorney Ward Akana today vehemently attacked Senator Willard Howland for laboring not in the interests of Hawaiian statehood but rather in the interests of "capitalism, feudalism and the Big Five."
>
> Mr. Akana claimed that the G.O.P. Senator from Hawaii would, if elected to the delegacy on November 2, "perpetuate the Big Five stranglehold on Island economy.
>
> "I have no faith in Willard Howland," Mr. Akana said in a

luncheon speech today before some 400 Union members assembled at the Union Hall. "I have no faith in the things for which Willard Howland stands. I do not believe he stands for the betterment of the people of Hawaii. I believe, on the contrary, that the only thing Senator Howland stands for is the betterment of the ruling class, the captains of industry, the sacred names of the presidents, vice-presidents and board of director members of the Big Five firms. I believe the Senator's impassioned plea for statehood, which has been made on every television and radio station in the Territory, in every city and town, on practically every farm and in practically every home in the Territory during these last several weeks—I believe this plea has been inspired not by Willard Howland's supposedly heartfelt desire for statehood, but rather by the cold business practicality issued and dictated by the Big Five."

Mr. Akana concluded his speech before the wildly cheering Union members by saying that "when we go to the polls on November 2 and cast our vote against Willard Howland and for Judge Adam A. Blanding, we will be casting a united vote against duplicity and the iron-fisted Big Five rule—and casting a vote for sincerity, integrity and the genuine champion of Hawaii's hopes for statehood."

Ward leaned back against the highly polished mahogany slab of George Hill's desk. He flipped open the silver box, reached for a cigarette and lit it with trembling hands. The color had drained out of his face. He forced himself to read slowly this time, with a stunned disbelief, every word of the story. When he had finished it the second time, he sat down in the oversized brown leather chair behind the desk and flipped on the interoffice communication system. His voice seemed clogged and he had to clear it before he told George Hill's secretary to call the Honolulu *Star-Bulletin*. When the unit buzzed again he picked up the receiver. "I'd like to talk to the city desk." He spoke slowly, struggling to keep the anger back in his throat.

"City desk, Ramsey speaking."

"Hello—this is Ward Akana. You're running a story about me on page—page eleven of section one. I was curious where you got that story."

"Just a moment, Mr. Akana. Yes—I have it."

"Where did you get it?"
"Just a moment."
There was a steady whir in the receiver and Ward could hear garbled voices in the background. Finally the editor said, "I'm not sure right offhand, Mr. Akana. I've just come on. The dayside city editor has gone home for the day. I'll check it for you, if you wish."
"Please do."
"Is there something wrong with it?"
"Yes. There was no such Union luncheon today. I made no such speech."
"Pardon me?"
"I said the story is all false. I made no speech today. And if I did make a speech, I certainly wouldn't have made that kind. I've been on Maui for the past three days and got back to Honolulu at two-thirty this afternoon. And I want to know just how in hell a story like that got into your newspaper."
There was another pause. "If you could hold on for just a few minutes, Mr. Akana, I'll run it down for you."
As he waited he relaxed his grip on the receiver. Beads of perspiration had formed on his forehead. He wiped them with a handkerchief and returned the handkerchief to his breast pocket.
"Mr. Akana?"
"Yes, I'm waiting."
"Mr. Akana, that story was from a news release that came from Rob Jessup in your own publicity department."
"The Union publicity department?"
"Yessir. I have the release right in front of me now. We had one of our men edit it but it's nearly word for word the way your p.r. department sent it to us."
Ward took a deep breath. "Thank you," he said. He flicked the receiver and told the secretary to have Rob Jessup come up to the office immediately. He folded the paper neatly and placed it on the center of the desk and stared at it dumbly for a few minutes. Then he bowed his head into his fists and knuckled the tension from his brow.
"Pretty hot stuff, eh Ward?" Rob Jessup said as he walked into the office and handed Ward a mimeographed copy of the news release. He was a tall, frail-looking man in his late thirties. He had a sharp, pale, nervous face, mouse-colored hair and small, hopeless

eyes. There was a hint of sourness about his mouth. "We got good play in the *Bulletin* and it's already made the afternoon radio and TV newscasts and is scheduled for all the evening news programs. I've just finished rewriting the lead for tomorrow morning's *Advertiser*. They should play the story up pretty good too."

Ward did not look at him. He sat behind George Hill's desk, his fists clenched into tight hard balls. He compared the newspaper story with the full release as the public relations department had written it. They were practically identical.

Rob Jessup, standing on the opposite side of the desk, switched the weight from one foot to the other. "Er, something wrong, Ward?" he asked, growing a little apprehensive. "We tried to give the release a little meat, you know."

"You did," Ward muttered.

Rob Jessup relaxed. "Well—I'm glad you liked it."

"I didn't say I liked it," Ward snapped, trying hard to dike the flood of fury that was moving through him in an ever-darkening current. He peered up at Jessup from beneath his dark brows. "You wrote this?" he asked flatly, holding the release in his hands.

Rob Jessup backed a little away. "Well, yeah. We wrote it and—"

"There was no Union meeting today."

Jessup stammered, "Well sure, I know that. But in the p.r. department we got to—"

"I didn't make any speech today."

Jessup tried a nervous grin that didn't come off.

"I've been on Maui for the last three days."

"Sure, I know that, Mr. Akana. But in the public relations department our job is to create news. You know what they say: a good newspaper reporter will go out and cover a fire and write about it for his paper. But a good p.r. guy will light the match to start the fire and then call the paper, hah-hah. That's about the way the cookie crumbles, as they say—that's about the way it goes."

Ward walked around the desk and Rob Jessup eyed him warily. "This whole story is untrue," Ward said, the color mounting in his face.

Jessup shrugged and smiled sickly. "Well, we've got to invent things, Mr. Akana. If we publicized only what the Union did, if public relations departments publicized only the truth, they'd have nothing to write about."

Ward rolled up the release and shook in under Jessup's nose. "This is a goddamned lie!"

"The whole damn business of public relations is a lie," Jessup said. "It's a form of literary masturbation. I can't change it."

"You can damn well change this!" Ward shouted. "I want this story retracted and I'll dictate to you now what I want printed in its place!" He grabbed Jessup by the shoulder and pushed him to the typewriter alongside George Hill's desk.

"Just a minute, Mr. Akana—please!"

"Don't just a minute me, you parasitical phony sonofabitch!"

"That's enough!" Jessup broke the grip. "I don't have to take this kind of talk!"

Ward shoved him into the chair. "Start typing!"

But Jessup bounded back out of the chair. "Look, Mr. Akana, stop shoving me around and get some sense into your head. We can't possibly get a retraction on that story without making the whole Union look ridiculous. I just work here and I do what I'm told to do, just like you. And I had orders to whip up something pretty damn hot—"

"You had orders to write this?"

"Sure I did! Did you think I just got a wild hair up my nose?"

"Whose orders?"

"George Hill's orders! Now take it easy!"

Ward shook him by the shoulders. "George Hill told you to write up a lie like this?"

"That's right, I did," George Hill said, hurrying into the office and stepping between the two men. "Now what the hell is going on in here, a Golden Gloves preliminary or something? C'mon, both you guys act your age!"

Ward turned on him, his face livid. "You ordered this written?"

"That's right, we're in a political campaign, remember? Now simmer down. What the hell's wrong with you anyway? What's wrong with that news release?"

"The whole damn thing is a lie!"

"So what? I asked you what was wrong with it."

"It's slander! It's cheap!"

"It's politics."

"I can't believe you'd do a thing like this."

"You can't believe a lot of things, Ward," George Hill said. "You got a little growing up to do. I told you before, we're not here to play marbles. We're playing for keeps. And if Willard Howland is such a grand old man, we've got to make him a little less grand. We're out to break Howland's back, Ward, and don't you forget it! You can go kiss and make up after the elections, but right now we've got to hit him with everything we can. Why the hell do you think we refused to accept the strike settlement offer—" He stopped suddenly. But he knew Ward had heard it. He hunched his shoulders and walked over to his desk. "Rob, you might just as well go back to work, the fun's over. You too, Ward."

Rob Jessup walked quietly out of the office and closed the door. Hill knew that Ward was still standing there, frozen in the middle of the room. He looked up at him. "Well?"

Ward did not move.

"If you quit playing Rover Boy I'll tell you what happened," Hill said.

"You just did."

Hill cracked a knuckle. "Okay, we did what we had to do," he said, getting up and starting to pace the room. "Management upped their offer to sixteen cents. You were there, then, and we all shook hands. But after you left, we decided not to accept the offer. The next day, when you were over on Maui, we met again, and management raised the ante to nineteen cents and we still didn't take it. Management upped again to twenty-two cents. Twenty-two-cents-an-hour raise, Ward. More than we ever expected. And we still didn't take it!"

"Why?"

George Hill stopped pacing and stood by the window looking at Ward. "Why? Because we had 'em over a barrel, that's why. If these wage-slaving bastards are willing to go up to twenty-two cents, then they must be pretty damned scared. They're beginning to hurt bad. And so is the administration backing them. The longer the strike lasts, the more dissatisfied the voters are going to get: dissatisfied with the administration and with the whole Republican crowd at Iolani Palace for not being able to do anything about the strike. And when the voters are dissatisfied, they throw out the administration and elect a new one. In other words, Galahad, the longer the strike goes on, the better our chances of electing Judge Blanding: the better our chances of defeating Willard Howland. Lesson number one in George Hill's political science course."

Ward felt a small choking movement in his throat. When he

spoke, his voice had a strange quality. "Is that why the strike was called in the first place?"

George Hill leaned back against the desk and folded his thick arms across his chest. He crossed his ankles and looked over at Ward and nodded his head. "Lesson number two: We had to get our own man in Washington. We renegotiated the contracts knowing it would cause a strike."

Ward shook his head. "I feel like a fool. I feel like I've been used. All along, I believed—and this must sound comical to you—but I believed we were calling the strike to help the workingman."

George Hill looked down at his shoes. "No, it doesn't sound funny to me, Ward. There was that, too. But basically, it was to knock out Howland. That's why I asked you, a long time ago, before Howland got the nomination, where your loyalties lay. I don't pretend to stand here in front of you and claim there's any comparison between a pontifical fraud like Judge Blanding and a man like Willard Howland. But unfortunately, we're not on Howland's side. That is, I'm not; the Union's not. I don't know what side you're on, Ward."

Ward slowly crumpled the newspaper release in his hands and tossed it on the desk. "And I guess I was sent over to Maui to be kept out of the way."

Hill looked at Ward with frank, level eyes. "Go to the head of the class."

After a moment, Ward turned and walked quietly out of the office. He drove aimlessly about the still harbor, tooling down one street and up the other, watching the pickets and the armed militiamen patrolling listlessly along the sunny piers or leaning with the slack acceptance of their lot against the sheds or against the leafy trees in the square, and when he did not want to look at the harbor any more he drove out Farrington Highway through Waipahu where the old sugar mill stood gaunt and idled by the strike, and across the wavering sunlight of the afternoon he could see the turrets of the warships at Pearl Harbor where bubbles of oil continued to seep out from the depths where the *Arizona* lay. The road was white concrete slab and it came winding and winding at him like a wide silver ribbon uncoiling through the deep red gut of the earth. Out along Kahe Point a breeze swept in from the ocean and he could see, on the mauka side of the road, the beginnings of the flushed, endless fields of sugar cane. He remembered his childhood names for the different fields: they were his Great Plains, his African Jungle, his Nuuanu Battleground.

Before they are harvested and burned, the cane fields shout with green. The stalks are slender and tall, waving gently in the breeze, and from far away they look like a slow, building, brilliant wave. The earth of the fields is rich red, the color of old copper in the sun. Sugar cane has been our curse and our blessing, he thought, racing by the green fields that stretched endlessly ahead of him now like summer wheat in Kansas. And it means to Hawaii the same as wheat means to Kansas, or coal to Pennsylvania, or cotton to Georgia. It is all in the textbooks and much of it is not pretty. Sugar cane is the backbone and the marrow and the empire builder; and while much of its story is not too pretty, it is not any dirtier than the story of cotton, wheat or coal. It is just that the unpleasantness has lasted much longer.

Under the blazing sun, Filipinos cut the cane. It is hot, mean work, and the plantations have the pay fixed so that the cutters cannot exactly wander home to the comforts of fine food and electric ranges after a day in the fields.

The Chinese coolie labor was the first to be brought in. But long ago they quit the fields and opened stores or wonderful restaurants like P. Y. Chong's used to be, and they married the happy brown Hawaiian girls and reared the loveliest children in the world. Then the thousands upon thousands of Japanese were brought in, during the late eighteen hundreds. But after their time of indenture in the fields, they quit to start small businesses of their own, and their children formed the 442nd Infantry Battalion and their grandchildren are studying to be doctors or lawyers at the University of Hawaii, or in Michigan or California. The Portuguese came next, but they balked at field labor, went instead to the machine shops where the work was easier and the pay was better. Finally the Filipinos arrived. They hold strong to the land today and wait to break away. They wear low black boots, their toes crackling inside the oven of leather, and light cotton shirts and dungarees and cheap cardboard pith helmets tied about their heads with dusty red bandanas to catch the breeze. They watch the car race by, then turn back to their cane. They are silent but prolific so there is nothing to worry about. There will always be cane cutters. And cheap, too.

And all this time, while the haoles ruled the land and imported cheap labor, the easy, regal Hawaiians sat on the beach, disdainful of the struggle for wealth and power. The haoles rule the land, the Orientals work the land, the Hawaiians enjoy the land.

He drove around the shoulder of the Waianae Mountain range and the highway cut through a fringe of Filipino shacks built around a gasoline station with a sign outside advertising saimin, and he had to slow down where a cane truck had spilled slippery stalks along a stretch of highway. When he slowed down he passed a young girl on horseback, riding easy with no saddle or bridle, just a rope bit tied around the horse's mouth. She was a brown girl, nearly all Hawaiian, maybe some Portagee or Chinese, it was hard to tell, and she wore dungarees rolled up showing lovely slender brown legs, and a red and white candy-striped T-shirt, and her hair was jet black and bounced down to her waist and she wore a frangipani blossom in her hair, and she sat that sorrowful bay mare like she was born on it. When he passed her, she smiled down at him with a warmth that could break his heart and he drove away slowly so he could watch her in the rear-view mirror; and somehow she knew he was watching her and he drove fifty, a hundred yards past her and she made him happy and heartbroken again with that smile and a farewell wave of her arm. But he had better forget all that, he thought, because he could never never turn back, and it was the highway and the heat again and the car bumped across cane railroad tracks, and he pulled in at last, into the hamlet of Nanakuli, where the life of the Islands pumped easily with the sun and the tides, much in the same way that life goes on in Salinas or Fort Wayne, although hotter, no doubt; and instead of the Smiths and the Williamses there are the Kobayashis, Wongs and Kealohas, and the eyes are not sharp blue, but warm brown and almond-shaped.

If you tried to say life was easier in this little town, that would probably be true, Ward thought, driving the car into a gasoline station. But if you tried to say life was happier—as so many of the romanticists have said—that would be conjecture and romance and not necessarily fact. And although you might have the odds on your side, you would never be able to establish it as fact. What could go as fact, he thought, was that the Kealoha family would be more miserable in Fort Wayne than the Williams family would be in Nanakuli.

He told the attendant to fill the gas tank. He crossed the highway and strolled along the deserted beach. The beach was fresh and sunny and warm in the late afternoon. It was lined with monkeypods in bloom. The tide was in and there was a clean breeze and a nice-looking surf rolling in against the shore. He realized that he had not been swimming for a long time.

He stripped down to his shorts, piled his clothes neatly on the sand, and dove into the water. He tried to swim through the rollers but they were very big and most of the time he had to dive beneath them. He swam slowly for a long time, tiring himself. He swam out beyond the breakers and turned in the quiet water and floated on his back. The water was buoyant and clear. He could feel the lift and fall of the swells as they passed him. Floating on his back, he saw only the sky, and for the first time in many years he imagined different shapes in the clouds. After a while he swam back to the breakers. He swam hard and caught a big roller and coasted in on it, face down, to the beach. He walked up to where he had left his clothes and sat down on the warm sand. It seemed to him for a moment that all the good things, the things that were fun to do, he hadn't done for a long time.

When he got back into town he knew he was through with the Union. He would find something else. He used his key to let himself into the front door and went upstairs to his office. He typed a note of resignation for George Hill. He would do one more job for the Union: he would fly to Molokai, tomorrow if possible, to settle the dispute over the unloading of the emergency hospital ship that called once a week at the leper colony at Kalaupapa. Then Ward Akana and the Union would call it quits.

He signed his letter of resignation and slipped it in an envelope and wrote George Hill's name on it. He dropped the envelope in the Out box on his desk. Then he picked up the telephone and dialed Willard Howland's Manoa Valley residence but got no answer. He placed a person-to-person call through the interisland operator, hoping he could reach Willard at Manoalani. It suddenly became the most important thing in the world for him to talk with his father. He waited for a long time, then he heard a slow, stricken voice that he recognized finally as Sloan's instruct the operator that Senator Howland could be reached at the Governor's office in Iolani Palace.

Ward lit a cigarette and dialed the palace. He managed to get through the Governor's secretary and finally to Willard.

"This is Senator Howland speaking," he heard his father say.

"Hello. This is Ward. I—I was hoping I could talk to you to-night. It's very important, Father—"

He could not pull back the word. He did not think he wanted to. There was a pause on the other end of the line. Then the unmistakable metallic click of the receiver breaking the connection.

After he had replaced the telephone receiver in its cradle, Willard Howland stared uncomprehendingly at the instrument. Ward's call had stunned him. He had listened just long enough to recognize Ward's voice. He had read the story in the afternoon paper. Ward's opinions had been made irrevocably clear to him in print: there was no need to have them reaffirmed by telephone. There was nothing left to say. But as he was hanging up the receiver, he could have sworn that Ward uttered the word "father." But it was unlikely, he thought, curiously watching the silent telephone as if he was expecting it to ring again. No, it must have been simply a similar-sounding word. His ears must be playing tricks on him.

During the campaign, Ward had criticized him often in the press and on radio and television broadcasts. But they had all been grist-mill political fodder; attacks against aims and policies and platforms, and Willard had accepted them as such. They had hurt, true, but the hurt had all been on a surface level, like a scratch or a bruise. The story today was an altogether different thing. It was a horrid thing. It was a deep, personal vilification. And reading it, Willard had felt a pain that was like a little bit of death.

He turned from the telephone and walked back to the vast circular conference table and resumed his seat. He gazed quietly out the window to the lush tropical garden below. He had always looked out of windows. Perhaps there was a small unbeaten part of him, he thought, that held on to the idea that if he looked long enough out of enough windows he was bound someday to see what he had always been looking for.

"Anything important, Willard?" Dwight Candles asked. He waited a moment. "Willard?"

Howland turned slowly from the window. "What? Oh—no. Nothing important."

"Maybe we should tell Mrs. Wong to hold up all telephone calls unless for an emergency," Dwight Candles said to the Governor. "If we don't, we'll be here all night."

"Yes, good suggestion," Governor Mike Balter said. He nodded to Casey Matasuka, his press secretary. "Will you see to that for us, Case?" The Governor folded his small, freckled hands together on the table and turned his attention back to the meeting. He was a short, jowly man with a large, veined nose and undersized eyes like the eyes of an old turkey, predatory, unblinking and a little obscene. He wore high-buttoned shoes and an unpressed gray Orlon suit, the sleeves of which were too short, exposing three inches of French cuffs. His high starched collar seemed to strangle the folds of flesh about his neck. He suffered chronically from head colds and he had a fear of drafts, so that indoors or out, he kept a battered Panama hat with a wide brim and a band of peacock feathers on the back of his head. From beneath the brim of his hat, wisps of feathery brown hair curled damply on his freckled skull.

Dwight Candles occupied the chair to the Governor's left. Secretary of Hawaii Frank Lorrin occupied the chair to his right. Mickey Shigita sat next to old Willard. Aside from Casey Matasuka, six other men surrounded the conference table: Senator Hal Evans from Oahu; Senator Castillo Rodriguez from Maui; Senator Tim Duarte from Kauai; Congressman Henry Kealohana from Molokai; Jay Walker, editor-publisher of the Honolulu *Advertiser* and Republican Central Committee member; and Whitney K. Frazer, editor of the Honolulu *Star-Bulletin*. The group comprised the hierarchy of Republican Party power in the Territory.

"Gentlemen, we needn't look so glum," Governor Balter said heartily. "This is a campaign strategy meeting, not a wake. We're as downhearted as a group of men at a funeral of a friend who owed us all money. Think defeat—be defeated: think victory—be victorious!" he said, emphasizing the point by slamming his right fist into his left palm.

"Well, I guess none of us here feels like drinking any victory toasts," Senator Hal Evans said with a smile. He was in his forties, a bald man with merry blue eyes and skin like porcelain. Tiny broken veins stood out in his pink cheeks. There was a heavy scent of shaving lotion about him and his fingernails were meticulously manicured. He smelled like the inside of a barbershop. "Anyway, I'm thankful I'm not up for re-election this year. Should I go on with these notes?" he asked, indicating a sheaf of paper he held in his hands.

"I guess you'll have to," Governor Balter said.

"Despite indications that this might be the first major Democratic Party victory in the Territory," Senator Evans read from his notes, "three weeks ago our tabulations showed Senator Howland held a commanding lead of five-to-one. It seemed, in other words, that as far as the delegacy was concerned, we were headed for victory. It seemed that way, until, and I trust you will forgive me for bringing it up at this time, until—the tragedy. To our dismay, gentlemen, the—the tragedy has had a damning effect upon the candidacy of the Senator. And we cannot delude ourselves for one second that the opposition party won't make hay out of it all. They're jumping all over it now, and they'll continue to jump even harder.

"Now, unfortunately, I must read you these latest poll tabulations, taken for us by the staff members of the Hawaii Visitors Bureau and arranged by Casey Matasuka at the request of the Governor.

"Since—since the tragedy, the polls have all but reversed themselves. Our heaviest loss, as far as the polls are concerned, has been on Oahu, the critical island, where Senator Howland now apparently is trailing Judge Blanding by a three-to-one margin. Kauai, Molokai and Lanai are indicating heavy Democratic swings. Maui is about even. And, thank God for small favors and for the popularity of Willard on his home island, the people of Hawaii still favor the Senator, but now by a smaller margin of only two-to-one.

"So you see, gentlemen, this tragedy has damaged our campaign. We are the victims of a horrible twist of fate. As unjust as it may seem to all of us, and most especially to you, Willard, the people, the voters of this Territory, are hypersensitive to the Howland name. I'm sure you can understand our position, Willard. It's bad. It's seriously bad. And something must be done."

"Like what?" Willard said.

"That's what we're here to discuss."

Willard gazed out the window again. Lately there had been a flatness to his campaign; an unfamiliar lack of response. The crowds attending his speeches were as large as they had been earlier during the campaign. But in place of the spontaneity, in place of the rush of cheers, there was now a polite cautiousness. Perhaps a suspicion of the whole Howland clan.

The newspaper headlines certainly had not helped him. There had been talk, and published reports, that he should step out of the race. Well, they could be damned, he thought. He refused to believe that the voting public, who had known him publicly for almost thirty years, would be swayed against him now because of a member of his family. As long as he himself stuck to his guns, then nothing could go wrong, he thought, wondering idly why he had grown so extremely conscious of things going wrong.

"Maybe now is a good time to discuss further the strike, yes?" said Senator Tim Duarte. "Maybe, as Senator Evans claims, he is not up for re-election this year, yes? But me, I am. And on my Island, on Kauai, the strike is a verra bad thing. Alla time, in my campaign speeches, like Senator Howland's campaign speeches, I say how bad this strike is to all of us and how the Republicans is going to end the strike. This I say to the voters on my Island. Yet we are four months now and still we have the strike. So the people on my Island they say, When are you going to do all these wonderful things to end the strike, Senator Duarte? They say, We have not worked for four months. We have not enough food, there are not enough supplies. You say you are going to end the strike but still we have strike. All talk talk talk, and still the strike. Now I say, What can I tell my people? We have campaigned that we will end the strike and still we have the strike, yes? What can I say?"

"The strike is no reflection on me or my campaign for the delegacy," Willard said. "I have no jurisdiction over striking parties."

"Sure, that's true, Senatah Will, but we had hoped, well, that maybe you could influence—you know—"

Willard frowned. "You thought one word from me and Ward Akana would call off the strike?"

Tim Duarte shrugged his massive shoulders. "All I know is that it's costing us votes. You and me. People are saying how we treat the strike like the weather. All we do is talk about it."

Dwight Candles leaned across the table. "Gentlemen, we all are aware now that the strike was called not as a matter of work and wages, but as a political weapon to be used against the Republican Party in general and against Willard Howland in particular. The longer the strike continues the more unified the Union voting block becomes. Twenty-five thousand members plus their families and sympathizers equals a solid-block vote of about one hundred and fifty thousand. And that vote is going to go against us, there's no doubt about that now. The Union will not consider settling the strike until after the election. However, we're getting a little away from the point. The purpose of this meeting was to, well, sort of stick our fingers in the dike and hold back the Democratic flood. Now let's see what needs to be done."

The Governor leaned across the conference table toward the two newspaper publishers. "One thing we need from you two gentlemen is more complete, enthusiastic support," he said. "Whit—this story today, this attack by Ward Akana, was not the kind of a story for you. It didn't have the merit to be printed in the *Star-Bull.*"

Whitney K. Frazer puffed stoically on his cigar. "Ward Akana is a power in the community," he said. "When he makes a speech before four hundred people, I've got to print it. When Willard rebuttals the attack, he'll be given equal space if not more."

"No," Willard growled. "I'm through fighting back against these attacks. My message to the people is purely our justification for statehood, and I'm not going to waste their time or my own by answering any more of these political straight-arms. I've had it, as far as that kind of campaigning is concerned."

The Governor looked over at Jay Walker. "Jay," he said, "just how in the name of God and the Republican Party can you validate your editorial that ran the day before yesterday?"

Jay Walker twisted uncomfortably in his chair. "I don't think we should discuss it at this time, Mike. My newspaper always has and always will continue to support the Republican Party. During a campaign, our editorial space is divided seventy per cent Republican and thirty per cent Democrat, just to keep the Democratic subscribers and advertisers happy. But I don't think it's wise to discuss that editorial now before—"

"Before me?" Willard demanded.

"I was going to say, before this group," Jay Walker replied, turning to Willard. "Senator, I have always considered you one of the ablest statesmen in the Territory. I said as much in my editorial. I have never wavered in my belief in your ability, your integrity, and your devotion to the cause of Hawaiian statehood. That too was made very plain in the editorial. But, speaking for myself as a Republican Central Committeeman, speaking for the Republican Party in general and for some of these gentlemen here in particular, I believe your candidacy for the delegacy has become a handicap for our party. And although I regretted the necessity of doing so, I felt an obligation to state that opinion clearly in my newspaper. Mr. Howland, I did so for the good of the Republican Party. Through no fault of your own, this tragedy, this terrible twist of fate involving your son and the Kahana lad, has brought irreparable damage to your campaign. And I think you will admit that. Whereas in the past the Howland name has been magic at the polls, this year, because of a tragedy over which you had no control, the Howland name has lost its gloss. The voters are wary of it."

Senator Castillo Rodriguez smiled weakly at Willard's stiff face. "Senatah, we discussed the mattah for a long time, huh, befoah Meestah Walkah published that editorial, huh. We decided, wit heavy heavy hearts, true, that the Reepublican Party would have a moah bettah chance wit another candidate, huh. Even at this late a date, huh. We had hoped, wit as I say, our hearts heavy, that you would remove yoahself as candidate. Maybe like, plead bad health, huh?"

"What it amounts to, Willard," said Senator Tim Duarte, "is that the Republican Party would do better if you dropped out of the race."

Old Willard looked at them each in turn with a fierce contempt. "When the ship begins to sink . . ." he muttered.

"It's not a question of that, Will," Dwight Candles said, getting up from his chair and walking around the table to Willard's shoulder. "It's simply a cold political reality."

Willard's head turned heavily in a gesture of a wild brood boar sensing danger, and his dark gold eyes burned into Candles'. "You too, eh Dwight?"

The color rose slowly in Dwight Candles' face. He spread his hands in a helpless gesture. "I'm committed to the party, Willard."

Willard nodded. He bowed his shaggy white-gold head, peering up at their faces from under his brows. "Is this the Party?" he said. "This table of twelve men with more Judases than even Christ could contend with? Do you call yourselves the Republican

Party?" He stood up angrily and shook his finger at the window. "The Republican Party is out there! The people will decide my fate, not the whimpering Judases of the inner circle!"

"Now, Willard—"

"Gentlemen, please," Governor Balter said, getting up from his chair and leaning his knuckles against the face of the table. "Please, gentlemen, we are in the same frail boat. Let's try to use a little less passion and a little more reason."

"No no," Willard roared. "The whole damned trouble with us, with the Party, perhaps with the world today, is that it's afraid to use passion over and above reason. Faulty reasoning, I might add." He looked down at the table. "How about you, Mickey?"

Mickey Shigita frowned. His index finger drummed against the table. He looked up at the faces of the men about the table. "Gentlemen, I believe Senator Howland should be made aware of the alternate plan you discussed before Willard joined us," he said.

The Governor coughed into his fist. Dwight Candles and Secretary of Hawaii Frank Lorrin exchanged glances. Then Candles looked down at Howland. "Willard," he said, "some of us here discussed the possibility of having Frank replace you."

Willard did not look up at him.

"Frank Lorrin would make an acceptable candidate," Candles continued. "Even at this late date. He's known throughout the Territory. As Senator Rodriguez pointed out, you could plead illness, or grief due to the tragedy. I mention this only as an alternative. Something we discussed. Solely for the good of the Party. Naturally, if Frank pulls in the votes, there would be a high Territorial vacancy that would have to be filled . . ."

"A deal," Willard muttered.

"A facing of the political facts," Candles said. "Pending Frank's success, you would be appointed by the Governor to fulfill Frank's term of office as Secretary of Hawaii."

"I don't want any part of it," Willard snapped.

"It wouldn't be a deal," Frank Lorrin said. "It would be a matter of putting our best foot forward. I don't mean to sound like I'm patting myself on the back. That's not it. Until this—this thing happened, you were our best man, Will. Now, to the regret of all of us, the public has lost confidence in you. It's simply a matter of political expediency."

"I won't step out," Willard said. "You'll have to push me out, damn it!" He turned to Mickey Shigita again. "Is this a unanimous feeling?" he asked. "I'd like to hear the answer to the question I asked a little while ago. How do you feel about it, Mickey?"

"With all due respect, I am inclined to disagree with some of you gentlemen," Mickey said, in a small dry voice. "I believe the Senator is the best man in the Territory to represent the people of Hawaii as Delegate in Washington. He will always have my vote."

Willard curled his old hands into fists to quell the trembling. His left shoulder suddenly ached, and he could feel the pain shoot down through his left arm.

"You will always have my vote too, Willard," Governor Balter said.

"I'll tell all of you gentlemen one thing," Whitney K. Frazer of the *Star-Bulletin* said, knocking an ash off the end of his giant cigar and leaning heavily with his elbows on the table. "Any crack-brain idea of dropping Senator Howland at this time would be political suicide. You think the people of this Territory are fools? You think they wouldn't know that Senator Howland had been axed within the confines of the old proverbial smoke-filled room, by a conclave of self-appointed potentates who hollered uncle at the first sign of a fist aimed at their faces? Gentlemen, to dump Willard Howland—and let's not mince words; that's what some of you were blatantly suggesting—to dump Willard Howland because of a family tragedy that was not of his making would be a disgrace to the Grand Old Party. It would be a breach of confidence. And we would be long in regaining the confidence of the voters. No election is ever assured, gentlemen, until the votes have been counted. Governor Tom Dewey will bear that out. We have not won this election, nor have we lost it. If we go ahead to win it, we will win it with dignity. And if we are to lose it, let us lose it with that same dignity. Let us not turn cowards. Let us not dare take the honor and dignity of Senator Howland and throw it out to the voters as some form of political or moral appeasement; as some kind of sacrificial offering to recompense the tragedy of his own son."

He became quiet and looked for a moment at Willard's bowed shaggy mane. Then he looked at each of the men about the table. "I need not tell you that what has been said in this room will never see print. But the guilt remains with us just the same, gentlemen.

The guilt and the shame were imbedded in the idea." He crushed his cigar noiselessly into the ashtray. Then he picked up his hat and walked out of the room.

It was after eleven o'clock when Willard got home. Mickey Shigita drove him up from Iolani Palace. The big Manoa Valley house was dark.

As Howland opened the front door, Mickey Shigita thought that the old man seemed half broken. His shoulders were stooped as if there was no reason to hold them straight. There were dark hollows underneath his eyes. His hands trembled. It seemed an effort for old Willard to keep his head high. Mickey made a mental note to phone Dr. Judd when he got back on the Big Island tomorrow. "Do you feel all right, Senator?" he asked.

Willard nodded heavily. "Yes. I guess so."

"If you want me to, I can pick you up and drive you to the airport tomorrow. What time are you flying to Molokai?"

Howland rubbed his forehead. "Molokai? Oh yes. I'd forgotten."

"Do you feel up to it? You have a speech scheduled at Kaunakakai at noon. A second speech at Kalaupapa at three o'clock."

Howland nodded and muttered something indistinguishable. He raised his head and stared at Mickey. "Yes. Yes, I can make it all right. I'll get to the airport by myself, thanks."

Mickey seemed to hesitate. He stood in the driveway and looked up into old Willard's eyes. "I'm—I'm awfully sorry this happened, Will."

Howland tightened the muscles in his cheek to form some sort of a weak grin. "Thanks, Mickey," he said, in a soft, almost inaudible voice.

Mickey Shigita looked up at Willard, and the old man could see the small Oriental face wrinkled up like a dried lemon, the eyes clouded. "Senator Will, why did they try and do that to you?"

Howland tried to laugh. "I don't know, Mickey. Maybe they all owed Frank Lorrin a debt."

"Seriously."

"Because they were scared, I guess. They're all honest men, as we have learned to accept the word honest. They were scared and they needed someone to toss out of the boat, for better ballast."

"You know what I noticed, Senator Will?" Mickey Shigita said.

"All through the meeting, even when they tried to—to dump you, there was no question of right or wrong."

Howland seemed to think about it for a moment. "Maybe it isn't that easy," he said. "I'm an old war horse. I grew up in a time when compromise was not the keynote to success. I entered political life more than a quarter of a century ago with the idea of doing some good for my fellow man. I thought if I worked hard and honestly, the people would benefit. I went my own way, perhaps an outdated way, without compromise. I was always afraid of compromise. If a man compromises one part of himself, then another part will suffer.

"As a Territorial Senator, I did not believe that I had the justification to compromise with what I considered the right. The first compromise is the hardest, making the second one easier, and down the line until compromise becomes a habit. Each bit of good work, then, becomes more difficult. Those men this evening were schooled in compromise. They were so eager to dump me for a compromise candidate because they are symptoms of the disintegration of public, private, and political morality. Our public institutions in this land have grown venal with self-seeking and corruption. We have suffered a massive lessening of human dignity."

Eucalyptus logs were burning in the fireplace when he entered the living room. He made his way around the obscure, shapeless furniture, and woke Coyama.

"Thank you, but you shouldn't have waited up, Coyama," he said. "An old man like you needs his sleep."

Coyama got up from the dark leather chair by the fireplace. He adjusted his bridge, then squinted through the gloom at old Willard. "Terefono terefono ring aw night. Is Mistah Ward Akana. He caw aw night."

"I'm not at home to Ward Akana," Willard said.

Coyama left the room. Willard tramped to the window, his footfalls echoing through the room like the slow sure cadence of doom. Down the slopes of Manoa, he could see the city spread out gently in the white lake of the moon. A feeling of nameless regret swept over him. His children had damned him, the leaders of his party had damned him, perhaps it would only be a matter of time until the voters damned him: and then the thirty years of dreaming would be over and the dream would become an endless elegy of discontent. Don't think like that, Old Man, he told himself. You have not been defeated. You may not be defeated, regardless of what those storm troopers of doom whimpered about at the palace tonight. You do not need them. You only need yourself. And you need faith. Faith is the most necessary thing in the world to a man. If defeat is to come, then let it seek you out. Do not walk out halfway to meet it.

He closed the drapes and tramped to the liquor cabinet and poured himself a tumbler of brandy. He sat down in the dark leather chair. He stared into the dying fire, sipping the brandy. He wondered with amusement what Doc Judd would say if he caught him with brandy. He wondered without amusement if he should have gone to Judd's office for the check-up as he had planned. He could still feel the hot bitter wires of pain in his left shoulder and arm. He would take a double TNT before going to bed, he thought; and maybe a few sleeping pills.

For a long time he thought about Sloan and Paul Kahana and about Aaron and about Ward, and then he thought about his wife Grace whom he had not thought of for many months now, and once again he thought of Garth, the wanderer, and he wondered if Garth would ever return home. And finally he thought about tragedy and whether tragedy stalked the Howlands or the Howlands stalked tragedy until each one of them caught up with it.

He picked up a copy of the *Star-Bulletin* and read Cobey Black's column. It concerned a three-hundred-pound clarinet player and his fight to be reinstated as a member of the Royal Hawaiian Band. The clarinet player had been fired by the bandmaster because he was forbidden by his doctor to march with the band on parade. But since the band was a civil service organization, the chief of that department in Hawaii ruled that the clarinetist could not be fired. Old Willard enjoyed the column very much.

Afterwards he dozed for a while and he dreamed that he was on a distant island, wandering alone along the haunted beach like a solitary and stricken Gulliver pouring his soul out to the wind. He must have leaned over on his left arm as he dozed, for the pain started anew and woke him. When he woke up he felt very much alone; and very old and tired. He did not want to go to bed as long as the pain continued. Nor did he have the energy to work over any of his speeches for tomorrow. At Kaunakakai, at Kalaupapa, he would simply speak to the people as he felt.

He stood up, with some degree of struggle and pain. He walked slowly to the bookcase. By the dull glow of the firelight he glanced through several books, then selected a slender volume of Dylan Thomas' poetry: one of Garth's hundreds of books that old Willard had never found cause to read.

He adjusted the studio lamp by the chair and scanned the pages. Then his attention centered upon one poem that Garth had underlined and he read this through:

Do not go gentle into that good night,
Old age should burn and rave at close of day,
Rage, rage against the dying of the light.

Though wise men at their end know dark is right,
Because their words have forked no lightning
They do not go gentle into that good night.

Good men, the last wave by,
Crying how bright their frail deeds might have danced
in a green bay
Rage, rage against the dying of the light.

Wild men who caught and sang the sun in flight,
And learn too late, they grieved it on its way,
Do not go gentle into that good night.

Grave men near death who see with blinding sight,
Blind eyes could blaze like meteors and be gay,
Rage, rage against the dying of the light.

And you, my father, there on the sad height,
Curse, bless me now with your fierce tears I pray,
Do not go gentle into that good night,
Rage, rage against the dying of the light.

Willard read the poem through a second time. Then he put the book down and rested his head back against the chair and closed his eyes. But he did not go to sleep. He did not think that sleep would come tonight. The telephone rang and he knew that it was Ward. It rang twelve times and then stopped.

Chapter Fifteen

A HIGH hard sun beat down on the flats of Kalaupapa.

Sister Melanie Anne hurried down the steps of Bishop House and across the tiny green park to the post office building, near the main Hansen's Disease Hospital operated by the Territorial Board of Health. As she passed the post office two small Hawaiian boys chased after her.

"Sistah An, Sistah An, de plane's comin'!" the older boy shouted to her.

"Look up dere, Sistah An," the smaller boy joined in. "De plane! Cap'n Bill's comin'!"

Sister Melanie Anne looked up at the small plane, banking like a silver bird over Molokai Lighthouse.

"See dere?" The older boy pointed for her.

She smiled at him and ruffled his hair. "Yes, I see it, Moke. Now you hurry over and be waiting at the strip for Captain Bill," she said.

She hurried down the dirt road along Kalawao Church, making a swift sign of the cross as she passed the modest stone cross that marked Father Damien's grave.

"I'll be right back," she said, half to herself, half to the cross. She never passed the cross without saying a prayer. This was the first exception.

A block beyond the church she reached a row of small, immaculately clean wood cottages. The street was shaded with royal palms. Bougainvillaea wound about the eaves of the cottages. Each cottage had a small lanai, a green lawn facing the Molokai coast, a fruit tree in the lawn and usually a cat or a poi dog sleeping on the lawn. Sister Melanie Anne went to the fourth cottage on the right-hand side of the road and knocked on the door.

"Norman," she called. "Norman, Captain Bill's here. Pearl is all ready to go."

Norman Pulawa had been lying on his cot. He got up and opened the door for Sister Melanie Anne. "I'm awreddy," he said. "I jus' packed Pearl's tings so she kin take."

"Good," she said. She looked at him thoughtfully as he walked out from the cottage into the sunlight. "Are you feeling all right?" she asked. She placed her practiced hand on his forehead. "Um, you have a little temperature."

"Da kine tube is annoyin' me," Norman said, pointing to the tracheal tube attached to his throat. "Throat nevah feels no good no moah."

Norman Pulawa had been at Kalaupapa for seven years. He was a slender Hawaiian in his late forties. He had been very active in the community—a director of the Boy Scout Troop, Tailtwister with the busy Kalaupapa Lions Club. For a while he even ran a little laundry business in the village. But during the last three months his eyesight started failing and lesions about his mouth grew severe and he had been forced to curtail his activities. He looked down with wide serious eyes at Sister Melanie Anne. "When Pearl's gone, are you movin' me to de hospidal?"

She smiled and took him by the arm to hurry him. "Crazy question," she said. "You're always asking about the hospital, Norman. I declare you're more afraid of that hospital than you are of the

Devil himself. I've told you a hundred times, I don't know if the doctors will move you to the hospital or not. Anyway, Pearl will be at Hale Mohalu only until the baby is born. Then she'll be right back here with you."

They walked up the road toward Kalawao Church. When they passed Father Damien's grave, Sister Melanie Anne squinted and looked across the park to the clock in the hospital tower. "We have time for a short prayer," she said. "Captain Bill can wait."

They knelt down on the grass at the railing surrounding the martyr priest's grave.

"What'll we say, Sistah?"

Sister Melanie Anne's deep blue eyes looked at Norman for a moment, then turned and looked at the simple cross. "Let's pray to Father Damien," she said. "Let's pray for the baby, Norman. What do you want the baby to be, a boy or another girl?"

Norman studied with bleak indifference the cross that the people of Molokai had erected to their martyr priest. "I jus' don't want de baby to be sick," he said. "Pleeze, Fathah Damyen, don't let de baby be a leper."

Sister Melanie Anne looked away. She bit her lip. "No no no," she said, trying to make her voice stern. "You *know* better than that, Norman. You *know* it's not hereditary. And how many times have I told you not to use that word! Now pray correctly."

They recited two Hail Marys and two Our Fathers, Sister Melanie Anne leading Norman in the prayers. Then they crossed themselves and hurried over to Bishop House where the hospitalized women were kept. Pearl was waiting for them on the steps of Bishop House. She smiled happily at her husband and patted her stomach, grossly distended with seven months of baby.

"We gonna get one moah keiki now," she said gaily. "Wondah if it'll be boy or girl baby, huh?"

She kissed her husband heartily and the two of them, with Sister Melanie Anne, climbed into the back seat of a waiting hospital car and started for the landing strip.

Pearl noticed her husband's gloom. "Eh, whasamattah you, bruddah?" She nudged him in the ribs. "Auwe—I know." She winked at Sister Melanie Anne. "Norman, dis time he hopes for numbah one baby boy, das his oney trouble. Las time wuz baby girl, remembah, Sistah? Well, dis time we get numbah one baby boy, you betcha!"

Norman smiled broadly. "Yeah," he said, taking Pearl's hand in his. "Numbah one boy!"

He reached into his pocket for his wallet and took out a photograph of their four-year-old daughter. He studied the photograph and scratched his chin reflectively. "Verra preddy wahine, huh?" he said, handing the photograph to Sister Melanie Anne.

"Beautiful," she said.

He looked at a second photograph, showing the girl with her foster parents in Honolulu. The babies never come back to the leper colony. The Territorial Department of Health, and various church agencies, find foster parents for them elsewhere in the Territory. The children never know. Their birth certificates are changed listing the foster parents as the real parents.

Pearl took the photograph from her husband's hands and studied the face of the girl. Then she nudged Sister Melanie Anne. "Eh, what's her name, Sistah?"

Sister Melanie Anne looked at the photograph and smiled. She had a warm, pleasant smile. "You know better than to ask that, Pearl. I don't know the girl's name and I don't know the foster parents' names," she lied. "And if I did, I couldn't tell you anyway."

At the landing strip, a dozen gleeful children and several adults milled about Captain Bill Holiday's Cessna biplane. Holiday was passing out bags of Hershey candy kisses to the children. Then he helped the colony's postmaster, Kale Kobayashi, lift the mail sack from the plane. Kale Kobayashi had been completely cured of Hansen's disease five years ago. But he had lived at Kalaupapa nearly all his life and he refused to leave. There was no place for him to go. He lifted the mail sack to his shoulder and waved goodby to Holiday. There was never much mail, but what there was was treasured.

Holiday walked across the strip to the hospital car where Sister Melanie Anne was lifting Pearl's suitcase from the trunk. One of the older children took the suitcase from her and carried it to the plane.

"Captain Holiday, I would like you to meet Mr. and Mrs. Pulawa," Sister said.

Bill Holiday tipped his yachting cap to Pearl and shook hands with Norman.

"Mrs. Pulawa is your passenger," Sister said. "You take good care of her, hear?"

Holiday grinned. "We'll get you all safe and sound to Hale Mohalu, Mrs. Pulawa."

Norman and Pearl walked solemnly to the plane, shaking hands with friends who had come to see Pearl off to Hale Mohalu, a confined Hansen's disease clinic at Pearl City, just outside Honolulu.

"Lots of activity out here today," Holiday said, glancing about the village. "That Union guy's out here to settle the hospital ship business, and I hear Willard Howland is due to speak here this afternoon."

Sister Melanie Anne grinned. "Yes, we're getting to be a busy little suburb."

Holiday lit a cigarette and watched Pearl and Norman walk to the plane. Then he looked into Sister Melanie Anne's deep blue eyes. "I understand you all are going to be my next passenger."

Sister sniffed the air about Bill Holiday. "Captain Holiday, I do declare you've been drinking already this morning!"

Holiday grinned and looked at his watch. "It's almost afternoon, Sister. And the Good Lord would never frown upon my shaking hands with Jack Daniels, seeing as how the Good Lord realizes how wonderful it makes me feel toward my fellow man."

Sister Melanie Anne frowned. "More people have gone to Purgatory and worse places for thinking the Good Lord wouldn't mind this or that little indulgence. You shouldn't drink like you do, Captain Holiday," she admonished him firmly. "But to answer your question: no, I will not be your next passenger."

"But I thought—"

"You thought wrong, Captain Holiday," she said sharply. She turned away from him a moment and glanced beyond the neat whitewashed rows of houses that marked the village, to the Molokai sea. "I've been here ten years, Bill," she said very quietly. "This is my work. This is my life, now. These are my people."

Holiday inhaled slowly on the cigarette. He watched the folds of the full, white nun's habit furl in the sea wind about her slender figure. He guessed she was about thirty-six, a few years younger than himself anyway, and he thought, watching her, that she must have been an exquisitely beautiful young girl. Her eyes were clear blue and deep as pools. Feathers of blond hair had come loose from her veil and brushed across the center of her smooth forehead. The lines about her mouth had tightened over the years, and lately her face had grown wan and pale. But she was still a beautiful woman.

She said, "I received word yesterday from Sister Superior. I can stay."

She turned and smiled at him and Holiday looked deep into her eyes. "Don't you sometimes feel that maybe—"

"No, I never worry about that, Bill," she said quickly. She gazed beyond the landing strip to where blankets of cloud hugged the sharp pali cliffs which isolated the Kalaupapa peninsula from the rest of the Island of Molokai. No road leads into the colony. It can be reached only by ship or plane; and only with the permission of the Territorial Department of Health. There were some two hundred patients at the colony now. In Father Damien's time, there were thousands upon thousands, sent there to rot and die by themselves.

"No, I don't worry about that any more than you do, Bill," Sister Melanie Anne said. "It is all a very misunderstood disease. It's almost impossible to communicate, if you employ basic health habits. A victim of Hansen's disease could marry a normal person and the normal person need not get inflicted with the disease. Babies are perfectly normal, like Pearl and Norman's, even when both parents are lepers.

"I keep thinking of what a horror it must have been for Father Damien. All those poor creatures shunted over here, outcasts of society, living in caves or dirty grass huts with no medical care until they rotted away. Now, we've just about got it licked," she said, smiling. "Until we do, I plan to stay here. This is my life and my work. I couldn't leave. I'm happy. It gives me a sense of fulfillment, working with these wonderful people. They need me and want me; and because of that, I need them and want them."

A mechanic, one of the lepers, had warmed-up Bill Holiday's plane. "Well, I guess I'm off." He smiled at her. "Want anything from the big city?"

"No thank you, Captain. Take good care of my patient."

"She looks as though she's pretty well able to take care of herself," Bill Holiday said, crushing his cigarette out against the concrete of the strip. "But the old man doesn't look good. He's looked worse and worse these past few months."

Sister nodded her head. "They both know it. Pearl's just being a good soldier."

Holiday looked over at Pearl and Norman, waiting by the plane. "It must be awful hard for a woman to go have a baby, knowing all along that the baby will be taken away from her forever immediately after birth."

They walked over to the plane. "Pearl has it harder than that," Sister Melanie Anne said. "She knows, even though she won't let on, that Norman won't be alive when she gets back."

Holiday climbed into the pilot's seat and waved good-by. Sister Melanie Anne leaned into the cabin of the plane and kissed Pearl and let Pearl kiss the crucifix that was tied to a belt of wooden beads wound about the waist of her habit. Pearl started to cry. "Take care of him, Sistah," she sobbed. "He's a good man. Hardly can see now. Please take care of him an' ask God to take care of him."

The little plane raced into the sky and banked over the sharp pali cliffs.

Sister Melanie Anne took Norman's arm and they walked slowly back to his cottage. For a minute she felt dizzy and thought she was going to faint. She held tight to his arm. She shook her head and the dizziness went away. She felt her forehead and her neck for fever. It was there again, as it had been all week, and much of the week before.

They passed Father Damien's grave and Norman stopped.

"Let's pray again, Sistah. Let's pray for a numbah one healthy boy."

They knelt down side by side before the stone cross.

Ward stood on the bridge of the hospital ship *Kanani* as it rode at anchor in the deepwater harbor of Kalaupapa. It was a converted eighty-two-foot motor vessel leased by the Territory as a hospital emergency ship. The chipped white paint of its hull was emblazoned by a great green cross. It called biweekly at Kalaupapa and other isolated points in the Islands which were inaccessible except for the waterways. An unwritten agreement existed between the Territorial Department of Public Health and the Union that the hospital ship would be worked despite the strike. This was the first occasion that the Union stevedores who worked the Kalaupapa wharf refused to discharge the *Kanani*'s cargo, which included mainly penicillin and various other medicinal supplies. Ward had left Honolulu on the early-morning plane for Kaunakakai, and when the dispute concerning the unloading of the hospital ship could not be settled at the Union local there, he had managed to get a ride with Bill Holiday across the mountainous width of Molokai to the Kalaupapa Peninsula.

It was a clear afternoon. From the bridge, looking northwest across the Molokai Channel, Ward could make out the hazy, peaked outline of Oahu resting on the curve of the world. A green squall was working its way across the channel.

"Looks like we might get some weather tonight," the captain of the *Kanani* said. He was a stolid, remote, taciturn Swede who was known throughout the Islands only by his last name, Sorrensen; an incorrigibly rootless and friendless old man who had apparently delegated his Christian name along with his hopes and promises, along with his home perhaps, his family and kin perhaps, back into the dust and inconsequential early chapters of his dreams. There was a rumor, long ago, that he had once lost a ship, then a wife, then a son. But no one knew just how or where the rumor started. His face was bitten deep by the moods of the sea and by the reflection of the sun and even the stars on the water; his mouth was a grim line, his eyes clear but defeated. He did not like things. He did not like man or the earth or weeds. He no longer even liked the sea. "There," he pointed out to the working squall. "We'll have trouble tonight."

"We might have trouble before tonight," Ward said.

"I don't know why." Captain Sorrensen shrugged. "You're the Union boss."

"It doesn't look that way."

"No. It certainly does not."

"I've given you Union authorization to unload cargo."

"You've given me sheets of signed printed paper. In triplicate. What I need is the men to do the unloading."

They walked to the edge of the bridge and looked down at the wharf. Several dozen persons milled quietly about the wharf, most of them patients. Many of these had the tracheal tubes attached like a loose vein to their throats. They stood expectantly in small groups by the shed, shifting their weight from one foot to the other, trying to figure out what to do with their hands. They looked shyly at one another, then to the argument at the foot of the gangplank. Ten stevedores blocked the gangplank. A group of Department of Health staff members stood a little off from the gangplank, staring sullenly at the unmoving stevedores. The young hospital doctor and the boss stevedore were arguing at the foot of the gangplank.

"Can those patients and some of the hospital staff unload the ship?" Ward asked, turning to the captain.

"They can if they can bust through those Union goons. They'd better figure out whether to swallow it or spit it out. I been here fourteen hours now. I can't set here all week."

Ward worked his way across the bridge to the deck and down the gangplank. The stevedores gave him a wide berth, all but the bossman, a dark giant named Watanabe who looked down at him with cold bemusement.

"What's the verdict, Doctor?" Ward said.

"Mr. Akana, if this is a Union jurisdictional dispute I wish you and Mr. Watanabe here would make up your minds who has jurisdiction and let us unload the ship. We've been bickering all morning. We have to move these supplies to the hospital without any further delay." He took off his field cap and wiped the perspiration from his brow with his forearm. He was a bronzed young man with good shoulders and an open face and pleasant manner. But he was out of his element here, Ward knew. He was being pushed by professionals.

Ward turned to the boss stevedore. "What do you say, Eli?"

"I say the stuff can't be moved, Mr. Akana."

"You're just going to turn the ship around without letting the hospital get its supplies?"

"Yeah," Eli Watanabe grinned, "I guess that's just what I'm gonna do." He stood over six-feet-four, built thick and square and like a rock. His hair was black and curly with long sideburns, and his pitch-black eyes were hard and coldly amused. He was a type that George Hill called a "Union necessity": the kind of a man who loves nothing better than to feel his fist crunch into another man's skull. He was not a stevedore. He was one of the Union musclemen, a one-man blitzkrieg whom George Hill would dispatch at a moment's notice to any part of the Territory where there was likely to be Union trouble. He was standing easy, his feet wide apart, his giant fists doubled and buried into his hips, the corners of his mouth pulled down into a cold grin. He looked so eager to crunch his fist into the bones of Ward's face that it made Ward a little sick at the thought.

"Take a look around you, Eli. What do you see?"

Big Eli glanced about at the faces of the patients. He turned back to Ward and grinned. "Touchin', ain't it?"

"These people need the supplies on this ship."

"Let 'em fly 'em in. The stuff can't be taken off the ship, Mr. Akana."

"I say it can." Ward turned to the doctor. "Can some of your staff help? And some of the patients, too. We'll need as many good men as we can get."

The young doctor looked warily from Ward to the stevedores. "Well—I guess they can. But I don't know, Mr. Akana. It kind of worries me."

"Don't let it worry you. I've given Captain Sorrensen authorization to discharge cargo. If the stevedores won't do it, we'll do it ourselves."

Big Eli stepped between the two of them. "Mr. Akana, case you don't know it, there's a strike goin' on."

"Not here there isn't."

"Yeah, here too. This ship don't get unloaded. Them's my orders."

"Who do you take your orders from, Eli?"

"Not from you, Mr. Akana. I used to take 'em from you. But not no more." He looked around at the handful of stevedores and laughed with them.

"From whom do you get them?"

"From Mr. Hill, of course."

"George Hill told you to stop work on this ship?"

"That's right, Mr. Akana. He called me last night to grab the first plane in the morning and get over here, just in case there was trouble. He told me that you'd probably be over here, startin' the trouble, but not to pay any attention to you, because you weren't with the Union no more, Mr. Akana."

Ward scowled. "Let me see those orders."

"Uh-uh. They're locked up inside here." Big Eli pointed to his head.

"There's plenty of vacant space for them up there," Ward muttered.

"Don't get nasty, Mr. Akana," Big Eli said, affably enough.

"That's what Mr. Hill said. He said how you might get nasty."

Ward walked toward Captain Sorrensen, who was leaning against the railing at the foot of the gangplank, and ripped two of the sheets from the triplicate authorization form he had given the captain. He handed one sheet to the young Department of Public Health doctor and held the other one up before Big Eli and the rest of the stevedores. "As highest ranking Union official present, I have just given written authorization for the discharging of this vessel's cargo in compliance with the Union's open agreement concerning the hospital ship. However," he said, leaning toward the patients, "we're short of hands. I have granted authorization to the ship's captain to use Union stevedores or anyone else present to unload this cargo, in case the Union men refuse. If we could get a handful of volunteers up here to help unload—"

Big Eli grabbed the paper from his hand. He read it rapidly. "Just what the hell kind of a stunt do you think you're pullin', Akana?" he said. "These orders don't mean nothin' since you ain't a member of the Union no more." He tore up the paper, tossed the shreddings into the air and grinned shrewdly as they fluttered down about him. "Pretty, ain't they?"

"Very pretty," Ward said, shaking himself.

Big Eli stood in front of him, his huge fists hanging easily at his sides. "Now what other orders you got to give, Akana?"

"Let those men through," Ward said flatly. Several of the hospital staff members and a group of the younger male patients had started filing toward the gangplank, but stood unmoving now as the stevedores blocked their way. One of the stevedores turned questioningly to Big Eli. "We gonna hold back a bunch of lepers?"

"Damn right we are!" Big Eli roared. He bulled his way into the patients and started pushing them back from the gangplank. "Okeh, all of you get back before we got to bust some heads open! C'mon, c'mon back—back up!"

One of the staff men approached him. "Look here, stop pushing these people! They're hospital patients."

Big Eli slammed a roundhouse into the staffer's face. He did not seem to put much energy into the punch, but the staffer drifted back ten yards and crumpled to the ground. "I said get back, goddamn it, now get!" He shoved and bulled his way about the crowd until the lepers dispersed from the gangplank. Then he turned and stalked angrily toward Captain Sorrensen and shook a huge finger into the man's face. "And I'll give you one word of advice, Skipper; you let anyone touch one box of cargo on this ship and you'll be sitting in the middle of a Union battle."

Sorrensen stared at him unblinkingly. "Don't try to scare me, big fellow. Go push those sick people around if you get a thrill out of it. But don't try and scare me."

"Okay, tough skipper," Big Eli roared, the veins exploding in his bull neck. "Just remember what I told you!"

Ward had moved up to the gangplank and the stevedores had broken ranks for him. "Now either you men unload this ship or I'll get the whole damn colony here to do it," Ward said, looking at the hesitant file of longshoremen.

Big Eli grabbed Ward by the scruff of the neck and spun him around. But when he swung, Ward moved in and under the fist, butted him in the stomach and brought his head up swiftly beneath his jaw, hard enough so that he could hear Big Eli's teeth crunch together. Ward drove a right into his heart and a left that split open his nose, and then Big Eli regained his bearings and started in on him. Big Eli's left burned across Ward's ear. He followed it with a right that exploded like a hand grenade against Ward's chest, sending him sprawling onto the gangplank. Big Eli lifted him up, holding him out straight with one hand, setting him up that way, then his huge fist bore in and broke over Ward's face in a black explosion. Ward fell back to the gangplank, bounced off the gangplank and rolled over on the concrete of the wharf. When Big Eli jumped him again, Ward dazedly put up his foot and caught the big man in the face. Ward shook himself free, tried weakly to get to his feet before the next charge. He could not see out of his right eye, but he turned fullface just as Big Eli rushed in for the kill. But before he connected, Ward glimpsed the butt end of a .45 automatic smash into Big Eli's face.

Ward blacked out then. He did not see Captain Sorrensen bring the automatic down again, hard on Big Eli's skull. Nor did he see Sorrensen crush his knee into Big Eli's groin. Big Eli keeled over at an impossible angle and vomited until he lost consciousness. Sorrensen walked over and gave him one last sharp kick in the temple. He looked without emotion at the huge form, confident that Big Eli would not get up any more for the rest of the day.

Sorrensen walked over to the group of unmoving stevedores,

his automatic in his hand. "Get away," he said. Then he turned to the young doctor. "Let's get this ship unloaded."

Slowly, the staff members and the patients walked up the gangplank, and with the third mate instructing them from the bridge, they formed a file from the cargo hold down the gangplank to the wharf and started unloading the supplies.

Looking out of the window of the Hawaiian Air Lines Convair as it circled Kalaupapa, Willard could see the village very clearly; the recreation area near the end of the landing strip, then the rows of outpatient cottages, the hospital for the severe cases, then Bishop House, the square, the steepled rise of Kalawao Church, the red corrugated roofs of the market houses bright against the ferny green of the hillside. At the mouth of the tiny harbor, he could see the hospital ship *Kanani* pull past the breakwater and rock a little in the swells of the open sea as it turned and headed for Maui. Before he left Kaunakakai, he had heard a report of some kind of Union battle aboard the *Kanani* involving Ward Akana. Maybe if Ward Akana had his skull cracked open, some sense would seep into it, he thought.

At the far end of the runway, where the plane would taxi to its stop, Willard saw that a wooden platform had been erected. The platform was in a grove of monkeypod, the rear of the platform toward the seacoast, and there were flags and bunting draped over the railing of the platform and behind it had been erected a giant-size photo poster of himself. There were a few people waiting on the platform and a crowd of about two hundred waiting for the plane to land. Musicians and a hula troupe were entertaining the crowd. The wheels of the plane touched ground and the engines were cut while the plane taxied along the ramp, and he could see down the neat, clean, palm-lined streets of the hopeful village of lepers. He remembered his friend Jack London's shocked grief upon visiting the colony almost a half century ago. Man is still enslaved by greed and disease and suffering and frustration, and man continues to outdo himself in order to display his utter inhumanity toward his fellow man with wars which are still waged with peace in mind; perhaps we are destined to wage perpetual wars for perpetual peace, because man, after the myriad centuries of walking stooped, has yet to master walking tall and straight,

Willard thought, looking out at the village—but man is trying. The leper colony here is evidence of man's attempt. And had he lived to see the result of this attempt, Jack London would have been spared a portion of his grief.

He descended the ramp. In the sunlight of the landing strip, the murmured welcome of the crowd startled him. But as he looked into the sea of faces, he remembered. The patients could not cheer. Nor could they shout a welcome. Most of them wore the tracheal tubes attached to their throats, their vocal chords warped, and they could not speak above a coarse, rasping whisper. They applauded and waved handkerchiefs, and old Willard grinned broadly at them and returned their waves with the Churchillian V-for-victory sign.

"One week from today," he said to them, as the applause died out, "you will go to your election booths to send a new Delegate to Congress to represent you. And I hope to heaven that you're looking at him right now!"

Willard shook hands warmly with the welcoming committee: Dr. Ned Grange, chief medical officer at the colony; young Dr. Dave Murphy, who had been at the wharf when the *Kanani* dispute broke out; several of the staff members and patients, including the grizzled, toothless and almost sightless self-styled mayor of Kalaupapa, Abraham Foxeyes Waipaho. A young girl with a smooth little face and dark eyes that could make up for all the eyes in the world came up to him and placed a red carnation lei about his shoulders. She wore crutches decorated with frangipani blossoms and her right foot was dreadfully disfigured, but Willard looked only into her eyes. A man could look only into her eyes, he thought, and he would need not look into any other eyes for the rest of his life. The hula troupe danced through the crowd, making an aisle from the landing strip to the platform. Willard followed the dancers. Several of the patients broke through the ranks of the crowd and walked up to him and placed leis about his shoulders. Willard stopped and chatted amiably with each. He shook a hundred hands. One of the nuns was unsuccessful in restraining her patient from barging through the crowd to Howland.

"Howzitt, Senatah Will!" Norman Pulawa said cheerily. "I jus' come up to wish you aloha."

"Thank you," old Willard nodded. He stared reflectively at Norman for a moment.

Norman grinned shyly. "Don't you remembah, Senatah Will? Norman—Norman Pulawa. I used to work for you at roundup time. Remembah now?"

Willard nodded heavily, his dark gold eyes softening as he looked at Norman. He clasped Norman's right hand warmly in both of his. "Of course, of course I remember now. An old man's memory plays tricks on him at times. How are you making it, Norman?"

"I ain't got no complaints, Senatah."

"And how is—how is—" Old Willard shook his head, cursing his worn, corroded memory.

"Pearl? She fine. She been gone to Honoluluh this moahnin' to have anothah baby. It'll make two." Norman grinned proudly and reached into his wallet and showed Willard the photograph of his four-year-old daughter.

"Norman," Sister Melanie Anne said kindly, "Senator Howland hasn't much time."

"No no, I want to see that girl," Willard said. He looked at the photograph and smiled with pride. "A beauty! An Island rose!"

Norman replaced the photograph in his wallet and as he did so, Willard looked at him steadily, noticing the tracheal tube, the faltering eyesight. An image was moving across the back yards of his memory, an image of a lean, wire-muscled teen-age youngster who could ride like a Cossack and brand more calves in a four-hour stint than any two ranch hands at Manoalani. He patted Norman on the arm and bowed with his old unfailing courtesy to Sister Melanie Anne. "Take care of him, Sister. Take care of yourself, Norman."

"Yessuh." Norman smiled but did not look into Willard's eyes. "Maybe sometime byanby I get moah bettah an' been go back to Manoalani an' work a roundup again."

"I hope so, Norman," Willard muttered.

Sister Melanie Anne exchanged glances with old Willard. Then she took Norman by the arm and crossed the strip of concrete to the front of the platform.

"You got my vote, Senatah Will," Norman's whispered voice reached the old man's ears. Howland waved to Norman and continued toward the steps leading up to the platform.

"You have my vote too, Senator," another voice told him.

The old man turned and felt a shock of surprise as he saw Ward leaning against the bannister of the steps. Ward's left arm was in a heavy cast, folded across his chest and hanging in a white cotton sling that was tied around his shoulder. There were ugly discolorations about his face. A bandage was affixed above his right eye, where the skin had been ripped away by Big Eli's knuckles. The eye was bluish-purple and grossly swollen, almost completely closed. Ward managed a weak quick grin. "I came to hear you talk—on statehood."

"You came, huh?" Willard surveyed the damage on Ward's face. "You look more like you were dragged here underneath a twenty-mule team." He rested his hand on the bannister and looked sharply at Ward. "Did you bring your goons with you to heckle me? Is the great vendetta still in full swing? I read in the papers last night that it was."

"I tried to call you and explain about that. The story was untrue. I made no such speech." Ward cocked his head to one side, squinting at the Senator. "And it was—never a vendetta, sir."

"Uh-huh. Just a difference of opinion regarding the merit of man."

"Perhaps." Ward looked down at the ground and slowly scuffed the dirt with the toe of his shoe. "Anyway, I've come to listen to you. And to wish you good luck. As I said, you have my vote, Senator."

"Your vote," Willard muttered scornfully. "There was a time, Ward, when deep inside me I would rather have won your single vote than the combined votes of all the members in that corrupt Union of yours. But now—"

"It's not my Union," Ward said. "I quit."

No reaction marked the unchanging granite of Willard's face. Ward looked up at him curiously, uncertain whether he had heard. "Did you hear me, sir?" He awaited. "Do you feel all right, sir?"

After a moment Willard nodded. "Yes, Ward, I heard you."

Ward reached up and with an almost childish gesture, covered old Willard's hand with his. "And please believe me, Father, it was never a matter of vengeance."

Slowly, Willard raised his old shaggy head and stared at Ward with a strangeness in his eyes, a quality that Ward had never seen before and did not comprehend. "It has always been vengeance, Son," Willard muttered in a soft, broken voice. "And I call you 'Son' because that is my debt to you and I am neither afraid nor ashamed. It is a debt which I have lived with since the day you were born and one which I have truly tried to repay, tried to make up for, without success: justly without success, for no man can repay the debt he owes his son, only the son can do that. And you have succeeded, your vengeance has been complete; your vengeance has abolished my debt to you and I need no longer look upon you as my son.

"A man's only true possession is hope," Willard said. "And since your birth, I had hoped, perhaps, for mercy; for grace, for luck, for the creeping of fate that would enable me in some way to repay my debt to you, which I have always considered a very large and heavy and perhaps monstrous debt. But there has been no mercy in our court, Ward. There has been, instead, the harsh awful symmetry of human justice, which claims that a man must pay, in some surprising shocking way, for everything he has done; and every part of his life is somehow equal to the whole. Your vengeance has equaled my guilt. There is no longer a debt between us, Ward. I've paid for you."

Old Willard drew himself up with a weary grace, his head lifted indomitably, his shoulders squared, his entire being a little stiffer and more rigid in bone and pride than Ward had ever seen it before, and as he mounted the stairs to the platform he said, in that same soft, broken voice, without a backward glance, "I don't want your vote, Ward. I don't need it now. I'd be ashamed of it."

Willard walked out across the platform, lean and slow-looking, his head bowed a little, the way a man does when he is out walking by himself and has something on his mind. He carried the wide-brimmed Manahiki hat in his hand, and the shock of white-gold hair spilled down across his forehead. He stood in the center of the platform, looking at the crowd.

They stood gathered around him, about three hundred now, motionless, their faces raised to him, their expressions a mixture of pride and something like humility too.

"I haven't many speeches left in me," Willard said. "Just as a man can issue no new reasons for honor and justice and truth, I can bring no new reasons for our statehood.

"I have heard the statement that Hawaii is doing fine as a Territory so why change her? To that I reply, such status of government never has and never will be adequate. It is an inferior status repugnant to the spirit of America. If this is what America intends, it is a denial of a trust.

"I have heard the statement that if America does not want us, then let us not want America. To that I reply from the foulest of Scriptures: an eye for an eye—were words emptier ever uttered? They are not for us. We cannot cut our cord from America. We in Hawaii have a love too deep and too strong toward America to ever permit our love to become diluted by a shallowness of spirit.

"We must keep faith in ourselves, our islands, and in our great nation. And that faith, which we have kept, will soon be answered; the wrongs righted, the star granted.

"And when that day comes, we will no longer be stepchildren of the nation. For we will have four representatives—two Senators and two Congressmen—voting for us in Washington. We will vote for the President, elect our own Governor, select our own judges to administer our courts. We will have closer ties with the Mainland, and the illusion that we are foreigners will be destroyed. Doubt will be destroyed.

"There was much doubt before 1941; before Pearl Harbor. There was perhaps legitimate doubt that the Japanese people, accountable for thirty-seven per cent of our population, had loyalties elsewhere. But our Nisei firmly removed that doubt. World War Two's 100th Battalion was formed from our Island Nisei boys as was the even more famous 442nd 'Go-For-Broke' Regimental Combat Team, described by my good friend, Mark Clark, as the 'most decorated unit in the entire military history of the United States'—Island Nisei boys.

"More recently Hawaii, still the whipping boy, has been charged with disloyalty within the ranks of its labor forces, with charges of left-wing and Communistic being hurled at the Union and its Fifth Amendment Leader, George Hill. It is true that Hawaii has a Communist problem. So does every state in the Union. But Hawaii has laws to combat it, and agencies charged with investigating and controlling it. We must keep a wary eye on both the Communists and the agencies charged with investigating Communism. For patriotism is a wonderful thing as long as it is not carried to a shallow extreme. Then, as Dr. Johnson pointed out, it can become the refuge of a scoundrel. There is the danger that we in Hawaii have too many super-patriots who, because of fear and hate and chronic inferiority or insecurity, condemn all those who do not think as they. Do not confuse nonconformity with disloyalty. Do not trample the individual.

"The individual must be allowed to think for himself. If his thinking is in disagreement with the majority, the majority must not stigmatize him as a traitor or disloyal. Perhaps the most truly loyal citizen the United States can have in times like these is the nonconformer. If a person maintains a nonconforming pattern of thought, he must not be reduced by the powers of state as an offender against society. Because when the holding of different opinions becomes a threat or a disaster for the individual, he will simply avoid the threat and the disaster by avoiding holding differing opinions. Then we will have totalitarianism. Because we have been attacked on that score from outside, we in Hawaii, I fear, have grown a little too prone and too quick to point and shout 'Communist!' at our neighbor, the individual, the nonconformer. And this has been one of the varied reasons that for so long has delayed our star.

"But no reason can delay it much longer. To continue to delay our equality would be a contradiction by America of its moral, spiritual and material leadership in the world."

He lounged a step forward, easy and soft-footed. Then it seemed to Ward, who stood by the steps of the platform, watching him, that the old man weaved unsteadily, flinching his left shoulder as if in pain. The fingers of his right hand gripped tightly about his left arm as if attempting to quell the pain.

But if there had been pain, old Willard recovered quickly. He looked down into the crowd, his shaggy white head turning slowly, his eyes stopping to rest upon a face here for a moment and then moving on to another face a few rows back.

"We have our destiny to accomplish," he said. "And we the people of Hawaii are equal to our destiny!"

The strange muted roar welled up from the crowd.

Willard waited a long time before he raised his hand to quiet the murmur that was, in its way, louder than a roar. His left hand hung limply in the pocket of his white linen coat. He changed his stance a little, leaning closer into the crowd, becoming one of the crowd, a figure that the crowd could see and feel and sense and laugh with and believe in; and Ward could see the stains of tears on many faces now, and he knew from old Willard's change in mood, change in stance, in attitude, in charge, the change in the very electricity of the air between Willard and the people, that he was up to it now; he would give it to them now.

"I ask you," Willard was saying, "to let me bring you the statehood and equality you deserve: not as a symbol of security with the greater nation across the sea, but as a gesture of salutation between free men and free men; of equal civilization not only across the vast expanse of empire that marks America, but also across the seas to Molokai. I ask for and demand statehood for Hawaii, for you people right here before me, who, as I, want respect without servility, allegiance without abasement, to the government which sixty years ago our ancestors and many of us ourselves accepted with pride but still as free men, so long as that government of the United States remembered always to let men live free, not under it, but beside it!"

The murmur rose again. Old Willard seemed to catch himself. His left arm became rigid at his side. He shook his head for a split second, trying to chase whatever it was away. He planted his feet wide apart, his legs stiff, his head a little at an angle, attentive, listening to the murmuring half-voices of the lepers. At the foot of the steps, Ward too cocked his head to listen. It was not simply a whispered murmur now. It was a hymn. The lepers had begun to hum softly in their coarse, muted voices. The humming seemed to start far back in the crowd, then moved forward as row upon row of patients raised their voices in "Aloha Oe." Ward raised his head and glanced past the platform, beyond Willard Howland's stiff, unyielding frame of rail, and he could see the faces of the lepers as they raised their voices in song.

"Your needs will be my command, your dreams will be my sword, your heart will be my power," Willard was saying above the concord of voices. "And I will not cease until the reality, the aspirations and the dreams have been united—"

His voice stopped. It did not trail off. It did not end in low key or in bombast like a voice that had planned to stop. One moment it was there, going on, word by word, above the concord of voices that filled the grove, then suddenly it was not there. The singing continued, but Willard Howland's voice did not. He stood at the edge of the platform for half a minute; mute, immobile, void of all discernible emotion. He did not seem to be noticing the crowd, or be even aware of it. Then with sudden decision he turned, his face flushed a dark red, and tried to walk stiffly across the platform.

But he buckled. His hands clutched his chest and the cords in his neck knotted like the roots of a tree. As Ward leaped to the platform, old Willard staggered backwards, his face drained gray, his mouth a twist of agony, straining for air but powerless to breathe. He swung his haggard and reproachful glance on Ward, and he seemed to try, in that last instant before collapsing, to grasp Ward's hand.

Chapter Sixteen

"YOU won't leave me alone, will you?"

"No. Of course not."

"Is that a promise?" Lei asked. "Please promise."

"That's a promise," Dr. Judd told her. "Now try and get some rest."

"I don't want any rest. I just want to have it over and done with." She looked up at him. "Does that sound cold? Or hard?"

Dr. Judd grinned. "No, it sounds very normal," he said. "Almost universal."

"Because I'm neither cold nor hard. I want this baby very much."

"I know you do, Lei." Dr. Judd leaned over and wiped the beads of perspiration from her forehead. "I don't want you to drain your strength. You're going to need all of it. Just try and rest for a while and save it up."

"Did you call Aaron?"

"Yes. I told you I did."

"I mean since then?"

"Yes. He'll be right over," Dr. Judd lied.

"You're not lying?"

"No."

"I want Aaron to be with me," Lei said. "I don't think a woman should have a baby all alone. Even if it's like—you know, like ours. Am I right or wrong, Dr. Judd?"

"You're right, Lei."

"And I'll tell you something else, Doctor. I still love Aaron. Very much. And I need him now, like all those nights when he needed me. I really need him now. I want him with me. I want to give him this baby. So he'll—"

She twisted her head into the pillow and closed her fists into tight little knots and waited while the pain shuddered through her. He wiped her brow. Her face was wan and gray. "How did that feel?" he asked her.

"I don't know. Yes, I know, but I'm afraid to tell you."

"Tell me."

"The pain doesn't feel good any more, Doctor. It just feels sharper and shorter. They're not big any more; not good any more. They don't seem to have any meaning now. They're just painful."

"They'll be good again soon. We just had a false alarm. Often this first labor is protracted."

"This isn't first labor, Doctor. You're fibbing to me now."

"No. It's first labor."

"What time did you bring me here?"

"Nine o'clock."

"What time is it now?"

"Three o'clock."

"Three o'clock in the morning?"

"Yes."

"This isn't first labor, Doctor."

"You rest; I'll do the diagnosing," Dr. Judd told her. "Do you feel any better?"

"Like dancing." She forced a smile. "Have you gotten any sleep?"

He shook his head. "When a man gets to be my age, he doesn't need any sleep. Or else he doesn't want any. He gets to feeling perhaps there aren't many days left, and he wants to make use of all the time he can."

"You look sleepy. Maybe you should lie down and rest too."

"Miss Wu is inside taking a nap now. Maybe when she wakes up I'll try."

"I don't like nurses."

"She's a very nice young girl."

"What if this keeps up, Doctor? What if it just keeps up for another five or ten hours?"

"We can't let that happen. I told you that."

"I know. But what if it just keeps up?"

"It won't. We'll give it a little more time. Then if nothing happens by itself, we'll make it happen."

"Will it leave a scar?"

"A Caesarean scar."

"I hoped it wouldn't mean a scar. I have no scars on me now."

"A scar or two is good for a person."

"I feel so bad and so ashamed of myself for being like this. For acting like this now, after being such a good patient for so long."

"You're still a very good patient."

"No, I'm not. If I was a good patient that baby would be up here now at my breast instead of down—" She bit her lip in pain. The pain bored through her, slowly, steadily, shockingly; then subsided. She opened her eyes and shook her head. "It wasn't a good one," she said. "It was just one of those empty pains. I wish those good ones would come again."

"They will."

"When?"

"Soon now."

"You hope."

"Yes," he smiled at her, "I hope."

"And if they don't?"

"I told you. We'll operate."

"And it will leave a scar."

"A small scar."

She closed her eyes. Dr. Judd mopped the perspiration from her brow with a wad of cotton. He felt her pulse. He did not like her pulse and he did not like the gray of her skin. He did not like her loss of strength and he did not like the lessening, jerky pains and he did not like the fact that it had been almost five hours now since he and Miss Wu had brought her into the operating room for that first false alarm; nor did he like the idea of the Caesarean with one of her kidneys almost a ruin with infection and the other kidney almost a ruin with strain and overwork during the last four months and most especially ruined with overwork these last six hours.

"What's wrong, Doctor?" She had opened her eyes and had been staring obliquely at him while he was taking her pulse.

"Nothing is wrong."

"It's almost like he didn't want to be born."

"Just give him time."

"You're sure it's going to be a boy?"

Dr. Judd nodded.

"I'm glad. I think Aaron will be glad too." She turned her head. The sprawl of her hair on the pillow was damp, lackluster. "Do you think maybe he doesn't want to be born, Doctor? Born—in sin?"

Dr. Judd leaned back against the straight wooden chair alongside the bed. "The Scripture says how we are all conceived in sin, but I don't believe in the Scripture or the whole rigamarole of Testaments and Bibles and Korans. Your baby was not conceived in sin but in love and need like all man is conceived. Now try and rest, Lei. Try and save your strength."

"I'm too afraid to rest."

"There's nothing to be afraid of."

She looked at him curiously. "I wasn't afraid at first. You know, when we first got here and you brought me into that room and the pains were so big—so big and fast and good that I thought I was going to explode him right out of me; do you remember? What time was it then, Doctor?"

"About nine-thirty. Ten o'clock."

"And what time is it now?"

"It's after three. It's Thanksgiving."

"Thanksgiving?"

"Yes," the doctor said, "and in a little while now it will be all over and although I wouldn't advise drumsticks and cranberry sauce, I'll think of something for you."

"Thanksgiving Day . . ." Lei mumbled. The pain coursed

through her and cut off the thought. And then it seemed to her that the thought cut off the pain. "It was no good," she said softly. "And now I'm more afraid than ever."

"There's nothing to be afraid about. Just rest."

"Do women die in childbirth any more?"

"No," he lied. "And let's not think that way. No one is going to die."

"But they still do die, don't they? I mean despite everything that's been done. They still do die."

"People die falling out of bed in the morning, Lei. But I'm not going to let you fall out of this bed and no one is going to die and in just a little while now you and your baby son will spend Thanksgiving Day together."

Lei tilted her head back on the pillow and closed her eyes. "I'm not afraid, Dr. Judd. I was just testing you. I'm not afraid because I'm late and I'm not afraid of pain and I'm not afraid of having the baby and I'm not afraid of dying or anything. I'm just afraid he won't be here with me. Maybe that's what's holding up his son; holding me up. We're waiting for him. We expected him to be with us. I just never dreamed that I'd be all alone."

"You won't be alone, Lei."

"I know. You'll be here."

"Yes. And so will Aaron."

"Yes, so will Aaron." She looked up mistily into Dr. Judd's warm yet sardonic eyes. "I'm very much in love with Aaron. Did I tell you? We had a fight and all that several months ago. He didn't like me this way; all blown up with part of him. And we fought. I told him I didn't love him any more; that he destroyed our love. And we stopped seeing each other. But I do love him. Not a bad love. You know what I mean—I don't want to cause him trouble or anything like that. But I do love him. Very much. I love him and I want his son very much and he'll be a fine son and Aaron will be proud. He'll be proud of himself and proud of me and proud of his baby son and he'll call his son Aaron like himself. He'll be proud of our love."

Earlier that night, when Lei had telephoned him from the private home in Kailua where she had been living since Aaron's trial, Dr. Judd had planned to drive her into Hilo. He had made arrangements for her at the hospital. But from her actions when he was driving her from Kailua, he did not believe she could make it all the way across the saddleback into Hilo. He took her straight to his home. She had been confident then. They had both been confident. His nurse had stayed on after hours and prepared one of the rooms adjoining his main office as a delivery room. He and the nurse, a slim, round-faced Chinese girl named Ethel Wu, had taken her into the delivery room and worked with her for more than an hour. Then, abruptly, the pains slackened, and after a while they moved her into the small bedroom of the guest cottage. The nurse had sat up with her for the first three hours while Dr. Judd tried to reach Aaron at Manoalani. Sloan answered the telephone and in her vague, distant voice told him that Aaron and Laura had flown to Honolulu that morning to sign the closing papers for the sale of their home.

Would they be back tonight?

Sloan did not know.

Was there a Honolulu number at which Aaron could be reached in case of an emergency?

Sloan did not know that, either. What was the emergency?

He left word for Aaron to call him immediately if he returned to Hawaii that night or the following morning.

Afterwards, he had lain down on the leather couch in his office and tried to sleep. But he did not sleep. He remembered that Aaron had tried to persuade Lei to undergo an abortion. Well, Dr. Judd had thought, it certainly would have been the best answer. He wondered if he would have performed it himself. Yes, he would have performed it. Presupposing certain medical knowledge, he would have performed the abortion. She was a lusty, full-blown, healthy-looking girl with the strength of a lioness, but the insides were all delicate and twisted. The vagina was twisted, for one thing; and there was anemia for another. And there were those wretched kidneys: one half inflamed through stress, the second totally infected. It would have to come out with the baby. And to top it all off, the slackening of labor pains; as if the baby itself inside the womb had received some mystic knowledge and given up the fight. Yes, he most certainly would have performed the abortion had he been aware of all the facts. As a medical man and as a human being, he had no argument against abortion.

Shortly after midnight he went in and sat with Lei. He read to her for a while from the wisdom of the Bhagavadgita and then, on a whim, he read her an entire book of Thurber's. She liked

Thurber the best and they talked about it for a while and he promised to read her another Thurber story the next day.

"Aaron?"

"No. It's me. Dr. Judd."

"Aaron?"

Dr. Judd stood up and leaned over her. The telephone rang, loud and rude in the dark hours of the morning. He turned and saw Miss Wu making her way to the desk. She picked up the phone on the second ring. She waited, then looked over at him, extending the phone but covering the mouthpiece with the palm of her hand.

"It's Aaron Howland," she said.

Dr. Judd walked down the hall and into his office.

"Prepare everything in the delivery room," he said to Miss Wu. "We're going to have to operate now."

She looked at him surprised. "Just you and I?"

"Just you and I." He took the phone from her. "Well, it's about time," he said into the mouthpiece. He waited. "No. Not yet. Yes, you're damn right. She's having a hell of a hard time. Where the hell have you been?" He waited again, his brows knit into a frown. Then he said, "You didn't *what?*" He waited while Aaron repeated the sentence. "Oh my God," he said. "I've heard everything now. Yes. Yes of course she's been waiting for you and asking for you—

"What's that? Yeah, you're damn right I do, if you ever want to think of yourself as a man again. I don't give a damn, Aaron. Come if you want. What? Yeah, the poor kid's been in terrible pain. No, no I don't understand that kind of thinking, Aaron. I'll never understand that kind of thinking. No. I think you're a shit."

He slammed the receiver back into its cradle. He stood by the desk for a moment, curbing his impotent rage. Then he crossed the hall and entered Lei's room. Miss Wu handed him the chart and he glanced at it surreptitiously for a second and handed it back to her, then focused his eyes on Lei, as if he could read all the things in her face that could not be read on the chart.

"Are you feeling any better?" he asked her.

Her lips cracked open slowly and she smiled at him.

"That was Aaron," he said softly. "He—he just got my message and he's racing right over here."

It seemed to cheer her. "Can I wait for him?"

Dr. Judd shook his head. "You've already lost much too much of your strength. I hoped the pains would start again, but since it appears they won't, the sooner we have the operation the better."

Lei moistened her lips with the tip of her tongue. She moved her hand into his for a moment and squeezed it tight. "Well," she tried to grin, "let's go and give Aaron a fine son."

Aaron lay dully on the bed, the backs of his crossed wrists resting against his forehead. His eyes had a bleak, drowned look, staring vacantly at the ceiling.

"He's going to operate on her now," he said. "A Caesarean."

Laura leaned up on her elbow. "Do you want to drive down there?"

After a while he said, "What difference would it make?"

"It might make a lot of difference to her. It might do her an awful lot of good, to know you're there."

Aaron did not stir. "I told Judd that I thought it would be all over by now. I told him I didn't want to be there; didn't want to wait and watch her agony."

"This is a different kind of agony," Laura said softly. "It's the kind of agony a woman loves. It's the kind of agony a woman is made for."

"Do you think I should go down there? I no longer know what I should do."

Laura studied his profile against the soft blueness of the night outside the window. "Yes," she said quietly. "I think you should be with her."

He turned and looked at her incredulously. "*You* think I should go down?"

"I think she needs you, Aaron."

He got up slowly from the bed and walked to the window. His eyes were utterly dull. His face was gaunt and haggard and forgotten, like the face seen in a gray dream. He had lost an enormous amount of weight. He no longer took care of himself: his dress was careless, his habits slovenly, most of the time he needed a shave, and often he would not be very clean. He had no appetite, and what little food he did force himself to eat he could not keep on his stomach; nor could he sleep at night without insulating himself with whisky. Although he was seldom drunk, he was never entirely sober. He had fled from the world of the living to the lost, broken world of the alcoholic. It had proved a thorough exile. An exile in which he seemed remote, apart from everyone, distant to everything in the world including his own burden. He no longer got up in the morning. The first thing a man must do in life is find a reason to get up in the morning. Without it, a man is beaten. Without it, a man never even gets started. He told himself that he had no reason. So he skipped the mornings, trying to escape from his own identity in restless sleep, and he wandered through afternoons of gray apathy into evenings of black remorse. There was within him no actual restlessness; there was not sufficient vitality in him for depression or regret—just a dulled, disinterested resignation.

He resigned his vice-presidency at Castle & Cooke, Ltd. The home in Kahala was placed on the market and sold. Plans were made to move to San Francisco, where he could recoup his forces, start a new life. But he knew there would be no new life. It was purely a fiction; a dream of man, a false vision, a forlorn illusion glimpsed a long way off down the dark hollow muck of the kaleidoscope. There would be no new life, simply because an errant God had deemed long ago that man must carry with him always his shattered emotions, splintered memories and corroded promise. But a man could soften these. He could retreat more seriously into the bottle: the lovely, liquid Miltown; the amber-colored anodyne against the futilities and neuroses and anxieties of our times; a bottle a day guaranteed to cure sufferers of self-disgust. You can buy it at your leading neighborhood liquor stores. Buy now, pay later. Comes in our convenient pint and fifth containers, and, for those of you who really have to get away from yourselves, our giant, economy-sized quart bottles are guaranteed unconditionally to put all the distance in the world between you and you. Sell me a case of those quart bottles, Aaron thought. Give me a hundred dollars' worth of distance, please.

He lit a cigarette and stared out the window into the garden. There was no moon, but the stars were low in the sky, the dust of their light making the sea gleam like dark glass.

Laura slipped a pale silk robe over her nightdress and joined him at the window. Her eyes searched his. "Do you want me to drive down there with you?" she said. "I will if you want me to. I'd just sit in the car, out of the way. She wouldn't have to know I was there."

Aaron turned and looked curiously at her. She took the cigarette from his fingers and inhaled deeply on it. The smoke was milky blue against the sky.

"You have a goodness I can't understand," Aaron said slowly. "This woman and I have caused you misery and pain. The standard script would be for you to resent her and hate her. Yet you stand here with me and tell me to go to her now because she needs me. I just don't understand."

She slipped her arm about him and leaned her head against his shoulder. "I don't ask to be understood. I don't even want to be understood. I'm your wife, Aaron. I want to be loved by you."

She walked thoughtfully to the head of the bed and took a cigarette from the pack on the headboard and lit it.

"I don't resent this girl—this Lei Villanueva," she said. "I don't hate her now. At first I thought I did. Do you know what my reason was, Aaron?"

He stood quietly by the window, watching her through the blue mists of the room, waiting.

"I hated her because I was on the losing team. I was a member of that vast, unheralded, overly criticized, almost apochryphal organization known as the American housewives approaching middle age. I married you when I was very young, and in the beginning it was a world of magic; of sharing your cycles of moods, hopes, dreams, frustrations, sharing life with you because I was your wife and I had to be a good wife; sharing our son with you, and sharing the tragedy of our son, yet keeping all to myself the sorrow of not being able to give you another son. I went through this saga of the American wife with you and it was most certainly not always a gay time but very often a black time, and the blackest time of all came when you looked at me with your eyes clouded by the fact that I was quite obviously no longer twenty-two. Somewhere along the way your eyes lost their power to see me and your hands lost their power to touch me and your heart lost its power to love me."

She dabbed a tear from her cheek with the sleeve of her silk robe.

"Lei Villanueva, when you get down to it, has brought me no grief. I thought at first she had, but I was wrong. She is just a girl who loved you. I don't condone adultery. It's ugly and it's threatening and it's painful. It's also a symbol: a symptom of this age of sensation that we're living in. And it's a more personal symptom:

for us, you and me, I think it was a symptom of a flaw in our marriage.

"Marriage isn't a senseless slip of paper," she said. "I know many people think it is. But to me, marriage is sacred. And the purpose of marriage is to have children. It's not a stupid, ritualistic slip of paper, but a spiritual and legal ceremony conceived to protect the emotional security of the children born of the marriage. And on that part, I—I—failed—"

"Laura, Laura, don't." He put his arms about her shoulders. "Don't talk like that."

"It's true, Aaron," she said, choking back her sobs. "That's why I can't hate that girl completely. Because I can't blame her completely. Nor you. Two people cannot be blamed for adultery. It always takes three."

After a while, he said, "What should I do about Lei?"

She answered him quietly, her composure regained.

"I think you should be with her now, I think she needs you there; and I think you need to be there."

He turned from the window and looked into her eyes. "Will you come with me?"

They waited silently on the couch in the main office for twenty minutes before Dr. Judd came out of the delivery room. He nodded to Laura and glanced with open contempt at Aaron. "Suffered a change of heart, huh?"

"Yes," Aaron said. He stood up. "How is it going, Doc?"

"It isn't going."

"What do you mean?"

"Just what I said. The kid doesn't want to come out. And in a way I can't blame him."

"How is Lei?"

"Very bad."

"What are you going to do?"

He untied the mask about his face. His face was wet and flushed and very tired-looking. "I'm going to do everything I can possibly do," he said. "And none of it sounds too good. Lei is very weak. The baby is reversed; not completely, just crouched kind of out of kilter. The umbilical cord seems to be wrapped around the baby's throat, and I can't tell right now if he's breathing."

Aaron looked at him hopelessly. "Is there anything we can do?"

Dr. Judd replaced his mask. "No. Not now there isn't.

When the doctor returned to the delivery room, Aaron sat down in the big old-fashioned leather-backed swivel chair behind the desk. He wondered with a ragged impotence why there was no sound from the delivery room. He wondered why the doctor did not send for him. Someday, he thought, lighting another cigarette, he would make it all up to Lei. And to Laura. And to Sloan. And to Paul Kahana— How could he make it up to Paul Kahana? And to the old man. And to himself. Yes, he had a lot of making up to do to himself.

His eyes darted restlessly about the office. He was careful not to lock glances with Laura. He looked down at his hands. His fingers were toying with a brass-backed calendar on the desk. A red ink circle had been drawn around Thanksgiving Day. His fingers seemed strange, as if they had a separate life and volition all their own. They flipped the calendar about so that he could not see the carefully compartmented days and weeks of Time, but saw instead the reflection of his own face in the back of the smooth brass sheet. The sockets of his face shone dark in the brass sheet, and his eyes were blank slits, like the eyes of a Modigliani portrait. It was, he admitted, a face that both expressed and inspired contempt; loathing. Dr. Judd had certainly looked at him in that manner. Dr. Judd, in a way, had treated him with loathing; pushed him around a little. A man who is thoroughly disgusted with himself is an easy man to push around. But it used to be different, he thought. It used to be . . .

The nurse came down the hall from the delivery room. He looked up at her expectantly as she entered the office. She nodded to him. "You may come in now, Mr. Howland."

He stood up. He exchanged glances with Laura for a moment. Then, with considerable hesitation, he followed Miss Wu into the delivery room.

Dr. Judd was holding the baby by its heels, upside down. He slapped the baby's backside. He slapped it a second time and looked at it crossly. The baby was very small and wet and wrinkled. Its face and its body was a dark red color. It hung very still, like a freshly skinned small animal at a butcher shop. Dr. Judd slapped it again, but still the baby did not cry. It hung from its heels, motionless, red, wet and wrinkled. Dr. Judd placed his free hand behind the baby's head and placed it on its back on a white table.

Miss Wu washed the wrinkled red lump and wrapped it in something that looked like white cotton. Dr. Judd took the mask from his face and leaned down over the baby. He placed his ear against the baby's chest and listened for its heart beat. He seemed to listen for some time. Then he took the baby's hands, which were about the size of a half-dollar piece, and stretched them back above the baby's mouth and breathed into it. He inhaled deeply and exhaled his breath in a long steady flow, forcing air into the baby's lungs. He repeated this for more than a full minute, like a bellows pumping life into a fire, forcing oxygen into the baby's lungs, until finally the clot tissue broke and the baby issued its first fierce, mewling, demanding scream.

Aaron stared dumbly at the infant. It did not seem to have anything to do with him. He crossed the delivery room and walked down the hall to the room where Lei had been taken. When he looked at her, he thought for a moment that she was dead. He realized, with a sense of shock, that he had never before considered the possibility of her dying. These things did not happen any more in childbirth. Now, as he stared at her, he considered it seriously: with humiliation, with outrage, with impotence. She looked dead. Her face was gray. Her body beneath the covers was rigid, immobile. It did not seem that it would ever move again.

He walked to the head of the bed and stood there awkwardly, dumbly, looking down at her gray wan face. He was certain now that she was dead. Then, looking for it, perhaps praying for it, he saw finally the slow, delicate lift of her breathing. Dr. Judd joined him.

"How is she?"

"Not good," Dr. Judd said. He looked tired. "No," he said, a minute later. "That's not correct. She's damn bad."

"Will she be all right?"

"I don't know."

Aaron shifted his eyes accusingly. "You don't know?"

"That's right. I don't know."

He walked out of the room.

Lei moaned. She opened her eyes and tried to smile at him. "I'm glad you've come," she said. Her voice was weak and very tired.

Aaron sat in a chair alongside the head of the bed. Lei put out her hand and he held it. "You mustn't talk," he said.

"It's over now."

"I swear I'll make it all up to you, Lei."
"What kind of a baby did we have?"
"A boy."
"Good. Is he all right?"
"Yes. Now he's fine."
"Do you love him?"
Aaron waited, and the thought flashed through his mind with irrevocable certainty: *She's going to die.* "Yes, I love him."
"We'll name him Aaron," Lei said weakly. She looked at him. "Is that all right?"
"Yes."
"I'm glad it was a boy and I'm glad he's all right. You wanted a boy, didn't you?"
"Yes. A boy is fine."
They were silent for a moment and he knew again that she was going to die. "I'm sorry, Lei," he said.
The nurse entered the room. "I'm sorry, Mister Howland, but you must leave now. Miss Villanueva must not talk. She's had a very bad time. She must rest."
Aaron stood up dumbly and looked down into Lei's face. She had closed her eyes. "I'm sorry, Lei. Oh God, I'm so sorry."
She opened her eyes and this time smiled up at him and the strength of the smile made him think that maybe she would be all right. "It was a boy?"
"Yes."
"I'm glad. You have a son, now."
"You really must leave now, Mr. Howland," the nurse said.
Outside the sky was lead gray with dawn. Streaks of pale canary-yellow were working their way through the gray. Aaron thought that it would probably be a warm sunny Thanksgiving Day. Dr. Judd stepped out of the front door of his office and joined him. They smoked a cigarette and watched the yellow burn its way into the sky.
"How is old Willard?" Dr. Judd asked.
"All right, I guess."
"Have you seen him?"
"Not since the day before yesterday. I haven't been up to his room. The nurse said he's getting along as well as could be expected."
Earl Judd made a noise deep in his throat. "How is Sloan?"

"We never speak."

"Don't you even see her?"

"No. She stays in her room. Or with the old man, sometimes. Or else she just disappears. Sometimes at night I've heard her play the piano. Late, late at night." He dropped the cigarette and heeled it out in the ground. He turned to look at the doctor. "Will Lei live?"

But before the doctor spoke, Aaron saw the dark and awful answer in his eyes.

"I don't think so," Earl Judd said. Then he went back inside.

Aaron turned slowly, his whole face suddenly going to pieces in a wash of misery, his features yellow with it, and put his fists up against the wall of the house and leaned his forehead against the wall of the house and wept silently. In a little while Laura came to him and touched his shoulder.

"Dr. Judd wants you," she said softly.

He walked inside like a wooden man. He prayed that Lei would not die. He wanted to die himself. He wished he had died that night long ago at the summit of Mauna Loa.

Miss Wu opened the door to Lei's room and motioned for him to come in. Dr. Judd was standing on one side of the bed. Aaron walked over to the other side. Lei did not look up at him.

"She's had a hemorrhage," Earl Judd said.

Aaron kneeled down at the side of the bed and started to cry. But there were no tears in him. Lei turned her gray face to him and smiled. Then she closed her eyes. There was a fresh stain moving through the blanket.

"You'll have to leave," Dr. Judd said. "She's starting to hemor rhage again."

She died quietly after the third hemorrhage. The sun had heaved up above the rack of cloud over Mauna Loa. It was becoming warm. Earl Judd cranked open the louvered windows of his office and the morning breeze stirred the curtains. He went to his liquor cabinet and poured himself four fingers of whisky and downed it. Then he poured himself a second drink and sipped this slowly, contemplatively. He left the bottle and several glasses on the desk but did not offer Aaron or Laura a drink. He sat down in the swivel chair behind his desk and glared with angry eyes at his thick hands wrapped about the glass; the hands which so recently had failed him. "In *The Bluebird,*" he said, "Maeterlinck states that we all seek happiness and find only death: does happiness lie within or beyond it?"

Aaron did not stir. He stood in mute shock in a corner of the office, like a wooden puppet after the performance had been concluded. Earl Judd turned to Laura. "Drink?"

She shook her head.

Miss Wu came into the office drab and tired and said how sorry she was. Earl Judd thanked her and told her to go home and get some sleep. Then he looked across the room at Aaron's sullen, broken back. "Do you want to see your son?"

Aaron made no move. He might have been carved from clinkstone for all his rigidity. Earl Judd repeated the question, a little softer this time. "Aaron? Do you want to see your son?"

Aaron slowly shook his head no.

Earl Judd swung his gaze slowly, questioningly, to Laura. She nodded.

He led her down the hall past the delivery room to a small, sunny adjoining room. Miss Wu had washed the baby and wrapped him in blankets and placed him in a small old koawood bassinet that the doctor had forgotten he owned. The baby was red-faced and wailing.

Laura bent down and picked him up. She looked into his face for a long time, studying it. Then, feeling Earl Judd's eyes boring into her, she looked up at him.

"I'm—I'm not sure I can," she said.

"Yes you can."

Dr. Judd walked heavily out of the room and closed the door behind him.

Laura loosened one corner of the blanket so the baby's face was clear. Her fingers moved gently across his forehead. Her mouth quivered and a large tear brimmed suddenly in each eye. Her lips came together and smiled sadly and mysteriously as she leaned to kiss the infant brow.

Chapter Seventeen

THERE is a lost quality to the soul of man. Each man's soul is mute and utterly alone and there is no voice for its hunger and only an echo for its despair. If one listened well upon any night of his history he might hear the sibilation of his soul, like the softened wings of bats at dawn, groping.

This lostness is perhaps the finest quality of man. It is the catalyst; it invokes man to search, to extend himself. It divides the wise men from the fools.

The wise man, satiated with his ancient human despair with humanity, surrenders himself to certitudes. He knows, for instance, that fulfillment slakes desire, knowledge rots dreams, the final harbor is not worth the journey, the combination of logic and skepticism can destroy everything in the world, including man's hope. The wise man knows that the soul was designed to remain lost.

The fool, exercising his ego until the final curtain falls at the close of his long drama of self, follows his dream. With a Phoenix-like scorn for, or unawareness of, his own limitations, the fool persists. He sets sail in his frail craft across the urgent oceans of his emotions, carrying with him always his buried needs and unspoken loneliness. And he searches, for in his fool's logic he has concluded that since he is searching, there must be something to be found. And somehow, he endures. If he finds nothing he is likely to shrug and say it is because man is too dumb to know what he really wants.

Garth Howland had always been considered that kind of a fool.

He was a tall, rangy, deep-chested man, with lean muscles laced tightly to heavy, angular bones. The backs of his hands, which now guided the sheets and tiller of his slim little ketch as it rode the swells moving up along the Kona coastline, were feathered with fine, coppery hair. His hands were large, sure, heavily calloused, with wide knots of wrists. His long fine hair was blown and tangled, the color of copper bleached by the sun. His dark, fine-boned face had a vaguely brooding delicateness which was neither weak nor sullen, but rather indicative of a permanent but controlled and somehow compassionate skepticism. His mouth, which at one time had been a proud scowl, was carved more softly now, set in the sad, cockeyed grin of a reluctant pessimist. He was strong somehow, and his eyes were strangely handsome; gray-gold, humorous, sardonic, undefeated eyes which had seen everything and believed in none of it. He had always been a peculiarly intricate creature, a little oblique; restlessly, impotently, outrageously alone in the world.

When he was fourteen he stowed away on a freighter bound from Hilo to San Francisco. He managed to slip away from immigration officials and started a zigzag tour of America, thumbing rides with motorists, grabbing freight trains headed in any direction, working occasionally for his keep, stealing on other occasions. A miner broke his jaw for him in a fight in Butte, Montana. He spent two weeks in jail at Joplin. He knew his first woman in an alleyway in New Orleans. After two months in New York he had saved almost two hundred dollars and he spent fifty of it for false maritime service credentials and worked a tramp steamer to Rio and São Paulo. He learned of man's never-measured capacity for brutality to man while working the tramp. From São Paulo he roamed his way south to Montevideo, then across the Rio Platte into Buenos Aires. Here, for ninety American dollars, he boarded one of Peron's beef steamers. Seventeen days later, he was wandering the Moorish waterfront streets of Cadiz when four Riff herdsmen fractured his skull and dumped him naked and unconscious in a doorway on top of a dead beggar. The next evening he was in the American Consulate offices in Barcelona and the following weekend he was back at Manoalani.

But when they landed him at Manoalani, he hit running, like a cat out of a sack. It was, he told old Willard, his time for wandering across the earth. He signed on as a crew member of the yacht *Ramona,* and sailed up against the winds into Balboa Harbor. He worked the fruit crop up through the San Fernando, San Joaquin and Salinas valleys, and on his sixteenth birthday he got drunk for the first time in his life at a place called Nepenthe in the dramatic Big Sur mountains south of Carmel. When he got back on the road the next morning he hitched a ride with a wheat rancher from Alberta who took him straight up the coast through the green hills of Oregon and the grays of Washington into Canada. He worked for three weeks as a dishwasher at the hotel in Banff. Then he lied his way into the Royal Canadian Air Force. A year and a half and eighty-three fighter missions later he had to his official credit six and a half Messerschmitts. Then, with a rather startling lack of military discipline and no sense of style, he went to his squadron commander and told him that he was through with the war. There was, he informed them the day he resigned his commission, no other possible attitude to assume concerning the war. He was not quite nineteen.

But he was not through with the war. When he returned to the United States he was drafted into the Army. He refused to fly; he refused with grim and steadfast determination any rank or rating whatsoever, and it was as an infantryman private that he slogged his way through the island-hopping massacres of the Pacific campaigns until one afternoon on a remote and needless island a mortar shell lifted him twelve feet into space and as he hung there, suspended, machine gun bullets ripped apart his right thigh.

He learned to walk again, first with a crutch, then with a

cane, dragging what they had left of his right leg. During the brief interval between wars, more out of curiosity than a desire to establish himself, he attended Scripps Institute of Oceanography at La Jolla. At night he worked as a police reporter on the San Diego *Union*. At school he took only the courses that interested him. They led to no degree, and they led to no idea of establishing himself, so he dropped out of school and quit the newspaper too and wandered up to San Francisco again. There he concocted a past history of newspaper experience which included the New York *World-Telegram* and the Denver *Post* and sold the concoction with conspicuous charm to the disbelieving Associated Press bureau chief, who hired him as a five-year man.

Two months later he was working the night desk in the Tokyo bureau and the following week he was in Seoul, again in war. As a war correspondent, it seemed that whatever campaign he was assigned to cover met with doom. He moved up through the bleak hills of Korea with the First Marine Division almost to the Yalu. Then the Red Chinese swarmed down, like the Sioux against Custer, and he had the Pulitzer Prize story of the Korean War tucked miserably in his hip pocket with all communications cut while he and what was left of the slaughtered American forces tramped back down the frozen peninsula in the most bitter, most causeless, most ignoble defeat in American history; all the way down across the frozen rutted wasteland from Chonjin to a still-posturing Douglas MacArthur. He was relieved of war coverage for a time and was sent on a treadmill replacing vacationing bureau chiefs: Calcutta, Ceylon, Bombay, Bangkok, where, despite the stench, he fell in love with the city and the early-morning misty reflection of the temple spires on the putrid canals; and then Hong Kong, where he felt most at home in the world and where he fell into what he truly believed was love with the eldest daughter of a Chinese minister.

And then again he was in a retreat—this time from Hanoi where he had been sent to assist the old war horse of foreign correspondents, Larry Allen, after Ho Chi Minh's guerrilla mobs finally battered the French Foreign Legion out of the fort at Dien Bien Phu. He was working in Hanoi for only a month when Pierre Mendès-France, just elected Premier of France, kept his word to the electorate that he would stop war at all costs. Hanoi was surrendered to Ho Chi Minh's Communists. So again there was that wild retreat, while women drowned their children in wooden washbarrels in the side streets of Hanoi and the tricolor was hauled down from the embassy building and he found himself, inexplicably, with a Communist price on his head and the Communist Army crossing the Red River just a few miles away. So there was nothing else but the road again, retreat, down the impossibly crowded road from Hanoi to Saigon, and when he reached Saigon he found bands of Communist terrorists roaming the streets, the alleyways.

It was through one of these alleyways that the three Maryknoll sisters came, herding with them, in double file, a group of (fourteen, he learned later) schoolchildren, and as they crossed the alleyway the terrorists showed up, hoodlums of sixteen or seventeen, and for absolutely no reason heaved the homemade bombs. When he saw the upper half of a little girl's body just pop up into the air like the unattached head of a jumping jack, then fall, tumble really, thuck-thuck-thuck, back into the smoke and the bloody debris of what used to be human beings, he choked back the bile that had risen in his throat and went after the mob. He caught the slowest one of them, the one who stumbled as the rest fled the scene, and he leaped upon him and they rolled over and over in the bloody, smoke-filled alleyway, their curses roaring above the whimpers of the dying children and the screaming approach of police sirens. By the time he looked down into the young terrorist's face and realized that the boy could not have been a day over eighteen years old, by the time he realized that, he realized too that the boy was dead, that he had choked him to death. When he handed in his resignation to the Associated Press, it was also, in his own mind, his resignation from having to observe, hear, feel and record the travail of humanity tearing at itself; it was his resignation from the civilization of mankind.

He purchased the ketch, obviously stolen, if the low price was any way of judging those things, from a dealer in narcotics and women in Macao. He got it over to Kowloon and worked on it there for a month, boarded supplies and a burly, spotted tomcat whose rickets made his walk seem like a rolling, bowlegged gait, and set sail. Without destination, and with a conviction of doing nothing constructive with his life, he arrived, quite naturally, in the South Seas. He spent almost four years in the South Seas, the anodyne islands.

Tahiti was not the answer, merely a wondrous interlude: the riotous nights at Quinn's Hut; the long contemplative strolls along the Quai du Commerce looking up through the gentle slope of acacias at the wide warm moon; the afternoons drinking wine with the velvet painter Leeteg sprawled against the jetties of the copra wharf, watching the schooners come in from New Zealand; the nights keeling the ketch through Matavai Bay, out under the beam of Point Venus lighthouse, with that girl aboard, the girl who proved Stevenson right when he called the Tahitians "God's best, at least God's sweetest work." He took the girl with him across to Moorea, then to Raiatea and Bora Bora where Bougainville thought he was "walking through the Garden of Eden"; then once more across the impossibly beautiful waters to Huahine, where they remained for more than a year living on the ketch in Papetoai Bay, the flooded cone of an extinct volcano which was, to his mind, the most beautiful anchorage in the world.

It was like learning to live again. The idyllic island, the languid mysteries of the nights, the kindness of the people, and especially the girl, soothed that taut and delicate futility of his. He forgot all about the gods turned clay, the scar he had made of himself. He no longer voyaged alone across the bleak and barren seas of his despair. He was no longer a casualty of civilization. He had become the fool again.

When the weekly copra boat came bringing him Willard Howland's letter concerning the political campaigns and requesting him to return to manage the ranch, Garth had read it with a mild curiosity, then destroyed it. He disregarded too the news broadcast from Papeete concerning the killing and Aaron's trial. But when the cable arrived from Sloan in care of the general post office in Papeete telling him of his father's heart attack, he knew, at last, that he had to return. And he knew also he was ready to return.

Silly fool, he grinned, there is no anodyne.

He hauled in the sheets of the jib. The ketch sped gaily and youthfully across the blue and drowsy waters, a small bow wave spreading a creamy fading fan beneath the forehull. He had passed Kealakekua Bay shortly after noon, working close to the coast, hungry for the sight of land again. It was, he told himself, too long and too hard a voyage by oneself. Ninety miles a day, up over the vast curve of the world; seven weeks against the prevailing trades. Thank God there was no big weather.

The Tahiti-designed ketch, which the girl at Huahine had christened *The Seven Little Sisters,* was thirty-two feet over-all, a little too much ship, he had discovered, for one man up from the Society Islands. But it was a marvel of compactness. Much of the time, he had lashed the tiller and let her sail herself. The cabin below had four bunks, an enclosed head, and a galley conveniently located under the forehatch so he could scramble, when necessary, to douse the jib or operate roller-reefing gear at mealtime.

There was still daylight, shining softly and with a tarnish, like the lining of a shell. And far up along the coast now, as if in the heart of the shell, he saw the old familiar rise of Manoalani. He leaned the tiller so the ketch hove a little to starboard, a little closer to shore, and as Manoalani loomed larger against its backdrop of lilac-colored sky, Garth Howland gazed at it with the quiet sensitivity of a man who had lived for a long time with his loneliness and who was now on good terms with it. And in his eyes there was a secret: it had been, at all times, a loneliness of his own choosing, a preferred loneliness—singular and bearable, completely unlike the inevitable and intolerable abject loneliness of the man who belongs to the herd.

He went to the cabin and took the binoculars and played them across the land. He picked out familiar boyhood haunts. Then he moved the glasses slowly over the entire frame of Manoalani, its face warmed now from the old sun into a shade of gold wine. Then, in the glasses, he saw the collies, Baron and Miss Brett. They were loping down the lawn toward the beach. And in a moment, following the collies, he saw Sloan and Dean cantering slowly. They were headed for the pier at Kailua Bay.

He set the binoculars back in their case. Suddenly, the feeling swept through him that he had spent all his life wandering through places he did not belong in just because it seemed, during those years, that he had no place else to go.

He checked the position of the brass-colored sun lowering across the Pacific. He guessed it was almost six o'clock. Christmas Eve. He was thirty-one years old, and he was returning home, and he knew, strangely, that it would not make any real difference. He was still the wanderer, the wastrel, the stray; the poet without a poem, the love-seeker cursed with the search for the unlikely Lorelei.

He brought in the mainsail and the jib and set the Diesel. *The Seven Little Sisters* chucked slowly into Kailua Bay. At the edge of the pier, he could see Sloan and Dean Kahana waiting quietly on their mounts, Dean holding the reins of a third saddled horse. Miss Brett leaped from the pier to the breakwater of lava rock and barked excitedly as the ketch came along. Baron stood placidly at the edge of the pier, waiting.

Garth waved. "Come on, old fellow," he said to himself. "It's time to tuck in your soul. You're home." And the word had for him a strange nostalgia, as if it brought him close to something rare and good.

Sloan arched her back. She nudged Willard's old white stallion forward along the pier. She could see Garth plainly now, catwalking across the cabin with the line in his hands, ready to toss it to Dean, who had dismounted and crouched far out at the jetty, waiting to bring the ketch alongside. She looked at Garth thoughtfully. He was still lean, bronzed, seemingly ageless. In his faded blue denim shirt and trousers and the white tennis socks and sneakers, he looked almost like a collegian, except for that limp and the sad cockeyed grin. If only Garth had been here all the while, none of those terrible things would have happened, she thought. If. If if if if: you've just got to forget that that stupid ridiculous little word was ever a part of your vocabulary, she told herself. You have got to teach yourself to forget what has happened and not let yourself think about what might have been. When that seemingly inexhaustible part of your mind starts working you over again, remembering things, then you simply must learn to snap off that part of your mind. And especially you can't let yourself start remembering any of it now, not with Garth here. He would be able to read it in your face in a second. He always did have that knack, or curse, of being able to see so damnably deep into people, as if he was seeing a part of himself. Perhaps that's what gives him that warm understanding he's always had of other people: seeing a part of himself in them. Perhaps that's what understanding is.

But anyway, don't think of anything now; don't let him read you. It would spoil his homecoming.

She dismounted suddenly, as if on impulse, the gloss of her dark mahogany boots flashing in the sun. She wore white cotton twill breeches and a man's black shirt in that ivy league style with the tiny pearl buttons tabbing down the collar. A slender pale neckerchief was tied about her throat.

She had grown very thin. Her cheeks were sunken. Her soft wild bright eyes were strangely vulnerable. Although her face had an almost gray pallor, there was the beginning of an underglow to her skin, like the sheen of a fine pearl. Slowly, cautiously, she was beginning to move out of herself. She had begun to move out of her hidden self when Dean had arrived at Manoalani for his Christmas vacation from medical school. They took long strolls along the beach together, and during the afternoons they rode far out across the rangeland, the way they used to do so many years ago. She had started talking it all out to him then and it made her feel better. The burden of her immutable grief was being shared. And he shared it willingly, almost eagerly, and after the endless bleak days of deadness and not caring, he had brought her up to the point at which life was coming back into her in a new way. Dean shared her burden and listened to her hour after hour, and slowly, with intuitive timing, battered down her moated wall of grief and stripped from her the fine veneer of self-pity. He showed her that self-pity could become a way of life; that she could fall into the pit of liking it, needing it, perhaps had already started needing it, started valuing the darkly mirrored reflections of her martyred picture of herself more than life.

"Dean," she said to him one night, cupping his face in her fingers, "I'm not sure that you understand exactly what has happened to me. I'm not sure I understand it myself. It's not pure bitterness, or resentment, or rage. I'm—I'm bewildered, Dean, I can't seem to cope with my emotions. I'm bewildered and lost and beaten not because I have been denied or because Paul has been denied—but because we have been denied so little; we asked for so little. We asked only to be left alone to our love and our happiness. And now, Paul is gone. And I am beyond love. I died then, when he died; a part of me just vanished, like a minor death, and there isn't enough left of me to ever love again."

"No. Please don't talk like that, Sloan," he had said.

"I'm being honest with you, Dean. I have no other way to talk."

"Sloan, try to stop yourself from remembering how bad things were or how wonderful they might have been."

She shook her head and buried it against his shoulder. "You know too much, Dean," she sobbed.

"No. I don't know enough yet. I'm trying to learn from you."

She looked up at him and there was a shine of tears in her eyes. "A long long time ago, when I was a little girl, I had one of those deep heart-to-heart talks with Garth. It was before he bought the boat; before he became a war correspondent. He was a little bit drunk, you know the way he'd get sometimes when he was blue, and I asked him what he wanted out of life. And he smiled at me and quoted a few lines from Sherwood Anderson. Those lines always used to come to my mind whenever I thought of Garth:

" 'I am a lover who never found his thing to love. It makes my destruction inevitable.'

"Now," she said, not looking at him, looking out beyond him at the black drawn sea, "those lines come to my mind when I think of myself. That's the way I feel now, Dean."

He had turned her chin to his face and looked into her soft eyes. "Promise me, Sloan," he had said, "that you'll try to forget those lines. Try to—well, not forget everything, but try to live with everything that's happened to you. Try to live."

And she had tried. She was still trying. She pressed her lips together in a soft smile and walked hesitantly, almost shyly, to the edge of the pier. "Aloha!" she called out to Garth.

He grinned up at her with quick pleasure. As the ketch was made secure against the pier, Garth bounded up from the deck and took Sloan into his arms and kissed her, lifting her completely off the ground and spinning her.

"Oh Garth, Garth, I'm so happy you've come home!"

He laughed. "You missed your beat-up derelict brother, huh?"

"Yes, darling darling Garth, I've missed you very much. We've all missed you and needed you!"

"Let me take a good look at my beautiful kid sister." He held her at arm's length and studied her. She seemed a stranger; broken and withdrawn and disenchanted, as if she herself had suffered a minor death; a Cinderella who grew up to become Isolde, the last light touching her profile of slackened flesh and cheekbone with a thin line of gold. She bowed her head shyly.

"I don't want you to look at me now, Garth. You always see too much."

He grinned and made one of his indescribable gestures. "Everybody else in the world grows uglier and older with time, you've grown more beautiful. I didn't think it was possible."

She slipped her arms tightly about his waist and rubbed her forehead against his chest. "You're such a lovely liar," she said. "You don't fool me. I know how I look. But I love those sweet kind lies of yours. I need them, now."

"They're not lies." Garth rubbed the scruff of her neck and kissed her head. He could feel her shoulders shake. He held them stiffly for a moment and raised her face to his. He looked directly into her eyes. "Hear me now, Sloan darling; they're not lies."

She dabbed at her eyes. "I'm sorry I'm all weepy. It's just that I'm so happy you've finally come home."

"And you believe me when I tell you how beautiful you've grown?"

She looked up at him with a curious flash of intensity, after which she slipped behind her façade. "Oh Garth, stop it."

"No, I'm serious. You're beautiful. I want you to believe it."

"I can't. Maybe I used to be. But not any more. Not since—"

"You're very beautiful. You're the most beautiful girl I've ever seen."

After a moment she grinned at him. It was the first eager gesture of youth he had seen in her. "Okay, I'm beautiful," she laughed impishly. "And so are you. You're beautiful too."

They laughed together and Garth tousled her hair.

"Yeah. I'm beautiful because I have less anger in me now than I had before," he said. "Less anger and less love. I'm getting old."

Dean finished with the lines and came over and shook hands with Garth. "Aloha. Welcome home. *Mele Kalikimaka*."

Garth grinned at him fondly. "Thanks, Dean. Or should I say, Thanks Doctor Kahana?"

"Not yet." Dean smiled broadly. "Not for another year."

"Not a year," Sloan said. "Just ten more months."

"Keep up the good work," Garth said. They walked over to the horses, the collies filing restlessly about them. "How's Kapi?"

"Good enough," Dean said. "She's staying at Manoalani."

As they reached the horses, Garth turned and stopped Dean with a motion of his hand. He looked up into the eyes of the big Hawaiian. "Look, Dean—I'm—I'm terribly sorry—"

Dean bowed his head. He traced the toe of his boot along the rib of the pier planking. Then he looked quietly at Garth. He nodded his head. "Suah. I understand, Garth."

They rode slowly through the rose and lilac colored twilight and as they rode Sloan told him everything that had happened and how it all happened, speaking to him in a distant, softly stricken way, so that Garth had the feeling that her voice was composed of the lost fragments of her splintered dreams. He eyed her quickly, curiously, his glance moving in a swift feathering appraisal across her face, her stooped shoulders, her hands folded in a pale silent embrace across the pommel of the saddle; and though she sought to form an answer to all the questions he asked, she lapsed at times into a forlorn passivity, a lostness, and he saw in her again what he had seen at the pier, a girl whom shock and tragedy had turned vague.

"How is the old fellow now?"

"Not good—but alive," Sloan told him. "Half-alive, I mean, like I am. Your being home will help him; like a tonic. Lie to him sweetly and kindly the way you lied to me—"

"I didn't lie to you, Sloan."

"Oh yes, I forgot. Well, lie to him anyway. And don't look at him too closely. His left side is paralyzed. Not from the hips down. He can still manage to walk. But up from the hip, his entire left side is paralyzed. His arm and shoulder and the left side of his face. And he keeps on trying to make his left hand work. Secretly, you know, when he thinks nobody is watching. He practically goes into a rage when his left hand fails to respond. It's not his first coronary, you know. He had one a long time ago, when I was in college. And apparently he had two during the campaign. He never told Doc Judd about the second one. It was a seizure a few days before he collapsed at Kalaupapa. I really didn't believe a man could live after all that. But Doc said Daddy simply refused to die."

"How did he take the elections?"

"He didn't," Sloan answered. "He didn't accept the election. He didn't know anything about the election until several weeks afterward. By that time he had become something of a hero; a martyr to the cause of statehood. You know, the newspapers drummed it up pretty big. It wasn't exactly dishonest, but it wasn't strictly on the level either. The Republican brass built it all up. In a way it was sickening. They more or less exploited Daddy's heart attack for votes. Frank Lorrin was rushed in as Republican nominee, those last few days before the election. But he was badly beaten by Judge Blanding."

"Adam Blanding?"

Sloan nodded.

"I thought he was a bail bondsman or something like that."

"Well, whatever he used to be, he's our Delegate to Congress now. And whatever energy Daddy has left, he spends it raging against the Judge." She turned and looked at him obliquely. "If you ever do get into a political discussion with Daddy, don't mention—don't mention Ward Akana."

"How is Ward?"

"Ward's fine. And Tani and the kids are fine."

"Will they all be here for Christmas?"

"No." She shook her head. "No, the chances are Ward will never set foot in Manoalani as long as Daddy lives."

She detailed the campaign and the bitter personal strife between Ward and Willard that erupted as a tangent to the campaign until its closing scene that afternoon at Kalaupapa, and she told how Ward had brought Willard to Tripler Army Hospital and then to Manoalani after Dr. Judd had given permission, and the bleak days while Ward had remained at Manoalani, solitary, unspeaking, waiting for the doctor's or perhaps a higher decision concerning Willard Howland, until that higher decision granted Willard Howland life, or a half-life as she put it, and that night, when they knew old Willard would live, Earl Judd and Ward Akana had dinner together down at the Kona Inn and Judd had put it frankly to Ward: It would be better that Ward did not go in to see the old man, not at least during this period of precarious balance, and that, as a matter of fact, it would not only be better, but was an absolute medical requisite.

Later, Sloan had tried to explain it all to her father, but at the mention of Ward's name the old man would slip into an endless black abyss, and after a while she had given it up.

"I'll call Ward tonight," Garth suggested.

"Yes, he'll want to hear from you."

They rode for a long time without talking. The ride was good, Garth thought. His legs were beginning to feel it and the muscles in his back and his stomach were vibrant and began to ache slightly because he had not ridden hard for a long time; but the ache was good. He could feel the shiver in his legs and he could smell the creamy white saddle soap-and-leather smell on his pants and the smoky horse odor on his hands, and he listened again as he had not listened in so many years to the muted, nostalgic sounds of a quiet man on a horse—the creaking of leather as he leaned back against the cantle, the regular walking of the horses, the scuffing of their hoofs along the road, the jingling of the bridle and bit as the horses chewed against them. He glanced over at Sloan who he knew had always been so good with horses and he saw that beneath her sensitive hands the ancient white stallion acquired once again his faded temperament and comeliness. As they neared the rise of land that marked Manoalani, the stallion reared a little and broke into a trot, the other horses following. But Sloan brought him under and they walked excitedly up along the searoad beneath the canopy of poincianas that lined the road. And, as he knew he must, Garth cautiously asked her about Aaron.

A white hardness swept her face. After a while she said, "Aaron's at Manoalani. Drunk most of the time. All of the time, I think. A ghost. The way he should be."

And very cautiously, Garth said, "Sloan, do you think you will ever be able to—to forgive him?"

"No."

Dean had ridden a little behind them most of the way, letting them talk to each other privately. Now he trotted up and fell into place alongside Sloan.

"I haven't tried to forgive him, Garth," Sloan said, staring straight ahead. "Maybe I'm one of those cursed people who can't forgive. But whatever I have become, I am what I am now, and Aaron is what he is. Both of us half-alive maybe; but it's better than being half-dead. I tried to convince myself that if I did not care about anything any more, then there would be no place inside me that could be hurt. But each time I saw Aaron, something terrible moved inside me. I tried to kill him one night."

Dean reached his hand over and covered hers. He tried to stop her. "Don't talk about it now, Sloan. Please."

She pressed his hand tightly and turned to him and an unexpected warm color flushed her wilted cheeks, freshening them, and she drew herself up, her back straight, and almost at once she was like a young tree rooted again in a field of rich earth with that unaccountable grace called life flowing through her.

"I can talk about it now," she said. "I can tell Garth. There was a time when I couldn't talk about it," she said, still holding tightly to Dean's hand but now staring straight ahead. "For all that long time when I didn't want the pain of being alive and remembering him, when I wanted so badly to die, during all that time I couldn't talk about it, but I can now. I talked about it to Dean and that's how I learned to talk again, and I can talk about it to you, Garth, because in a way, I've learned to live with it—I'm still learning—at least now I know I must keep on living because that's what people do. They go on, somehow.

"But I did not believe Aaron should go on. I did not believe any of that story he told at court; that business about it all being a mistake. I believe he knew what he was doing and I believe he meant to kill Paul and he did kill Paul and so one night I tried to kill him." She caught her breath.

"It happened the night after he was acquitted. I didn't sleep at all that night; sleep hardly ever comes any more, and about midnight I went downstairs and tried to play the piano again—you know, like I used to do when I was in high school. I can't play at all any more, I wish I could; the feeling is still there, maybe even deeper now, but my left hand is no good any more, just terribly no good. I guess it's because I didn't keep it up, no discipline. But I tried to work chords and harmony that night, and later, it must have been early in the morning, the dead cold hours of the morning, I started playing the Greig Concerto, almost like I played it in high school, remember? Except that I was hitting all the wrong notes, but the funny thing was I didn't care because it felt good, it felt awfully good, as if I was losing all my emotions into it, and I played it for a long time, all three movements, over and over again until my hands were like claws and there wasn't a drop of feeling left in my blood; that is, until I didn't think there was a drop of feeling left. But there must have been that one drop because I did try to kill him.

"I gave it up after a while and blew out the candles and just sat there exhausted on the piano bench in the living room, staring at the shrouds and all the hooded furniture, and then I heard his footsteps on the stairs. I watched him staggering in the stairwell, not clearly, just his dark hopeless form, and then I saw him lurch against the front door and open it and stand there uncertainly in the bright slant of moonlight that poured into the hallway and he stood there, white and blue and needing to be dead, the dark shadow of fatality and doom across his face, and just before he staggered out of the house I saw the revolver in his hand. I stared at the revolver for a long time and thought how cool and clean and deadly it looked in the bar of moonlight and how perfectly designed it was to end Aaron's dreams now that they had become nightmares, and I knew what he intended to do but I didn't want to give him that chance, that final satisfaction. So when I watched him stagger across the lawn with that revolver glinting blue and cool in his hand, I went out of the house and followed him down to the beach—"

Dean reached across and shook her shoulders. "Please stop it, Sloan darling, please stop!"

"I wanted him dead; truly down in the pit of my soul I wanted him dead and I followed him to the beach thinking what a great wash it would be inside me after I killed him."

"Sloan!"

She gasped. She turned sharply and stared with chill displeasure at Dean. The color had drained from her face. Her eyes were bright with fury. Her hands were trembling. She stared full into Dean's face for almost a minute and whatever it was she saw there made her turn and spur the ancient stallion savagely and gallop on ahead of them, the collies loping incuriously alongside, across the green velvet lawn and the macadam that curved slowly toward Manoalani.

Kapiolani Kahana walked soundlessly into the hallway. She was wearing a dark green holoku, and for the first time since her son's death she wore an hibiscus in her hair. She went to Garth and put her arms around him and kissed him. "God bless you foah comin' home," she said.

She led him by his hand to the door. "He's been watchin' you foah the last four hours. He had me get him them binoculars and wheel him to the front of the house so's he could watch you sail up almost all the way from Keahou."

Garth opened the door to the living room and stepped inside.

He shut the door quietly and stood leaning against it, both hands behind his back resting on the massive brass doorknobs. For a moment, he could not see very clearly. In the vast volcanic rock fireplace at the opposite end, a fire had been started, and the flames licking into the dark wood made the rest of the room obscure. Then he caught the reflection of the flames in the gloss of the piano; then again in the coated paper of the packages beneath the tree. The tree was in one corner, decorated but unlit. As his eyes became accustomed to the gloom, he made out the form of old Willard, a surprisingly small figure, seated on his leather chair across from the fire. He was covered with blankets against the evening chill, his shock of white-gold hair fallen across his skull, his deeply hollowed face warmed and mellowed by the firelight as the late afternoon sun would warm and mellow the rugged western slope of Mauna Loa. He sat with such immobility, without even the lift and fall of breathing, that Garth thought for a moment that maybe he was dead. Then, still without any apparent movement, Willard said, "It took you a long time, Son."

Garth let out his breath. "Hello, old fellow," he said. "I understand you refused to die."

"I didn't refuse. I just postponed it. I thought I'd kind of hang on and watch the way you'd mess up the second half of your life, you've made such an unthinkable mess of the first half."

Garth laughed softly. "Hell, you're not sick at all. You're just the way you were when I left."

He crossed the room to old Willard's side and stood there for a moment, looking down at him. And then, guided by an impulse he did not completely understand, he knelt down with characteristic plunging movements and put his arms about old Willard's shoulders and kissed him on the forehead. It seemed to shock Willard, and he sat there motionless for a moment; then he shook away irritably, muttering something indistinguishable under his breath. He pushed Garth away gently. "Get us a drink, Son; get us a drink."

Garth stood up and eyed him speculatively. "Are you sure it's all right?"

Willard's old skin bunched across his brow. "Don't come in here, in this house where you were born, for the first time in what? —in five, six years?—and start any foolish arguments with me! Get me a drink! Over there."

Garth walked behind the piano to a koawood chest and opened the top. There was a half-empty whisky bottle, glasses around it, and a full bottle of brandy. Thank the Lord for small favors, he's laying off the brandy, Garth thought. He poured himself a drink and poured his father a light one.

"Bring the bottle over," Willard called to him.

He went over, bottle and glasses in hand. There was a decanter of water and a bowl of ice on a table near the piano and he pushed the table along too.

"Does Doc Judd know you're taking your evening nip?" Garth said, leaning back against the table. "Are you supposed to have a drink now and then?"

Willard took his glass and sipped it. "Earl Judd couldn't write a prescription for a rabid dog," he muttered. He scowled at the drink and handed the glass back to Garth who poured in another jigger of whisky at the old man's insistence. "And there isn't a man born of woman who isn't supposed to have a drink now and then; a man owes it to his sanity to get drunk once in a while. It's the only way he can muddle through. And as for my doing what I am supposed to do or not doing what I am not supposed to do, I've long ago quit worrying about that. If a man worried about that, he'd never get out of the womb." His right hand came up slowly, his skinny fingers wrapped about the highball glass in a toast. "Welcome home, Garth. Aloha."

Garth leaned over and clinked glasses. "To you, old fellow."

"How long are you home for?"

"It depends." Garth shrugged. "I'm really not sure; no plans—"

"How long, Garth?"

Their glances locked. Garth raised his glass. "For good, Old Man. I'm home for good. Let's drink to that. Let's drink to my being home again and to your living to a graceful old age."

"There's no such thing as a graceful old age," Willard muttered. He drank slowly. A little amount of the whisky seemed to placate him. Garth had the feeling that the old man neither wanted nor needed the whisky but merely demanded his right to have some if he chose. The blankets came only to Willard's chest, and above them Garth could see that his father still clung to his mode of dress, the white linen shirt and familiar black string bow tie visible beneath a blue silk lounging robe. His hands were lumps of bone and vein wrapped in porcelain.

"I saw you several hours ago, sailing out along Kealakekua Bay. I followed you all the way into Kailua with the glasses. I kept on trying to place the last time I saw you."

"Years and years ago," Garth said. "You were just a kid when I left."

Willard smiled slowly; a half-smile, the left side of his face like frozen wax. "And now that neither of us are kids any more, are you all through running away?"

Garth shrugged. "I'm not so sure that I have been running away. Any man who goes off on a different track, the herd points a finger at him and says he's either a crackpot or he's running away. I read somewhere that in a world of fugitives, a person taking the opposite direction appears to be running away."

"You read somewhere," Willard muttered with contempt. "Your mind is full of all the tattered useless things you've read and half read; that's been your trouble all along, Garth. Your mind has been inundated by carbon copies of wet philosophies that have taught man nothing, except perhaps to promise without practicing, to aspire without attaining. If the ghosts of those dead philosophers of yours could open their mouths, the earth would crack with their laughter. There is absolutely no sense in reading a book unless you can put what knowledge you gain from it to use. And after you've read sections of the Bible and *Huckleberry Finn*, you don't need to read anything else at all. Not that I have anything against reading or learning things; I don't think it's too harmful, except that it makes a person unhappy and unfit for work—and I might add, you have mastered both characteristics with consummate ease—and it seems to me that the more useless knowledge a man assembles, the smarter he becomes, the stronger his tendency to run away. Like you." He turned his disapproval coldly upon Garth. "You were running away, Garth. You've been running all your life from the way the world is to the way you'd like it to be. And you've never found it. I told you long ago, in my letter, that the reason you've never found what you've been looking for is because it didn't exist. Shake off the dream, Son. It's tough enough to grasp reality. When a man cannot find peace within himself, he's a fool to search for it elsewhere."

"I have been almost every place in the world," Garth said, shaking his head in that kind of charming futility of his, "and every place I've been, people are running away.

"I think it's because something has gone wrong with us. Something is changing in the world. Man has no place left on earth to explore. He can't push westward any more; he can't find land to clear. He can't find a way to exhibit his valor, so slowly he's giving up his valor. He can no longer find means or reasons to exhibit personal human dignity, so he's losing his grip on human dignity. Not even in war can a man show dignity and valor. I know war, old fellow; I'm practically an expert on war. I'm thirty-one years old and I've been through three or four of them. In the next one, Science, with its rockets and missiles and hydrogen bombs, will take all personal dignity out of war; it will reduce war to cold, impersonal, precisioned death. In a war like the one that's coming up, if a man shows valor he'll be a fool; it will be a dramatic stunt."

Old Willard's face assumed an expression of mild concern, stolidly watching his son. "You're a lost romanticist," he said. "You want to lead a cavalry charge into the Kremlin."

Garth shrugged. "Maybe."

"There's no maybe about it, Son. You talk like some—some South Seas beat generationist."

Garth laughed. "I hope not. I hope I'm talking like a thinking member of the human race—before the human race either stops thinking or stops talking or both. I know only that things are more brutal, more coldly devastating, more hopeless now than they were when I was a kid. There are no heroes any more. Do you know why? Because a true hero insists upon accomplishing something worth while. And when he does, he is placed upon a pedestal of fame, and fame today, thanks to the moral and intellectual glut of Hollywood and Washington, has become an end in itself. In this, the golden age of press-agentry, inescapable media of communications, television, movies, radio, magazines, advertising, newspapers, celebrities have been made famous not for accomplishing anything of value, but precisely the opposite: for doing nothing.

"Celebrities are famous today because they get drunk in fashionable bars, because they are caught in the wrong bedroom, because they smoke a certain brand of cigarettes, use a certain type of brassière, shoot one of their fellow celebrities, enter Menninger Clinic, commit suicide—even because they wear a certain kind of menstrual padding. And when the real hero mounts his deserved pedestal and takes a look about him, he becomes revolted and parachutes off somewhere and tries to finish his work in anonymity, like Robinson Jeffers up at Tor Tower or Sibelius in the mountains of Finland, or, the prime example, Dr. Schweitzer in the Belgian Congo. The real heroes of this world are declining to mount the pedestal of fame. They know that the addled, television-cultured masses do not want real heroes, but frauds; they do not want to admire people who have done something, but they want to admire people who, like themselves, have done nothing.

"If a real hero arose, he'd be ignored or maybe even stoned by the great depersonalized citizenry, because he would not, could not, be a carbon copy of what the image makers in Hollywood and Madison Avenue have drummed into the soft American brain as hero type. People don't want a real hero: what they want is a celluloid reproduction of themselves that can have sensations for them; and most important of all, they want a reproduction of themselves that can be happy for them. Because if you look around the world, you look around at the faces of people, especially in the big cities of America, and you'll realize that the normal state of the adult human being is a qualified discontent. Because he's in a box. Either he placed himself in a box or he let society shove him in the box and slam the lid. And he either is too afraid or else he's unable to jump out of the box and run away."

"Run away?" Willard asked.

Garth looked up, his eyes sadly quizzical. "Well, if I've been running away like you claim, that's what I've been running away from: society's box. Man's fretful, anxious, admitted futility and badgering insecurity. I am running away from man's colossal devaluation of man; from his fall from grace in his own eyes. I am running away from man's cheapening dehumanization of himself."

Old Willard eyed him with a face like that of a heavy hawk. "But you yourself are not insecure, is that it, Garth?"

Garth grinned. "Yeah. I've worked insecurity to a perfection." He sipped his drink. "But I honestly don't feel as if I've been running away. I've seen people run. Thousands, hundreds of thousands in Asia and Europe are running away; but it's a physical running away, a flight from starvation or slaughter. In America people are running away from themselves in some sort of intellectual retreat—a spiritual flight from their own emotional self-abuse."

He stood up and walked over to the fire and stared into it, chuckling softly, as if he was laughing at himself. "I don't know," he said, "I decided I didn't want to have anything to do with America once the circuses folded. And now they've got big ships calling on Tahiti and Bora Bora. Tourists pouring all over the Quai du Commerce, hurrying nowhere or less. In Quinn's Hut one night I was sitting at a table drinking a glass of fine French wine and looking out across Papeete Harbor at the widest whitest moon in the world, and the palm trees were black and languidly still against an indescribably beautiful sky—and then someone came in and played an Elvis Presley record in the jukebox." He chuckled to himself again. "Hell, I don't know. I'm just kind of enthusiastically disillusioned."

They had another drink, and later, Kapiolani and Laura entered the room. Kapiolani went about the room lighting lamps and the massive wheeled chandelier. Then she lit the Christmas tree. It was a forlorn little tree, balancing its brightly painted ornaments with a gaiety of spirit that failed to prevail through the rest of the room. The presents wrapped in their splendid ribbons and twine seemed somehow mute and abject beneath the branches.

Coyama padded in from the kitchen and wrinkled his face at Garth. "Aahh, Mistah Garth, you stay home now, numbah one!" He set a huge wassail bowl of tarnished silver on the table by the tree. "Merry Christmas, Merry Christmas!" he said.

"Pour yourself one, Coyama," Garth said, walking over to him. He looked into the bowl. The eggnog was steaming. Coyama poured and Garth handed the cups around to everyone.

"You're looking very well, Laura," Garth said easily.

She looked up at him with brittle eyes. Then she managed a wry grin. "You mean, under the circumstances."

"No, I mean you are looking very very well. Good. Pretty." Garth grinned and sat alongside her on the davenport.

"You're a wonderful liar and I've always loved you for it."

"How do you feel?"

"I don't know how I feel," Laura sighed. "To tell you the truth, I'm trying not to feel—anything. That's a hard thing to do around Christmastime. Especially for an old sentimentalist like myself. But I'm trying."

Garth stared into the fire. She studied the back of his head, the bronze curling vigor of his hair. He smelled a little bit like iron, she thought, contemplating him; like an old leaf fallen in the garden. "Would you help me, Garth?" she said softly.

He turned to her. "Of course I will."

She bowed her head slightly and stared at the rim of her eggnog cup, flicking her fingernails with nervous daintiness on the side of the cup. "Garth," she spoke so softly that he had difficulty hearing her, "Aaron has had—" She raced her tongue across her lips; then continued: "Aaron has had an illegitimate baby. A son." She paused, as if waiting for Garth to speak, but he remained silent, attentive. "It's a wonderful little baby, all fat and cheerful and bubbling; you'd love it. He's really wonderful. He's—he's not all haole; the girl, the mother, was a mixture. She died," Laura said in a whisper, glancing up at Garth from the corner of her eyes. She hesitated, then she said, "I want to adopt that baby, Garth."

Garth felt he should say something. He looked at her for a moment. "Can you?"

Laura nodded her head excitedly. Her eyes became quite round, unafraid. "Yes. There's nothing to stop me. There are no grandparents on the mother's side. Her only relative was a brother, a young boy who was in a way involved in that—that terrible killing; but he's up in California now. The baby has no one, except me . . . and Aaron."

She placed her cup down and tightened both her hands restlessly on his. "I went to church this afternoon, Garth. It was the first time I had been inside a church—except for the . . . the wedding—in years. I went to church all by myself and prayed. I prayed that Aaron and I would adopt the baby. I prayed for more than an hour. I begged Aaron with everything in me to adopt the child. To give the child a home, or perhaps give us a home, give Aaron and myself a home because of the baby. But I couldn't get through to Aaron. He doesn't want anything to do with the baby. And finally, I called Earl—Earl Judd—and asked him to talk with Aaron. That's where Aaron is now. They're discussing the baby. At Judd's office.

"Garth," her fingers tightened about his hands, "if Earl Judd fails with Aaron, will you try? Will you help me in this?"

Garth looked down at her trembling hands and covered them with his.

"The baby is Aaron's own son. His own flesh and blood. And

the baby deserves a chance. Aaron will listen to you. Try, Garth. Please. For me and for Aaron as well as for the baby's sake."

"Sure. I'll try, Laura."

The collies wandered into the room, serene, independent, yet friendly. Miss Brett inspected the wassail bowl for a moment, then joined Baron as he lay at old Willard's feet. Sloan and Dean followed the collies into the room.

"We took the station wagon back to the harbor," Sloan said. "We collected your gear for you, dear brother, including this rugged little monster." She tossed Rickets and he scrambled across the rug, pausing to hunch and flex as he passed the two serene collies, then continued his way to the davenport where he leaped up alongside Garth and stared at him accusingly for a moment. Garth laughed and rubbed his neck.

"Get that goddamn thing out of here!" old Willard cursed.

"He's a good cat, old fellow. A little beat-up like all of us here."

Willard insisted on walking to the dining room table. Kapiolani brought him his battered white linen coat. It took him more than a moment to doff the robe and slip into the coat. They ate gravely, each with their own thoughts. Their talk had a strange tempo: they would either slip into periods of protracted awkward silences, or else, with self-conscious and obvious efforts to break the silence they would all begin talking at the same time, inundating each other with shy brittle chatter until, self-consciously again, they grew silent. What little conversation was held concerned Garth and his travels and his plans, possibly because among the others there was a twisted incommunicability as if when they turned to look at each other's faces, they saw, surprisingly, each other's hearts. And the scar that had been carved in their hearts.

Midway through the meal, the telephone rang. Sloan answered it. She was gone a few moments, then reappeared and beckoned to Garth. When he joined her in the hallway she said, "It's Ward. He wants to talk to you. Whatever you do, don't mention it to Daddy."

Garth looked at her skeptically. Then he went to the phone and talked a long time with Ward, then with Tani and finally the children. He resumed his place at the table and looked directly into the heavy hawk-faced, hawk-eyed countenance of his father. "It was Ward Akana," Garth said. "He called to wish you a Merry Christmas."

There was not a sound at the table. Each of them seemed to be stilled, as if time itself had stopped; as if a movie projector had jammed and the people on the screen had been frozen in mid-action. Then the projector whirred again and they all looked self-consciously down at their food. Willard's old seamed face brooded above them all, dissolute, remote and almost insufferable with arrogance.

"There is something I should tell you, Garth," he said.

"There's something you should be told," Garth said.

"The reason I am not in Washington as Delegate to Congress is Ward Akana."

"I've heard that isn't so."

"I am telling you it is so. And we won't discuss it, Garth, please. As long as I live, that man's name will not be mentioned in this house, nor will he ever set foot in this house. You've been gone a long time, Garth, and many things have happened. None of which I care to discuss."

They had cordials after dinner in the living room, before the massive fireplace in which logs burned briskly, and upon old Willard's request, Sloan went to the piano and played several Christmas carols with stoic indifference, Willard gravely listening not to her, but to the singing of Manoalani years ago. As she was playing "Silent Night," voices rose to the melody, and she looked outside and could see the holiday-lighted truck pull up at the entrance to Manoalani. They walked to the door, Garth taking old Willard's arm and tramping with terrific slowness. On the ramp of the truck there was a Christmas tree, and the boys' choir from Kailua High School was serenading. They sang "God Rest Ye Merrie Gentlemen" and "O Little Town of Bethlehem" and finally, "*Adeste Fidelis*," and the little group on the veranda of Manoalani applauded them and wished them a Merry Christmas. And as the truck turned and departed, a low winter moon, thumbed partly away like an ancient half-dollar, rose low in the sky; and in the white lake of the moon, Aaron stood before them with his baby blanketed in his arms.

He was sober. He hugged the baby in the crook of his right arm and his eyes moved with opaque questioning across each face of those who stood slightly shocked on the veranda, watching him.

"This is my son," he told them.

Later, they walked along the shore into the very heart of the moon. The night was timeless and very soft; the sky was a violet arc above them in which stars now flowered like pale and tarnished petals of the amber rose.

"I just had to get out of that house," Sloan said. "When I saw him there, with that baby wrapped in his arms, I just had to get away."

"I know." Dean put his arm around her shoulders and drew her close. He loved the scent of her; it was fresh and clean and wonderful, like the odor of a young tree. The odors of people are very rich, he thought.

They walked quietly along the beach, listening to the night, listening to the old voice of the ocean, listening to the whisper of their steps in the sand.

"When I saw him there, I knew all at once why I didn't kill him that night. Why God or something made me miss him. It was God, I'm sure now. I almost shrieked when I saw him with that baby, because I understood, then, the power of God. I understood then that God all along knew something I did not know and that's why He made me miss him."

Dean remained quiet. He heard the sibilancy of her voice, moving again through the story, putting it all out in front of her now, or behind her really, now that she understood it, and he thought: If she wants to talk about it now, I won't stop her. I saw no reason for Garth knowing about it, but if now that she understands, she wants to talk it all and completely out of herself, it is because she needs to get it all and completely out of herself, and then I hope to God it will be as if it never happened.

". . . and when I reached him, caught up to him that night," Sloan was saying, "he was about a mile up along the shore, toward Waiaka, and he was staring out at the sea like a stunned, hopeless animal, and from time to time he looked down at the revolver in his trembling hand. I watched him for a while, thinking to myself, Pull it! Put it to your head and pull the trigger! He did put the muzzle to his head, twice I think, but neither time did he pull the trigger. Both times he simply put down the gun and buried his head in his hands and wept. And then he heard me.

Aaron turned. His face was a wash of despair. He held the revolver poised, the webbed butt harsh and wet against his palm.

"What are you doing here?" he said.

She stood at the edge of the sand dune, her shoulders slumped, her hands spread against her stomach, her fingers hooked faintly so that the tip of each nail dug into her skin beneath the blouse. She was looking straight at him, her eyes narrowed as if she were looking into a strong sun. "I've come to watch you do it," she said.

Aaron took a slow step toward her, then stopped. He balanced warily, his eyes bright with dread. "I can't."

"Yes you can. Go ahead."

"No," he said thickly. "I can't. I tried twice before."

"I know. I watched you. I'll leave and then you'll be able to."

Aaron shook his head. He was weeping. "No, no," he wailed.

"Do it!" she screamed. "Do it! Do it!" She seemed oddly like some silken machine of hate or revenge which had waited idle too long, and now, awakened with the opportunity before her, with the object of her fury before her, would function solely upon that hate and would continue to function upon it until the object had been destroyed. "Do it, for God's sake!"

He wavered and shook his head. "I can't," he murmured, in a weak drab voice. "I wanted to, I wish I could, but I can't. I just can't squeeze." He staggered down to the shoreline and fell to his knees, crouching, his body jackknifed, his elbows buried into his thighs and his spread trembling palms covering his face. There was no moon, and the wavelets which moved up and sloughed indeterminately about his knees were dark, soundless. He threw the revolver up along the beach. "You do it."

The gun looked terribly beautiful in the sand. Two webbed deer antler plates, worn almost smooth of their ridges, were set skillfully into either side of the butt so that the grip they formed was set clean to the fingers. Sloan's fingers moved over the cold hard feel of the gun. When she picked it up, it came so willingly that she could hardly believe it was in her hand. It balanced steady in her hand, waiting and eager and hating anything she pointed it toward. It seemed almost alive, an extension of herself, resting coldly and easily in her hand, the perfect steel glinting with the cold detachment of a tiger's eyes, waiting for the kill. She aimed and held her breath and pressed the trigger. The shot echoed through the night. She pressed the trigger again. Aaron screamed in terror. She pressed the trigger again. Her hand was unsteady now and she gipped the revolver in both hands and fired again.

Aaron was racing headlong down the beach. She stood on the little sand dune and continued firing at him until she heard dimly the click of the empty cylinder. She looked thoughtfully at the revolver, hot and smoking in her hands; then she dropped it into the sand and walked away.

And it is over, Dean thought. It has to be over now.

They had reached the dark wet tidal boulders surrounding Waiaka, and Sloan said quietly, "Now I know why I missed him. And I'm thankful I missed him."

They were silent for a time, like grave children. Then Dean said, "None of that evah really happened, did it, Sloan?"

"Yes, it really happened. You know it really happened."

"No. I've forgotten it. You forget now."

She turned in to him and buried her head into his shoulder, murmuring, "Dean, Dean, Dean." And he kissed her hair and her forehead and he held her close in both his arms as if he was trying to make the two of them one and he said, "I love you, Sloan. I've loved you all my life."

She looked up at him. "What are we going to do, Dean?"

"I don't know. All my life I've only wanted one thing to make me happy. But, wanting that one thing, wanted everything. And it's you, Sloan. It's always been you."

She walked a little away from him, her back to him.

"There's something you don't know, Dean. Something even Paul didn't know, although I wish now I had told him. Dean," she said softly but with no shame. "I'm pregnant."

She turned after a moment and looked at him. He seemed immobile against the boulders, standing like a king and smiling sadly at her like a clown.

"Did you hear me?" she asked.

He nodded heavily. "I heard you."

She looked up at him with the utmost clarity and walked slowly toward him and she could feel within herself an almost reluctant starting, but a starting nevertheless, as if she understood that with his help she would be able to track down and capture that sweet kind myth again, and her face had in it the passionate ecstasy of a child. "But you have to understand, Dean, I'm proud of it. I'm happy and glad I'm carrying his child because that way he'll never be so—so completely dead."

He could feel his heart strangle as he took her in his arms. "Sloan, I love you with everything in me that can love. I always have. When we were kids I used to dream of lovin' you and marryin' you, but it always seemed like I was out trying to pick up roses and gettin' stuck by the thorns. I still want to marry you, Sloan. I wasn't meant to be alone. And I know that without you I'll always be alone. But with you, I wanted to bring years of love; years and years of love, Sloan, and love would wash away everything else." There was a pain in his heart like glory.

She was crying softly and she let him kiss her. She was crying because she had become aware once again of an old mislaid sorrow which seemed to haunt her with the absurdity, the total oppressive impossibility of any human being trying to communicate with and perhaps weld the soul, heart and mind of another human being in a world and time where nothing was ever what it seemed to be, and she thought: I am afraid to balance his soul, his heart, in my being. I am afraid of having the responsibility of his happiness in my hands. I am afraid of the overwhelming responsibility of love. I hope and pray to God that He will change me soon. Because I do not want to be afraid of love.

"Will you marry me, Sloan? Please darling, marry me and we'll have love and we'll never be alone or afraid any more."

She swung her gaze at him, her eyes opaque as smoke. And she leaned in to him and kissed him. But she did not answer him, and she did not form the answer in her own heart. But when you are in love, she thought, and you are loved in return, then at night, when it is dark, you never have the feeling that you're all alone or frightened or feel like crying.

Behind them, the sky became suddenly crimson. They turned to look at it. The crimson was spreading swiftly across the eastern sky like a false dawn. They walked hurriedly up the sand dune to the road, and far away they could glimpse the bright flash of flame spiral into the sky from the summit of Mauna Loa.

Chapter Eighteen

THAT night the vast sphere of the earth spun upon its axis, steadily, inflexibly, committed in unvarying orbit to its course around the sun. Tranquil, seemingly undisturbed by atoms or by man and his history of insane splendors and agonies, scornful of that power which bound the sweet influences of the Pleiades and loosed the bands of Orion, it hung there against the black prehuman dignity of the night, singularly brilliant among the high impassioned ecstasies of the stars.

It was a dying earth, soon to be a moon. Yet even in death it was proud, absorbing all its magnificent vigor from the sun, which rode, that night, deeper into Capricorn.

The swords of the sun bit into the earth. At solstice they stabbed through the hot liquid core to the strata magma; up into the seething batholith where they mixed with gas and flaming torrents of basalt. As the pressure increased, the mass surged upwards 1,800 miles through the bowels of the earth. It pressed against the inner crust of the earth until it escaped through one of the deep abyssal fractures of the crust, roaring upwards to explode furiously across the land through the festering wound on the back of the old volcano.

Up in the high country of Mauna Loa, a herd of wild goats fled at the spasm. An old boar threw up its head indignantly. The muscles in its chest swelled with taut fury. It swung its outraged eyes upon the erupting summit for a moment, then turned and trotted stiff-legged down the slope.

Christmas twilight was oppressive as a cloak: as a ceaseless, sulphuric cloak which neither wavered nor drifted in the hot faint sibilance which was not strong enough to be a breeze. The island suffocated with it. Manoalani, beneath the cinnamon-red implacable sky, was heavy and heat-soaked like a sodden veil. The broad avenue of palms drooped as lifelessly as banners in defeat. The sea beyond them was reflectionless and mocking.

All along the Kona Coast the people came out of their houses to look up at the mountain. Farmers and small coffee ranchers leaned against their fences and gazed speculatively at their crops, ripe now and ready for harvest. Then they stared up at the mountain—hoping. The men stood silent and motionless, their boots not planted into the soil as was their custom but resting lightly upon it, almost apologetically, as if fearing a new series of temblors. From the doorways of the houses, the women watched their men. Then, with timid, hesitant steps, they walked out and stood beside them, their eyes searching the faces of the men for terror, or disgust, or resistance, or defeat. The children stood nearby, barefoot, a Christmas doll or perhaps a soldier clutched in their arms. They watched with wide curious eyes the expression on their parents' faces. Then, the bravest of the children grinned and said: "Pele's returned."

The woman smiled faintly at him. "Go back in the house and play."

But the child stood quietly. "Will the flow come this way?"

"Go back inside and play," the woman said.

And suddenly, the child burst into tears and the woman picked him up and pressed him warmly into the folds of her breasts and after a while the child stopped crying and all this time the man watching the mountain did not speak or show emotion of any kind.

Only the mountain prevailed: vast, untamed, unconquerable; proud of its lusty glamour, aroused and smoldering now, charged with turbulent power, hurling into heaven its fountains of flame while far below, the people watched, and the earth waited, and the wild boar bitterly quickened his pace.

"Ah, here it is," Garth said, leaning back against the railing of the veranda, a volume of Shakespeare open in his hands. "It's in *Henry IV*. I don't know what made me think it was in *Lear*. Listen:

"Diseased nature oftentimes breaks forth
In strange eruptions: oft the teeming earth
Is with a kind of colic pinched and vexed
By the imprisoning of an unruly wind
Within her womb
Which, for enlargement striving,
Shakes the old bedlam earth and topples down
Steeples and moss-grown towers."

"My God, poetry!" Willard fumed. "The whole southeastern pastures might be burned out and you sit there reading poetry! Jesus Christ!"

"Always name-dropping." Garth grinned, putting the book aside. "What do you want me to do, old fellow? Mutter a few Hawaiian prayers and raise my hands and order Pele to cease and desist?"

"I expect someone in this household to get their tails out to the eastern grazeland and bring the cattle in from there. We've got about three hundred head in the east pasture alone and I want them cleared out. If the rift opens up where it's supposed to, that's the end of the east pasture, but it doesn't have to be the end of those head."

"What do you mean, If the rift opens up where it's supposed to?"

"We were listening to the radio reports earlier," Sloan told him. "The volcano observatory expects the northwestern slope of the mountain to open up, about five miles down from the summit."

"When?"

"Tonight or tomorrow. As soon as enough pressure is built up underneath."

Garth paced restlessly across the veranda, forgetfully dragging a little on his bad leg. "Damn. I'm sorry old fellow," he said to Willard. "I didn't know."

"Well, now you do." The old man had been sitting for a long time in the fading light of the veranda, his booted feet propped angrily against the lower railing. He had spent most of the day watching the eruption, his old, fabled rage surfing through him. Eight temblors had rendered the island during the day. The last three seemed exceptionally strong, coursing through the crust of the earth with undulatory, stomach-sinking spasms. One of the huge glass windows of the living room had blown out and splintered against the veranda in a brittle cascade. Willard had cursed it vehemently, not bothering to look at it, keeping his thunderous gaze upon the mountain. He seemed not much more than a shadow of his old powerful self. Yet he sat painfully erect and implacable in his white linen suit and black tie and boots, and only the shadows about his darkening eyes told how deeply he had been stricken. It was as if his heart, spent now and wearied of struggling, abdicated of all dreams, poured blood through his body in slow debatable beats, like the lava pouring from the summit, wearing away his flesh. The old collie dreamed fitfully against his chair, his forepaws switching occasionally as he relived the proud and ancient gallops of his youth when the mountain was full of wild boar scents that maddened the blood in him and the end of the hunt was valor. He barked indolently in his dream and Willard dropped his old boned hand on his head and said softly, "Hush, Baron."

Sloan leaned gravely against a column of the veranda, Dean standing so close to her that she could feel his heart hammering against her breast as if it were in her own chest.

"Where's Aaron?" Garth asked.

"Probably getting drunk up in his room," Sloan said. "Probably anesthetizing himself so he won't know what's happening."

"No, I'm not drunk," Aaron said. He had walked quietly and unnoticed out from the dark gloom of the house into the paler gloom of the veranda. He leaned against the side of the house in a leashed and brooding repose, watching the volcano with eyes that had grown dark and restless and behind which lurked an old thin sorrow. "I haven't had a drink in a week," he said.

Sloan looked at him with bleak eyes. "Not even one tiny little gray drink? How are you bearing up under it?"

"Please, Sloan," he said simply.

He walked to the end of the veranda and joined Laura who rocked there in an old chair, cradling the baby in her arms like a sheaf of grain. Sloan watched them for a moment. "Touching little scene," she said.

"Ease up, young lady," Willard muttered.

Abruptly, Sloan walked stiff-backed into the house.

Kapiolani Kahana came out to the veranda, wearing a savagely flowered holoku and carrying a serving tray of drinks and coasters. Old Willard reached for a drink but she made him take his medicine first, then made certain he got the drink she fixed purposely weak for him. "The radio jus' reported that the rift opened up down the northwestern wall," she said. "Pahoehoe lava comin' down the slope. They say about eleven miles an hour."

Willard grumbled. "Which way?"

"This way," she told him.

"Goddamn! I guess I'll ride into that east grazeland myself and herd those cattle out," Willard cursed.

"We'll get 'em out tomorrow, Senatah," Dean said.

"Tomorrow," Willard mimicked with disgust. "Tomorrow there might not be any cattle left. Four hundred head in there," Willard protested. "Four hundred head and everybody sitting on their goddamn duffs—"

"You said three hundred a minute ago, old fellow."

"I said four hundred! Goddamn it, I'll saddle up myself and get them." He turned and bellowed the length of the veranda. "Aaron! Your addled old man was hoping perhaps some of his sons would try and save some of their cattle!"

Aaron stood up. "I'll ride in at dawn," he said. Then he looked curiously at Dean. "If you want me to go in with you."

Dean looked at him for a moment, then turned away. "Don't make no difference to me. We'd moah bettah need three or four men."

Willard looked up at Garth. "And what are you planning to do? Catch up on your poetry reading?"

Garth grinned easily. "I'm driving up to the volcano observatory. Dr. Jaeger's calling a meeting of representatives from all the ranches and villages along the coast."

"What in hell for?"

"Explain what's happening up in the summit crater. Tell us about what we can expect."

"I know what we can expect," Willard muttered. "Especially if those cattle aren't cleared out. I've been to those meetings. Just jabber jabber jabber; greatest bunch for talking. Cycles and sunspots, sunspots and cycles."

Garth sipped his drink and looked fondly at the old man. "I wouldn't discount that talk. They've got Mauna Loa pretty well pinned down by that theory of sunspot cycles: a minor disturbance every year and a half, a serious eruption on an eleven-year cycle, and a major catastrophe on the hundred-and-thirty-two-year super-cycle. When the sunspot activity reaches a peak, radioactive waves are sent toward the earth in clouds of electrons, moving with the speed of light, and their energy is transferred into the core of the earth, setting up inner earth shakewaves, and the old volcanic ball starts bouncing."

Willard looked at him heavily. "And you believe all this drivel? These immense vulgarities of misapplied science that weaken the fine dream of man and soil his mind?"

Garth lit a cigarette. "I believe only that science is trying in its own way to explain. I believe those cloistered, timid little men with the pinched faces and the big glasses and dreamy eyes are trying to establish a few truths, old fellow. They have, for example, linked all phenomena of earth with sunspot activity: the weather, magnetism of the poles, radio reception, the growth of trees and sugar cane, the richness of the hide on those cattle out there, the lake levels in Africa, and especially the eruptions of Mauna Loa; they've linked them all to a definite relationship with sunspot activity."

Willard brooded a moment. "Science and all its acids and wax and answers!" he grunted. "I don't believe these precious god-damned scientists search as devotedly for truth as they claim. They work from a theory that truth is the rejection of beauty, and then they go and bisect things, searching for the end of beauty. They look at an orchid and tell you just how much carbon is in a petal but they can't tell you its color. Tell me," he swung his contemptuous gaze upon Garth, "what cycle do the scientists claim forced

Mt. Ararat up from the flood so Noah could land his ark?"

Garth studied his father curiously. "You ride a few cavalry charges of your own, old fellow."

Willard turned away. "Those cattle must be brought to safety. I'm only interested in my stock, not in sunspots, not in anything in those geophysical bulletins from the observatory, or in any cycle or in what the scientists say. Like every other breed of man, they overrate themselves. They think their accomplishments are important, profound, powerful. But all you have to do is open your eyes and look up there at that erupting volcano and you'll realize how truly insignificant man is. The mastodon, the saber-toothed tiger, all the noble powerful creatures perished while an absurd ape swung down from a vine and for a brief moment fools himself into thinking he rules the earth. Your scientists," he muttered contemptuously, "have discovered and told us everything about an erupting volcano except why."

Above the grave restlessness of the palms, the sky curved like a red, metallic, intolerable bowl, and the windless air exuded a thin odor of resin and burned heat. The first stars shone, dusty and savage. Garth descended the stairs and walked across the lawn toward the ocean. He felt suddenly and inexplicably lonely, and as he walked, he grinned at himself with derision: the emotional eunuch wandering speechlessly down the endless lane of man's immemorial sadness.

His leg had started bothering him again and he leaned against the trunk of one of the palm trees, his ankles crossed, his arms folded across his chest, his head back against the tree. In the distance, he could see the steam cloud mushrooming up in the sky, two miles above the summit of Mauna Loa and still rising, like the cloud over Hiroshima. He guessed the cloud would probably reach four miles by morning. The wonderful thing about volcanoes is that their grace is still savage and pure and cannot be either defended against or contaminated by man, he thought. God has claimed the creation of the earth and yet the earth is imperfect, as if from its own original sin of existence; as man is imperfect; as, reasonably, God too must be imperfect, limited, cursed equally with His original sin of existence. Just as the flaw in man courses through him from the pit of his soul to his finger tips, so the vast abyssal flaws of the earth course through it from the batholithic core to the summits of the old volcanoes like Mauna

Loa. And as the flaw in man is the seed of his destruction, so will the flaw of the earth bring about its destruction. But will the flaw in God bring about His destruction?

Man and God are weary, Garth thought. The earth too is already weary; already a dying cinder. There was a time when the earth was a white-hot sphere like the sun; and, pursuing as it must its temporal destiny, there could come a time when the earth would be a dead cold thing like the moon, a casualty of the second law of dynamics in the frigid interstellar space of the macrocosmos. Mars first, when Phobos, which even now had almost reached its limit of approach, explodes into it. And in time earth, when the moon returns to 11,000 miles and bursts, its fragments perhaps becoming trapped in orbit into a trail of ash, like the rings of Saturn, to curse the poets and amaze the stargazers of planets yet unborn.

But not in our time, Garth thought, gazing up at the volcano. We are yet in the time of heat: the time of Vesuvius and Krakatoa and Mauna Loa; the time of sweet thunder.

Professor Norton Jaeger listened absent-mindedly to the thunder. Piled on the desk before him were the day's newspapers with their bold headlines concerning the eruption. He had read the stories carefully, with an increasing distaste for their inaccuracy, then he pushed the papers aside. The rest of the news did not interest him: war, strife, pathos, the devious delights within Sodom and Gomorrah. Always, when he glanced at those stories chronicling the decay of the human race, he felt a stirring of pride at his own singular profession in which he was pitted against natural forces and not against his fellow man.

He was a burly, shambling man with an ironed brown fifty-year-old face and a taciturn manner. His close-cropped hair was the color of smoke. His mouth was square and dryly humorous. His eyes were deep-set and very sober, and they fastened curiously now upon the steam cloud that had risen more than three miles above Mauna Loa's summit. It was rising approximately fifteen feet a second, orange colored at its base, turning to a smoky yellow-green higher up: filled with silicate slag and dust and basalt fragments, and the fine glasslike filaments of lava called Pele's Hair, which, he knew, would be carried by the wind to some distant slopes and start forest fires. He gazed questioningly at the volcano, as if awaiting an answer that would not be forthcoming.

Professor Norton Jaeger had spent his entire life among the volcanoes. He had grown to love them, much in the same manner that a sailor might love the sea or a pilot the sky; all of which, he thought, might be an indication that knowledge is the key to love. He believed the volcanoes were a force upon the earth either useful to or antagonistic to man. They must be useful to man, he reasoned, because there was no natural phenomenon on earth ordained antagonistic. Despite the tragedy of Pompeii, despite the death and destruction wrought upon Martinique by Mt. Pelee, despite the various havocs wrought upon his own island by Mauna Loa, he felt certain that there must be eventual good in an erupting volcano. Man's task was to discover that good. If man could only know more about volcanoes, more about the inner earth, perhaps he could discover and harness that good: harness, for instance, the magnificent energy of the volcano. It often appalled him that the great leaders of nations and companies, the powerful ones on earth who employed scientists and spent millions of dollars in an attempt to reach the moon, would not spend a dime to investigate the inner earth and all the wonders it must yield. They see visions of the stars and the moon, he thought with an old thin dismay, but they fail to see the visions of the earth.

He turned from the window and moved his burly quizzical stare across the faces of the visitors assembled in the laboratory of the Hawaii National Park Volcano Observatory.

"In the old days it was easy," he said. "When there was an eruption, the ancient Romans would glance across the Tyrrhenian Sea to the island of Vulcano, an ash speck off Cape Calava at the northernmost point of Sicily. This was the domain of Vulcan, the smith god, and it was the entrance to the nether world. The Romans figured that Vulcan was down preparing arms for Mars. The old Hawaiians believed that the eruption was caused by Pele's return; or Pele burning her lover Lohiau in revenge. But today, we're not that lucky. We want to know exactly what is happening, why it is happening, and what we're liable to expect. Okay," he said, getting up from behind his desk and walking over to a corner of the room. It was a long rectangular room, three walls of which were covered with various geophysical charts and graphs of the two volcanoes, Mauna Loa and Kilauea. At the far end of the room stood a long table divided into four sections, a draftsman's stool at each. On the nearest stools sat two junior volcanologists, plotting the day's lava course. Behind them, stretched along the width of the laboratory, was a knee-high topographic mock-up of the Island. Alongside this, was the main seismograph. Professor Jaeger went to the seismograph and the group of men assembled at the meeting crowded around him at his suggestion.

"This is a comparatively simple little gadget," he said. "Kind of a sensitized pendulum that swings at the least shock inside the earth.

"Christmas Eve, and all day yesterday, you folks felt perhaps seven or eight major tremors in the earth. They were strong enough so you could actually feel the earth quiver. But this little gadget," he indicated the seismograph, "started feeling them a month before. A week before Christmas, it recorded seventeen quakes. The following day, thirty-four quakes. That's when we sent our first press release to the newspapers and radio stations and alerted the Island's civil defense posts that some activity could be expected. During the entire week before Christmas, this machine continued recording the mounting tremors; here," he pointed to a pinned-up chart upon the wall directly behind the seismograph, "is its record. Ninety-seven tremors the following day; then one hundred and seventeen, three hundred and sixty-nine, and so on, until on Christmas Eve and Christmas Day it recorded a whopping six hundred and eleven tremors—eight of which were strong enough for you to feel.

"These tremors all centered in Mauna Loa. Kilauea, as it is right now, remained comparatively quiet, responding only with sympathetic tremors to the bigger volcano west of it."

"How many tremors have been recorded today?" Garth asked.

Professor Jaeger checked the readings on the seismograph. "Two hundred and . . . seventeen; so far. We don't know how great the full twenty-four-hour total will be."

"Does that indicate that maybe the eruption is tapering off?"

Dr. Jaeger grinned. "It would seem to, but we don't think so. I'll show you why."

He went over to the topographical map and with a pointer traced a line from the raised papier-mâché head of Mauna Loa northwestwards. "Roughly, this is the way the lava—pahoehoe lava—is flowing out of the summit; straight northwest. But here," he indicated a spot on the map in which three red-headed pins had been stuck, "is where the northwestern rift zone opened up yesterday evening. The entire northwestern slope of the mountain is still swelling. There might be fewer tremors, but that's only because now the lava has two great holes out of which to pour, instead of only the summit. We weren't worried about the summit flow. It's slow and congealing quickly. But this northwestern vent, which is about four miles down from the summit, is dangerous. The flow from the summit is joining it, like a tributary stream of a great river. They are combining into one great northwest flow."

"It looks like we'll be spared this one, eh, Mr. Jaeger?" Brock Tavares asked. He was a tall, dark-faced man with clear eyes and a thatch of undisciplined iron-gray hair. He wore levis and boots and carried a Stetson in his hand. Garth recognized him as the foreman of the vast Parker Ranch.

Professor Jaeger nodded. "Unless the flow changes direction, it appears that the Parker Ranch will be clear of it. However, the Howland Ranch is in for trouble."

"How much trouble?" Garth asked.

Professor Jaeger rubbed the tip of his nose with his thick, blunt fingers. "It's difficult to tell, Garth. You've got about fifty thousand acres in grazeland along Mauna Loa's slopes, isn't that right?"

"About right." Garth indicated an area on the map. "This area here comprises what we call our eastern grazelands. Dad sent Dean Kahana and Aaron and some of the hands into those grazelands this morning to clear the cattle out."

"Good." Professor Jaeger looked up at Garth. "How is the Senator?"

"Just like the volcano: erupting." Garth grinned. "He's worried about the lava flow. How bad do you think it will hurt us?"

Jaeger shook his head doubtfully. "It's difficult to estimate. I'd hate to guess. Never have believed in guesswork."

"Well, what's the worst it could possibly do?"

"It could easily wipe out all that grazeland, Garth. It's good you're herding those cattle out today. They're directly in the present path of the flow. But of course, that's not the worst that can happen. The worst is that the flow can pick up speed as it descends the slope, endangering the entire Kona Coast from Kealakekua north to Kailua."

"That would include Manoalani."

"It certainly would," Professor Jaeger said. "I flew across Mauna Loa yesterday, when the northwestern rift zone opened up. Colonel Green here, from Hickam Air Force Base, was kind enough to make the flight possible. We got a good look at the flow. It's picking up speed now. And it's headed directly toward Kailua and the coast." Professor Jaeger turned and exchanged glances with a youngish-looking Air Force lieutenant colonel. "We're going up again tomorrow morning, isn't that right, Colonel?"

"Yessir. About eleven-thirty."

"Could we take Mr. Howland here with us? He could get a good picture of the lava flow from up above. Maybe arrive at a few ideas about how to best defend his land."

"It would be a pleasure, Mr. Howland," the pilot said.

"Thanks. I'd like to very much."

Professor Jaeger looked about the room. "How about Doc Judd? Doc—" He spotted him among the men. "As chief of the civil defense along the Kona Coast, you would get a pretty good idea of what to expect from up there. Can you come with us?"

Earl Judd shrugged. "I don't see how I can make it. We've called a civil defense meeting tomorrow morning at Kealakekua."

"Perhaps in the afternoon," the Air Force colonel suggested.

"The afternoon would be fine," Doc Judd said. "If there's anything still left of the Island."

"By tomorrow, Doc, we should have enough indication from the lava flow to know whether or not to evacuate Kealakekua. There is a group of Army Engineers down there now, dynamiting five miles outside the village, trying to establish a ditch deep enough to delay the flow if it reaches the outskirts."

"When do I order an evacuation?"

"When and if the flow reaches that ditch."

"And we are to move north along Mamalahoa Highway straight to Kailua?"

"That's correct."

Dr. Jaeger walked briskly back to his desk. "It could be said that a volcano is similar to a boil or a pimple on the surface of the skin; the hot poison mounts steadily through the system. The outer layer of skin pyramids into a conelike shape and the eye of this cone must be lanced or popped in order for the pent-up poison to find its release. It's a crude way of describing it, but it makes its point. Here"—he went to the small blackboard behind his desk and upon it drew a large circle with two gradually smaller circles inscribed within it—"here is the earth.

"This outer line represents the crust of the earth. It is crystalline, cooled basalt, about twenty-five miles thick. When the earth first cooled it shrank in size. In so doing it left deep abyssal fractures or flaws in this crust, leaving it weak, irregular, composed of mammoth mosaic blocks which pitch and roll constantly, bounded by planes of weaknesses and known faults. The greatest of these known faults is right underneath where we're sitting now—the great girdle of fire stretching from the Aleutians straight down across the floor of the Pacific. The Hawaiian Islands are volcanic products of this fault, which winds like a vein down through the twenty-five-mile crust into this middle layer of earth here"—he indicated his drawing—"which we call magma: a glassy, highly gas-charged basalt lava, approximately two thousand degrees Fahrenheit in temperature. This acts as an eternally restless, eternally seething force chafing against the inner surface of the earth's crust. When the pressure of this force becomes too great—because of sunspot energy, an astrophysical pull, a magmatic shift of gas pressure—it seeks release and surges upward through one of these cracks in the earth's crust and pours out, still two thousand degrees Fahrenheit, through the volcano—in the present case through the summit and the northwestern vent of Mauna Loa.

"The pressure of this internal mass accumulates at a fairly even rate through the years. The summit and the vents of Mauna Loa act as a kind of safety valve; the weight of the island itself acts as the spring control on the valve, opening when the pressure inside has gone beyond a certain power. Once, about every eleven years—and we've discovered this to be in direct relationship to maximum sunspot activity—this underground pressure, which has been building gradually all the time, forcing itself up through the summit crater and through the various rift zones which break up the mountain into blocks, this pressure reaches its limit. The mountain swells. The safety valves are opened, and we have a major eruption."

"Professor Jaeger," Lieutenant Colonel Green interrupted, "do you anticipate any need for bombers?"

Norton Jaeger gazed thoughtfully out the window. "I hope not. Right now we don't anticipate having to use them. The last time we had to bomb Mauna Loa was in order to redirect the lava flow away from Hilo. Now, however, with the flow moving in the opposite direction—northwest—it has a long way to go before it causes any great damage: that is, except to the grazeland and perhaps some coffee fields on the upper slopes. Twenty or more miles northwest into Kealakekua, about twenty-five miles northwest to Manoalani, thirty miles northwest into Kailua. We would not call the bombers unless Kailua itself was threatened. And I pray to God that won't be the case."

During the night the old boar trotted almost continuously down the slope, rooting his way northwest, keeping ahead of the burning river of lava. He had halted several times, but on each occasion his rest had been unsatisfactory. The lava kept pursuing him relentlessly, pushing him on. Farther down the slope he entered a forest of lehua and fir trees. He remembered the smells of the forest. Many years ago he had been trapped and almost killed there by a hunter and two dogs. But he had outwitted them and escaped. Pleased with himself, thinking he had now outwitted this new enemy, he burrowed into the sweet-smelling needles that matted the floor of the forest and went to sleep. But soon he was awakened by a great blast of heat. The entire forest was burning. From their roots to their tallest branches, the fir trees were wrapped in flames like Roman candles.

The old boar raised his head. He sniffed the air. The scent was a mingled one, strange and alarming. Before he recognized it, he saw the pheasants scamper from the brush, their feathers flaming. Flightless and terrified, they plunged directly into the oncoming flow.

The old boar got to his feet. He snorted fiercely at the fire and shook his head in rage. Then he turned and continued his stiff-legged bitter retreat down the slope. He remembered again that stand he had made many years ago against the hunter and those dogs and he would like to make such a stand now against the flaming river, but he did not know how.

At eleven o'clock the following morning, December 27th, the drowsy village of Kealakekua seemed an actual physical embodiment of its name—"The pathway of the gods." A mile west of the village was the sea, thirteen hundred feet below the sheer pali cliffs of the Kona Coast. Thirteen miles to the east of the village came Pele's advancing flow of fiery lava.

"We're going to have to evacuate," Earl Judd said. "We might just as well start now."

He stood quietly on the front steps of the Kealakekua coffee mill. He could see almost the entire village, sleepy and languorous beneath the wavering rays of the sun which slanted palely through Mauna Loa's cloud. The village was choked with heat. The main street was a blistering slab of tar; a continuation of Mamalahoa Highway which circled the island. It curved slowly into the heart of the village, past the shacks of fishermen and coffee plantation workers, row upon row of small, identical two-room wooden houses with corrugated tin roofs. The houses leaned gently against the slope of dirt roads that led into the main street. Ragged green lawns and thick foliage splashed with orchids and poinsettias garroted the houses. Chickens and goats and scrawny poi dogs and shrieking children wild and soft as animals and cheerful with filth and holiday clamored about the houses. The heart of the village was two hundred yards long: a drugstore, a grocery and hardware, a gas station, a feed and grain building, all in the same block, their yellow-painted fronts long faded, heat shimmering from their tin roofs. Across the main street was the post office, a low wood building, one wing of which constituted the town hall. At the south end of the street was a squat Buddhist Mission, and at the north end the freshy painted Congregationalist Church, the stopped four-faced clock in its steeple claiming ten past six. A row of monkeypods shaded the street. The tallest building in the village was the Kealakekua coffee mill. From its front steps Earl Judd and the Hawaii National Guard captain who stood alongside him could see across the roofs of the stores, past the coffee fields, green and heavy and doomed now, to the grazeland of the Howland Ranch and Pele's burning flow. They could hear the spaced detonations as the Army Engineers continued dynamiting a trench to clog the flow. They could see the front of the flow moving sluggishly across Howland land; black, crackling, serpentining its way toward the village. The front of the flow appeared to be about six hundred yards wide, forty or more feet high; smoking.

"You think we should get started now and not wait until it hits the engineers' trench?" the National Guard captain asked. He was a tall, bulky Japanese named Hirozawa.

"I don't see any point in waiting," Doc Judd said. He watched the lava river a moment more. Then he shook his head and walked somberly into the coffee mill.

It was like an oven. The sacks of coffee beans had been trucked away the day before. The mill now was practically vacant. A group of National Guardsmen and civil defense volunteers were talking quietly among themselves around a table at the far end of the mill as Doc Judd and Captain Hirozawa joined them.

"I wish I could bring you good news," Doc Judd told them. "But I guess you've figured by now that all news is bad news. We're going to have to evacuate Kealakekua. Everyone and everything."

"Except the land and the houses and the crops," somebody said.

Doc Judd nodded. "Except the land and the houses and the crops," he agreed sadly. He leaned against the desk and they grouped about him, grave and childlike. As his eyes moved across their faces he was surprised to see Sloan Howland enter the mill —a shadow at first, as she stood in the doorway—then slowly walk across the floor and stand remotely at the rear of the group.

"I'm glad you could all get here," Doc Judd told them. "We've had our training. We've run through emergency drills. Our plans for evacuation have been established. Now we put it all to a test."

He and Captain Hirozawa spread an Army Engineers' map of the Kona Coast area across the table.

"The procedure for the evacuation is simple," Doc Judd explained. "A National Guard regiment will line Mamalahoa Highway from the village six miles north to where the Kuakini Highway fork comes in. We are all to march north. Nobody is to stop at Kanialiu, which also is to be evacuated. We go straight north to the Kuakini fork; then north again along the Kuakini Highway past Manoalani to Kailua—if necessary. And it looks as though it might become necessary."

"Hea, Doc Judd," one of the men interrupted, "why we no go south, huh? Why we no go down byanby to Napoopoo or City of Refuge, huh?"

"Because the best plan is to stay in front of the lava flow, not to head in a direction where we might be trapped by another possible break in a rift zone. If we headed south, and a second rift zone opened up, or if Kilauea erupted, we'd be directly in the path of its flow. Napoopoo, Honaunau, City of Refuge, Kealia and Hookena—all the villages south of here—are scheduled to evacuate farther to the south if it becomes necessary. From here north, we evacuate to the north."

"Auwe—I got plenney cousins down south along the coast," the man protested.

Doc Judd laughed. "We'll make plenty of new cousins along the road north."

"What time you think we moah bettah start, huh Doc?" a big Hawaiian-Japanese rancher asked.

"We should start this afternoon. The village should be completely evacuated by tomorrow noon. Each area captain is responsible for the people in his area. By nine o'clock tomorrow morning, you should see to it that all the people living in your area have their possessions out of their houses, stacked on their lawns and ready to be placed into the National Guard trucks for transportation north—"

"Includin' the pigs an' the goats, Doc?"

"We've got livestock trucks," Doc Judd replied. "There will be a fleet of thirty National Guard trucks to help move you. We should be able to get all valuable possessions out safely. Those who want to start moving north today should be encouraged to do so. For the rest, we should make sure that they start gathering their gear and belongings this afternoon. They should assemble as much as possible today and get their stuff out alongside the road so we can make swift pickups tomorrow morning and clear out of here."

"Tell me, Doc Judd: since we no gotta move till later this aftahnoon, maybe byanby you can come ovah an' take a look at Lehua for me, huh?"

Doc Judd looked at the big Hawaiian fisherman curiously. "What's wrong with Lehua?"

"What's wrong: what's da kine alla time wrong? She's plenney big hapai!"

"Again?"

"Suah," the fisherman grinned, "why no?"

The crowd laughed. "Okay," Doc Judd said, shaking his head. "I'll get over there this afternoon. We don't want any babies born on the road. What does that make? Nine?"

"Auwe, nine. Eleven! You musta missed out on two of 'em," the fisherman roared.

"Incidentally"— Doc Judd raised his hand to quiet the laughter—"if any of you run into difficulties—people refusing to leave, that kind of thing—you know how stubborn some of these old-timers are, scoffing at the volcano—then call either myself or Captain Hirozawa here and we'll help you out." He caught Sloan's attention. "Miss Howland—ah, Mrs. Kahana: has the Red Cross made emergency preparations at Manoalani?"

"Yes," Sloan answered, almost inaudibly. "There is a mobile field unit at the house now."

"Will there be cots available?"

"Yes," Sloan said.

"In that case," Doc Judd continued to the group, "you can instruct the people in your area that as they move north along Kuakini Highway, there will be Red Cross facilities and rations at Manoalani, in the event that some of the older folk will want to pull up there for overnight instead of going all the way to Kailua."

When the meeting was over, Sloan walked up to Doc Judd as he and Captain Hirozawa were leaving the mill. "Can I talk to you for a second?" she asked.

He joined her and they strolled down the steps of the coffee mill and out along the main street of the village. "You know," Doc Judd said, his eyes sweeping across the village, "the plans are perfect, but they'll probably all go wrong. These people won't leave their land until the last possible second. And even then, they'll try to think of some way to save it; and by that time, the neat, orderly evacuation we've just planned will be a shambles."

Sloan nodded. "Could we go have a cup of coffee?" she said quietly. "I want to talk to you. About something else."

Professor Jaeger said, "How do you like the looks of it from up here?"

"It looks like hell," Garth said. "Literally: it's as though you could see right down through the crust of the earth into hell."

Lieutenant Colonel Green turned from the controls and grinned at him. "It would be a real hell soon enough, if we were to have any engine trouble right about now."

They flew in a slow arc about the summit of Mauna Loa.

Colonel Green held the altimeter at fourteen thousand feet. The fiery summit was a little more than three hundred feet below them. Updrafts caught the fuselage and at times the small Cessna biplane hove sickeningly, but for the most it droned over the summit steadily enough. They had attempted to make a complete circle about the volcano, but the eruption cloud hovering over the northwestern slope was so filled with lava dust that they could not see, and the sulphuric smoke was so strong that they gagged with it. The cloud was now more than four miles into the sky, its crimson and gray billows obscuring the sunlight.

Garth, sitting in the co-pilot's seat, craned his neck and stared out the window.

The fire pit of Mokuaweoweo was a sea of blood. All along its three-mile belly, fire fountains spiraled up into the sky. The sprays were white with heat as they shot upwards, turning crimson as they fell back into the pit or spilled across the summit down the mountainside. Cinder cones swelled within the pit. The main cone belched to a height of three hundred feet. A red molten flow oozed from its heart and poured down the slope. A three-hundred-yard section of crater wall broke down and tumbled into the pit. Through this break the red river flowed ceaselessly down the northwestern crags of the volcano. Jet after jet of immense proportions shot into the sky like frothy geysers, glowing incandescent lava which descended in cascades of gas-charged flaming rock, like an enormous firefall, to rape the land.

The noise was terrifying. It was as if the entire labyrinth of the volcano, with its rumblings, its whirlwind rushings of gas, its pealing thunder of cascading lava rocks, the blastlike detonations deep in its crater, its shuddering spasms, all had joined in a great choral debauch of the land.

"We can slip in a little closer to the pit if you want to," the pilot suggested.

Professor Jaeger nodded. He was crouched between the pilot and Garth, his hands braced against the backs of their seats for balance. "Not too close though." He pointed to the fire pit. "Only two weeks ago, the lava in that crater was jet black and seemingly docile, with just tiny streams of red veined through it. Now look at it—a blood lake."

The lava lake was incredibly beautiful, Garth thought. It was a caldron of liquid fire. The waves sloshed and exploded against its walls, breaking down a wider gap in the northwestern wall and flowing out over it. Steaming whirlwinds were set in action by the rushing gas. Fountains ejected their frothy lava five hundred feet above the rim of the crater, and these cascaded in ribboned cataracts down across the mountainside.

The volcano seemed to shudder for an instant. Then a blinding explosion shattered the crater.

"Get out! Pull out quick!" Professor Jaeger yelled at the pilot. The plane banked sharply, as if out of control. Then it straightened and nosed away from the summit.

Garth and Jaeger stared back at the summit. The sudden blast seemed to have pulverized the crater. Ton chunks of flaming clinker lava, hurled from the fire pit, began dropping from the cloud now like meteors. One plummeted across the path of the plane, not fifty yards ahead of it. Garth caught his breath, then watched the massive volcanic bomb fall to the slope and explode, a flash fire starting about it.

"Close . . ." Colonel Green said. He had a grin on his face but his brow and hands were clammy with sweat.

"Too close," Garth said.

The plane descended the long northwestern slope of the mountain, traversing it almost in the manner of a glider. Garth watched the summit flow ooze down the slope, devastating a swathe of land six hundred yards wide from Mokuaweoweo four miles down to the flank eruption.

"This is the baby we really have to worry about," Professor Jaeger said, indicating the flank eruption. "This is the one that will cause the trouble."

The rift opening along the northwestern slope of Mauna Loa was about seventy yards wide. Gases and fire fountains five hundred feet high poured out along its mile-long stretch. The biggest concentration of fountains was at the lower end of the stretch. Steam and pumice spouted up from the spatter cones. Everywhere Garth looked, the burning lava was inundating the mountainside; rumbling, fountaining, drooling, massively destructive over the land. The flow from the summit crater met with the rift flow at one junction and fanned outward like the hood of a cobra, igniting a strip of forest. The mammoth body of lava trailed northwest down a valley formed by two older flows. Its tongues pushed forward here and there, burning red; exploratory. As it flowed, the lava changed in character from the issuing aa or clinker-type, which was rough and spiny, to the smooth, billowy, almost satiny pahoehoe lava, vitreous, glassy-skinned, swift-flowing. Its bulbous tongues gushed with unreasoned violence down the slope: fluid, crackling, rasping, sections of the front almost sixty feet thick; forking and reforking and joining forward again in insensate, intricate patterns, writhing, convulsing in fantastic, deadly shapes—a river of death which left nothing living in its wake.

"Look down there," Colonel Green said.

A herd of wild goats was trapped in a curve of lava. They galloped in all directions like mice chittering through one of those scientific mazes designed to observe their reactions. Garth watched until the curve of lava started swooping in on the trapped goats.

"They've come all the way down from the upper reaches of Mauna Loa," Professor Jaeger said. "And they damn near made it to safety."

The lava river covered the herd. Years later, a section of jawbone would be found, or perhaps the snub of horn, preserved perfectly in an airtight cover of ash.

Professor Jaeger nudged Garth on the elbow. "There's a section of your grazeland."

It was a sheet of flame. A prairie fire rushed down across it from the slope. Miles ahead Garth could see the dust and the brown bobbing of the cattle being herded to safety. "I'm glad they got them out this morning."

"Up there," the pilot pointed. "Looks like a break in the flow."

Professor Jaeger narrowed his eyes at the black smoking countryside. "It is a break in the flow. And it's a bad one."

As Colonel Green banked the plane farther down the mountainside, they could see that the great river of lava had split into two streams. It split against a century-old lava barrier, built up like a levee a hundred feet high. Instead of lumbering over it, the lava pooled against it and divided. One stream rumbled almost due west, vesicular and ropy, its front widening to a thousand yards, moving in against Kealakekua and the Kona Coast. But the other stream broke off in a sharper northwest direction. It was moving very fast, along a narrow front only two hundred yards wide. It moved in a couse almost parallel to Mamalahoa Highway, almost parallel to the fleeing herd of cattle.

"Follow it," Professor Jaeger told the pilot.

Colonel Green kept the airplane directly above the new river of lava. They could see the herd of cattle very clearly now, and far to the west they could see trucks moving up along Mamalahoa Highway.

"Look up ahead there!" Professor Jaeger said excitedly. "That's just what I was afraid of!"

Three miles ahead of them, the river of lava bent and started curving west. It ran along a high promontory, then cascaded down over the Howland grazeland and started roping its way straight west, across the path of the cattle herd, toward Mamalahoa Highway and the coast.

"They might be trapped down there!" Garth said, watching the westward flow begin to cut across the path of the herd.

Professor Jaeger shook his head. "I think they'll beat the flow. When they see that they're blocked, they'll turn the cattle west and try to beat the flow to the highway. It looks as though they have the time to do it."

"We'd better try and warn them just the same," Colonel Green suggested.

Professor Jaeger slipped on a set of earphones and established radio contact with the Hilo tower.

"This is HCS-one one eight nine seven to Hilo tower. HCS-one one eight nine seven to Hilo tower, how do you read me?"

Jaeger waited. Then he said, into the speaker:

"Notify Hawaii National Guard headquarters and Civil Defense: a fork of the main lava river has broken off and is moving at an estimated ten to twelve miles an hour northwest, paralleling the Mamalahoa Highway. Approximately five miles north of Kealakekua, this flow has turned almost due west." He repeated that portion of the message and then he continued: "If it continues in its present direction, it should cross to the coast approximately at the intersection of the Mamalahoa Highway and the Kuakini Highway sometime late tonight or tomorrow morning. Notify Hawaii National Guard and civil defense headquarters: the Mamalahoa Highway northbound will be blocked by this flow."

He repeated the entire message a second time, then placed the earphones back in their clip on the control panel.

"If that flow crosses to the coast and blocks the highway to the north," Garth said, "and the main flow goes into Kealakekua, blocking the highway to the south . . ."

Professor Jaeger looked at him soberly and nodded.

"You've got your own answer," he said.

Colonel Green banked the plane low over the advancing cattle herd. They flew in so low over the grazeland that Garth could make out Dean Kahana in his bright red shirt, riding behind the herd, waving at the plane.

"Isn't there any way we can warn them? Signal them?"

"Not from here there isn't," Colonel Green said. "They should be able to see that second flow soon enough."

Professor Jaeger craned his neck, his angry eyes studying the lava flow. "Let's get back," he said.

A little more than an hour after he had watched the airplane disappear beyond Mauna Loa, Dean sensed the increase of heat. The trade winds which blew perpetually across the vast domain of Howland grazeland had stopped for once. The air was thick. Not a blade stirred. The red-gray leagues of cloud piled over the big vega were hot as molten glass. From them came the oppression felt by every living thing on the grazeland.

Dean spurred his roan up along the ridge of a grazeland mesa. The horse's chest was flecked with foam; the pelt dark with sweat. When he pulled his horse to a stop, Dean could see steam rise from the animal's flanks.

"Rest a minute," he said. He unscrewed the lid from his canteen and drank deeply. He poured water into his hand and rubbed it across his grainy face. His skin felt like rawhide being soaked. He wore chaps, spurs, heeled boots and a red work shirt which now was sopping wet, clinging to his back. His back and legs ached. His lungs felt congested from sucking in the sulphur and carbon fumes of the lava along with all the cattle dust. He removed his Stetson and poured some of the water over his head. It refreshed him for the moment. But he knew that soon the thick, steamy feeling would return.

All day long the grazelands had been unbearable with the heat. When they were working the eastern cup early that morning, a hot hard rain teemed down on them. Lightning had crackled from the clouds. Ash and burning cinder and volcanic bombs chucked down upon them from the sky. Several of the cattle had been badly burned. Two had to be shot. And there were probably a dozen head lost somewhere on that black smoking slope, Dean thought. But almost four hundred head had been herded out safely, and these rumbled by him now, howling, hawking, their eyes bulging, their horns sticking out like pickets: a churning mass of hoofs and white-faced heads, pounding red clouds of dust and hides and flies. Point riders loped along the sides of the herd, top hands who would know just how to handle any emergency—stampede or lava flow. The dust and heat of the herd walled against the heat of the earth and the sky. The swing riders shifted back and forward on their wiry ponies while Aaron and another paniolo trailed behind, keeping the laggards moving.

Aaron saw him. He cut his horse from the herd and cantered up the mesa and pulled in alongside him. "It looks pretty good from up here," Aaron said.

Dean pointed back along the trail. "We're out about four or five miles northwest of the flow. If we keep ahead of it, we're okeh."

Aaron swung one leg over the pommel of the saddle. "You did a fine job, Dean, getting all these cattle out safely." He reached into his shirt pocket for a pack of cigarettes. He extended the pack to Dean.

"Smoke?"

Dean shook his head. "No thanks." He remounted, feeling self-conscious with Aaron's cavernous, uncomfortable eyes boring into him.

Aaron lit a cigarette. Then he raised his canteen to his lips and took a long drink. "Water! Clean, cool water," Aaron said. "I'm strictly on the wagon now. For good."

Dean sat uneasily on his horse, watching the herd. He wished Aaron would leave. Aaron was trying too hard. It was embarrassing to listen to him.

"Look up there at that summit," Aaron pointed. "It seems as if life has been one dreadful nightmare since that day when you and I rode up there to hunt. Remember?"

Dean's jaw was clamped so tight that his teeth ached. He turned and glared angrily at Aaron. "Look, Mistah Aaron—it's been no nightmare for me. It was all verra real. I'd rathah not talk about it."

The color drained from Aaron's face. He swung his foot back into the stirrup. He kept his eyes averted from Dean's. "Okay, Dean, okay. I don't blame you. But you can't blame a man for trying, Dean. I've got to try."

Aaron turned his pony and trotted down the ridge. But before he got to the bottom, he pulled up sharply. In the distance, he could see the new fork of lava cascading like a firefall down the promontory and starting to river its way across the grazeland. He watched it for a moment, spellbound. Then he turned to Dean. "That's going to cut us off!"

Dean had seen it at the same time. He heeled his horse and joined Aaron at the bottom of the ridge.

"We'll have to turn the herd west," he said. "We'll have to ride them straight west to the coast and then move them up along Mamalahoa Highway."

"We can't get a herd like this on to the highway. If they started evacuating Kealakekua this afternoon, the highway will be jammed."

"We'll have to take that chance. There's nothing else we can do. Look at that stuff coming!"

The flow cascaded down from the promontory in a brilliant three-hundred-foot leap to the grazeland. It serpentined across the grazeland now; agile, swiftly destructive. Three grass fires raged in its wake. Its first blast withered the leaves and trunks of a grove of slender ohia, the hot ash cremating the trees. A finger of lava swooped up about the taller trees, sheathing their trunks with solidified ash. The front of the flow curved west about a mile ahead of the herd. The front-riding paniolos had already started turning the herd west, speeding them up, trying to make it to the coast highway before the flow cut them off.

From his position, Dean could see both rivers of lava: the new fork rumbling seaward about a mile northwest of him, and the sluggish main flow several miles south, advancing steadily seaward toward Kealakekua. Both flows covered the prostrate land with their massive death, encircling the herd and the villages along the highway west of the herd in a gigantic pincer attack. Pele, Dean thought, gazing at the flows with both hatred and despair: goddamned whore.

"There's a gap in the flow," Aaron said. "See it? Right underneath the firefall coming off the bluff."

The promontory bluff was about three hundred feet high. The lava poured over it like a waterfall of fire. And directly underneath its overhang, Dean could make out a clear path: a tunnel about thirty yards wide and two hundred yards long, like the pocket inside a waterfall. At the far side of the tunnel lay the vast rolling sweep of unscarred grazeland leading to Manoalani.

"I see it," Dean said. "But we suah as hell couldn't drive a herd of cattle through it."

"I wasn't thinking of the cattle. I was thinking that we could ride through it. If we get trapped."

They galloped their horses across the grazeland and soon caught up with the front of the herd. The grazeland was an uneven, faceless plain. Its pitch and roll slowed the herd. But it also slowed the lava flow. By sundown, Dean and Aaron and two of the veteran ranch hands raced their horses a half mile ahead of the herd. They spread out in a northward curve along the ruts of Mamalahoa Highway. As the herd approached, each man rode into it, forcing the lead cattle to swerve in a northward arc along the highway. In thirty minutes the entire herd had been swung north along the highway and back onto safe Howland grazeland north of the flow. The last few straggling heads had to be whipped across the highway, but they beat the lava flow by several hundred yards.

Dean reined-in his mount. He and Aaron and one of the ranch hands watched the flow simmer west and cut across the highway. The front of the flow was only a hundred yards wide and about twenty feet high. Mamalahoa Highway seared as it spilled across it. Two telephone poles flared brightly for a few minutes, then toppled over into the flow.

Dean looked at them curiously. Then, on sudden impulse, he turned his horse and started cantering along the lava flow toward the sea.

"Where are you going?" Aaron called.

Dean did not bother to answer. He spurred his roan into a gallop, rounding the front of the flow and heading back to the highway on the other side.

"Dean!" Aaron shouted.

But Dean was riding at a full gallop now, back south along Mamalahoa Highway.

The ranch hand rode up alongside Aaron. "Just what the hell is he up to?" Aaron said.

The old Hawaiian paniolo wrinkled his face. "Wit da kine telehfon wires down, maybe he figures dose people at Kealakekua don't know 'bout did flow, blockin' dem," he said. "Maybe he figures de only way to warn 'em is to ride down an' tell 'em."

The lava had completely crossed the highway now. It rolled to the edge of the pali and was pouring down the cliffs into the sea. The noise as it hit the sea was deafening. A great steam cloud began rising from the water.

Aaron and the old paniolo watched it for a moment. Then they turned their gaze south along the highway. But the river of lava and the smoke and the gathering dusk obscured their view.

"He's way down dere now," the Hawaiian said. "You no can see him no moah."

"But he's riding right back into the trap," Aaron said. "He's headed straight back into the main flow."

"Yeah. He suah as hell doin' dat," the old man agreed. "But he knows de one way to get 'em out of de trap."

The wild boar had made it safely down the northwestern slope. When he had reached the grazeland he stopped short. The hair on his back lifted. He saw the great herd of cattle and the men on horseback riding northwest. Here was a danger he knew. The men confused him. He knew he could not trot out across the grazeland; not with the men present. And he knew he could not turn back up the slope. The flaming river which had been pursuing him for three days and nights now had become a personal enemy, one which seemingly he could not escape.

He found a little gully running along the edge of the grazeland. He descended into it, rooting his trail through brush and scrubs of panini cactus, being careful to keep far behind and out of sight of the men riding herd. He saw the firefall pour over the promontory and the new river of lava burst across the grazeland. When the herd veered toward the coast, he stopped and watched it warily. He decided to cut straight across the grazeland to the coast.

It was twilight when he reached the highway. He could no longer see the herd. But he heard the hoofbeats of a horse galloping down the highway toward him. He trotted off the highway and hid himself in the brush. He saw the horse fall and roll over the man, then get up, shake himself, and canter down the highway. The man did not move.

When he could no longer hear the horse's retreating hoofbeats, the boar scampered up to the highway and looked at the man incuriously. He ducked his head and scraped his tusks against the road and snorted angrily. Then he turned his head and looked frankly at the advancing lava flows. He started to bleat.

Later, when Dean regained consciousness, the first thought that flashed across his mind was of his father. And the way his father had been killed: *The twist of a pony's foreleg on a trail he had ridden a thousand times. . . .*

His head cleared. He opened his eyes cautiously. He could see the tops of the trees sawing above him against the choking blue-gray vault of the sky. The road felt warm beneath him. The pain in his leg was like fire. When he tried to move he almost passed out. There was a battering pain at the backs of his eyes and inside his forehead. Nausea uncoiled through his throat. He turned his head and vomited. It did not make him feel any better.

He took a deep breath and leaned up on his elbows. His eyes searched the darkness for the pony. He knew he should not have galloped the pony. A strong little quarter horse that had been worked hard since dawn and was too exhausted to lift its hoofs. He should not have galloped him in the bad light of dusk. He should have been watchful for heat cracks along the highway. He should have been more alert and held the reins higher to check a fall. But he had not done any of those things. And now, he could not see any trace of the roan. He hoped the horse was safe, wherever it was.

He lay his head back against the warm road and closed his eyes. He tried to listen to the pounding of surf against the tidal boulders far below him. The ocean sounds louder and greater at night, he thought. But he could not hear it. Its roar was drowned out by the crackling of the burning lava rivers converging toward the highway.

He opened his eyes and sat up, braced on his elbows. You are in one hell of a fix, he told himself. Just how do you plan working your way out of it? What can you do now? Just lie out in the middle of the highway until a truck comes along and rolls over you without seeing you? You were going to show them how to get out if they were trapped. You were going to lead them to that path underneath the firefall. You turned out to be one hell of a hero, all right. Just lie helpless and wait for a truck to roll over you.

He listened to the lava crackling over the land. Far away, he could see the flames of the approaching flow. Hell, he thought, no truck will roll over this part of the highway. It's probably all closed up.

He tried to crawl over to the embankment on the ocean side of the highway but the fire in his leg flared so painfully that he almost lost consciousness. He waited a while. Then he took a deep breath, and keeping his legs immobile, using his hands and elbows to propel himself, he dragged himself to the ocean side of the highway. There was a three-foot ditch along the side of the road and he rolled into it, screaming from the pain in his leg. He lay motionless at the bottom of the ditch, waiting for the pain to ease. Then, on his back again, he worked his way tortuously up the embankment. His lungs worked spasmodically and he lay for a long time on the slope of the embankment, catching his breath. The slope was covered with pili grass and lehua haole scrub. He moved his hand restlessly across the grass. It was hot and dry from the lava blasts. Farther to the east there was a file of languid palm trees and behind them a coffee field was burning.

When he felt better, he leaned up and moved one hand across the stretch of left thigh. Halfway between the hip joint and the knee he could feel a sharp-peaked swelling. Then as his fingers moved across his rough trousers, he could feel where the thigh bone had snapped off. It was pressing upward against the skin.

He felt drained and exhausted. He leaned back on his elbows and stared at his leg. It was lying at an impossible angle. It was hurting very badly now. Bile rolled up through his throat and he swallowed it and it only made him feel worse.

He gazed into the darkness and tried not to think about the pain. He realized that it was almost impossible not to think about pain when it is your own pain and it is very severe. But he forced himself to think about the horse. He felt very stupid for permitting the horse to fall. If the horse ran south along the highway, toward the evacuees from Kealakekua, and they sighted him, then they would realize something was wrong and they would search up along the highway for him. And if they didn't . . . There was no point in thinking that way, he told himself. He would not think about the horse, or about being or not being found, or about the pain of his leg, or about the approaching lava. He thought of Sloan for a long time, visualizing her, not any particular part of her but the whole glory of her. Then he thought of a thousand other things and faces and people, but each time his mind would return to Sloan again, and he thought about how he still had a chance for that glory if he was found and he tried very hard to keep thinking about that chance as he sat quietly on the embankment, listening to the approach of the burning lava. He fought hard to keep from passing out again. He searched his mind to set up a plan of action for when the lava river reached the opposite side of the highway.

Idiot, what good would a plan of escape do you? You couldn't put it into action.

No. But I can plan it anyway.

All right then, here's your only plan: you can crawl the half mile to the edge of the pali. Then, when the flow comes, you can either roll over the pali thirteen hundred feet to the boulders and the sea below, or you can sit back and fry. It's all your choice.

He saw dim shapes scurry across the highway. A family of quail raced single file in that peculiar way of theirs down the ditch and up the embankment a few yards away from them.

He stared at them curiously for a moment. They did not seem to fear him.

"Fly away," he said. "Shoo, birds, fly away."

Then he realized that the baby quail could not fly.

"Goddamn it!" Doc Judd roared, "they've got to get out of there!"

Captain Hirozawa shrugged his shoulders. "Do you want us to carry them out bodily?"

"If that's the only way they'll leave, we'll have to."

They worked their way swiftly through the crowds that jammed the main street of Kealakekua. The village, and the highway especially, seethed with activity. All during the night, Mamalahoa Highway and the little dirt roads lancing into it were packed with people rushing here and there with unseeing eyes. The main street was lined bumper to bumper with cars and old trucks, wagons and trailers in which was piled everything the people owned. And the gardens surrounding the small frame houses were littered with furniture, bric-a-brac, wooden bedsteads, machinery, stoves and refrigerators, television sets and old radios. The people grouped about the porches and gazed up at the volcano speculatively.

But they refused to move during the night. They would look at the volcano, and at their homes, and at the row of stationary vehicles on the main street, waiting. But they refused to evacuate this village in which they were born and reared and married and raised children, until they were certain that there was no other choice. They would leave, but only at the last possible moment.

As Doc Judd hurried across the main street from the coffee mill he could see the smoking flow beginning to pour into the south edge of the village and he knew that this was the last possible moment. The caravan that had lined the main street during the night, waiting, had started to move at dawn, and now, almost eight o'clock, was well on its way, rolling solemnly but without panic north to Kailua: fishermen and coffee plantation workers, ranchers, small farmers, tenant farmers, shopkeepers, mill packers, rich and poor, dark, tan and haole, women with children, old Chinamen with their vision almost gone, the dying, the crippled, several women far gone in pregnancy. Many of the people were barefoot, some rode horses; children, still with their holiday feeling, ran gleefully along the caravan; some rode on the backs of farm cows, others led goats. As many as three families jammed into an old debatable Buick. Pickup trucks were piled unbelievably with the possessions of a lifetime—chairs and tables, mattresses and blankets, a trunkful of memories, a broken Shinto shrine, bundles of farm equipment spliced by wire, framed pictures of ancestors, the pump handle of a well, pots to cook in, bathtubs—and in one case, an entire bathroom; lanterns and buckets and clothes and shoes and food, a wooden cupboard painted bright red, cartons of dishes. A great strapping Hawaiian woman more than sixty years old strode along the highway, her grandson perched on one shoulder, a television set on the other.

Hawaii National Guardsmen were spaced at intervals along the highway, directing the mass exodus. The people who owned no vehicle of their own loaded their possessions onto National Guard trucks, then jumped aboard the trucks themselves and joined the procession northward. Lines of weariness bit into the faces of the refugees. Lines of disenchantment drew about their mouths. Their eyes were bleak and puzzled, but undefeated. They had lived fruitfully all their lives upon the rich tablelands of Mauna Loa's northwestern slope, and they would return to it.

Above the village, the sky was ghostly unreal; a thick, suffocating blood-red cloud. A hot volcanic rain whipped through the streets. Captain Hirozawa led Doc Judd up an alleyway off the main street and then along a curving dirt road. Chickens scattered at their advance.

"Here's the house," Captain Hirozawa said. "And there's the old fella right there."

It was a little wooden tenant shack that seemed on the verge of collapse. Unlike the other houses in the village, it was completely in place. Not a single piece of furniture had been moved. The lawn was neat and uncluttered. Behind the house the wire chicken coop was still latched, the fowl skittering nervously to and fro. There was absolutely no evidence of intended flight. Quite to the contrary, Doc Judd thought, it seemed that the house and its owners were determined to stand firm.

An ancient, wrinkled Japanese farmer sat placidly on the porch, rocking back and forth in his chair. Several of his neighbors were talking to him in Japanese, gesticulating vigorously, pointing to the lava flow. But the old man just grinned at them and shook his head, rocking back and forth and listening to their entreaties with stoic politeness. He was bald. His face was the color of, and had the furrows of, an old raisin. But there was in it a dignity, an ancient peace which gave Doc Judd the distinct impression that the old farmer had found the security for which the rest of the world hungered, and consequently was assured that it had not disappeared from the earth.

"What's the old fellow's name?"

"Moto," Captain Hirozawa answered him. "Sesue Moto."

"You're kidding."

"No. That's his real name."

Doc Judd walked to the rickety steps of the house and rested one foot against the lowest step.

"Mr. Moto, you speak English?"

"No," the old man answered distinctly.

"You don't speak any English?"

"No."

Doc Judd wiped his brow with a handkerchief. His shirt was sticking to his back like a wet sheet. Perspiration streamed down his cheeks.

"Mr. Moto, you must leave here."

"No." The old man smiled peacefully. There was not a single tooth in his head.

"You do not speak any English at all, Mr. Moto?"
"No."
"But you do understand me when I tell you that you must leave your house."
"No."
Doc Judd turned hopelessly to the National Guard captain. "Okay," he said, "you tell him. Make it clear to him and explain why he's got to get out."
Captain Hirozawa grinned at the old man. The neighbors who had gathered about him started jabbering at him once Doc Judd had given up, and Captain Hirozawa elbowed through these people now and spoke to the old man in Japanese. Doc Judd watched him. The captain was friendly yet firm. He alternated between insistence and cajolery. But the old man merely continued shaking his head no.
Mr. Moto did not exactly stand up: he seemed rather to unhinge himself into an upright position, into a debris of time-rotted joints and angles, his body older than the sun; and he led the way inside the house, walking slowly, with the worn and intricate fragility of the very old. It was a dark, hot, dusty shack. On a cot in the far corner a white ghost slept. Captain Hirozawa whispered to Doc Judd that the ghost was the old man's wife.
Doc Judd did not believe the woman could weigh more than sixty pounds. He bent down before the cheap cardboard Shinto shrine that stood alongside the bed and listened to her heartbeat. He was surprised at its evenness and strength.
"Mr. Moto does not believe she can be moved," the captain said.
"Tell him that we'll take her with us. She can be moved. Explain to him that I'm a doctor and I say it's all right."
It seemed to take forever for the captain to get the message across to the old man. But finally Mr. Moto grinned and bowed; then pointed excitedly to the Shinto shrine.
"Yes," Doc Judd said. "The shrine too. Everything that's in the house. Tell him we won't leave anything behind. It will all be safe."
In a few minutes a National Guard truck and an ambulance pulled to a stop in front of the house. The neighbors hurriedly moved the Motos' scarce possessions into the truck. Doc Judd watched silently from a corner of the house as the old farmer

helped his wife to her feet. He wrapped her tenderly in a robe and blanket, and then the two of them kneeled before the shrine, oblivious of the commotion around them. They remained there for a long time in prayer, the sibilance of their lips droning ceaselessly through the room while lazy insolent flies buzzed about their heads and the room was stripped bare. Finally the ancient couple padded soundlessly from the house and descended the stairs, helping each other with slow reverence. At the bottom of the steps they turned and stared at their home with the forlorn passivity of ancient Orientals; and as one of the neighbors walked from the house carrying the Shinto shrine, they turned again and moved with their terrific, undefeated slowness to the ambulance. The volcanic dust hung heavily in the air while the ambulance tooled down the rutted road toward the highway; and, Doc Judd thought, gazing after them, it would be in the air a long time after they left.

By ten o'clock that morning, Kealakekua was an inferno. From the steps of the coffee mill, Doc Judd gazed south along the village which seemed a tinderbox of noise and flame and trembling earth. The lava flow had rumbled through the southern section of the village and one explosion followed another in earsplitting succession. Torrents of sparks pierced the sky and descended slowly, almost lazily, through the murky clouds of blood-colored smoke. From far up the highway he could hear the rise and fall and roar of many voices, growing constantly louder, like the breaking of a great surf against the shore. He could see the Buddhist Temple and the row of stores next to it burst suddenly into flame. A squadron of National Guardsmen was strung out across Mamalahoa Highway, arms linked, walking north through the village ahead of the flow; making sure no one would be trapped behind. Ahead of these Guardsmen, the last of the straggling evacuees hurried into the waiting trucks. Two ambulances tagged along at the rear of the processional and as these drove slowly past the coffee mill, Doc Judd turned to Captain Hirozawa and said, "Well, we've got everybody out."

Captain Hirozawa seemed bitter. There were unmistakable wounds in his eyes.

"Is this your—your home village, Captain?" Doc Judd asked, eying the young man thoughtfully.

"Yes," he said quietly. "It was."

"Are your people all right?"

"Yes," the captain answered, gazing bitterly at the blazing village. "They left early this morning. I made sure of that. Everybody is safely out of town now, Doc Judd."

To the south, they could see the vast relentless flow coiling down and mauling the village like a monster serpent with a fifty-foot head, striking venomously. Thin little ripples of fear that started in Doc Judd's stomach coursed outward through his entire body so that the fingers that rubbed the strain from his brow were cold even though he was perspiring heavily. He could feel his temples begin to throb from the heat. The smoke and sulphuric dust burned his nostrils and lungs and he started coughing.

"We'd bettah get out of here ourselves, Doc."

As they got into their jeep, there was a sudden crash of timbers falling nearby. Doc looked up and saw a thin tongue of flame lick through the roof of the coffee mill.

"We'd bettah hurry," the captain said, firing up the jeep.

They pulled quickly out from the alleyway behind the coffee mill. Ahead of them was a tunnel of fire from the buildings that were burning now on both sides of the highway. A glare brighter than a dozen suns dazzled their eyes. The scorching heat seared their skins. The roaring, crackling, crashing inferno beat down against their ears in painful waves. For an eternity, it seemed, they were in the midst of a flaming, wrathful torrent. Then, as the buildings started collapsing into the highway behind them, they made it out of the flame tunnel.

Captain Hirozawa sped north along the highway, catching up with the tail end of the caravan. As they neared Kainaliu the trees thinned out and the tall flames cast monstrous shadows across the highway.

"The caravan seems to be slowing down," Doc Judd remarked.

"Look over there. One of the Howland Ranch horses."

As Doc looked in the direction the captain indicated, he saw a badly cut and frightened roan gelding with the familiar HR brand on its rump, loping along with the caravan. Several men were chasing it and one finally coaxed it close and grabbed its loose reins and mounted it.

A mile north of the village of Kainaliu the caravan came to a halt.

"Pull over to the far side," Doc said. "Let's see what's going on."

A patrol car of National Guardsmen bore down upon them from the north and came to a stop alongside them.

"The highway's blocked!" one of the Guardsmen shouted. He jumped quickly out of the patrol car and went to the jeep. "Mamalahoa Highway is impassable up at Kuakini. A flow of lava has crossed the highway. It's blocked for about a hundred yards."

Doc Judd stared at the youngster with disbelief. "My God, are you sure?"

"Yessir."

"When did this happen?"

"We're not sure, sir. Last night or this morning."

"Christ! There's no break in the flow?"

"No sir. We sent a jeep inland to scout the flow. It's pouring over Kuakini Bluff—that old lava barrier—straight across Howland grazeland and the highway to the sea. Nothing can get across."

A crowd had gathered about them. Doc Judd said nothing. He continued staring dumbly at the young Guardsman. The youngster shuffled his feet uncertainly. He looked up at Captain Hirozawa.

"Those people up there—at the front of the column—they're not too good, Cap'n. They're scared. And I guess I don't blame 'em. I'm scared too."

"Things will work out," Captain Hirozawa said. "At Kailua and at Hilo they must know that we're trapped. They'll send in 'copters."

"Incidentally, Doctor Judd," the young Guardsman said, "we found one of the paniolos from the Howland Ranch up near the front. He was lying in a ditch. His leg is broken."

"When did that happen?"

"I don't know. We found him a couple of hours ago. Maybe he was riding down here to warn us."

"You're sure his leg is broken?"

"No doubt about it, Doc. He's unconscious most of the time. He's been in pretty bad pain. We gave him a shot. But he's been in awful pain."

"All right. I'll drive up there with you." Doc Judd's eyes roamed across the crowd that had gathered about the two cars. He looked past the crowd to the long file of immobile cars and trucks trapped along the highway. "You'd better stay here, Captain. I'll be back as soon as I can."

He followed the youngster to the patrol car. The people separated to form an aisle for him. Now that they had digested the news that the northern escape was blocked, they stood about like dreamwalkers, their eyes focused panoramically, not seeing any detail but seeing instead the whole vista of the Kona Coast, burning now on three sides of them—and the thirteen-hundred-foot pali cliffs west of them. There was in their faces no panic yet; no hysteria. But Earl Judd knew that there soon would be.

When the evacuation first started, the eyes of the people showed strain and sorrow; as if, the worst having happened, they had nothing more to fear. They had feared the eruption and the ruination of their homes and lands and fields and village by lava. They had feared the loss of all their years upon those fields; and the loss even of all their worldly possessions. And as the evacuation started, the people knew that they had lost their homes and their fields and their village and the worst that could happen to them had happened and it was not too unbearable after all. Now they understood for the first time that the worst that could happen had not happened; had not even threatened to happen until now. Yet they remained silent, mute, without horror. Whatever lay buried in their hearts had not yet moved to their faces.

As he looked at their faces, they all turned south, as if on signal, as the boiling muck of lava completed its devastation of Kealakekua, rumbled to the edge of the pali and poured down in a flaming cascade to the sea. Explosions shattered the air as the lava hit the ocean waters. A huge cloud of steam scudded up into the sky.

In a few moments, Doc Judd thought, Kealakekua Bay and the monument marking Captain Cook's discovery of the Islands would be buried beneath the lava. Pulverized coral reefs and blocks of lava would be hurled upward from underwater explosions; and fragments of sharks and strange deepwater fish would float to the surface, belly-up and boiled. The village of Kealakekua and the Captain Cook monument were now only memories.

Doc Judd got into the patrol car, slammed the door behind him, and the young Guardsman turned the car slowly north. Up ahead of them, Doc recognized the furry white head of Reverend Kamuela. He was standing on the top of the cab of one of the

National Guard trucks. A large crowd had gathered about him. He held a prayer book in his hand and he was reading to the crowd. The people looked neither right nor left, but straight down at the ground, their eyes vacant, inward. They seemed like ghosts.

Reverend Kamuela's arm was raised toward heaven and his voice carried resonantly above the rumble and hiss of lava.

"In his despair, Job bowed his head and cried: Out of this earth cometh bread, and under it is fire. The stones of it are the place of sapphires, and it hath dust of gold. Yet if my lands cry against me, then thistles will grow instead of wheat, and cockles instead of barley.

"And the Lord said to Job: Who hath measured the waters in the hollow of his hand, and meted out heaven with a span, and comprehended the dust in a measure, and weighed the mountains in scales and the hills in balance? Where wast thou when I laid the foundations of the earth? Whereupon are these foundations founded? Who laid the cornerstone thereof, while the morning stars sang together and all the sons of God shouted for joy?"

Doc Judd listened a moment more as the people started singing a hymn. Then he nodded to the young Guardsman and the car continued north along the highway. Doc Judd turned and watched the old Hawaiian preacher through the rear window. He was still standing on top of the truck, his hand raised to heaven, while behind him, the dark mountain hung unbearably in the distance; the mountain, Earl Judd thought, that had produced these fertile lands and for a time loaned them to these people and now was reclaiming them. Let it reclaim only the land, Doc Judd prayed.

The sun moved directly overhead. Up at the Kuakini intersection, where the front of the caravan was trapped and halted by the new lava flow, a little Hawaiian girl jumped down and stood by the tailgate of her father's truck. Her eyes were wide with fear. In the ditch alongside the highway—not fifteen yards from where she stood—she could see the wild boar, glaring angrily at her.

The boar snorted. Then, with erratic decision, he bounded up from the ditch and stood for several seconds on the edge of the highway, in full view.

The little girl screamed. Her brother leaped from the truck to the highway and threw a rock at the boar. It struck the animal's shoulder and he backed off a few spaces and raised his head belligerently. The children's father hurled a spade at the boar. In a few seconds a dozen people started throwing rocks and pots and anything they could lay their hands on at the boar. A pack of timorous curs yipped at him.

But when the boar retreated inland across the rolling grazeland, the dogs grew bolder and gave chase. Several of the children and a few grownups joined in the chase. Two men on horseback galloped inland after the boar. The lead horseman held a rifle in his hand but he did not shoot yet for fear of hitting the children. A jeep with three National Guardsmen rumbled down the ditch and up the inland embankment. In a few seconds, the jeep was rocking across the grazeland, leading the chase. None believed the old boar represented any true danger. He was just an ugly thing, universally despised; an object against which they could release their fears and wrath.

The boar loped inland along the lava flow. He had been running for so long now that his heartbeat, his muscles, had grown immune to the punishment and functioned now not like animal organs but like the sockets and joints of a perpetual motion machine. He was running nowhere and fleeing from everything and his rhythm-hypnotized muscles flowed smoothly and insensately and he sensed that if he ever did stop running they would scream in agony. But as yet he was not particularly exhausted and not exactly without hope and he did not especially dread the lava rivers any more, nor did he wish especially to outdistance the men. He ran with a hypnotic steadiness and no attempt at guile. He was far beyond outrage now, and beyond bafflement and, to a point, beyond suffering. He had reached a point where his instinct for life had changed into a savage and invulnerable curiosity concerning his capabilities of being further affronted; what next could be invented by lava or man for him to bear? He was mesmerized. Flight had become his way of life. He loped inland a mile and a half until he reached the promontory over which the day before he had watched the firefall of lava cascade down into the grazeland. He heard the rifle reports behind him. The first two shots missed him. But the third thudded burningly into his rump, spilling him. He got up quickly and galloped north. He found the brown earth through the lava flow. It was a path thirty yards wide underneath the overhanging promontory. It stretched out before him more than a hundred yards, like a tunnel. He raced through it to the clear open country on the opposite end.

The horsemen galloped through after him. Then the jeep. When the horsemen reached the clear country on the other side, they caught their last fleeting glimpse of the old boar darting in a zigzag path back up the mountain slope. One of the riders took two final shots at him. When the noise died away he looked grimly and disappointedly up at the mountain slope.

"You get the sonofabitch?" his companion asked.

"No." The rifleman shook his head.

The jeep had come to a stop and one of the Guardsmen pointed up the mountain. "There he goes."

But the boar was out of range.

The driver of the jeep set the vehicle in reverse and turned around. "Well, it was something to do."

The horsemen trotted alongside the jeep back through the lava break. When they had gone through the break and had turned back toward the highway, it was the driver of the jeep who first realized it; understood it. He slammed the jeep to a stop and looked dazedly at his companions. "My God!" he exclaimed.

The rifleman pulled in his horse and swung his gaze toward the break in the lava. "Sonofabitch!" he said. "And to think, we nearly killed him."

They went as fast as they could back to the highway and the caravan.

Sloan dismounted and looped the reins of her horse around the fender of a Red Cross mobile unit which had been stationed at the northern end of the lava break. She was, she thought, no good at all. She wished she could be of some help. But her nerves were on edge. All she could do was pace restlessly about the edge of the tunnel-like lava break, waiting for Dean to be brought through. She chased from her mind any doubts as to his being found. He had to be found.

It was not yet sundown, but the light was shifting rapidly and the first stars had come out. Sloan had ridden from Manoalani to the cutoff flow early in the afternoon, when she had learned from Aaron that Dean had ridden back down to Kealakekua to warn the civil defense of the cutoff flow. She had ridden back and forth along the northern bank of the flow, searching for a way across. But she had not ridden inland far enough to discover the break. She had not ridden to the break until she saw, by midafternoon, the dust of the first cars of the caravan rolling slowly northwest through the break.

When the boar hunters had returned with word of the lava break, a bridge had been constructed over the ditch alongside the highway. Slowly, all during the afternoon, the caravan rolled across the bridge and inland along the south bank of the flow, the cars and trucks and wagons pitching awkwardly across the grazeland. By midafternoon, the lead jeeps and the horsemen who had ridden after the boar led the caravan through the lava break.

Impatiently, Sloan watched the people come through. Their heads were held high, undefeated and imperishable. They laughed and made improbable jokes concerning Pele and the lava flow. As dusk settled, the headlights of the cars and trucks were turned on and luau torches were lit at the northern side of the tunnel for the vehicles to guide themselves by. Sloan could see the long single file driving slowly northwest across Howland grazeland, free of the lava flow now, heading toward the continuation of the highway.

As the last few cars and trucks rumbled safely through the lava break, Sloan walked to the edge of the path where a tall National Guard captain was directing the traffic.

"How many people are still left on the other side?"

Captain Hirozawa looked at her tiredly. "Not many now. Maybe a dozen cars and trucks. A few ambulances. Everyone is safe."

"I'm looking for a Howland ranch hand. He rode down to Kealakekua last night. Just when the flow crossed. I haven't seen him come out."

"Probably in one of the last few cars."

"Dean Kahana—do you know him?"

Captain Hirozawa searched her face. "Oh—I recognize you now, Miss Howland. Mrs. Kahana," he corrected. "No. I don't know him." He continued directing the caravan traffic, waving his arm to guide the advance of the trucks and cars as they rumbled out from the dark overhang.

"I heard something about a Howland paniolo earlier this afternoon. He got hurt somehow. I think Doc Judd might still be with him."

"Hurt—" Sloan gasped.

"We've been pretty busy. I might have heard wrong."

"Where is Doc Judd?"

"He's on the other side, at the end of the caravan; waiting until everyone else is out safe."

Sloan mumbled thanks and hurried past him.

"Hea wait! You can't go in there!"

But she had worked her way to the entrance of the lava break and was hurrying past the oncoming cars and trucks. When she reached the southern side of the break, she saw only seven trucks waiting to drive through. She peered into the trucks, but did not see Dean. Behind the trucks were two ambulances, and she ran down toward these.

"Sloan!"

She whirled around.

"Sloan, what are you doing here!"

She saw Doc Judd skip down from the running board of the first ambulance and trot toward her.

"Doc, have you seen Dean? God, I haven't been able to find him! He rode down last night to—"

Doc Judd hugged his arm about her shoulders and quieted her. She was trembling. "Easy, easy: he's all right." His voice sounded even more tired than he looked. "Come on," he said, leading her to the rear door of the old-style Red Cross ambulance. "He's in here. I didn't get finished setting his leg until about a half-hour ago."

"His leg—?"

"Broken. He's pretty well doped-up; but he's all right."

It was dark inside the vault of the ambulance. When her eyes became accustomed to the dark, she could see his head stir against the pale sheets of the cot.

"Here, Sloan," he whispered.

She knelt on the floor and wound her arms about his neck and kissed him. "Oh my God, my God, I was so scared! I was afraid I had lost you too, Dean."

He tightened his arm about her and in a few moments the trembling ceased. The ambulance rumbled through the lava break and started on its way across the grazeland toward Manoalani.

They held each other very close and in a little while her thin passive hysteria slid out from her heart without a sound.

Willard Howland stood bleakly on the veranda, an old tattered king watching his empire burn before the onslaught of the enemy. He was leaning forward, his hand wound tightly about the railing; his dark eyes, which had seen too much too long, bitterly traced the course of the first Hickam Field bomber as it roared overhead.

Garth stood beside him. "If your eyes were antiaircraft batteries there wouldn't be a plane left in the sky."

Willard did not answer him. He stiffened perceptively, his head still low, his eyes following the flight of the bomber the way the eyes of a hawk would follow distant carrion. He watched the bomber turn and level off just above the flank eruption. When the first bombs exploded against the northwestern slope of the volcano, his body seemed to become more rigid. His face became dry and bloodless as a dead moon, and swallowing the dark-veined rage that swelled in his throat, he turned to Garth and said, "The goddamn eruption ruined what? Forty thousand acres? The bombers will ruin the rest."

"We can't get our backs up, old fellow," Garth said quietly. "It's got to be done."

"Have you convinced yourself of that?"

"They've got to try and save Kailua."

"At Manoalani's expense," Willard muttered heavily. "That bombing is going to redirect the flow away from Kailua, straight through here."

"No, you know better. They're trying to explode the source tunnel. If they can score a direct hit on the source tunnel, it will clog up the entire flow. The fronts of the flow won't get fresh lava energy and will stop moving."

"If—" Willard said with disdain. He turned his eyes to the volcano as a second plane released its bombs against the slope.

A thin midmorning sun spread its pale light upon the veranda and upon the uncropped lawn that stretched to the sea road. The lawn was littered with debris. More than a hundred evacuees from Kealakekua had camped at Manoalani during the night. Although all of these had gone on into Kailua earlier that morning, the lawn was still covered with rows upon rows of Army cots, several tents, crudely assembled lean-tos, and an assortment of cooking pots and pans, plates, blown paper and a variety of litter. The veranda too was in a shambles from the people who had eaten and slept on it. The caravan of evacuees, when they had made it safely out of the trap through the lava break, had descended upon Manoalani like a flood. The lawn and veranda and living room and dining room and even the stables had been turned into overnight sleeping quarters. All through the night there was a constant turmoil: people were cooking and washing and lifting and putting down and moving and gabbing and waiting in line at the toilets and at the two mobile Red Cross units. Dogs and goats and cattle and children endlessly crisscrossed the area, adding to the confusion. All during the burning night, the lawns of Manoalani were covered with prostrate men and women, too tired or weak or scared to go on any further. The night had been unbearably hot, and the flies swarmed through the house, fat and insolent and bold. The evacuees chatted softly among themselves, restless, and the steady stream of cars and trucks from Kailua rolled across the lawn with volunteers bringing freshly cooked meals.

Laura and Kapiolani Kahana, and later Sloan, after she had first gotten Dean settled for the night in an upstairs bedroom, worked tirelessly among the people until almost dawn. And now, toward noon, the people had all departed and old Willard gazed with disgust at the soiled lawns until the sight so sickened him that he could look at it no longer and he swung his eyes to the volcano again, cursing in a bitter steady unrepetitive stream the Air Force bombers as they poured their black staccato slashes into the slope.

After a while, Aaron and Earl Judd drove the ranch station wagon over the macadam and pulled to a stop in front of the main stairs leading to the veranda. Doc Judd stepped out of the wagon and mounted the stairs, grinning at Willard. "That's a pretty shade of purple you're wearing on your face," he said. "You look as though each exploding bomb is giving you a separate attack of auricular fibrillation." His fingers circled old Willard's wrist and counted the pulse beat at over two hundred. "Come on inside, Will," he said gently. "We're going to have to knock that down."

"I don't want any of your goddamned horse pills," Willard

said, shaking away Doc Judd's hand and tramping heavily ahead of him into the study. "Trouble is, you've been running this evacuation as badly as you run that abortion mill of yours down by Keauhou."

Doc Judd got him to lie down on the couch in the study and injected a shot to bring down the blood pressure. As he was putting away his syringe, he said, quite matter-of-factly: "In case you haven't heard, Senator, I don't own an abortion mill any more. There's no more abortion mill or home or office, and no more drydock. There's no more Keauhou. It went last night."

Old Willard stared at him mutely for a moment, shaking his head. Then he rested his head back on a pillow and closed his eyes. "I'm sorry, Earl."

When Willard dozed off, Doc Judd joined Garth and Aaron on the veranda. "He should rest peacefully for the afternoon," he told them. "Be sure you keep the old guy under wraps."

"Do you want a drink, Doc?" Garth suggested.

"Not yet. Too much work still to do. Maybe I'll come back tonight and have twenty."

"It'll be here waiting for you."

"If there's anything left of the house by tonight," Aaron added.

Earl Judd frowned. "Well, we can hope for the best," he said without conviction. "Where is Sloan?"

"Sleeping," Garth informed him. "She and Kapi and Laura worked until dawn with the evacuees."

"When she wakes up, tell her that I want Dean moved to the hospital at Kailua. I've reserved a place for him there. I think old Willard should be taken up there too."

"It'll take a bulldozer to move him away from Manoalani," Garth said.

"Pretend it's some kind of a trip for him."

"He wouldn't fall for that. He plans to stay glued to the veranda as long as Mauna Loa keeps erupting."

"Well, somehow you've got to move him out of here tonight. Don't let him get the idea that you're evacuating Manoalani. He's not too bad now, considering everything. But if he starts suspicioning that Manoalani's being given up, he'll fly into a rage. And it could well be his last rage. I don't want him to be around when that flow starts moving in close."

"You don't give us much of a chance, do you, Doc?" Garth asked.

Earl Judd glanced fondly at the house, its massive entranceway, the peeling columns of the veranda. "I've known and loved this place for nearly a half century. It's withstood some strange and terrible things, and it's known some truly wonderful times too, but I don't think it can make it through this."

"What about tonight?" Aaron asked him.

"You should be all right tonight. Especially if those bombers break up the flow. But if they don't, then before noon tomorrow you should have everything you want to save moved out of here."

From the co-pilot's seat in the lead bomber, Professor Norton Jaeger looked down at the island with utter dismay. The flow, now in its sixth day, including Christmas Eve, inundated the island from the summit of Mauna Loa northwest more than twenty miles to the Kona Coast. The lava river had widened as it descended, devastating the entire northwest slope of the mountain and a swathe of coastlands from Kealakekua north beyond Keauhou to the Kuakini intersection, and it was still serpentining northwestward now, up along the coast toward Kailua.

Five planes had been dispatched to divert the flow. Their bellies were loaded with five three-hundred-pound testing bombs and twenty six-hundred-pound TNT bombs. The test bombs had been dropped. Now each plane flew across the northwestern slope of Mauna Loa at twenty-minute intervals in an effort to bomb the source tunnel of the eruption.

Professor Jaeger grinned without relish at Colonel Green. "Well, bombing the source tunnel worked against Hilo some time back. Let's hope it proves the trick that will save Kailua."

Colonel Green banked the plane and leveled off at an altitude of 10,000 feet, approximately 4,000 feet above the rift-zone eruption that had been designated as the prime target.

"You want me to hold on a straight line down the slope?" Colonel Green asked.

"That's right. We're not interested in the summit eruption. We want to destroy the flank eruption. That's the one that's causing all the trouble." Jaeger pointed to the rift zone just ahead of them down the slope. It seemed to him that the flank eruption had not diminished since the day he and Garth had flown over it. A row of immense cinder cones had been built up along the fault and from these fire fountains continued to shoot into the sky, the lava spiraling up two hundred feet, then cataracting down to begin its slushy, smoking flow across the land. If anything, Professor Jaeger thought, the activity seemed greater now than it had several days ago.

"Underneath this rift in the volcano slope," he explained to Colonel Green, "is a deep subterranean lava cave. It is the main source of supply to the flow. This source tunnel feeds the lava out from the inner mountain mass to the fronts of the flow up there near Kailua. The underground lava chamber is only about a hundred yards wide. To knock it out will take pinpoint bombing. We need a direct hit. If we can destroy this source tunnel, explode its guts so that the debris will pile into it and the pent-up gas underneath can escape, then the lava will be cooled and lose its energy. It will just pool and gurgle for a week or so but it won't move, because the tunnel system linking the front of the flow with the source will be broken up. The front will lose all energy and come to a stop, before"—he crossed his fingers—"it gets into Kailua."

Colonel Green grinned at him. Then he pushed the button on his intercom system. "Pilot to bombardier, pilot to bombardier, we are approaching target."

And a second later he said, "Over target."

Craning his neck, Professor Jaeger could see the explosions far below as the bombs broke into the rift zone. They made two complete runs, but the source tunnel gave no indication of suffering a direct hit. They peeled off and the second bomber flew in.

The wild boar trotted stolidly along a trail worn deep by cattle and horses. He came to a sloping mesa and paused a moment, warily. Beyond the rim of the mesa he could see flame. He smelled the thick odor of lava. He decided to skirt the mesa and move on north, where the skies were clear blue. The bullet wound in the muscle of his hip did not bother him. He felt quite strong. Almost confident. He would get far north under blue skies and sleep and eat for a week.

He plunged around the mesa. The bomb exploded thirty yards ahead of him. Tons of clinker lava were hurled into the air above him. A fragment the size of a basketball smashed down against his shoulder, searing his fur and hide. The shock more than the actual pain caused him to panic. He galloped blindly up a gully. In his nostrils was the scent of his own burned hair and hide.

The bank of the gully was unsure. He missed a step and rolled over, kicking. He struck a ledge of burning lava. He leaped from it and began running wildly again, his back in flames. He saw the plane come in again and he shook his head at it in his old blending of impotence and rage. He bared his tusks and managed to utter his final cry of defiance before the bomb tore the earth from under him.

That evening Sloan listened to the dark iron of the bells at St. Peter's Church. Seven o'clock. She had dozed off in the chair alongside the bed in which Dean lay motionless.

It was dark in the room. Through the window she could see the turning sky, lilac-colored and deepening with night. A hot breeze stirred the curtains. She stood up and walked to the window and closed it.

"Hello."

She turned toward the bed. "How long have you been awake?"

"Ten minutes," Dean said. "I've been watchin' you."

"I guess I fell asleep. I'm a rotten nurse."

"You're the best nurse in the world."

"How do you feel?"

"Like havin' you closer to me."

"You must be getting better," Sloan grinned.

"I love you."

She sat down on the edge of the bed and took his hand in hers and bent over it and kissed it softly several times and pressed it against her cheek.

"Sloan—"

"What?"

"Come into bed with me."

"Dean—"

"Come into bed with me."

"No." She turned and lay down next to him on top of the bed. She put her arm about his head and pressed it gently to her breast.

"We're almost all alone in the house," she said.

"Where is everybody?"

"Doc Judd came back after dinner. He insisted that everyone who could, clear out. Laura and the baby, and Coyama and your mother went to Kailua for the night. He came up here to see how you were but you were sleeping. You had a temperature then—you're still burning up, for that matter—and he decided maybe it would do you more good to sleep here for the night. He's reserved a room for you at the hospital tomorrow."

"Where's the Senatah?"

"Sleeping downstairs in the study. Garth and Aaron are staying here with us tonight. Just in case. Then tomorrow, you and Daddy go into the hospital."

"I'm not goin' into any hospital."

"Yes. You and Daddy both. You can play chess together . . . or something."

"They won't get me in any hospital and I doubt they'll get the Senatah."

"Did you hear the bombers this afternoon?"

"Yes. I think so."

"They kept it up all afternoon. I thought they'd waken you. Daddy was on the veranda all afternoon, cursing them. I thought he'd have apoplexy. They're bombing grazeland—they were toward the end, I mean."

"Did they hit the source tunnel?"

"We think so."

"Has the flow stopped?"

"No. It's slowed down. It's only moved about a mile this afternoon. If it hasn't completely stopped, all its energy and drive have been bombed out anyway, thank God."

"Then why do we all have to get out of here?"

"Just a precaution, I guess. Doc Judd was worried mainly about you and Daddy. Since neither of you can move any too well."

"We won't have to move."

"I don't think so either. But if we have to make a move tonight, Garth and Aaron can help you."

"We won't have to. You'll see."

"I hope not. The radio report said the bombing was successful and Kailua was out of danger."

"So are we. What are Garth and Aaron doing?"

"Garth is out at the stables. We've kept half a dozen horses here. There was no room for them in the van. Garth is saddling them so we can move them out the first thing in the morning. Aaron and some of the hands moved the downstairs furniture out on the vans before supper. The piano, all the living room furniture; they've even taken the chandelier. It's strange-looking downstairs now, all bare and brooding. Almost defeated. In a way . . . it made me feel that Manoalani itself was surrendering. Daddy watched them move the furniture. That was when Doc Judd was trying to persuade him to go to the hospital tonight. Daddy looked so sad. Crestfallen. I've never seen him like that before. It was as if, you know—his children had disappointed him, his health and heart had buckled, his dreams of the delegacy had all gone up in smoke, and now his land . . . I nearly cried, watching him. But after they had stripped the living room bare, he seemed to look at them—Aaron and the rest, and Doc Judd—with contempt. You know that look of his; all that fierce old arrogance burning in his eyes. He just turned his back to all of it and walked into the study, his hands feeling every speck of wall and drape and bannister, as if the house itself was the last thing he could rely on; as if everything else could fail him, but Manoalani would remain."

She traced her fingers along the profile of his face. His eyes were like dark stones and there was an expression on his face as if he was waiting for the pain to start after being hit. She leaned over and kissed him and there was no pain.

"What are you thinking about, Sloan?"

"Us."

"Are you happy now?"

"Yes. Very happy, in a way." Her face was serious. "Yes, I am happy, Dean. I've learned at last to accept the past and everything that's happened. I've learned that pain need not be pointless if you can direct its result. I've learned it purposely. Because if I couldn't accept the past and its burden and pain, then I would have no future, for without one there can't be the other and only out of the past can you make a future. And I want the future."

He tried to turn to take her in his arms, but he was unable to. He reached for her and she moved close to him, kissing him. "Oh God, Sloan, I love you so much. I want you near me all the time."

She got up hurriedly and went over to the door and bolted it. She returned to the bedside and began unbuttoning her light cotton dress, and as he watched her, he could see in her face the fine yielding courage and dignity of woman; the glory she had always been to him.

Many years afterwards, the people of the Kona Coast were to speak of that final, dying spurt of lava with reverence and a mystical awe: for it has been in the need and nature of man since Adam to worship gods of thunder, and to attribute to natural phenomena a symbolic and oftentimes macabre spiritualism. Years afterwards the people of the Kona Coast were to say that Pele had directed that ultimate flow: that she had looked down upon it out of her red lidless eye while in its smoke somewhere, dawn held like a breath suspended, and the flaming river curved along the macadam beneath the high solemn grace of the palms into the colonnades of Manoalani. They were to say that it was an act of vengeance, and only Sloan knew differently. But she was never to utter a word about it.

She awoke at that time which was neither day nor dawn nor night. There was a reflection of flame upon her bedroom window. Dean was sleeping soundly. She slipped out of bed and wrapped a robe about her nightdress. She tiptoed to the window. Outside, the stables were blazing. She could see Aaron hurrying toward the stables to set the horses free. A flame galloped frantically across the lawn, then rolled over and went out. The horse stood up for a moment, dazed and screeching in pain, then collapsed. The fetid stench from the stables almost nauseated Sloan. A scream started up from her stomach. She shrank back from the window and clapped her hand to her mouth, feeling that she was going to vomit.

She fled from the room and hurried downstairs. Her teeth were chattering, but so great was her shock that she was not aware of it. The front doors were opened wide. When she reached them, she stopped suddenly and slumped back against the wall of the veranda. She could see, at the foot of the stairs, her father standing rigidly and defiantly with his back to her, while forty yards down the macadam the dark red-veined smoking torrent of lava curled toward Manoalani. The blast of its heat was insufferable. The massive columns were browning and beginning to smoke. The face of Manoalani had taken on a burnt color from the heat.

Sloan screamed. Her face twisted grossly. Her fists were

clenched tight and her eyes were squeezed shut. She screamed several times and then buried her face in her hands and sank down on the steps. But in a second she was on her feet again, unsteadily. It was as if she was suspended in a steel grip and she did not recognize Garth until he slapped her sharply across the face.

"Snap out of it! C'mon, Sloan, snap out of it! Get Dean!" Garth shouted at her. "Go up with Dean! We'll be right up for you."

When he released her, she slumped back against one of the columns. It felt like a hot bar against her back. She was breathless and dizzy and sick to her stomach and she stared with sleepwalker's eyes at Garth as he led old Willard down the length of the veranda and hurried him inside the station wagon. "I'll be back as soon as I get the old fellow down to the Red Cross unit on the highway," Garth called to her. "Get Aaron to help you with Dean. Bring him around to the back of the house."

Sloan watched the station wagon plunge across the lawn to the searoad. Then she turned and for a second she watched the mountainous lava rumble toward the veranda. She hurried into the house and up the staircase. She tripped on her robe. When she fell, she cut her head against a corner of the bannister and she froze for a moment on the stairs. She tried to collect her scattered emotions. She tried to breathe more easily. If she could only get one deep breath, way down into her lungs; a clear breath. If her heart would only stop hammering for a moment. She rose dizzily and continued up the stairs. When she reached the bedroom, Dean was sprawled across the floor. He looked up at her helplessly. "I—I tried to get out of bed and make it to the door myself. I thought I could get out by myself," he said.

She stooped over him. "Can you move?"

"I think so."

"Put your arm around my shoulder."

She helped him stand. His bedclothes were soaking wet. His skin felt as if it were on fire. He shuddered violently, then gritted his teeth in an effort to overcome it.

She tightened her arm around his waist and they hobbled to the door. The heavy cast on his leg made their movements tortuously slow and awkward.

"Aaron will be here to give us a hand," she told him.

When they reached the head of the stairs, the entire forward wing of Manoalani was in flames. Smoke curled upwards at them and for an eternity, it seemed, she coughed and reeled on the staircase.

"Get blankets," he told her. "And wet them down."

"Can you stay here?"

"I'll have to."

She raced back to the bedroom, stripped the sheets from the bed and took a blanket from the closet. She pushed open the bathroom door and turned the shower on full force, dousing the sheets and the blanket. She wrapped the sheets and the blanket about Dean and herself, and slowly they started down the curving staircase. She missed a step once, stumbled, and almost lost her grip on him, but recovered. When they were four steps from the landing, Dean's foot caught in the dragging sheet. She saw it happening and tightened her grip on him. But his weight plus the weight of the cast was too much for her. They fell back against the curved wall of the stairwell and tumbled to the landing.

She landed on top of him. She was unhurt but the wind was knocked out of her. Dean was knocked unconscious by the fall. She rolled over on the floor, sucking in deep breaths. When she looked at his inert form, all panic fled her. It was as if the fall had steeled her nerves. She did not scream; she did not even wince. She slipped out of her robe and with it beat against the little lines of fire that shot swiftly around her. The study was gone now, and the front doors and colonnades were hissing sheets of flame. The drapes in the living room were torches, and flames licked swiftly through the immense koa wood beams.

She straddled Dean and hooked her hands under his armpits. She started pushing him along the floor, a lunge at a time. She pushed him through the smoke-filled dining room toward the kitchen and the back door. Her nightdress caught fire suddenly and she slapped at it with her hands and rolled over on it. There were deep gashes on her knees. The cut on her head had started bleeding again. Her loose hair was flowing about her shoulders and it was a second or two before she realized that that dreadfully sickening smell that engulfed her was from her own hair scorching. She lunged harder with Dean. His body seemed to weigh a ton. It was like pushing a mass of lead along the floor. The flames shot all around her now, writhing, fiery snakes. She knew she was screaming for help and she knew she should stop screaming in order to conserve her strength but she could not stop.

The beams of the dining room crashed behind her. She stood up, staggering and coughing, and pushed open the swingdoor of the kitchen and set it, and made her way through the smoke to the sink and vomited. She hurried back to Dean and pulled him through the door to the kitchen. She had no strength left to pull him any farther. She stood up quickly, thinking she was going to be sick again. Her head felt light and spinning for a minute, then she fainted, crumbling to the floor in a corner of the kitchen. The cupboards and the great center table were starting to burn.

"Sloan! Sloan baby!" Aaron bent over her and slapped her face lightly, trying to revive her. He lifted her to her feet and bent her head into the sink and turned the cold water on over her head. She blinked her eyes at him and became steadier.

"Aaron—Aaron, help me with Dean—"

"C'mon, baby." He lifted her in his arms and carried her out the kitchen door. The air seemed to revive her.

He carried her across the warm lawn of the garden to the banyan tree. He had tethered Willard's ancient white stallion and a gray gelding to the banyan. The horses pulled against the tree, their eyes wild, their hoofs stamping thunder into the earth.

"Get on the white," Aaron said, when Sloan seemed to have recovered her senses and strength. "Get up on him and bring him over to the kitchen door."

Sloan mounted dumbly and quieted the old horse. She trotted him to the kitchen door. Aaron had run on inside the house.

In a minute he staggered out, carrying Dean across his shoulders. He propped Dean roughly across the rump of the horse, directly behind the saddle. He took the rope from the paniolo saddle and lashed Dean securely with the rope, winding the ends of the rope about the horn of the saddle, then knotting the ends quickly and pushing them into Sloan's hands.

"Keep him braced," Aaron told her.

"Aaron—look!"

The bay gelding had broken away from the banyan tree and was galloping wildly down a clear path behind the banyan and up along the northern draw of the garden.

It was the only escape remaining. Every other inch of Manoalani and the gardens was an inferno of flame and crackling lava.

Aaron and Sloan watched the bay disappear up along the northern draw. In a second, Baron and Miss Brett loped through the path and out along the draw, barking and yelping as they ran.

"Follow them!" Aaron said. "It's the only safe way left!"

The old white was prancing nervously. Sloan kept a tight grip on his reins with one hand while she braced Dean with the other. She turned swiftly and stared wide-eyed at her brother. "Aaron—how are you going to— Get on behind Dean! Hurry, Aaron!"

But Aaron slipped behind the old white and he slapped him now hard on the rump and the horse lunged ahead in those great strides of his, up along the path. Aaron watched them make the turn beneath the banyan tree, which had suddenly burst into flames. He heard Sloan call his name once—twice—then gallop up the north draw and out of sight.

As he started running after them, the side wall of the kitchen blew out. The burning timbers struck him with the force of an explosion. They knocked him across the garden. When he got to his feet his shirt was burning and his arm swung loosely and uselessly at his side, as if it had been jerked out of its socket. His face was twisted with fear and insult and surprise. He staggered and fell to his knees and dimly, he thought he could hear Garth's voice calling out to him. When he raised his eyes to look for Garth he saw the blazing sheet that was the rear wall of Manoalani come down on him.

New Year's Day the trade wind went dead. The air was leaden and moist, hanging limp without a murmur. The gaunt ruin of Manoalani rose against the pale afternoon sky, stark, desolate and profound: a long, veined rectangle of blackened foundation rock. The immense smoke-stained chimney towered above the ruins like a massive tombstone. Two of the enormous veranda columns still stood upright, charred into black ash. A third column, half-burned away, had fallen backward and lay tranquil now in its smoking desolation across the charred remains of what used to be the living room.

The entire coast was a smoke-blackened wasteland. Every grove of trees, every well-remembered path, every field and hill was piled high with cooling lava. No distant cattle lowed, no birds sang, no wind stirred the crusted arches of the remaining trees.

Garth gazed quietly over the land. An old thin despair gripped his heart as he looked at the ruin of Manoalani. He drew a deep shuddering breath. "There's no use staying here any longer," he said. "There's no use looking at it."

Old Willard did not answer him. He walked a little away from him and stood alone on the gentle rise of land where the silk oak had held strong. The granite of his face had become slack gray flesh. His hand wrapped bitterly about the head of a cane which he dug into the earth in front of him. His tailed white linen coat was disheveled, his body hunched beneath the still massive shoulders, and he stooped forward with a slower, grayer hint of his old rage.

"They found Aaron, you said?"

"Yes, Father. They found—"

"What was left of him."

"Yes sir." Garth nodded quietly. He tried to tell from his father's expression whether the old man would finally break. But Willard said nothing more. He stood, like a weary gray ghost, his eyes flicking across the smoldering ruin of Manoalani and its lands.

"Father?" Garth said, moving to his side. "We'd better go. Come on, old fellow, let's get back to Kailua."

But Willard was not looking at his lands any more. He was looking beyond them at the passionately eternal summit of Muana Loa. It was quiet now, subdued, its wrath completed, its dome rising peacefully above the rack of cloud.

"Come along, Father."

"Pele," Willard muttered with disgust. "The miserable bitch."

The old man raised his head, a little finely, a little tragically. His back stiffened and his jaws clamped tight and Garth knew now that old Willard would not crack.

"We should be getting back, old fellow," Garth said. "There's nothing we can do."

After a while, old Willard turned and started tramping back toward the station wagon, Baron and Miss Brett trailing at his heels. "What do you mean, there's nothing we can do?" he demanded, out of some bitter and implacable reserve of undefeat. "We can start rebuilding. We can keep the cattle in the northern pastures and start clearing that glut away from Manoalani as soon as it cools. We can build that old house again."

Epilogue

GRASS grows now, over the cinders where Manoalani once stood: young blades of pili grass weaving gently like peacock feathers through the fields of lupin and buttercup that flower now, where the flames once flowered.

There are no fires on the land. The cinder cones remained, but they have consolidated into tuff and the tourists poke sticks into them. The river of lava has cemented into dark glassy rock.

Garth completed the new ranch house late last year. It sits high atop an old lava barrier on the slope of the Judd Trail. It faces southeast—the grazeland and the sea and the passionately eternal volcano. From none of its vistas can be seen the gutted remains of Manoalani, nor the lava rock cross that marks Aaron's grave.

Garth manages the Howland Ranch now. He is content with

it. Sometimes at night, there is that moment of aloneness; the thin celibate despair of the seeker. But he has lived with it for so long now that he recognizes it before it comes and he shrugs his shoulders and works that sad broken grin of his. It is like welcoming an old friend.

Trees which did not yield to the lava flow bloomed early and very green this year. In the valley beyond the trees, the grazelands have been reopened. From the lanai of the new house, you can see the cattle at pasture, their backs to the seawind, and you can hear the distant bawing of the herd.

Perhaps at night, when the clouds furl silver against the dark sky beyond Mauna Loa, and the trades saw through the tallest branches of palm, there is a loneliness, a disenchantment about the new ranch house. But on Sundays, it is a live gay place.

Kapiolani Kahana drives up from Kailua for the late afternoon barbecue. She sold her house at Nanakuli and moved back to her home island. She works at the Kona Inn and sells baubles to tourists, and at the Sunday afternoon barbecues on the lanai of the new ranch house she pantomines the tourists in outrageous fashion.

Laura Howland used to be a constant weekend guest. She would bring the boy, young Aaron. But of late she has been keeping company with a young Naval lieutenant commander and her visits are rare. They plan to be married this fall, at St. Peter's Church.

Dean and Sloan and little Melani visit every weekend. They do not stay at the ranch house itself, but in a small cottage built behind the house in a grove of young ohia. Dean has started practice in Kailua. He has arranged his schedule so he finds time every afternoon to take Sloan and little Melani off in his fishing boat and spend an hour or more in the channel after striped marlin. Melani is a big-eyed girl, full of life and mischief. Yet there is something about her that constantly burdens Sloan. When she does not know she is being watched, little Melani sometimes will stop and stand utterly still, poised and solemn as a young tree, her dark head turned a bit, listening to a faraway sound, her face a portrait of the ultimate gravity of childhood.

Doc Judd predicted that Melani would be a boy. And the prediction makes Sloan laugh. There is no brittleness to her laughter now. For a long time she did not laugh at all. She would spend her solitude wandering endlessly along the nighttime beaches, throwing her soul to the wind, watching the surf and trying dimly to collect her scattered passions. But she is well over that now. She laughs fully: a rich wonderful laughter that is heard from very few women, and only when they are completely in love and loved in return.

"Come on, Sloan," Garth chided her. "Let us all in on the joke."

They were all out on the lanai—Sloan, Dean, little Melani, Kapiolani and old Willard—and they were waiting for the coals to burn white before putting on the steaks. Sloan placed her drink on the table and reached over to squeeze Dean's hand.

"I hope the joke is on Doc Judd again," she said. "If his prediction yesterday is as true as his prediction about Melani, then everything is perfect. Dean and I both want a boy this time. And Doc said flatly that it was going to be a girl."

Miss Brett nuzzled about little Melani, exploring. Then she went and curled at old Willard's feet. Willard gazed down fondly at the collie and rubbed her head. She misses Baron, Willard thought.

Then he raised his head and turned his dark gold eyes toward the searoad, far below, and the eternal volcano beyond it. His vision had become very bad, but he could still see well enough to make out the cloud of dust rising along the cutoff road that wound from the searoad up to the ranch house. And in a moment, he could see the Kona Airport taxicab tool its way up the road.

"Visitors?" he grumbled.

Garth put down his drink. "Yes—in a way."

The group on the lanai became very quiet. They watched Willard uncertainly as he swung his gaze accusingly at Garth. "What visitors?" he demanded. "Who would be coming up here without my knowing about it?"

Garth watched the airport taxi swing up the road and turn into the dirt driveway of the new house. "An old friend," he said.

Willard's face became stone. His eyes were bright and implacable. He got to his feet with unbelievable slowness, as if in his gray old years he was almost incapable of the effort.

First Garth, and then Dean went to his side as if to assist him. But they stopped and glanced quickly at each other, then backed away from the old man. They could see the strange way Willard stiffened, the manner in which his head swung high with a semblance of his old arrogance, as he watched first Tani, with the baby Melinda in her arms, then the twins, Matt and Mark, and Barbara and finally little Chris jump out from the taxicab. And, at last, Ward Akana.

Garth watched his father nervously. "Our—our guest of honor, the United States Senator from the new State of Hawaii, back from his first season of Washington politics," Garth said, forcing his voice to sound light and carefree. "He's—he's come over to—well, to get your ideas about how to straighten out the mess in Washington."

But old Willard had pushed past him and tramped heavily to the edge of the lanai, where he stood, his booted feet spread wide and planted firmly, almost defiantly, in the earth. It was as far as he would go and no farther, and he seemed to draw himself up there in that gesture of old pride and indomitability, his head high, his shoulders painfully stiff, watching Ward Akana walk up the narrow lane that led to the lanai.

Ward walked as a young man walks, but Willard could see the lines about his face; and he thought, Dedication is rare—when you meet it you can always see the marks it leaves on a man. Ward looked tired. His face was thin. The hair about his temples had turned to the color of chalk. He stopped suddenly, several yards down the lane, and looked up into the face of his father. Both of them seemed to remain fixed that way for an eternity; a rigid scene out of space and out of time.

Ward grinned. "Hello, Father," he said.

Old Willard bobbed his head several times. His white-gold mane stirred in the breeze. His mouth was working. "Washington," he muttered, to no one in particular. "Well, I guess I can figure out a word or two of advice for you." And with his cane he smashed open the gate to the lanai and tramped heavily down the lane toward Ward.